Raven Blue

—JP Ishaq—

Raven Blue

"Epitaph on an Army of Mercenaries," from *Last Poems,* by A. E. Housman, written in1917.

To my parents, Kristin and Mousa, who got me started,
And to the friends who keep me going.

Epitaph on an Army of Mercenaries

A. E. Housman

These, in the day when heaven was
falling,
The hour when earth's foundations fled,
Followed their mercenary calling,
And took their wages, and are dead.

Their shoulders held the sky suspended;
They stood, and earth's foundations stay;
What God abandoned, these defended,
And saved the sum of things for pay.

Table of Contents

Overture: A Dream of Better Days

The unraveling Earth was held together at the seams by the roots of a single alien tree. Standing tall in the dwindling afternoon sunlight, the tree seemed eternal, supernatural, even dwarfed by the looming gray towers on all sides. The towers were full of dimly lit windows grimy with soot; one of those windows was home, but the little boy still did not know which.

He returned his attention to the strange tree. He had barely learned to scrawl the word "TREE" in his lesson book when he saw a picture of one, but he could tell right away that this one was different than the other ones in the courtyard between the buildings. It was taller, straighter, with bright orange leaves. The other trees had no leaves. They were stunted, gnarled things, and they did not look like the pictures in the book. "Da, what's so special about this tree?" the little boy asked.

Off between the trees, the man stopped sweeping the path and propped his broom against a bench. The little boy watched him approach, his footsteps ringing out against the cracked concrete slabs. Surrounding them were the packed masses of millions of people, but for the moment they were the only two people in the world.

The man knelt beside his son, leaning in. He was tall in the boy's eyes, and he was thin, but not as thin as he had been. His stern face was assembled around gentle, tired eyes. He smelled of earth, of nature. His voice was low, conspiratorial, as though the information he was about to impart was their little secret. "Well, Leon, this special tree is a *d'kad* tree. Your mother brought it from the planet Tagea when it was just a seed, and she … changed it, to make it better."

The little boy frowned. How could you change a tree?

The man saw that the boy was confused, and he smiled. "Maybe she can explain it to you, someday. She understands it better than I do. I just look after the gardens. But you see, the soil here is poisonous to many things."

"Is that why we can't grow veg—veg…." The boy paused, trying to form the word. "Vegetables?" he finally managed, enunciating each syllable carefully.

7

"That's right. But these special trees are very strong. They're not afraid of the poisons. They can *eat* the poison, and they can stay healthy. So, they grow big, strong roots under all the sick trees, and they suck away the poison so the other trees can get better."

The little boy nodded sagely. "So, it's a doctor tree?"

The man laughed softly. "Yes. It is. Now, what else do doctors do?"

"Does the doctor tree give the sick trees medicine?"

"Sharp boy," said the man approvingly. "Your Ma taught the tree to give the other trees nutrients and vitamins, like the ones you take in the morning. They drink them in through their roots. And when the other trees are better, they can help us clean the air and make the whole world better."

While his father got back to work, Leon played in the grove of sick trees surrounding the vibrant survivor as its leaves turned to tufts of flame in a beam of weak sunlight. The little boy marveled at this tree, wondering if all the trees would look like that soon.

From time to time he heard snatches of sound from the city beyond the buildings, the constant roar of Crossing. He missed the quiet of home, the gentle sway of the palmas in the tropical breeze, but he knew it made Ma and Da sad when he said it, so he kept it to himself.

One of the other tenants was crossing the square, an old woman stooped with age, wearing a brightly colored scarf on her head that the little boy thought was very pretty, especially against the drab buildings. She caught his eye and waved, smiling a toothless smile, and went on her way, slowly picking her way over the broken paving stones.

A shriek cut the air, angry and mechanical. Crossing had many sirens: bridges going up, bridges going down, shield officers searching districts, shield officers closing districts, shield officers opening districts, factory shifts starting, factory shifts ending. The little boy had learned them all, and his parents had made sure he knew the air quality sirens, too.

Da had been tending the trees across the square, but it seemed only an instant before he crossed it and scooped the little boy up in his arms. He covered the distance to the nearest building in long strides and opened the front door. He deposited the boy on the floor and hit the large red button on the wall. Nothing happened. "Cheap motherfuckers." The inner door was locked, too.

"Stay calm, Leon, okay? We have to run to another building. I need you to hold your breath for me. Can you do that?" The indulgent smile he had worn as he taught his son about doctor trees was gone; now he looked angry and frightened, and that made Leon frightened, too.

As they took off across the courtyard again, the trees had already begun to disappear from view, consumed by an angry brown cloud that rolled toward them, funneled between the buildings. It seemed to chase the man and the boy, long fingers of fog outstretched.

Leon did not cry out. He trusted his Da, and he knew he would protect him.

"It's all right, son. Just hold your breath, okay? It's a contest; let's see which one of us can hold our breath the longest."

This hardly seemed the time for games, the little boy reflected. He obediently held his breath as the cloud closed around them.

Leon could barely see the next building through the fog, but suddenly they were at the door and Da flung it open. He recognized the spider-web pattern of cracks on the door's glass and the graffiti painted on the vestibule wall. This was their building.

"What about Mrs. Galloway?" Leon asked as his Da set him down.

"What?" his father asked, hand paused over the red button that would lock down the vestibule and prevent the poison from getting in. The newer buildings had automatic scrubbers and purge systems, but the Loyalty Park Projects did not.

Leon pointed through the cracked glass. Mrs. Galloway was struggling toward one of the buildings, her scarf pulled down over her face, her white hair streaming free.

"All right, Leon, I need you to stay here. If you see black smoke, I want you to push the red button. Even if we're not back. Promise me."

Leon was a good boy who did what his parents told him to do, and he nodded sharply, though the thought terrified him. His Da had told him what would happen if the black smog got in. People could get very sick. Some might die.

Da pulled out the handkerchief Ma had given him, the one with the birds on it, and wrapped it tight around his nose and mouth. He hugged Leon tightly, took a deep breath, and opened the door. Tendrils of gray-brown smog crept in the vestibule as the door closed.

Leon could barely see his Da or Mrs. Galloway through the swirling cloud and the smudged, cracked glass of the door. The haze closed its shifting maw around them. The trees disappeared, the swing set disappeared, even the tall gray buildings disappeared, and Leon was alone. His breath was loud in the little room between the sets of doors.

He did not know the word for claustrophobia, but that was what he felt, trapped alone in the little room as the world vanished behind a muddy shroud, his hand trembling, the button within easy reach if he saw the dreaded black smog.

He started as his Da slammed hard into the door, half carrying Mrs. Galloway. He opened the door and the two of them spilled into the vestibule, panting and coughing.

"Alex, thank you!" the old woman wheezed. "I don't know what I would have done."

Leon's Da pulled down the handkerchief, stained with soot. Where it had covered his face, his skin was clean, but above it his forehead and the bridge of his nose were stained dark brown. "Nice weather we're having, isn't it, Mrs. Galloway?"

Leon hugged his father and the three of them watched as the poison cloud swirled around the courtyard before receding into itself, seeming almost disappointed. The *d'kad* tree emerged from the gloom, standing tall and defiant, its fiery leaves undimmed by the noxious assault.

The first rays of morning light crept through the apartment window, waking Leon. His gray-green eyes fluttered open, and the red tree disappeared, replaced by the ceiling of his apartment. He wasn't a child any longer and the bittersweet scraps of memory fluttered away. All but the memory of that smog, that he seemed able to smell for years after leaving Crossing, after leaving Terra.

Rachel yawned and sat up in bed, her hair a wild black tumble. "Are you all right?" Even wrenched out of sleep, she was beautiful, her blue eyes bleary but sparkling as they focused.

"Yeah. I just …. I was dreaming about home."

"Baby, your nose is bleeding."

Leon rolled out of bed and went to the bathroom to wash his face. He coughed bloody phlegm into the sink. It was as though he had brought that out of his dream, but he knew it was a souvenir of his trip to Aethaleia, a world so poisoned it made Old Terra seem like paradise. He held a towel against his nose, staring his tired reflection in the face.

Clean-shaven for the first time in years, Leon's long, solemn face looked younger, though his eyes looked old and weary. His fingertips drifted across the scar on his cheekbone and the abrasion on his chin, healing but still raw. Rachel stepped into the bathroom behind him, and their eyes met in the mirror.

"It's because of that place you went, whatever was in the air there. Isn't it?" Rachel crossed her arms.

Leon nodded. His recollection of his father, so faint to begin with, vanished, replaced by the memory of Aethaleia. He and his friends had braved dark, deserted streets on a world emptied of its people by an insidious biological weapon. At least, that was what Leon had been told. He didn't quite believe it.

"What did you dream about?" Rachel asked, to distract him.

"I had a dream about my Da," he said wistfully.

Rachel turned the taps in the shower. "Let's get you cleaned up, then we can go get some breakfast and you can tell me about him."

First Aria: The Last Bastion of Vali

The angry wail of the sirens tore Emma from dreams of lost tranquility, and she scrambled from her bed, terrified. That sound could mean only one thing: their illusion of safety had crumbled.

Emma's panic passed quickly as she reasserted control over her trembling limbs and gathered her wits. There were other possibilities, she told herself. It could be a false alarm, or a drill. *I wish.* A fresh jolt of panic coursed through her, threatening to undo her resolve, but she suppressed it and began to dress.

Karda had shown her how to strap on the heavy armor plates so they wouldn't slide around, but in her fear Emma forgot where everything went and found several straps hanging loose. The armor was too big, too unfamiliar, and she threw it aside in frustration. She had to get to her station, in case she was needed.

The urge to turn on her comm and find out what was going on was hard to resist. Karda's lessons stayed with her, though, and she left it off, off and dark and unable to give her away.

As she passed the small mirror mounted above the sink in the corner of her quarters, Emma caught sight of herself and paused. Her face was drawn, haggard, a shadow of its former beauty. Nearly a year under the blackout had taken a heavy toll on her, mind and body alike. She hated not knowing. Not for the first time, she cursed the blue tint that was beginning to show on her skin, the mark of all Cincon Augments. The thought of turning now was too much for her. Emma had been blessed: only half Cincon, her skin tone had shown none of the typical pigmentation, and she had escaped notice until recently. Her father had been lucky that way, too, but her mother … some said it was better her mother had died in childbirth. Blue would never be beautiful in the Valinata Enclave.

Emma threw open the metal door of her hut and stepped onto the packed, rocky ground of the main yard, breathing in Mandolin's humid air. It was still night. She looked left, then right along the rows of identical dwellings. They were little more than gray metal shipping containers, four meters on a side and partitioned into two sections, living quarters and a water closet. They were all concealed beneath camouflage netting, the effectiveness of which was dubious at best. It was a far cry from the bungalow she had shared with Kent on Fidelity. She still missed Kent sometimes, but the Valinata had called her, and she could not have refused.

Mandolin had been settled as part of the Valinata's Cartography Initiative, a drive to locate and harness resources to stave off economic starvation. Mandolin had been a beautiful world to settle, and Emma had seen no view to equal that of the suns climbing over the horizon, rays of light diving playfully through the fronds of the tall palmas. But there were only a few thousand colonists, and the sense of isolation after the hustle and bustle of Fidelity had been profound.

The Mandolin colony was a frenzy of activity now, though, directionless and panicked. Colonists ran across the yard, looking for friends, loved ones, or any figure of authority to tell them what to do. Karda's hand-picked security team was trying to restore order, but they were tiny islands of calm in the storm. At one end of the compound a long line of uniformed Valinata Space Force sojieri watched silently, making no attempt to help Karda's men. The siren continued to blare from the loudspeakers atop the pylons, and Emma ran toward the central station, the sprawling amalgamation of prefabricated modular buildings thrown together at the camp's center.

Four thousand people, crammed together on a few acres of ground and surrounded by uncounted kilometers of wilderness which seemed to creep closer every day, no matter how thoroughly the crews cleared it. The new growth was striking, the pale, wispy stems of fresh palmas jutting bravely out of the dirt. Emma trampled them in her haste.

The siren stopped, and Emma halted, surprised by the abrupt stillness, the sudden vacuum of sound that occupied the space of that awful wail. She willed herself to move again and made for the door of the station. Two of Karda's guards stood before the entrance, and they raised their rifles, nervous themselves and clearly uncomfortable with the big, deadly weapons. They shouted a warning, and Emma paused long enough for them to recognize her and wave her through.

Inside, Dr. Harris was shouting orders, trying to get a handle on the situation. He was the colony's heart and soul, keeping them all grounded. In the control room banks of computer terminals sat dark and useless, as ineffective as the rest of their technology. A holographics projector now served as a table, strewn with paper made from the palma fronds. It had been Harris's idea to cut off all contact with the universe, and they had put their faith in him. As he saw Emma enter, a fleeting smile shot across his face. "Emma! Thank God, you're here!" His right hand was pulling at the end of his beard, a sure sign of his agitation. "The comms room is locked, and we can't get in! We think a signal's been sent out."

It was like a punch in the gut, and Emma drew in a sharp breath. *A signal ... who would do that, and why?*

Before she had a chance to ask, a uniformed sojier stepped forward. It was Lieutenant Hall, who commanded the VSF detachment standing idly by outside. "What do you know about this?" he snapped, voice full of suspicion.

"Emma had nothing to do with this," Harris promised.

Emma looked up at her interrogator and saw the contempt in his eyes. *How can Harris trust a dirty Cincon?* they seemed to ask.

"I'll get us in right away," Emma said quickly. She had purpose now, and that made all the difference. No longer just a bystander, she could take some comfort in Harris's protocols. Compared to the colonists waiting helplessly, she was lucky.

The comms room was not far from the main control room. When Emma reached it, she had to push past the five security officers trying to break through. She recognized their chief, Vendac the Sheff'an, whose dark brown scales allowed her to blend in with the palma trunks when she hunted for food. She saw Emma and made way for her. "Finally! Get it open!"

The door to the comms room had been reinforced at Karda's suggestion, to thwart any colonist who might give in to the temptation to reach out and contact someone. Three keys had been made: one for Emma, one for Karda, and one for Frye, the other comms officer. Emma fumbled with hers for a moment before she plunged it into the reader. There was a click, and the lock popped open. She quickly pushed it open and stepped inside.

Three keys had been made: one for Emma, one for Karda, one for Frye. Frye was leaning back in his chair ... sleeping? No, not sleeping. They had been chosen for their loyalty, for their dedication to duty (the same dedication that had made it possible for Emma to leave Kent behind on Fidelity). As Emma drew closer, she saw the dark, glistening red bib of blood covering his open throat and chest. Beside his lifeless hand, the TRANSMIT light was blinking steadily. Emma ran forward and shut off the comm. "I don't understand," she said. "There's no message, just an open band."

Vendac was by the door, long tail whipping back and forth. "What do you mean?"

"The ... damage ... is done," came a weak voice from behind them. They turned to see Karda sitting propped against the wall. He had sounded the alarm. His hands were pressed to his belly, trying in vain to hold in his guts. A long knife lay beside him, its blade shining wetly.

Vendac and Emma ran to their leader, the man who had organized them, who had kept their spirits high with his promises and his practicality. With him they had known that they could survive, that even if they never again reached out into the stars, they would have a future on Mandolin. Now he was dying, coming to a sad end in a dark room.

"Sir!" Vendac hissed, furious. "Who did this?"

Karda, that most noble of Tageans, turned his head toward them, his dark eyes regarding the two women. "O'Connor. It was Tyler O'Connor."

The name came as a shock, and Emma felt faint. "No, sir, you must be wrong. He and the VSF are here to protect us."

Karda flicked his pointed ears twice, an emphatic no. "Trust me, I ... got a good look at him when ... he gutted me." There was bleak mirth in his voice, and it broke Emma's heart. The Tagean's dulling eyes fixed on her. "He said ... you'd know where to find him."

Before she even knew what she was doing, Emma was on her feet and running, running down the hall, through the control room, and past Dr. Harris. Vendac caught up with her easily. "Where are you going?" she demanded, her nasal crest flared in anger.

"Get everyone out of the colony, into the mountains!" Emma shouted back. "I'll deal with Tyler!"

Whether or not Vendac understood her or not, Emma did not know. But the Sheff'an slowed her pace and stopped at the door as Emma pounded down the stairs and back onto the soil. She pushed through the throng of frightened colonists as the news began to spread. Karda's security forces and the VSF sojieri were shouting curses at each other, and it was only a matter of time before a gun went off.

Emma sprinted into the woods, bound for the place she had shown Tyler. Why had he told Karda that? *"You'd know where to find him,"* he said. *Why me, and why is he doing this?*

The night was cool, pleasant despite the humidity, and unseen animals hooted and rustled through the bushes. Heedless of their calls or the fronds whipping against her face and exposed arms, Emma tore through the brush, tears streaming down her face. The sweet musk of the jungle flooded her nostrils. Perhaps it wasn't too late, perhaps she had cut off the signal before it was triangulated. Perhaps there was no threat, and their blackout was nothing but a paranoid overreaction. Perhaps … if only the universe could be so simple.

Up ahead the trees thinned out and finally ended along a rocky cliff face. Emma was nearly three miles from the colony's perimeter, panting, her vision blurring from the effort of her prolonged sprint. Her feet skidded in the gravel as she came to a stop. Spread out before her was the vista of Mandolin's primeval equatorial basin. Broad rivers glistened in the moonlight, silver-chased ribbons winding their languorous way through the dark jungle. Through the branches to her right, Emma could see Tyler O'Connor, sitting with his feet dangling over the edge. Instead of the joy she usually felt when she saw him, now his face seemed to stand for all the disappointment and betrayal in her life.

Once it had been her goal to study untouched worlds such as this pristine Eden, but that goal was a delusion. As a Cincon Augment, her test scores and her ambition were secondary to her genetic composition. It had never occurred to her that the universe could be so cripplingly unfair, that she should be kept from university because of chromosomal modifications inflicted upon her by the very government that denied her applications.

16

A Human contaminated with Rukadj genes to make her a more versatile worker, Emma had gestated in three months and reached sexual maturity in seven years. After that, she aged far slower than unmodified humans, but she was prone to numerous disorders as a result of the genetic hack job. The Cincons had been created for a purpose, and when that purpose had been served, the Valinata had not known what to do with them. So they had been left to their own devices, second-class citizens with few rights and no voice. The discovery that they could breed naturally, and with other Humans, no less, had caused the Vali leadership considerable distress.

When Emma had finally been offered a scholarship, she had been ecstatic until she learned that it was from a school for outcasts, with little funding and a poor curriculum. Instead, she had volunteered for the Valinata Civil Service, hoping to find some outlet for her skills. The VCS had sent her to Mandolin. And then war had come.

War with whom? No one seemed to know, but Dr. Harris and Karda had decided to close off Mandolin's contact with the rest of the galaxy, severing the hypercomm ansible connection to avoid giving away their position. Since their voluntary blackout, they had reactivated the comm system only once: to rescue a stricken Valinata Space Force transport that had limped into the system, guiding the vessel to safe haven. The ship had carried Lieutenant Hall and his men … among them Corporal Tyler O'Connor.

Emma had never seen a ship crumpled like that, a result of the gravitic drive field failing and the lightspeed conduit closing upon the stern half of the ship, crushing it and more than thirty troops inside. The remaining VSF sojieri had been grateful for their deliverance and their shelter, promising to abide by the rules of the colony. They had never explained the circumstances of their retreat or the state of the Valinata Enclave at large, but they had been a welcome addition to Mandolin's small population. At first, they had made a pretense of respecting Dr. Harris's authority, helping with the harvest and building shelters and silos. Lately, though, the VSF lieutenant had been exercising more and more authority, authority born of the guns his men carried.

But Tyler O'Connor was different! He wasn't a trigger-happy warrior or a blind follower taking Lieutenant Hall's words as holy gospel. He was smart and funny, and he had befriended Emma despite her blue skin. What could have made him turn traitor?

Pushing through the branches that separated them, Emma decided she had to ask. She had shown him this picturesque outcropping during one of their picnics. It was a sweet memory: he had appeared out of nowhere one day, toting a small medical supply crate filled with food and even a bottle of Karda's prized wine. Charmed, Emma had led him to her favorite spot. She had rebuffed his clumsy advances gently, but they had remained close friends.

He looked oddly at peace for a man who had just committed two murders and possibly doomed the entire colony. His chiseled, youthful face no longer seemed dashing and impish but blank and menacing. There was drying blood on his sleeves, and Emma found herself wishing it was his. She moved up behind him, trying to be quiet, looking for a weapon and wishing she had taken the knife he had used on Karda and Frye. It would have felt right.

Emma lost her footing momentarily and sent gravel skittering toward O'Connor. He turned slowly and looked at her. "Emma!" he exclaimed cheerfully, joy lighting his features. "You came!"

Was he out of his mind? He sounded as though she was responding to a dinner invitation. "Tyler," she began, keeping her voice even. "What have you *done*?"

His brow furrowed. "What … I did it for you! For *us*!" he declared. "This was the only way." He stood up and reached out to her. "You know I love you."

Emma recoiled from his touch. "You *love* me? You hardly *know* me!"

Tyler O'Connor's eyes moved back and forth as though he was reading. "But I've seen how the lieutenant looks at you!" he stammered. "I had to protect you from those narrow-minded bastards. Who knows what they might have done? The Celestials don't *care* about your skin color! They can fix you, and we can be together in paradise!"

The Celestials. Emma felt her blood run cold. So it was true. They existed, and O'Connor had called to them. Like a great weapon they would home in on Mandolin and burn it from the universe. "'Fix' me," Emma said softly, "because there's something wrong with me."

O'Connor's frown deepened. "No, I didn't mean.... What did I say?" He seemed not to remember. Suddenly his idiosyncrasies, his flightiness, weren't charming quirks. He was unhinged. Had something happened to him when the conduit spat his ship out? They said the conduits could do strange things to a person, especially to the weak-minded. "I love you, Emma. We're going to be together in heaven, with the Celestials."

"Oh, you're not going to heaven, Tyler," Emma hissed. Without realizing she was going to do it, she lunged forward. Cincons had been bred to be strong as well as subservient; while Emma had never been violent, she was certainly not docile. Her fingers curled around O'Connor's neck, squeezing. He struggled, trying to break free, and his foot slipped off the edge. They went down together, dropping from the outcropping and onto the steep shale slope. Stone dug into Emma's back and sides as they tumbled, but she refused to relinquish her grip on O'Connor's throat, even as a jagged rock sliced open her forehead. As they fell, she kept on squeezing, feeling his vertebrae popping and his windpipe slowly collapsing.

They landed hard. O'Connor was already dead when a rock stove in his head, his life choked out of him. Still Emma refused to let go, squeezing until she heard something crunch. Then she fell back onto her rear, kicking his lifeless corpse as she backed away on her hands and feet. Leaning against the rock face, she rested her head against the cool stone. It was sticky with her blood when she pulled away. Her whole face was throbbing, burning, and she tore a strip from her shirt to wrap around her forehead. She marshaled her strength and began to climb.

She could hear the explosions before she was halfway up the slope. Still she pressed on, her hands digging into the loose shale, her palms cut to ribbons by sliding stone. Tears were streaming down her face, not from pain but from grief. Emma could hear sporadic gunfire echoing through the forest, followed by more explosions and loud, sizzling hisses like grease frying. Had the VSF and Karda's loyal few turned on each other, or was it something worse? If the Celestials had truly come to call, then Mandolin was done, a paradise toppled. Over everything was a haunting moaning sound that seemed to come from everywhere at once.

When Emma reached the top of the outcropping, her breath caught in her throat and she let loose an involuntary cry of terror. The forest, the beautiful forest, was ablaze. Animals fled out of the trees, predator and prey side by side, heedless as they ran in vain for safety. Many tumbled over the cliff with yelps of pain and surprise. Emma could only stand and watch. Plumes of black, oily smoke billowed over the colony clearing, framing a monstrous black ship that hung over it all. Kilometers long, the vessel seemed suspended in time as well as space, a snapshot of a prehistoric nightmare. Suddenly a volley of green fire erupted from its belly, hammering the woods and the colony. Emma fell to her knees, cupping her face in her hands. It was over. It was all over. She forced herself back to her feet and faded into the jungle.

First Movement:
Pariah

1: Revelation

There was a place beneath the Coalition's royal palace beyond the reach of tourists or the press, beyond all but the highest security clearances. No guest had ever ventured there, and though the windowless passages were attractive enough to pass muster, none ever would. Innocuous-looking potted plants and sculptures lined the black-tiled hallways, no doubt concealing surveillance equipment, defensive countermeasures, and security gates that could snap closed at a moment's notice and stop an artillery round if the need arose.

Grand Admiral Hakar walked solemnly through the corridors, feeling small as he organized his thoughts. At this late hour, the palace was quiet, tomblike, and his mind was racing. *Just a few months ago, the galaxy still made sense. It feels like a lifetime since then.*

He had been awakened by an emergency priority message, rising to find a quartet of Falcon Guard sojieri outside his apartment door. They were dressed in finely decorated but still lethally functional dress armor of glossy black with purple trim. It seemed fitting that he would be jolted awake on the one night in the last month he had been able to fall asleep, and adrenaline warred against fatigue as he walked with his solemn bodyguard.

The Falcons were surprisingly quiet in their crystal-clad armor, intimidating even though Hakar loomed over them all. Once a society of nomadic raiders, centuries of warfare had honed them into a relentless and unmatched fighting force. Pushed to the fringes of the galaxy as the major powers grew, they joined the Coalition out of desperation; met with suspicion, they nevertheless swiftly became the empire's elite guard. They had never fully integrated with the Coalition Royal Defense Force command structure; their mystique and their undeniable prowess were enough to inspire awe even in an experienced veteran like Hakar.

He and his escort passed through security checkpoint after checkpoint. The whole labyrinth was electronically and physically shielded. Hakar had been down here only once, at the fall of Emperor Telemon. An air of desperation had permeated the refuge then, as the deposed monarch had rallied the palace guard for a last-ditch defense against the Royal Shield detachment that had been sent to arrest him. It had been Hakar who had convinced the guards to stand down. Had he done it out of loyalty to the Coalition? Or out of self-interest, to secure his place with the next administration? He didn't like to dwell on that question.

Those who knew him described Hakar as noble of feature and bearing, and while his elegant snout and piercing, coal-black eyes certainly looked the part, inside he felt anything but. His fur was graying, his once-tailored uniform hung off his frame, and his outwardly graceful stride felt uncertain and ungainly. The face he saw in the mirror each day was that of an estranged friend, at once familiar and hard to place.

They reached the end of the gently sloping corridor, and Hakar stopped. *What a gauntlet. Probably designed to strike fear into the hearts of the unworthy.* Before him was a black wall that seemed to ripple like liquid even though it was motionless. It was the shell of the command bunker, made of solid trykon crystal reinforced with interlocked layers of metal and stone, enough to stop anything short of a gigaton Worldbreaker missile. Only a direct threat to Tagea, the throneworld of the Coalition, would have been enough to open this deep, dark underworld.

After another bioscan, a seam appeared as a door detached and slid outward, and Hakar was hit by a blast of cool air. The bunker was kept at positive pressure, to keep out unwanted contamination in the event of a biological attack. Hakar ducked through the portal, the Falcons following one by one.

Inside was a different world. One might have expected the command shelter to be cramped and utilitarian, a bunker in all but name, but it was not. In addition to serving as a safe haven for the Coalition's highest-ranking leaders, it was designed as a sanctuary to preserve culture and history. Consequently, art adorned the warm sandstone walls, which climbed to a vaulted ceiling that simulated sky and bathed the chamber in what seemed like natural moonlight. A row of purple and silver banners hung on the far wall displaying the Coalition standard. Beneath them waited a platoon of Falcon Guards in a riot of colors. Representing all their order's major cadres, they stood silent and motionless before a small and unassuming door.

Hakar knew that the cavernous chamber was only one of many. Doors on all sides led to hydroponics gardens, living quarters, laboratories, and medical facilities, anything the royal entourage would need to survive a protracted siege. Sojieri and workers with special security clearances bustled about in a hushed sort of panic, checking supplies and making the space ready for just such an event. The space was ornate, almost cathedralesque in its design, an ostentatious monument hidden from public view. It was chilling to think that Hakar might live out the rest of his days down here, while his wife and child lived and died worlds away.

Trying futilely to push aside the thought, Hakar stepped through the ranks of Falcons to stand before the door. The angular petals irised open.

His Falcon bodyguards remained outside, joining their comrades while Hakar walked into a well-lit and well-appointed conference room. Though modest, this room was the nerve center of the refuge, a spot from which to command resistance, to rally troops, to maintain contact with whatever was left of the Coalition in the event of catastrophe. It had never been needed. *Someone had better be overreacting*, he hoped.

A dozen or so of the Coalition's highest-ranking political and military leaders occupied the room, looking uneasy. At the head of the table stood Empress Atyre Kra'al, the first Prross to rise to the office. Usually garbed in elaborate gowns, Kra'al looked thuglike and fearsome in slacks and a simple blouse, the rolled-up sleeves of which revealed the ritualistic tattoos covering her arms. They also crept up her neck and along her snout, elaborate depictions of her accomplishments. Beside her stood Grand Admiral Bosh Telec, her Sanar defense advisor, appearing small and frail at the arm of their thickly muscled ruler. His exposed skin gleamed wetly in the lights.

The high grand admiral, da-Fon Pirsan, and Grand Admiral Doran Motayre stood to the side, speaking in hushed tones and towering over the rest of those present. To Hakar's tired mind they resembled a sword and a hammer, Pirsan lean and elegant, Motayre blunt and brutal. And yet their personalities could not have been more dissimilar from their appearances. They broke off and took seats flanking the empress. The rest of the grand admirals who made up the Star Chamber that oversaw the Coalition Royal Defense Forces were faces on a bank of monitors at the front of the room. Abroad with their fleets, they joined the meeting via hypercomm ansible. Also joining remotely were the chaplains of the Falcon Guard, impassive and silent. It was expensive, but it allowed for realtime communications across the vast gulfs of space. Several regional governors were also listening in, though not in realtime.

Kra'al locked eyes with Hakar. "We're still waiting on signal authentication," she said tensely. Hakar nodded in the Human fashion and took a seat beside Telec, listening to his colleague's rasping breath. Drinks were set out alongside a plate of sandwiches in an absurd parody of normalcy. No one had touched them.

Joseph Winters, the Human Grand Admiral, looked ashen-faced. Hakar couldn't tell if the effect was from the signal quality or something else entirely. "Your Majesty, I still don't know what would cause her—"

"Let's just wait until we see the feed," Kra'al snapped.

Telec whispered something in Kra'al's ear. She was about to reply when an alarm chirped. One of the monitors on the far wall began displaying lines of text as well as fragmented images. The assembled personnel watched in consternation as transcripts and snatches of video played across the screen, interrupted occasionally by screeches of garbled audio.

"That's coming over the Valinata whisper network," observed Hakar, rising to get a better look.

"I don't understand," Kra'al confessed. "How are they transmitting to us?"

Hakar peered closer as he explained. "The Valinata Space Force has been effectively neutralized, along with their centralized command. But we've been working with some of their remnant fleets, and one of the conditions of granting them asylum was total access to their military datanets, including priority communications. This is Coalition data being sent across their system."

"That sounds like a last resort," one of the finance ministers pointed out.

Very possibly, Hakar admitted to himself. *This is going to take time to fully decrypt and analyze, time we probably don't have.* A fragment of data in the corner of the screen caught his attention. "There," he exclaimed, pointing. "Can someone pause that there?"

One of the technicians manipulated the feed. Hakar stepped even closer, the glow of the display bathing his graying fur in ghostly, flickering light.

"Admiral Hakar, we can't see the feed. Please tell us what you see," requested Joe Winters, concern evident in his voice as it crackled over the speakers.

"This was part of an emergency data export sent from *Champion*. Full SOS." Hakar frowned. "What happened to Admiral Rodriguex?" He turned to look at the others.

Telec looked uneasily at the empress, then at the image of Joe Winters, who was Flora Rodriguex's commanding officer and mentor. The dark-skinned Human looked positively furious, and now Hakar understood why. Telec spoke calmly, though. "It appears she and the Dragon Valia fleet remnant holding position over Calama left a token force to protect the region before staging an assault on Valinata space."

"Why?" Hakar blurted out, realizing he was playing catchup to what everyone in the room already knew. Why would Joe Winters send her out there? Or did she go rogue? Hakar didn't know Rodriguex that well, but her record was unimpeachable.

Voice even, Telec answered, "Our intelligence assets in the Zoh Hegemony have been conducting a comprehensive dump of every database they can find, and Tanis Ruin keeps coming up."

Hakar's frown deepened. The Zoh Hegemony was one of the Coalition's member states, although a reluctant one at that. However, its position along the Emerald Veil, the Coalition's border with the Valinata, had given the CRDF front-row seats from which to watch the breakdown of order. The Zoh's long-standing tradition of espionage had bred exceptional surveillance assets that were instrumental in collecting data for the Coalition.

"That doesn't answer why she would abandon her post," Joe Winters said, anger creeping into his voice. Hakar supposed he hadn't authorized the action or even been notified.

"Or why she armed her flagship and several other cruisers in the fleet with tier zero ordnance including antimatter and nuclear missiles in the gigaton range," added Empress Kra'al, livid. "She also managed to bypass the formal notification process, which shouldn't have been possible."

Surprisingly, it was the high grand admiral who spoke. The scales on Pirsan's neck turned a deep shade of ochre. "I overrode the protocol. We received actionable intelligence that Raven Blue forces staging at Tanis Ruin were preparing to strike at Calama and capture the conduit bundle. I had no choice but to act quickly."

The room was stunned, but they could assign blame later. Hakar returned his attention to the main display and gestured for the technician to continue playback. It was hard to make sense of the data as the garbled stream of images and audio streams collided and overlapped, but Hakar's eyes were focused. "Wait, what the hell is that?" The technician was slow to react, and Hakar snapped his fingers impatiently. It took several moments to find the precise point in the playback—only a few frames, obscured by interlacing lines of encrypted characters

"Any chance you can clean that up?" he said, tone conciliatory. He felt rude for snapping his fingers. It was one of those Human gestures he had picked up along the way without realizing it.

Slowly the image came into focus, the lines of characters removed. The quality wasn't good, but there was no mistaking what they were seeing. As the feed was shared with those grand admirals watching remotely, their expressions grew troubled. Open space and a fog-shrouded planet formed the backdrop; it was Tanis Ruin, Hakar assumed. In the foreground was a large space station built on the Valinata Sakrin-Westfield pattern, a sprawling spider web of a fortress. The station was in ruins, surrounded by a glittering cloud of debris and … ships. So many of them, the now familiar mottled organic-looking vessels of Raven Blue.

That wasn't what had caught Hakar's attention, however; to the right of the planet and the station was a hole in space—that was the only way he could think to describe it. The anomaly seemed to shimmer and ripple, its edges ragged with bursts of gravitational energy that illuminated the seemingly endless stream of black warships emerging from within.

"What is that? Is that a ... *conduit*?" blurted Grand Admiral Tarah Charok, the Sheff'an representative to the Star Chamber. Her voice was soft, awed, and barely audible from the speakers.

"A fucking huge one," Joseph Winters added. The Human grand admiral's hair was snow white, standing in stark contrast against his dark brown skin. Though a century Hakar's junior, Winters was a brilliant military strategist and wise leader. "How are they keeping it open? It would take incredible amounts of energy to sustain such a bridge. At least...." Words failed him.

"Special Projects was working on a gravity ram that could theoretically tunnel like that," Charok said. She sounded positively excited. "They couldn't manage more than a meter for a few milliseconds. We scrapped the project. It wasn't feasible."

"Well, it looks like someone made it feasible," Winters put in. "Maybe we can ask them how they did it. I'd also love to know where it leads."

"Goddess help us if they've managed to weaponize it," said Grand Admiral Vara Najo. Like Kra'al, she was Prross, with a blood-red hide covered in angular tattoos. While they differed greatly in matters of politics, their shared heritage and the fact that few Prross left the homeworld bound them together.

"They don't seem to need the edge," a senior defense minister muttered. The image had shifted again, a magnified view of the planet. Figures scrolling across the screen showed no enemy activity on the ground, although cloud cover could have obscured some of it. Enemy ships in orbit, however, were being highlighted, the screen filling up at an alarming rate. *Too many to count, too many to fight in open warfare*, Hakar realized solemnly.

"It's clear to me that we need to begin preparations—" Kra'al began, as the screen suddenly went dark.

"I'm sorry," said a voice from the back of the room. Hakar turned to regard the speaker. He couldn't have picked the spymaster or his companions out of a lineup to save his life, but he knew enough to listen. The Human man leading them stood by the console controlling the presentation, his hand on the keyboard. "We need to classify this until we can verify—"

"I'm sorry," Kra'al retorted mockingly, "Classify it from whom? You do know who is in this room, don't you?"

"With all due respect, Your Majesty," the man said evenly, his gray eyes never wavering, "until we can assess the validity of this data and the threat it represents, we need to stop all transmissions." There was a hum as the terminal ejected a datakey, which the agent deftly plucked and deposited in a pocket. The screen had gone dark. "I will personally deliver this to Triatha central control for analysis."

"You sounded the alert," Hakar said, locking eyes with the man.

"No, sir. We haven't confirmed it yet, but we have reason to believe Admiral Rodriguex initiated the full lockdown as a protective measure when she realized she was about to be overwhelmed." Almost as consolation, he added, "It is my sorrowful duty to inform you that her flagship has been destroyed and she has been killed in action."

The room had already been quiet, but the hush that fell over it now was oppressive.

Hakar glanced at Joe Winters's face on the screen. The Human admiral's mouth tightened and his eyes narrowed, but he said nothing.

It was Cratos Mindor who spoke first. "They never should have engaged," he said softly. "Not while our scanners are still having trouble with persistent lock." Coalition forces had been unable to effectively scan and lock onto Raven Blue vessels in early engagements. With the vast majority of ship-to-ship weaponry controlled by sensor-computer interlink, this was a serious problem. Mindor's point was a valid one, but unpopular.

"They should have retreated, you think?" snapped Motayre in a voice like rock breaking. "And abandoned the colony?"

"What of Talriis?" the empress asked, apprehension in her voice. Hakar wondered, too. The Fifth Fleet had been guarding a colony of millions in addition to holding open Calama.

The agent paused. "While most of the inhabitants had already been successfully evacuated, one of the major habitat stations was caught between elements of the fleets. We estimate civilian casualties of approximately twelve million."

A disgusted murmur rose from the assembled senior parliamentary ministers, but Kra'al waved them down. "We need to send in a relief fleet at once, to look for survivors and regain control."

Joe Winters spoke, voice cold and tinny over the speakers. "Your Majesty, I am requesting authorization to redeploy my fleet to Calama. We can be ready in a few hours."

"Admiral," said Kra'al, keeping her own voice even, "I appreciate the gesture, but I have other plans for you."

"My condolences, Joe," added Grand Admiral Najo, "but Admiral Daris and I are already en route. Be reasonable."

"And where were *you*?" Winters snapped back at her. "Your fleets were supposed to be at Calama already, not playing escort for CRAG." Najo and Daris had been waylaid as their fleets joined up with troop carriers and fortress layers from the Coalition Royal Army Ground's 1046 Legion.

"Joe, this isn't productive," the empress said softly. "Our enemy is out there." She paused to glare while the spymaster and his retinue left the room with their precious cargo. "Raven Blue have proven themselves ruthless, even barbaric, but they strike with purpose. Those worlds not rendered uninhabitable in the course of invasion are occupied in a consistent manner. Population centers, agricultural resources, and even industrial centers have been kept largely intact."

"Only to deter nuclear or antimatter strikes," interjected a general.

"That kind of thinking is going to get us in serious trouble," objected another.

Hakar sighed, embittered by the sniping. "As far as we can tell, they are not in the habit of slaughtering civilians. We should remember that. And those worlds that have been nuked lifeless are just as likely to have been destroyed by unfocused counterattacks. CRDF precision is our best asset, not mass destruction." Military outposts had been razed, picket fleets swept aside by the fleet pouring out of that wound in space. They would need surgical precision to repair the damage. He pointed to the darkened screen that had only minutes before shown them their clearest view of the enemy. "We have seen the kind of force they can bring to bear through just one of those singularities, if that's what it was. And we have to assume they are capable of generating more, and that what we have seen is only a fragment of their full naval capabilities. We need to make recapturing and holding Calama our top priority, otherwise we hand them the keys to everything from the Yangtze Tradeway to the Crown Road."

That was a terrifying thought to those present, and rather than focusing their anger, it seemed to explode like a bomb. Soon a dozen conversations had erupted regarding how best to protect the largest trade routes that ran through the Coalition and, in the case of the Crown Road, passed right through the home systems of most of the charter species.

With natural authority, Kra'al gestured for quiet, her claws raking through the fear. "Focus," she growled with barely contained anger. "I am in the presence of some of the finest minds in the Coalition. You're no good to me if you panic." She turned to regard Hakar with her liquid, golden eyes. "Admiral Hakar. Continue."

Hakar mustered what authority he could and faced the room. "Since the Raven Blue threat was assessed, we have been planning contingencies to deter invasion. Calama and its conduit bundles are the most straightforward path of attack, but over the decades we have seen that that region of space is as hard to attack as it is to defend." He could see that his words were hardly having a calming effect, but he forged ahead.

"Still, Raven Blue's strategy relies on the force of sheer numbers, meaning that they will require large trade routes to move their fleets rather than split their navies via smaller intersystem conduits. Other likely avenues of attack would be the Gates of the Arc in the Amanra Crescent, the Benez Traverse through the Tears of Alkyra, and the Zoh Strait of Helios."

One of the senior finance ministers coughed politely, managing to observe etiquette even in the midst of this crisis. "Admiral Hakar, we can certainly count on the Zoh to reinforce their territory. The Gates of the Arc and Calama sound defensible from what you tell us, but the Tears of Alkyra are no longer Coalition territory. What realistic options do we really even have for reinforcing that region? And what can we do to help?"

As to that, Hakar wasn't sure. He didn't say that his younger sister was living in the Tears of Alkyra and that he was terrified for her, but he couldn't chase the thought from his mind. Luckily, Empress Kra'al rose from her seat and raised a hand to forestall further conversation. "We're not going to solve the tactical issues here, but as to the issue of parliamentary support, that's an excellent question."

Drawing herself to her full, imposing height, Kra'al may not have been going for intimidation, but in that moment she hardly seemed like the "safe choice" she had been seen as eight years before. "Until now, you have all been tremendous in your support and your discretion in dealing with this matter, including the unfortunate secrecy with which we've had to treat Prime Minister Somerset's murder. We are moving into uncharted territory here, and public opinion about our actions in the coming weeks is going to be very difficult to predict. I hope I can count on all of you for your continued discretion as we gradually begin to release details of the threat across the border. More importantly, I hope I and the rest of the Coalition can rely on you to act according to your consciences and not out of interest for approval ratings. The work we are doing here may prove very unpopular, but it is vital that we carry it out with singular purpose and not let historic political rivalries or territorial disputes get in the way of progress." She paused, looking thoughtful. "No, it's not progress. Something greater. Salvation.

"Many of you may be harboring thoughts that we made a colossal mistake leaving our border undefended as part of the negotiations with the Valinata over the last few years. You may also think that we've watched and waited too long as this latest situation has gotten out of control. Think whatever you wish, but what's done is done, and right now we need to stop the bleeding. I'm not interested in assigning blame any more than I am in carelessly getting into a shooting war. I insist that we continue to make all reasonable attempts to contact Raven Blue and achieve a diplomatic solution to this violence, but I want all territories and all fleets on alert. Do any of you disagree?" No one spoke. "Good. We also need to begin serious discussions with our counterparts in the Commonwealth, the Shar'dan, and the Aradon Dominion. We could have stood shoulder to shoulder with the Valinata against this, and now we are left with one less potential ally. And now we need all the help we can get."

Kra'al's remarks were unprepared but elegant, nonetheless, and Hakar remembered why he had thought she would make such an effective agent of change after Telemon. Still, the veteran admiral found himself dreading the new dawn. The fragile peace of the Coalition, so precarious to begin with, was definitively at an end.

The empress had always impressed Hakar with her ability to maintain a clear head, and never more than now, when faced with such an absurd level of destruction and when their vaunted intelligence assets had failed so appallingly in warning them. Sometimes her desire for objectivity made her seem stubborn as she waited for evidence, but now it was exactly what they needed to temper their fury. Had Rodriguex forgotten this? Had she charged blindly into a battle she could not win, arrogant in her previous victories? Pride and battleships were always a lethal combination.

Kra'al's deceptively placid reptilian eyes narrowed to slits of amber. "If there are no other immediate orders of business, let's all get started. I'm sorry, everyone, but I don't think we're going back to bed. We will not, however, use this facility just yet. You can all return to your offices and homes."

High Grand Admiral Pirsan adjourned the meeting. One by one the monitors winked out as the admirals and politicians abroad severed their comm connections. With an undertone of barely contained panic, those left in the palace bunker hurried to leave it as though simply being there might cause its existence to become a necessity.

Trailing the empress and her bodyguards, the officers and minsters of parliament were subdued. Motayre and Pirsan discussed the defense of the throneworld; the big Vodroshoyan tried to whisper, but his voice echoed anyway.

Telec placed a webbed hand on Hakar's shoulder, pulling him aside as the others passed. All around them, the refuge preparations continued even as the guards stood down. "Are you all right?"

"Hardly."

"We knew this day might come, my friend."

Hakar flicked his ears and shook off the hand. "Did we? We gambled and lost." Somewhere in the depths of space, that awesome fleet was mobilizing, uncoiling in the dark. And it was hungry. He looked at the staff working to secure the bunker in case it was needed and realized how pointless it would be to hide down here as the universe burned down around them.

Telec had said something in response to Hakar's words. The Tagean looked back at his colleague. "What was that?"

"I said that the house can't win every time."

Hakar frowned.

§

On Eve life was settling into a semblance of normalcy. Leon had achieved a strained equilibrium, drifting between Rachel and the Jackal Pack Mercenary Legion. One thing had become abundantly clear to him, however: after facing the nameless horrors on the fallen Valinata world of Aethaleia, something had to change.

They weren't nameless horrors, though, were they? Whatever those things had been, Hakar had given them a name. *Raven Blue*. And while the admiral had told Leon that they were hallucinations brought on by a Valinata biological weapon, Leon had trouble believing it. He trusted Hakar and he always would, but he trusted his own senses, his own instincts, more.

The Coalition Star Chamber had said that the Valinata or a rebel faction within the Vali had deployed a toxic agent against the people of Aethaleia. Those who hadn't been killed outright by exposure had torn each other apart in an orgy of violence and terror brought on by the agent's waking nightmare effect.

Leon would have been unable to dispute that had he not recovered data from the computer of Moira Traveler, the Valinata scientist his team had been sent to rescue. They had not been able to save her, but perhaps she had saved them. The data contradicted the Chamber's claims, and although Leon had never thought to trust the word of anyone from the Valinata over the commanders he had once served in the Coalition Royal Defense Forces, the information on the recovered hard drives could not be ignored. If only the CRDF had not confiscated it, forcing him to attempt to rebuild from memory what little he had understood. He just hoped they were putting it to good use rather than filing it away in some archive.

Leon could spend only so long dwelling on the data from Aethaleia before he started to feel as though he were running in circles. Or perhaps he was just losing his mind. What the Coalition had called Raven Blue, the Vali had called Abaddon. Abaddon, Angel of the Abyss, the Destroyer. It certainly could have been the codename for a weapon of mass destruction, something to pacify rebellious urban worlds, but Leon was sure it was actually a reference to a newly discovered sentient species. Who exactly had discovered whom, though? Raven Blue had conquered Aethaleia and who knew how many other worlds in the span of months, perhaps a little over a year. All of it happening just over the border, and somehow, through some dark miracle, no one had known.

Upon returning to Eve, Leon had done his best to reconstruct the results of Moira Traveler's research, jotting down the bits he could remember. He was disappointed by the glaring gaps in his memory. A stack of papers sat by his elbow, covered in the scribblings of an obsessed man trying to crack an unsolvable riddle. It didn't help that, while he knew that what he had seen had been real, it was so far beyond his wildest conception that he couldn't quite believe it.

"Anyone in there?" asked Rachel, standing at his shoulder. How long had she been there?

Leon smiled sheepishly. "Sorry, just trying to figure this out. I thought you were spending the day in the city with your friends."

"Well, Zenna was on call at the hospital and she had to go in, so the rest of us got lunch and called it a day." Rachel slipped off her jacket and tossed it on a chair. "By the way, we tried this new wine from Devona. Cori says it's the next big thing, but I can't tell the difference between it and that cheap Triathan cabernet that Stephen got me for my last birthday." Rachel walked to the kitchenette and pulled a bottle of vodka out of the cabinet. "I'm having a drink. You want anything?"

"Isn't it a little early?" asked Leon.

Rachel smiled and pointed towards him with the neck of the bottle. "Says the man with the empty Hais glass next to his elbow."

Leon winked up at her. "I guess another couldn't hurt. But I have a meeting in twenty minutes. I need to keep a clear head."

"My father always said that the key to being a functional alcoholic is to remember the functional bit." Rachel handed him a fresh glass of whisky.

As Leon took it, his smile faltered. "You really don't talk about him much."

"That's because I hate him. But he did give great advice." Rachel poured herself a generous amount of vodka.

Leon watched her stand on tiptoe as she inspected the contents of a cabinet. Their kitchenette didn't see much use—neither of them knew the first thing about cooking, so most of the time they ate out. "Do you think the base PX has olives?"

"I don't think I've ever seen olives on Eve, but we could see about ordering some. You want me to go check?"

Rachel smiled a knowing little smile. "Don't worry about it. You look like you're pretty focused." Gratefully, Leon turned back to his papers.

There was something undeniably appealing about this domestic life at which they were playing, but somehow Leon knew it was a façade, plastering over deeper fractures. Or was it? It was true that Rachel had left for months without giving him a reason or saying goodbye. But she had come back, and that had to mean something.

It should have been easy to turn his back on Jackal Pack, to hang up his weapons and retire. Then again, tempting fate had become almost second nature. He was still attached to this place, this life, and these people.

Rachel approached, sipping her drink. "What are you working on, anyway?" Since his team had returned from Aethaleia, Rachel had not pressed Leon for information, allowing him to come to grips with what he had seen and done. How could he tell her about the streets lined with uncounted dead or about the giant, roaring monstrosity they had half-glimpsed between buildings as they fled the ruins of a world?

"You haven't looked? I haven't exactly been hiding it."

"No. I figured you'd tell me if you wanted me to know. It's not my business, is it?"

"It's technically none of mine, either." The original data had been sealed and classified by the Coalition, and Leon had been told not to share the details of the mission with anyone. At the moment, his loyalty to his former commanders was outweighed by bitterness at the way they had swept the issue under the rug. "I don't like keeping things from you."

A strange expression passed across Rachel's face, but she said nothing. Leon handed her a piece of paper that he felt was representative of the rest, mainly because half of the things he had written were crossed out. "It's a genome. The most perfect one I've ever seen."

"This doesn't look like any genome I've ever seen. It's a ball?"

"Yes," Leon said, glad to finally be able to talk about it. Raptor, Jeric, and Asar all knew, but they seemed completely uninterested in reliving the mission or discussing anything that reminded them of it.

Before becoming a mercenary, before becoming a sojier, Leon had studied to become a genetic engineer and follow in his parents' footsteps. That part of his past was one of the few things he and Rachel could discuss without turning it into an argument. She seemed to sense his nostalgia for that more peaceful past and nurtured it. She read one of the lines he had written and then crossed out. There was a cluster of question marks beside it. "The genes have been rearranged?"

"I thought so. You see, this species, whatever it is, has its genetic information arranged differently than we do. You know we have ours arranged in a double helix. For a long time, scientists on Terra thought that was the only way genes could work. Of course, now we know about all the other architectures, but this … this is unique. All the information is presented on the surface of this sphere, and then a protein reads the surface for replication."

"How does it know which way to read? I thought genes could only go in two directions."

Rachel was perceptive. "That's exactly what I've been trying to figure out. Of course, I can't, not without data, live samples, and someone a hell of a lot smarter than me. I can't even begin to imagine how it might be possible. With this sphere it can be read in any direction, the bases hit in any order. That means there's an almost infinite possibility of protein assembly, and I can't ... I just can't wrap my mind around it."

"That's wild," Rachel said, frowning. "Where'd you find out about this?"

"From...." Leon paused. "It's complicated."

Rachel understood immediately. "Never mind. So I take it this is some sort of new organism."

"Yeah, and I just don't understand it. It violates every rule I know."

"So why do you think the genes were rearranged?"

"A hunch, I guess. At first I figured there's no way a species could evolve with this kind of flexibility. They would have been too vulnerable to mutation, and they never would have progressed past single cells. So I assumed that the genome had evolved in a linear pattern like ours and *then* been arranged in this format. But that would be impossible. This genome codes sixty thousand genes with a number of base pairs roughly equivalent to what we would find in Terran bacteria."

"More genes than Humans," Rachel noted.

"A *lot* more. Twice as many. And that can only be achieved with the sort of flexibility this sphere configuration gives it."

Rachel was quiet as she processed the information. "What else have you got? Why isn't any of it on the computer?"

Leon shifted uncomfortably. "I could get in a lot of trouble for this, with the kind of people I don't want to be in trouble with. I figured it would be best to keep it away from any network access."

What little he had told her was enough to land him in a Coalition prison, but trust had been one of the biggest obstacles they had faced, and they were still climbing over it. "It's nice to see you with purpose like this, Leon. You don't usually get this enthusiastic about things. I'd love to see you do this kind of work more often."

Leon didn't know what to say to that. The beeping of his computer's appointment reminder spared him from having to think of a reply.

§

The day was waning, the sun painting the clouds in crimson velvet as it fell toward the horizon. The Three Sisters hung in the sky, a porcelain triad of moons, and the Jackal Pack troops who weren't on duty were beginning to file toward the mess halls and the on-base pub, the Desher Vaux.

General Jon Rockmore and Colonel Irún Akida watched the steady procession of sojieri from the window of the general's office. Customarily, the courtyard was raucous, full of laughter and ribald jokes. Lately, however, the mercenaries trudged like miners after a long shift, quiet and morose. Rockmore had instituted a lockout on all contracts in the wake of the perceived threat from the Valinata. It and the constant drilling were taking a toll, and the secretive return of Leon and his team aboard the *Faithless Bitch* had sparked speculation that was far from idle.

General Rockmore was a generally stolid man, not prone to wild gesticulation or temperamental outbursts. His face looked as though it had been carved from stone by a sculptor who needed more time to practice his craft. Scars crisscrossed his weather-worn face, the worst of which was a deep, puckered gash that traveled along his right cheek and jawline. Age had done little to diminish him, and despite the snow-white hair and beard, he looked powerful, with thick arms and hands that looked capable of breaking a rifle in half. Even so, his mind and his heart raced.

Colonel Akida was very different. Where Rockmore was tall, Akida was short, and where Rockmore was broad, Akida was slim. His hair was a black so dark it appeared to have a blue tint. His skin was unmarred by the violence of their lifestyle, and though he was a killer, his fingernails were clean, as was his conscience. He was impatient, but he hid it well.

The door opened, and Leon Victor entered and saluted. He had shaved off his beard following the mission to Aethaleia. It was strange to see him clean-shaven and though his stubble was growing back grayer than before, the man looked ten years younger. Except for the eyes: Leon Victor's gray eyes looked haunted and weary with the long years of his life.

The general returned the salute, glancing at his watch as he lowered his arm.

"I hope I didn't keep you waiting, sir," Leon said.

"It's all right, it gave Colonel Akida and me some time to talk about you behind your back," he joked. "But we have to get down to business." He waved the two colonels to their usual seats and retired to the big chair behind his desk. Three glasses of water had been set out on a silver tray. "I've decided to lift the contract lock."

It was interesting to watch the two colonels' reactions. In the Tagean tradition, Rockmore had elected to groom two successors, two men to run the Jackal Pack Mercenary Legion's day-to-day operations and command four of the legion's six combat brigades. They were polar opposites, their tactics mirroring their personalities: Leon was loud and brash, Akida quiet and methodical. And yet the two were remarkably similar in many ways, as well. They put duty before everything else in their lives, as though in penance for hidden sins. Loyalty was among their chief virtues, and they both cultivated atmospheres of excellence among their battalions. Longtime rivals who seldom had a kind word for one another, Akida and Victor nevertheless thought in synch quite often. Right now they had to work hard to suppress their joy. Both had very profitable jobs lined up for their units, and they were anxious to begin work again. There was an instant when a mutually contented look passed between the two arch-rivals, and Rockmore almost laughed.

"As of next week the Jackal Pack Mercenary Legion will be back in business. And now that all our troop carriers are fully repaired and refitted, we can ship our people out even faster. I know deployment efficiency has been an issue for both of you, and after the Korinthe job, I'm taking that to heart."

"What do you mean, sir?" asked Akida.

"I'm exploring options for small outposts deeper in core territories."

The smile on Akida's face was amused, disbelieving. "Franchising, sir?"

"It was Colonel Victor's idea, and after giving it some thought, I find I agree."

Akida ran his hand through his hair, brushing a few stray locks into place. "Not a bad idea, I confess."

Rockmore picked up a pen and twirled it idly. "I'm hoping that one day soon we can have forces on call within hours of any spot in the galaxy, even larger garrisons if it's feasible. Bases in the Shar'dan, in the Commonwealth, the Aradon." Rockmore hesitated. "Maybe even the Valinata...."

It was a compelling thought, and Leon and Akida knew they would be the ones to lead those new garrisons.

"Even better, I've bought a new fighter carrier to replace the *Coyote*, bringing our strength back up to four. It was second-hand, from the Shar'dan, but it just needs a bit of polish. Gorgon-class, eight-squadron capacity. *Star Wolf* has also been fully overhauled," the general said proudly. "The dockyard is just finishing the hull work."

"I didn't think we'd ever get that tub battleworthy again," Akida admitted. Jackal Pack's single heavy patrol cruiser, the *Star Wolf* had been Rockmore's pride and joy at the legion's incorporation. A heavily modified, heavily armed and armored Shar'dan Confederacy Dragon-class battle cruiser, she acted as the primary sentry for Eve. But it had been years since she had seen battle, even longer since she had been properly refurbished. Most of their naval work was conducted by their modest complement of destroyers, corvettes, and fighter carriers. The last time Rockmore was aboard *Star Wolf*, the bulkheads were stained from leaking pipes, half the weapons were inoperational, and much of the crew had seemed inexperienced.

"Oh, she's ready. She may not be as maneuverable as some of the more modern Coalition Royal Navy boats, but I daresay she's more heavily armed than anything in her tonnage class. And she's got a few new surprises, including a neutron beam that can cut right through a defensive grid." Rockmore crossed his arms and leaned back, satisfied. The contract lock had upset many of the mercenaries and annoyed more than a few investors, but it had given them time to get their house in order. "Anyway, brass tacks. You both flagged your crews for missions, and those contracts are still open."

"My crew can be ready in twenty-four hours," Akida put in eagerly.

"Excellent. And Leon? I know you had planned to lead the Mekon DaVoi operation yourself, but you don't have anything to prove here. Captain Braeburn could take it on, as well."

Rockmore had expected some reluctance from Leon after the close call on Aethaleia, but it seemed his words had provoked the colonel. After the barest hesitation, Leon said. "Thank you, sir. I'd rather just get back to business." There was a defensive edge to Leon's voice. He didn't like being coddled, and he hated being protected. "I'll discuss it with my team." *And Rachel*, he thought to himself.

"Very well. The client has made some changes to the contract since you had a chance to review it, owing to the dynamic nature of their situation. They want a full platoon, so I'll need you to review your enlisted roster, choose some NCO specialists to lead them, and handle requisition with Major Craf."

Originally, it had been a mission for four mercenaries, the same team Leon had taken to Aethaleia: Raptor Merikii, Jeric, and Asar Abu Seif. Since Asar had been gravely injured, Rockmore had sent him home to be with his wife and newborn daughter. Leon already had a second unit in mind: each of the three officers present commanded two of Jackal Pack's six brigades. Leon led the Third and Sixth brigades, comprised of mixed forces of infantry and heavy infantry, mechanized armor, and light aerospace support. While neither colonel was obligated to do much field work, both of them were fully committed specialists in addition to their administrative duties. It kept them sharp, it kept them in touch with their people, and it brought in revenue.

Rockmore was turning to Akida when Leon interrupted him.

"Sir, I plan to make Traxus the operational commander and put her in charge of the platoon. She wants the work, and she needs the experience." Leon looked uncomfortable. "With your permission, General."

It wasn't as simple an issue as replacing a platoon's lieutenant, which in itself was problematic. Traxus Tachai was the younger sister of Grand Admiral Hakar, a powerful Coalition flag officer who had been both friend and foe to Jackal Pack over the years, handing out penalties at least as often as he handed out contracts. The issue was compounded by the fact that Traxus, as her clan's future matriarch, had gone against the family's wishes by joining any sort of military at all. She had made her upstart brother complicit in her rebellion, further damaging his reputation in the eyes of the family. Tageans may have administered the bulk of the Coalition's interests, but sometimes it was easier to be a Human. Putting Traxus in harm's way against Hakar's explicit wishes could jeopardize Jackal Pack's already tenuous relationship with the Coalition Royal Defense Forces and their discretionary budget.

Akida looked annoyed that Leon would even broach such a sensitive topic, but Rockmore was inclined to give his men the benefit of the doubt. "Tell you what, let me run another assessment of the client, do a little poking around. If everything looks clear, you've got my blessing to take her. She's done well in command exercises, but keep her out of trouble."

"Yes, sir. Anything goes wrong, I'll have Raptor sit on her."

"Very well." With Leon satisfied, Rockmore turned to Akida. "As for you, Irún, I'm still not sure I'm comfortable with your team supporting Tendur Famis's outfit."

"Actually, sir, I have another issue I'd like to address first," Akida said languidly. "I had a long-term corsec contract in the Aradon lined up for a company of my light infantry, but the Indigo Specialty Group undercut us on the bid while we were in lockdown."

Leon sat up straighter, and Rockmore frowned. "ISG? That's the third time they've poached a client. Leon, didn't a few of their people used to run with your old Mourning Star team?"

"Jaimie Cota and Luxinha Farseen," Leon confirmed. "I haven't spoken to either of them in years. Lux wouldn't give me the time of day, and I'm not sure what kind of clout Jaimie has with them."

Rockmore looked disappointed. Corporate security—or corsec—was hardly their most lucrative market, but it tended to be stable. "Maybe I'll get in touch with them and see if we can agree to some sort of jurisdiction on this sort of thing. Anyway, back to Tendur Famis. He used to be a slaver, and most of his crew were slavers, too. I don't want Jackals subordinated to that kind of activity."

Now it was Akida's turn to be defensive. "I understand, General, and up until a year ago, I would have agreed with you. I did a little research, though, and it looks as though he turned state's evidence in the Shar'dan in exchange for clemency. I guess they liked his information enough to put up some of the capital for his new operation."

"This mining colony on P'trop. And you really think he's gone legitimate?"

"Heidi analyzed the financials, and everything seems to check out."

"If the Shar'dan helped set up his mining operation," Rockmore mused, "you'd think they could help him defend it."

"P'trop is in the Free Trade Zone," Akida said, shrugging.

"Free fire zone is more like it," Leon said smugly. It was an accurate nickname. The Shar'dan Confederacy, trying to follow the examples of the Coalition and Unified Commonwealth, had deregulated vast stretches of resource-laden systems. That policy had had an unintended consequence, however, with private firms militarizing against one another, the colonist pioneers caught in the crossfire.

"Famis isn't the only one with marauder problems," Akida said haughtily.

"He wouldn't even be the only one to hire those marauders to knock off his own shipments so he could sell them on the black market for a higher price, tax free," Rockmore pointed out. "But it's your call, and I trust your judgment. Do me a favor, though, and keep backup on standby, at least a platoon and a frigate. And have your old colleagues in the SRG keep an eye out." The truth was that Akida probably didn't have many friends left in the Shar'dan Republican Guard, but it couldn't hurt to ask. "That's it for now, gentlemen."

The two colonels saluted and turned for the door. Leon even held it open for Akida. Aside from that, things were finally getting back to normal. Rockmore allowed himself a glance at the portrait of his wife, Theresa. It still hurt to look at her picture sometimes, especially as night fell. Even all these years later, it felt wrong to sleep alone.

§

Hakar sighed. It was hard to be patient and coach people to come to the same conclusions he had reached months ago. Still, he had been facing down Telec and Kra'al on his own for so long now that circumventing normal channels was becoming an old habit. When had subterfuge become so comfortable?

Grand Admiral Cratos Mindor sat before him, looking tired. Short, slim, and well-mannered, Mindor had a knack for going unnoticed until he felt like stepping forward. Well, it was time for him to step forward, yet he was digging in his heels. "When Her Majesty said she had something else in mind for me, I didn't realize she wanted me playing politics. There are thousands of people better qualified to lead negotiations with the Dias Traverse than I."

"But no one who will try harder than you."

"Potential rebellion on one side of the empire, a war starting on the other. And I'm supposed to play marriage counselor for the Tez'Nar. I feel there are better uses for my skills."

A seasoned leader and a grand strategist in the old tradition, Mindor had spent his autumn years drawing up literally thousands of scenarios and battle plans for the CRDF. He knew the CRDF's capabilities inside and out and could recite whole chains of command and fleet compositions. He could do the same for the militaries of the neighboring powers. In short, Cratos Mindor was a man with a singular gift for numbers and facts, which was likely why the ambiguity of their present situation caused him so much discomfort. Moreover, he came from an aristocratic family, and his pride was prickly.

It had surprised them all when Empress Kra'al had selected Mindor to lead the diplomatic mission rather than one of the more obvious candidates from parliament or the consular corps. It had surprised them even more when she had subordinated his main battle fleets to Grand Admirals Daris and Najo to help seize and hold the conduits at Calama. It made him an admiral without a command, depriving the rank-obsessed man of much of his status.

"I've never even considered visiting the Traverse," Mindor mumbled into his morning Kaf.

"The ride to Ezai is long. You'll have plenty of time to get excited." The Dias Traverse, home region to the feathered Tez'Nar, had been a hotbed of political unrest for years. Recently, dissidents led by the Dias Liberation Front had threatened to light the fuse, and whole planets were on the verge of open rebellion. While the Coalition had far more pressing matters than the Dias, they couldn't very well let it get worse, or they would have to tie up valuable military resources there, as well. Whatever Hakar thought about how the Coalition had marginalized the Dias, he had a war to win.

Mindor's office in the Tagean Ministry of Defense was lavishly appointed even though he rarely had cause to use it. In the last two years, he had been on Tagea for a total of twelve days. This latest visit was to be a brief one, as well. Through the window Hakar could see across the Plaza of Unity to the Coalition Chambers of Parliament, the massive edifice shrouded in fog. The Tagean officer sighed. "I still think you should take a larger escort."

"From where? My fleets aren't mine anymore. And we already have battleships looming over the Dias Traverse, Hakar," Mindor said haughtily but tiredly. "The DLF barely recognize our authority as it is. Holding a fist under their nose will *not* endear us to them."

The Dias Liberation Front, the organization at the forefront of the Dias Traverse independence movement, had been responsible for murder and mayhem in their efforts to be heard, but they were not nearly as intractable as they seemed. They had agreed to meet with the Coalition leadership and the loyalist Dias governors on the condition that they choose the location. Ezai was neutral ground, all right: a barren, airless planetoid with a population so small that selective breeding laws had been enacted to preserve genetic diversity.

"They respect warriors, Cratos," Hakar pointed out. "You'll have far better luck than any politician." He felt a stab of regret as he remembered that Prime Minister Adam Somerset had been brutally killed by the mysterious Raven Blue, along with his entire retinue. The massacre had been covered up until the Star Chamber could figure out just what they were dealing with, but that couldn't last. In the meantime, they needed the Dias on their side: the Tez'Nar of the

Traverse were master shipbuilders, and their fleets were almost uncannily coordinated.

"I still feel that having a grand admiral at the negotiating table will be seen more as a threat than a show of respect. And as to your Special Projects interests, I fear that the kinds of things you're talking about may exceed our mandate."

"They may," Hakar said guardedly. "Let me worry about that. You heard Her Majesty: we need to put aside our personal feelings in order to preserve what little momentum we have.'

"I don't believe she was specifically referring to this sort of sub rosa inquiry. Using Special Projects resources to sweeten the pot for the negotiations is a low move."

Hakar frowned. Bribing potential dissidents with their own military contracts was a gamble. "I don't mean to insult you, but do you actually think it's unethical, or is your queasiness simply because you don't want to be the one to put your name on it?"

"A little of both," Mindor admitted. "But I will do what needs to be done, I assure you."

"I'm glad to hear it. I'm not asking you to go behind her back. We have her tacit support. We simply need to give her some distance from it."

"Joseph was right. He told me you had your back against the wall," Mindor said accusingly. That stung. The Niaotl rose from his chair and walked to the credenza by the far wall. He poured water from a crystal carafe into two glasses and brought one to Hakar. "This is a very strange bribe to offer. I don't believe you would have considered it a few years ago."

"We weren't on the brink of total war a few years ago," Hakar snapped. Mindor may have been an aristocrat, but he was also disconcertingly blunt and didn't seem all that concerned that he had insulted Hakar. "Listen, I'm not happy about it. But we need to extend the proverbial olive branch, as Joseph might say."

"Humans and their idioms," Mindor muttered.

"Can you think of a solution that will get a quicker response?" Hakar asked. "A *feasible* one," he clarified, forestalling Mindor's inevitable argument. After all, the DLF and the other regionalist groups in the Dias had always been very clear about what they wanted. "I'm told that the Dias have some of the best bioengineering programs in the Coalition. We need experts we can rely on."

"Biowarfare has always been a touchy subject, especially if we're talking about focusing on a genetically homogenous enemy. I don't need to tell you how politically dangerous that could be." Mindor's round face was pinched, thoughtful. "And working from Valinata data … not to mention without the actual samples. I'm no scientist, Hakar, but doesn't that violate the integrity of the research?"

"It does, conventionally." *Yes, he's right, every damn thing we take from the Aethaleia data could be in doubt.* "But we have to work with what we have. I don't think there will be any shortage of samples before long."

"Did you have someone in mind to head this biowarfare program?"

Yes, but Leon Victor is long gone. "Whoever it is needs to be committed to results, not observing pro forma." Hakar couldn't believe his own words. It was true what they said about power corrupting. But he wasn't doing it for the power, he was doing it for the sake of the kingdom! *That's what the corrupt always claim as their defense. It's as bad as saying "I was just following orders."*

"Hakar, are you all right?"

"That's irrelevant." He instantly regretted his words. "I'm sorry, Cratos. Listen, the data from Aethaleia are only fragmentary, but it's the best lead we have. We can worry about covering our asses, or we can do what needs to be done. The deadline for proper methodology has expired."

"You don't *really* suppose it's as bad—"

"I *know* it is," Hakar said finally. "This is no hypothetical scenario, my friend. This is no war game. What this *is* is a fight that could be an end game if we let it become one. Meanwhile, I'm not going to be the one worrying about budget cuts and parliamentary inquiries. I'm not talking about preserving my career. I'm talking about *serving*. Serving the Coalition that we swore to protect at all costs. *At all costs*, Cratos, even at the cost of our lives and our reputations."

Hakar realized he was shaking. It was strange that planning this ruse had allowed him to speak more candidly than he had in a long time. Although he didn't like Mindor much, he trusted him implicitly. "I couldn't care less what the history books make of me at this point. Doubtless, I'll be vilified, if I'm remembered at all. But we have to ensure that there will be history books for us to be remembered in. You may think I'm exaggerating for dramatic effect, but I've seen what these people are capable of. They don't operate on any principles we would recognize. I don't like it, but maybe we have to be a little more flexible with our own."

When Mindor had left for his ship, Hakar went and sat in his office, feeling riven. What sense of legitimacy, of righteousness, did he have left to him? At what point did a person become so morally compromised that they lost their bearings on honor? Hakar feared that he was already seeing that point in his rearview mirror.

2: Eye of the Storm

The empress looked up from her work, sparing a glance through her office window for the busy cityscape. She let her gaze rove across the palace grounds and the gardens blanketed in winter snow. How long had it been since she had taken the time to stroll along those paths? Certainly not recently, as her metabolism prevented her from enjoying northern Tagea's mild but long winter.

Hakar bowed slightly. "You wanted to see me, Your Majesty?"

"Thank you for coming, Hakar. You know that I trust you implicitly?" she asked absently, returning her attention to her work, her clawed hand moving gracefully as she wrote.

"Yes, Your Majesty. And I thank you for it." Where had *that* come from, and where was it leading?

"I understand that Daris and Najo have arrived at Calama."

"Yes, and they've begun operations against the enemy as well as recovery and salvage for the Fifth Fleet. Mindor's fleets are not far behind."

"Very good." Kra'al put down her pen and waved him to a seat. Hakar moved a stack of files to clear a chair and sat facing her. "I've seen too few reports of survivors."

The thought raised a lump in Hakar's throat. Rodriguex's commanders and crews had been valiant, and it did not appear that many had retreated. But here and there, escape pods and partial wrecks had been found with pockets of survivors on board. More often, the rescue ships found only flight recorders, playing back silently to themselves as they drifted through the long, cold dark. "Far too few," he agreed.

"Resistance?"

"Plenty," Hakar confirmed. "But not nearly as much as we had anticipated. Either the enemy has already moved through in force or they've withdrawn."

"Seeing as we're not knee deep in reports of Raven Blue attacks, I'm inclined to believe the latter. It probably won't be for long, though."

There was nothing to say to that. She was absolutely right.

"Have you heard the signal picked up by the carrier *Scotland*?" Kra'al asked, reaching toward her keyboard.

"I have not," Hakar answered, puzzled.

"You probably should have received it before I did. Tell me what you make of it." She called up a file and hit a key. The noise that played back to them was obscured by static, but there was a distinctive moan, low and mournful, like some great injured beast. It was primal, haunting. And Hakar recognized it.

"We received a signal like that from Shra, following the incident with the Valinata carrier group at Calama a few months ago." He said it breathlessly, as though unable to believe it.

This recording was much longer than the first he had received, and Hakar listened to it play through two more times, each time trying to decipher a pattern. The moaning was punctuated periodically by whistles and clicks. As before, the recording filled him with dread.

"Have we really had no luck with decryption?" she asked.

"No, Ma'am. We ran the last one through every comscan, algorithm, and codebreaking suite at our disposal. No one knows what it is, but it *is* consistent with other signals we've received from sweeps of the Valinata Whisper Network."

"Maybe they'll have better luck with this one," Kra'al offered doubtfully. "You still believe it's be a language?"

"If Raven Blue is a homogenous species as we suspect, it could be, and it could be completely unfamiliar to us. None of the databases or linguistics experts we've managed to wrangle from the FLASH Center have had any better luck isolating patterns."

"You can't even say for certain that it *is* a language, although I admit it does sound like a vocalization of some sort." This was perpetually disappointing. With the introduction of the FLASH battery, civilization had leapt forward: centuries ago, enterprising scientists from across the different powers joined together to develop a consistent interspecies method for implanting latent neural pathways in developing children. This imprinting included enough linguistic data to make communication across languages and vocal physiologies possible and relatively easy. It was the reason Kra'al and Hakar could communicate so well, even while speaking their native tongues, and it had facilitated technological and cultural renaissance in nearly every generation since the system's establishment. Coming across a species that could not or would not communicate with the Coalition, even when hailed directly, presented yet another challenge in the long list of barriers to understanding and making peace with Raven Blue ... or defeating them.

"Some people have suggested that Raven Blue may therefore not be sentient," Kra'al mused, tapping her pen against the desk, "but I imagine that is absolute bullshit to anyone who's seen the data or fought them firsthand. We need information, we need to understand them, and we need to be able to beat them."

The empress leaned back in her chair, tossing her pen aside. "That's not why I called you here, but I did wish to keep you informed."

"I didn't think it was, Highness."

"I have redeployed Joe Winters and his fleets to the Amanra Crescent. He has to hold the Gates of the Arc. Parliament has authorized a ninety-day defense maneuver until we secure enough support for an official deployment."

"That's good." Hakar waited tensely, but he feared he knew what was coming.

"I am rejecting your request to redeploy to the Tears of Alkyra."

"But Your Majesty—"

"I agree with your assessment that the Tears will be among the enemy's likely paths of advance, and that can work to our advantage. I'm also smart enough to know that you have family there, and I understand why you would pay special attention to Eve. I will happily dispatch a royal escort to retrieve your sister and anyone else you want removed. But we need to think strategically."

Hakar was stunned by the bluntness of her response. She wasn't wrong, but she was putting billions of lives in the crossfire. "I can't condone funneling the enemy through a populated region that way, Your Majesty. The Tears may not be part of the Coalition any longer, but that doesn't mean we can simply abandon them."

"I don't intend to abandon them," Kra'al snapped, clearly insulted by the accusation. "But there are greater forces at work. You may not be aware, but the Cosmographic Advisory Panel has projected that the Benez system, the regional capital, will soon travel out of phase, temporarily fragmenting the major conduits there." She adopted a mirthless smile. "It will become a series of dead ends, unsuitable for an attack avenue."

It was true that star systems moved along the conduits, the connections tenuous, always shifting, stretching, contracting, or breaking ... sometimes to be reformed, other times permanently lost. Hakar wasn't sure he was comfortable relying on the cosmographers, however. "How long do they say this phenomenon will last?" he asked, still unconvinced that they could afford to leave the scattered worlds of the Alkyra undefended.

"It's unlikely to last more than a few months," Kra'al conceded. "These things are hardly exact. But if we can predict the phase, so can they. They wouldn't be foolish enough to try and claw through that. It would take months instead of days."

"And if they tried? It would turn the Alkyra into a warzone."

"And that's why I have you to draw up contingencies. If the worst happens, you will lead the counterattack."

She wasn't giving him a choice, Hakar saw. He was smart enough to join her rather than fight her on it. "Very well, but may I suggest that we take a more active role there?"

"You may suggest anything you wish. But please don't lecture me on obligation. It was Telemon who vowed never to intervene in Alkyran affairs. I'm merely following his precedent," Kra'al said acidly. Her disgraced predecessor had begun the gradual removal of all Coalition assets in the Alkyra trade sector, partly as a way to mollify the Valinata but also in recognition of the sector's independence. Hakar felt that Kra'al was showing uncharacteristic pettiness in following that example.

The grand admiral steeled himself for what was bound to be a grudge match. "Telemon violated his oaths to the people of the Coalition, and he'll be forever hated for it."

"Hated? They still call him 'Uncle Franz.'" Kra'al sounded petulant now, and Hakar frowned.

"Telemon gave himself the nickname. People just ... went along with it." The truth was that most people *had* thought of Telemon as an uncle: the sort of alcoholic, lecherous uncle that families prayed would not come to holiday gatherings. Nevertheless, Kra'al had a point. There was no familiarity between her and her people. She was never "Auntie Atyre" or anything of the kind, always at a remove, always The Empress.

Hakar decided to go on the offense. "I agree that the Coalition can't simply storm the Alkyra, but we need more than a token presence. The regional base on Eve is a shadow of its former capability and has almost no aerospace assets. We need a force familiar with the Alkyra, a force which could take full advantage of the stellar configurations and respond quickly to any crisis, buying time for us to deploy."

"Your rapid response fleet idea refuses to die," Kra'al said, faintly amused.

"Not quite. I would like you to approve a contract offer to a professional Ronin organization." Hakar paused, waiting. The empress harbored a well-known disregard for private military units in all their forms—"disgraceful" was one of the kinder adjectives she used to describe them. Part of the platform of her candidacy for the monarchy had been more stringent sanction systems to prevent mercenary companies from operating in Coalition space.

"'Professional?' Mincing words again, are we?" Kra'al's eyes narrowed in suspicion or amusement, he couldn't tell. "You have someone in mind, I take it. Go ahead, I'm listening." Her tone implied *Not for long.*

"Yes, Ma'am. The Jackal Pack Mercenary Legion is located on Eve, near the apex of the Alkyra, with easy access to most of the sector. We've hired them for sensitive missions before, and they've always exercised discretion."

"Right. Your affair with the underworld continues. I shouldn't have invited you here tonight." Her hissing Prross Shar was laced with poorly masked disdain. She drummed her claws on the ebony desk. "That last reconnaissance job didn't go too well from what I understand. Oh, don't act surprised. I knew what you were up to." She paused for a moment, and her expression grew more conciliatory. "I appreciate that you're trying to think outside the box, Hakar, but it seems to me this is like trying to patch a hull breach with a piece of tape. I'm unaware of any Ronin outfits with sufficient personnel or materiel to make a difference. And even if they could, I don't trust them. I pay attention. I know about Jackal Pack, I know about Leon Victor, and I know how they operate. It's going to take a lot to convince me it's not a complete misallocation of funding." She leaned back in her chair, her tail thumping once against the floor. "Go on, then, convince me."

Hakar withdrew a mem from his briefcase and handed it to her. It summarized Jackal Pack's resources from combat assets to financials and contained glowing testimonials from former clients including members within the governments of the major galactic powers. She snorted occasionally as she scrolled through, but her eyes were focused on the information while Hakar talked. "Many of their units are independently operating commando squads, but all told, they can wield a full infantry corps, with armor, naval support, artillery, and logistics. Nearly fifty thousand personnel altogether. And their leadership is top of the line, all ex-military. The vast majority of their officers have command experience, much of it in clandestine or frontline operations." Hakar paused, to see if Kra'al was still with him. She was listening intently. "As a matter of fact, I believe they can act extremely effectively as a forward recon force or as fast-response skirmishers. They have proven proficient in small-unit actions against much larger enemy concentrations, and more importantly, they're adaptable. In fact, one of their teams obtained the Aethaleia Sequence."

Kra'al brightened a little, but she still seemed skeptical. Good news was hard to come by these days, and she was naturally distrustful of anything that sounded too good to be true. "The Aethaleia data will come in handy, I'm sure, but it will take more than that to sway me. It says here that their commander in chief's last official rank was that of brigadier general. The rest of the leadership doesn't break colonel. They seem a bit ... overextended."

Nodding gravely, Hakar tried to keep from getting defensive. He knew that he had to be objective to get what he needed. "I'm aware of that, but I can testify to their administrative and command capability. As I said before, the majority of their force functions as independently operating units at the company level. Their actual regular force is little more than a division. General Rockmore commands and administers two brigades, and each of his executive officers is in charge of two more. I realize you have your reservations—"

"I do," Kra'al said, cutting him off. "I seriously question the ability of this strangely small command staff to maintain discipline and organization of a full corps in the heat of battle or over the course of an extended campaign. Looking at these mission summaries, I am impressed by their accomplishments, but the entire force has never been in the field at one time. In fact, the largest cohesive force fielded by Jackal Pack has been a single brigade, commanded by a single colonel with oversight by this General Rockmore. They are Ronin, Hakar, a *lot* of Ronin, but that does not constitute an army. I have no doubt that they are the top choice for assassins, smugglers, bodyguards, spies, and private security, but I need armies."

Hakar stood silently, feeling his opportunity slipping away. He knew Kra'al well enough to realize that arguing with her once she had made up her mind would shatter whatever say he had in the matter.

When she spoke again, she surprised him. "Still," she said thoughtfully, "using contractors as a commando force might have merit." She smiled absently, but her gaze was predatory. "You may have something here. We can send them into hotzones to act as spotters or at the very least use them to draw fire."

Hakar's face fell. "Your Majesty, I hardly consider these sojieri expendable. They're highly specialized and highly skilled."

"But in the end they are simply criminal combatants." Kra'al exhaled through her razor-sharp teeth. "I suppose they have proven themselves useful in the past, but this could be far beyond their capabilities. I also question their loyalty in the face of a prolonged conflict, not to mention their impact on the morale of our own troops." She looked the grand admiral in the eye. "You really think they can bring something to the table?"

"Yes, Highness. They can go where we can't, and do what we can't. You said you trust me, and I trust them. I hope that counts for something."

Kra'al gave in graciously. "I wish you wouldn't use my words against me like that, but I *do* trust your judgment, my friend. I have since I was crowned. Even so, I will have to convince the others, and that will be difficult if *I'm* only half-convinced. Not to mention negotiating with the Alkyra Trade Council." She gave him a meaningful glance. "Granting them a blanket sanction will take some time, and I hope you understand why I am reluctant to allow these pirates free range about our space."

Hakar cleared his throat. "Naturally, Your Majesty. I've taken the liberty of looking into their current sanction ratings, and they are cleared at the highest levels of private operators. I believe I can get them affordably, and with guarantees. They're in the line of fire, and they know what's at stake." He sat with his hands clasped between his knees, awaiting her decision.

Kra'al did not keep him waiting long. His reliability and his ingenuity had earned him some credit with the monarch. "Very well, Hakar. You want my approval, and I won't give it, but I will give you my permission. Get everything they have available: ships, tanks, sojieri, any illegal arms or weapons of mass destruction they might have. Assure them that there will be no repercussions for disclosure." Her mouth split in a serrated smile, but the expression failed to reach her eyes. "Should I write you a blank check?"

Hakar smiled in return. "You won't regret this, Highness. I would be proud to have any of these officers serving under me. You will be, too."

"I'm glad to hear it. I expect a full proposal *with* an ironclad contract in a week. Assuming the Alkyra Trade Council agrees to our intervention, I'd expect you to conduct a strategic assessment of the area yourself. Your fleet can leave once I've confirmed this with the cabinet." Kra'al picked up her pen. "Good night, Grand Admiral Hakar. Oh, and Hakar?"

He turned back.

"I hope you're not doing this out of some misguided sense of loyalty or friendship. We can't afford to let personal issues affect our judgment."

"Never, Majesty."

§

Grand Admiral Mindor stepped off the launch's ramp and onto the airless world of Ezai, accompanied by a cadre of marines and officers. The lights of the planet's single colony—an old frontier bunker complex from a long-forgotten war—gleamed invitingly in the cold distance. Ezai was not in reality a planet but a moon, orbiting a dying gas giant that reminded Mindor of the third planet in his own home system, red and orange with a few meager rings.

It was easy to forget just how close the Dias Traverse and the Tagean Corridor were to one another, separated by just a few dozen light-years. It took Mindor's command staff only a few days to reach Ezai, but it might as well have been at the remotest edge of the galaxy. It was unloved and forgotten, yet the fortunes of the entire Dias Traverse hinged on the decisions that would be made here.

Mindor had gotten over his sense of bewilderment, even resentment, at being chosen for this task. Now he was eager to try his hand at politics as well as war. Though Mindor knew there were many ambassadors and parliamentary ministers better qualified for such negotiations, he couldn't help thinking that this might be the first step on a path to the high grand admiral's seat. Success here would make him a true power player. The thought brought to mind Prime Minister Somerset, cut down so ruthlessly.

Having been granted nearly absolute negotiating authority was nearly as terrifying as it was invigorating, but Mindor took the responsibility given to him by Her Majesty and the parliament seriously. He had spent most of the journey studying, reading, planning. The Dias Liberation Front and their allies wanted fairly simple goals: wealth and the quality of life that came with it.

Staving off invasion by Raven Blue was far more important than suppressing the Dias uprising, and Mindor had been gently, subtly instructed to give in on whatever front was necessary to secure allegiance. That did not, however, mean that he intended to roll over. He would do his best to represent the Coalition's long-term interests, so that even when the approaching war with the Ravens ended, the Dias would be secure, loyal, and free of this senseless violence.

His overture, including thinly veiled promises to establish Special Projects divisions and military research and development facilities would mean direct investment by some of the largest corporations in the galaxy while also giving the Coalition Royal Defense Forces a better foothold in the region. He hoped and believed it would be well received.

Mindor understood that the Dias region had been marginalized over the preceding decades, but he felt little in the way of guilt and nothing in the way of responsibility. He did not believe it was the Coalition's job to coddle economically backward sectors. His own homeworld of Citakk was largely mountainous, rocky, gifted with the bare minimum resources needed to sustain life and facilitate the development of a sentient species. And yet the Niaotl had carved vast fortresses out of those mountains, mining ore, cultivating underground gardens and forests. They asked for nothing. Their harsh crib had raised a hardy race, and it was no wonder the mountain clans had swiftly conquered the Niaotl of the grasslands and forests, establishing a world government far more unified than those found on Tagea, Terra, or the other homeworlds.

The grand admiral put aside his ruminations. He was here to extend a helping hand, after all, however he might feel about it. And the people eking out an existence on this dustball needed it, that much was immediately obvious. Ezai was as dead as a world could be, and it was with that thought that he understood the DLF's tactic. Setting the negotiations here would give them an incredible psychological advantage. Only the most cold-hearted brute could ignore the plight of the Dias Traverse as illustrated by these impoverished colonists, who had to import everything and pay dearly for it with whatever they could earn from the arts and crafts they cobbled together from scrap. Their chief export was some sort of potent mushroom used in gourmet cooking, grown in musty old warehouses beneath the surface. Mindor did not intend to let sympathy for their poverty sway him.

Nevertheless, Ezai might be an ideal setting for more sensitive operations. There were few people to pry into their doings. Almost reflexively, the admiral began tallying costs and predicting numbers of personnel required to staff defensive stations and ground emplacements, find a full-time commander.... The costs never seemed to end.

It was unfortunate that they had been forced to land so far away from the colony, but Ezai was prone to severe dust storms. Even now, swirling clouds reduced visibility to a hundred meters. Over their heads the grit had whipped into a frenzy that could have tossed the command shuttle into the buildings of the colony had they tried to land any closer.

The world looked cold and uninviting through the curved dome of his helmet, the only thing between him and asphyxiation. Grand Admiral Cratos Mindor was the last in a long line of naval officers who traced their service back to the dawn of Niaotl space travel. Duty was ingrained in him, and he would put up with much in the name of that duty, whether or not he had thought the Empress up to her office. He had always known it was a changing universe, and one had to adapt or become obsolete.

The low gravity and the canned sound of his breath reminded Mindor of extra-vehicular combat training in his youth. There had been nothing finer than standing on the outer hull of a ship with nothing between him and a nebula but the thin skin of an exo-suit. He had marveled at the void, felt its icy gaze on him in turn. He had been hot with the flush of excitement, even as the temperature outside approached absolute zero. Once, during a training exercise, he had been knocked from the hull, his boots' magnetic clamps malfunctioning. As he had tumbled, outbound for a crystalline blue nebula that looked like nothing so much as a bottomless, world-swallowing ice cave, Mindor had found himself enchanted. A rescue vehicle had towed him back long before his oxygen had come near to depletion, but he had been breathless with emotion. He had never felt so alive as at that moment.

It was telling, then, that instead of exhilaration all Mindor felt now was inconvenience. It had been decades since he had been in an airless, low-gravity environment, and it had long ago lost its enchantment. Perhaps Hakar would have found some enjoyment in it, and he knew Motayre would have. *Probably would have gone bounding off like a child.* To say Ezai was airless was not entirely accurate; however, the planet's atmosphere was so thin that rebreathers were required outside the pressurized habitation domes. The least the colonists could have done would have been to send a vehicle or some sort of welcoming party, but he supposed he shouldn't be surprised at the cold reception, this deep within the DLF sphere of influence. He wasn't looking forward to being a guest in this peculiar frontier town.

The colony had been built into a large asteroid crater to shield it from the strong winds and the dust storms they produced. Inhabited by only a few thousand colonists, the bunker complex itself had been designed to support a garrison of nearly a quarter of a million. Enormous hangars, tunnels, and refrigerated warehouses honeycombed the crust of Ezai. They would be perfect for Special Projects' new Red Labs. The crater's puckered rim was visible from time to time between gusts of debris. A wound in the world, it sloped into the sky and nearly obscured the lights of the buildings sheltered within the crater. But there were the tops of sentry towers, beacons of cold light reaching into the colder oblivion of space.

As Mindor and his retinue drew closer, he was able to make out colonists gathering along the lip of the crater, watching. Among them were members of the DLF leadership as well as the Coalition-friendly Irachan government.

There was movement beside Mindor. The commanding officer of the marine detachment, a Human sergeant major named Simon Munroe, appeared out of the dust. Clad in a broad-shouldered, towering EMMA suit, Munroe was an intimidating bodyguard. The EMMA—short for Enclosed Mechanized Main Armor—concealed his face beneath a death's-head helmet and made everything about his features exaggerated, terrifying. While the light infantry were the most widespread of the CRDF ground forces, the heavy infantry was by far the most recognizable, the most iconic. Encased in massive suits of powered armor that conjured images of chivalrous knights of old, they were the ultimate melding of person and machine, the suit operated principally by a neural interface. Such a suit could turn a person from a simple sojier into a nearly unstoppable force, capable of absorbing enormous amounts of damage and fighting in environments that no other sojier could even enter, including deep space. With the suit came awesome firepower in the form of the CL-84R "Cougar" pulse rifle, an upscaled squad assault machine gun that was impossible for anyone but a powered armor-clad marine to handle.

"Admiral, permission to speak freely?" Munroe asked, his voice clear over the comm despite the howling dust storm. Mindor waved for him to go ahead. "I don't trust these DLF or our so-called supporters among the Irachans. You should let us check the crowd."

"I just want to get inside, Sergeant," Mindor said. "I assume they'll wait to shoot us until they hear what we have to offer."

"Very well, sir." Munroe withdrew.

"He's right, you know," pointed out one of the other officers. Mindor turned to look, a simple motion made awkward by his stiff suit. Rear Admiral Tasinto, a pale-furred Niaotl with hauntingly dark eyes, had not yet begun her combined-arms rotation to determine whether or not she could rise to Grand Admiral and command mixed forces across theaters—what was referred to as menagerie, or zookeeping—but Mindor had little doubt of her abilities.

"Perhaps. But we must treat all these people as our equals, whether we want to or not."

"Of course, sir. But since we have to work long-term with them, it behooves us to demonstrate our authority."

Tasinto had been raised in an egalitarian society, and her brashness was to be expected. Mindor couldn't hold her upbringing against her. Someday he knew he would retire. And then one of his executive officers would replace him, either Geran or Larador. And then Tasinto might move up to fill that vacancy, and her attitude would be their problem. In fact, all the officers accompanying Mindor were candidates for Vice-Grand Admiral, the best and brightest from his armies and navies.

What would the DLF make of that? The Coalition had sent their finest officers to parley with rabble. They walked onward.

§

The Tez'Nar were so focused on their ambition that they would have failed to notice anything less than a supernova in their own system. Liriket Nephor, too, was Tez'Nar, with bright pink plumage and a prominent skull crest. But though he was one of them, he felt apart, alone. For months he hadn't belonged anywhere … anywhere, that was, but the sweet embrace of death.

With Ezai suddenly awash with comings and goings, it had been a simple matter for Liriket to insert himself into the daily pattern. Everything had gone as predicted until now, and once again he found himself marveling at the prescience of his benefactors.

He had been given one chance and one chance only. It had been a miracle when the Celestials had freed him from the camps, offered him a chance to live. All he had to do was kill for them. Liriket did his best to avoid notice as he moved through the crowds of mingled colonists, Irachans, and DLF rebels. The Irachans and DLF were posturing, mixing only reluctantly, and it was easy for Liriket to pass as one or the other as it suited him.

Now as the time drew near, he set to work. How had he come to this? A few months ago he had been a man with a family, working five days a week behind a desk and coming home to leftovers. It had been a routine life, but Liriket was a man who liked routine. Until recently he had never held a gun, and now he might have to use one. On a person. *It's not a person, it's an obstacle.*

It hadn't been difficult to come to Ezai and pose as a dock worker—after all, stacking crates required little mental effort and left plenty of opportunity for observation. His only real moment of panic had come when it was time to build the bomb. But then a strange calm had come over him, seemingly guiding his dexterous hands through the measurement of compounds, the wiring and placement of the detonator, with a fluidity that could ordinarily come only from experience. From there it had been a simple matter to replace one of his exo-suit's air tanks with the dummy tank that contained the bomb.

Only now did that decision begin to look foolish. He had come outside with the other workers when news of the CRDF admiral's arrival had reached them. With only half the suit's regular air supply, he would have had air to spare, assuming the admiral's delegation had touched down at the colony's main pad. To his dismay, they had landed outside the crater and were making their way in on foot, adding nearly an hour to the wait. The heads-up display projected on his suit's scuffed visor informed him that he had less than an hour's worth of oxygen left.

His beak clicking rapidly out of nervousness, Lirket withdrew from the crater lip, back toward the colony buildings. It was time to unscrew the bomb and place it out of the way where no one would stumble upon it until he was ready.

Clumsily he reached around the back of his suit, trying to get a grip on the tank, but the angle was awkward. He cursed and leaned against the wall of one of the modular surface structures, trying to give himself a little leverage.

"What are you doing?" rasped a voice in the Zetzoy tongue, with an accent so cultured it could only be one of the Irachans. Liriket looked up, trying to come up with a reasonable cover story.

Standing over him was an Irachan Home Guard, clad in ceremonial exo-armor that was painted a rich blue and topped with a crested golden helm. His weapon was slung over his shoulder.

Liriket's mind blanked. He was no spy; he didn't know the first thing about talking his way out of anything like this. His beak clicked a few times helplessly as the guard looked at him questioningly.

"Trouble with your air supply?" asked the guard finally, giving Liriket his way out.

"Nothing serious," he said in his own native language of Fiig, trying to sound casual. "I can handle it."

"Let me see," said the guard, gesturing for Liriket to turn around. "I used to service exos for dock maintenance. They were bulky, deep space models, not like yours. Shouldn't be too different, though."

"Really, I'm fine," Liriket insisted, now afraid.

"Nonsense. You'll never reach it like that." The guard forcibly turned him around and began examining the tank casing. His mind racing, Liriket tried to think of a way out of this. He couldn't blow his cover or the Celestials would destroy everything he had left, which was admittedly not much.

Against his better judgment, Liriket had hidden a small pistol in one of the airtight storage compartments on the torso of his exo. Now he was glad he had. He reached for it, popping the compartment's seal. He didn't want to do this, but he felt those icy fingers of calm massaging his conscience, guiding his hand. Clumsily, he pulled out the weapon, realizing how difficult it would be to handle while wearing the thick exo gloves.

"Well, here's your problem," the guard said, puzzled. "Your secondary tank isn't even hooked up. The scrubbers don't work on a one-valve configuration. You're burning through it double-time. Give me a moment."

"I told you, not necessary," Liriket said. His feathers had fluffed inside the suit, pressing against the padded lining. He raised the gun, hoping it would fire. He didn't know how to work the safety, and he didn't have a spare clip. He wouldn't have known how to reload it even if he did.

"What is this?" exclaimed the guard. "The coupler doesn't rotate. Is this even a real tank?"

Liriket turned around and shot the guard in the face before he could raise the alarm. Even in the thin atmosphere the report would carry, and people would wonder what it was. Hopefully, the howling storm around them would buy him time. He watched the guard crumple, shocked by the consequences of his action.

Somehow Liriket had deluded himself into thinking that the visor of the helmet protecting him from the elements was a solid wall of impenetrable glass. Seeing it punctured so easily, that neat little hole in the center, nearly unmanned him. Little cracks spiraled outward from the hole as the suit depressurized, and the glass blew out in an instant, slowly settling at Liriket's feet, jagged snowflakes in the dark. The guard's face was a red ruin, caved in, and the body sank to the ground in a puff of dust. Liriket felt his bowels loosen and knew that he was now committed to the act.

Realizing he didn't know what to do, Liriket began to panic. He was on a time limit, but the madness of the situation seized him in its grasp. Running out of oxygen, he still had to carry out his mission, or his death would be a painful one.

He saw shapes in the dust, people drawn by the commotion. He ran back toward the safety of the crowd, breathing shallowly, his chest tight. All around him stood his fellow Tez'Nar, their eyes fixed on the approaching CRDF delegation, barely visible down below in the swirling dust.

Most of the people in his immediate vicinity were DLF, recognizable in their dingy, secondhand exos with yellow armbands and sloppily painted insignia. However, here and there Irachan guards were searching the crowd, clearly alerted by comm reports. Liriket still had to get to a safe distance before he set off the bomb....

It was then that he remembered he was still wearing it, with no inconspicuous way to remove it. He closed his eyes, feeling that strange sense of calm flooding him. And then it vanished. He was afraid. There were Irachan guards moving through the DLF ranks now amid the very vocal protests of the rebels. It had all gone so perfectly, but now it seemed Liriket would be caught and killed like a rabid dog. The icy fingers around his brain slackened, replaced by a cold dread as he gave in to his natural fear. It made sense: he had never been a brave man or an adventurous one. His wife had once told him that if he ever tried anything exciting it would be the death of him. In the end, she would be proven right.

Knowing what he had to do to escape the wrath of the Celestials, Liriket moved deeper into the crowd, hoping to avoid the guards for just a few minutes more … until the admiral climbed the hill.

Liriket turned his head, trying to spot pursuers. It would have been an innocuous enough motion any other time, but wearing an exo, he had to tilt and rotate his entire torso. A professional would never have made such a simple mistake, but Liriket was no professional. There was a knot of guards searching the crowd behind him, and the movement gave him away.

"Stop!" one of them yelled. Liriket broke into a run, pushing through the DLF as they watched in confusion. Suddenly he felt something bite into his arm, and there was a hiss of escaping atmosphere as his suit began to depressurize. He had been shot!

Then the burning sensation began, and he felt warm blood streaming down his arm within the suit. When had he fallen? He had to get up, had to keep running.

He pushed himself to his knees, his arm burning with the effort, feeling as though it was twisting free. He let out a cry and looked around him. The guards stood in a circle, their weapons aimed right at his head. They were shouting orders, but he was in a haze of pain as he rested back on his haunches.

"Raise your hands!" shrieked one of the golden-helmed guards. There were people gathering around them, Irachan, colonists, DLF, all together as they came to see what was the matter. They pushed and shouted curses at one another.

In a moment of clarity, Liriket realized that if anyone ever found out who he was and what he had done, they would assume he identified with the Celestials, that he was fighting for them, a willing martyr. That could not be farther from the truth. He would strike a blow not for freedom, not for religion, not for any ideal. This would be a victory for fear, a blow struck for hate, enslavement. Perhaps it was better that he would not survive this, that he would join his family in the afterlife. He didn't want to live in a world where nightmares came to life. Most pawns had the advantage of ignorance, not knowing they were being sacrificed. Liriket could see the whole chessboard as though he were already a ghost looking down on it. Where his pawn had been, there would be only a crater. He pressed the button on the detonator. He was going home.

§

As Munroe watched the fireball rise into the air, he realized that he would have to get blood on his hands after all. He felt a knot forming in his stomach even as a cold relaxation massaged his mind.

The explosion would have been larger in a richer atmosphere, but as it was, Munroe could hear the pops of secondary explosions as the fire was propagated by oxygen tanks rupturing, turning each individual into a personal inferno. After that came the faint pop and rattle of small-arms fire as the surviving rebels and loyalists turned on one another.

The marine detail had arranged itself around Grand Admiral Mindor in a tight circle, their Cougar autorifles pointed outwards. The officers, too, had their service pistols out, their eyes fixed on the colony through the domes of their helmets. There were more explosions, these the muted thud of distant grenades. The comm bands were frighteningly silent.

How had this happened? Munroe was only supposed to act as the Judas goat, leading Mindor and his retinue to slaughter. He wasn't supposed to have to kill the officer he had followed for six years. Something must have happened to force his Tez'Nar ally to move forward early. Munroe had to move quickly or the evening might still end poorly. *Who are you kidding? The night will end poorly. You'll be a murderer. And a traitor.*

Having spent a lifetime learning to master his fears, Munroe was ashamed to be ruled by them in the end. But he had been on leave on Ressa when the Celestials came. He had seen what they were capable of. No punishment the CRDF could give him held a candle to their hellish wrath.

Munroe knew that he was alone and that he could never hope to shoot down all his comrades in their thick armor. He had to separate them, draw Mindor away.

"Sergeant Omireth, take the squad and move up in force. Find out what's going on," Munroe said, putting as much force as he could into his quaking voice. "I'll get the admiral back to the shuttle for immediate evacuation."

He was the squad leader and had the command in the event of an emergency. Even so, he was surprised when Omireth and the others obeyed without question and thudded away, their boots kicking up clouds of dust.

"This way, Admiral," Munroe said, waving Mindor and his retinue back toward the shuttle. The admiral was shaking, dismayed by the attack that had been meant for him.

If only we had landed at the colony as we were supposed to.

When they had gone almost a kilometer, Munroe dropped back, allowing the officers to pull ahead. The marines' EMMAs would have stood up to a few rounds from a Cougar, but these officers' exos were unarmored, meant for agility and style rather than protection. Munroe raised his rifle and put his finger on the trigger. There were tears streaming down his face.

Mindor sensed that his guardian had dropped back and half-rotated as he bounded across the bleak landscape. "Sergeant Major, what…."

Munroe squeezed the trigger, and the Cougar bucked in his hands. The report of the big rifle was quieter than it would have been on a world with a richer atmosphere, but the recoil shuddered up his arm as the large-caliber shells left the barrel to tear through their targets.

Grand Admiral Mindor was the closest, and his body jerked and tumbled. His exo depressurized, spewing gaseous oxygen and crystallizing blood into the cold, thin atmosphere. One shot shattered his faceplate, leaving a frozen expression of horror on the admiral's face. Almost instantly crystals began to form on his fur and over his glazed green eyes. Munroe felt sick, but he kept shooting as Mindor's body tumbled in the low gravity.

The other officers reacted quickly, but their service pistols barely dented Munroe's EMMA. It was like the pealing of a thousand church bells as the bullets ricocheted off his armor, tolling the death of a great man and the damnation of the betrayer who had slain him.

One by one the commanders of the Ninth Royal Line were killed, their suits punctured, their innards exposed to near-vacuum. Slowly their bodies settled to earth, their blank eyes staring skyward into the uncaring eye of the gas planet.

Munroe lowered his rifle, staring at the carnage. Admiral Tasinto's head was splattered all over the inside of her helmet. He had known her. She had joked with him on the shuttle. And Mindor had given him his sergeant major's chevrons personally. Munroe began to run.

He could hear his own comrades chattering on the comm, their voices full of confusion and anger. "Shots fired, shots fired! Get the fucker!"

"Who? Who fired?"

"The—the fucking *sergeant major*! He killed the grand admiral!"

"Forget the goddamn Tez'Nar, get Munroe!"

Munroe continued to run as the dust storm died down, and the last of the swirling particles settled to the ground. The grim scene was lit with cold, bright moonlight A dozen bodies were visible, limbs splayed.

"Oh, *Jesus*! He wiped out the whole Niaotl command."

Munroe put on a burst of speed as his own marines began to fire on him. At this range even the electronically-assisted aiming systems would have trouble picking off a moving target. The EMMA was programmed to move for the wearer under extreme circumstances, and so he could sprint far faster, and for much longer, than he could under his own strength. So could his fellow sojieri, though. He was lucky he had a two-kilometer head start.

Rock and debris leapt up around him in little puffs as the marines peppered his position. One bullet rang off his armor, and he could hear the hiss of escaping air.

"Call for aerospace support," snapped Omireth. Two fighters had stayed in low orbit during Mindor's landing, in case of trouble.

They were hardly antipersonnel weapons, but they were dangerous. Munroe ran on, realizing that he didn't really care if he lived or died. If he did manage to survive, he would have to live with the memory of what he had done.

A new voice broke into the channel, that of Commander Sharon Dodd, the lead pilot. "Sergeant Omireth, we copy your request. What the hell is going on down there?"

"Just bring down Sergeant Major Munroe."

"Tough to do it at this speed. Switching to rockets."

"Your call, Commander. I don't care if there's a body."

Munroe only had a minute or so before the fighters were in range. He ran on, the concentrated oxygen in his suit making him feel strong, giddy.

The first rocket streaked in when he was still a kilometer from the shuttle, exploding a hundred meters to Munroe's right. He felt himself lifted and tossed to the left in a swirling tornado of rock and dirt. He thudded down hard, rolling in the dirt. He was still disoriented as the suit automatically righted itself and resumed the course on which he had set it. Another rocket struck a few hundred meters ahead of him. Munroe ran through the smoke and the shower of debris.

One of the pilots tried their luck with an energy beam. The bright blue streak of light carved a swath in the soil of Ezai, turning the dirt to glass. Munroe almost lost his footing as he skidded through it. He had to get to the shuttle. They wouldn't risk firing near the shuttle, would they?

The crew had taken up positions behind the landing gear and were unloading on Munroe as he drew closer. Their sidearms were nearly useless against his armor. He ran toward them, firing in carefully controlled bursts. One went down, then another. The pilot ran for the ramp of the shuttle, and Munroe shot him in the back.

There were explosions in the sky above, and he saw a trailing fireball arcing, uncontrolled, across the sky. There was a telltale green flash, followed by another explosion. The fighters were under attack. Up there, somewhere, was a great ship the color of midnight. He should not have been surprised that the Celestials would come to watch this test of their servants.

Had the Celestial Mother come to press him to her twisted bosom? An invisible spirit of fury, come to punish the Coalition as she had punished the Valinata?

Though he could not see the ship, Munroe knew that it would jam all signals but his. And he still had work to do. As commander, his comm unit could interface directly with the shuttle's long-comm and transmit his words across the galaxy.

"This is Sergeant Major Simon Munroe," he said, his voice quaking with fear and guilt. "The DLF have broken the cease-fire and killed Grand Admiral Mindor and his staff! We are outnumbered. They've destroyed our air support. Requesting immediate reinforcements!" He allowed the transmission to fade away in static.

Suddenly Munroe felt the sense of icy calm slackening, releasing him. In its place he felt an uncontrollable desire to look upwards. He did so, searching the star-strewn expanse for his masters.

"I did what you asked of me!" Munroe cried aloud. He felt a presence behind his eyes, probing. "Please let me go." He had been promised freedom by this dark succubus with its gently waving tentacles. But now he was helpless before it once again, reduced to begging.

He could not see it, but it could see him, and Monroe stood transfixed by its gaze. He cried out as a painful keening began in the soft tissue of his brain.

The Celestial Mother was calling him. Munroe's nose, eyes, ears, and mouth began to bleed. Tears mingled with the blood as he pleaded for release. He did not receive the escape he sought. He gurgled, choking on his own blood. He coughed, and dark red spattered against the clear curve of his helmet's visor. "No, please," he moaned, unable to see through the curtain of his own blood. Then he collapsed in the dust at the foot of the shuttle's ramp. He barely felt the first bullet when it hit him in the back.

3: Aftermath

"I understand, Your Majesty." Hakar was crestfallen, but he kept his head up before the empress. There was no sense arguing. "Colonel Victor is a good sojier. I would have vouched for him myself."

"You wanted my signature. This is my condition." There was no animosity in Kra'al's voice, and no sympathy, either. She looked regal and inspiring as she led the way down the long broad hallway. The city of Sherata was ghostly through the fog, looking gray and dour by comparison. Days of rain had melted most of the snow, and the canals were swollen.

Hakar felt acutely exposed having this conversation on the move, with Kra'al's bodyguard and attendants swarming around them like a school of fish.

Kra'al gave him a warm look. "I promise I'm not trying to be punitive here, Hakar. I appreciate your position, and I appreciate your loyalty, but you are too visible to associate with someone so notorious. It won't take much to derail this entire plan of yours, and the wrong name on the roster will almost certainly do it. Under ordinary circumstances I would be very reluctant to reach out to private military contractors, but I'm a practical woman, and I recognize that these circumstances are very extraordinary.

"Jackal Pack may only be the first of many private outfits we hire in this conflict, but that makes it essential that we keep things clean, that we maintain credibility, and that our conduct, as well as theirs, be above reproach. It's been less than ten years since his indictment. His proximity to these operations is not something I want to contemplate or anything the administration will tolerate."

"Are those your words, Your Majesty?"

"Hakar, tread carefully here. My position is delicate, too. And yes, those are my words. Some of the words *other* people have used to describe Victor to me included 'maniac' and 'rabid,' hardly inspiring." That stung, but Hakar held his tongue. "You know some people actually miss Telemon, and they see Victor as the chink in the armor that brought him down and punched their meal ticket. Everyone

72

else sees him as just another example of what was wrong with the last administration. No one save you is clamoring to have him reinstated."

"Ma'am, I'm not asking to have him reinstated, merely—"

"I trust you, but the word got out. Parliament has been exemplary in putting aside partisan politics to get things moving for us, but all of the senior ministers have been very clear on this issue. They don't want a war criminal anywhere near our troops or the cameras."

"Victor isn't a war criminal, Majesty. It never progressed past—"

"His honorable discharge was by the most marginal technicality and you know it," Kra'al snapped. "If you hadn't been able to abort the court martial, how do you think it would have ended? Quite differently, I expect. And as far as the court of public opinion is concerned, he was found guilty long ago. War criminal or war criminal-adjacent, it makes no difference to the average citizen. In fact, if I had been able to extradite him when I was crowned, I would have made an example of him."

The empress held up a hand as they entered one of the vast bullpens where several hundred palace staff were seated at their terminals, going about the business of keeping the empire running. There were dozens of rooms like this one dedicated to different government functions. With trillions upon trillions of citizens scattered across thousands of worlds, the bureaucratic machinery of the Coalition was vast indeed. The room was large and open, sunlight filtering in through windows in the dome above. An ornate mosaic decorated the curvature of the dome, under renovation by workers who clung to a scaffold far above.

Hakar waited while Kra'al greeted the staff. It was remarkable how easily she could flip the switch from pragmatic decision-maker to regal monarch. Her effect on the people was impressive, and Hakar saw smiles all around. He simply couldn't share in the revelry, and her words had cut deep, very deep. *"I would have made an example of him,"* she said.

As the retinue reached the other side of the office, Kra'al turned back to him. "I know that Victor was your protégé, and I know that his discharge was highly politicized. But I read his file. Even the

Heavenfall dossier that everyone tried so hard to keep secret. He was an exceptional sojier … a long time ago. He's a mercenary now. There's nothing you or I can do. Unless you think maybe he's worth committing political suicide over."

"No, Ma'am."

"I'm glad to see that you can be objective about this. We have to focus on the big picture. You want Jackal Pack included in your fleet, that's fine. It's your budget to squander as you wish. But I've been very public in my condemnation of mercenaries, and if I'm going to modify my position I have to do so very carefully. What we will *not* do is bring in a man who makes us look like a group of barbarians by association. Am I clear? At some point I'll have to go before parliament and ask for more funds."

The grand admiral clicked his tongue slowly. He saw her point and had to admit that it was a valid one. Whatever his personal feelings about Leon Victor, they couldn't afford another misstep, especially one that might associate them with the disgraced regime. Hakar was still too close to it for many. He resolved to find a way to make it up to his exiled champion. "I'll convey our decision to General Rockmore."

Kra'al was in the midst of responding when Hakar's comm beeped urgently. Her own comm was chiming as were those of several of her aides. Something was happening, and as he looked down at his personal computer he saw the priority alert.

The empress's bodyguards were already circling her, preparing to rush her to safety, but she shrugged them off. "Not now," she said gruffly. "People are watching." She continued walking casually, her gown trailing behind her as her aides found out what was going on. The staff watched nervously, and Hakar could already hear the murmuring.

Her desire not to panic the workers was admirable, but Hakar hoped it wasn't foolhardy. He answered his comm quietly as the retinue exited the office.

"Mindor has been killed," Motayre told him, not mincing words. Hakar staggered under the weight of the news. The palace suddenly felt cold and inhospitable, the fog outside oppressive.

"*What?*" he whispered. A glance at Kra'al's face, which had taken on a sudden claylike pallor, told him that she had received the same news.

"Not just that. His executive officers were murdered nearly simultaneously, as well."

"How ... how did this happen?"

"A bomb aboard Vice-Grand Admiral Larador's ship. The entire bridge tower was destroyed. Vice-Grand Admiral Geran was shot four times in the shower. She was still alive when she was taken to sick-bay, but she expired shortly thereafter."

"The killers?"

"Geran's killer, a Human ensign named Lydia Gillette, managed to shoot herself in the head before being captured. Larador's assassin is assumed to be among the dead, but the Service say they don't know who it was. As for Mindor, it appears the DLF decided to make a bolder statement."

"Hakar," Kra'al said sharply. "We must speak."

"I'll talk to you about this later," Hakar said to Motayre and hung up. He turned to regard Kra'al. "Your Highness."

"I take it you heard the news." Kra'al sounded shaken, her voice thick with grief and anger. "Telec has just informed me that the Ninth Royal Line has just been decapitated. All three of Mindor's main fleets are leaderless, and the nearest likely candidates were all killed with him on Ezai."

Surreptitiously, more royal guards had joined the entourage, forming a protective circle around the empress and her aides. Hakar noticed that the safeties of their ornate but functional assault rifles had been switched off. Was the threat that immediate? Reflexively, his hand drifted to his own sidearm. Its cold weight was reassuring.

"This is unbelievable," he muttered. He was trying hard to think of some way that this could be a mistake. It was overwhelming news, the sort of catastrophe it was possible to plan for but never expect. "If the DLF—"

Kra'al snorted. "*If?* It seems very clear that the DLF were responsible for this act of terrorism. By the time our forces arrived at Ezai, they had killed the entire marine detachment. They and the Irachans were still shooting when our ground forces hit the dirt."

Up ahead, the guards were forcing people out of the way. Kra'al moved to stop them, but Hakar reached out a calming hand. "Maybe it's for the best, Your Highness. We can't be too cautious at the moment."

Kra'al blinked, and her expression seemed to clear. "Poor Cratos. He didn't even want to go to Ezai. It's awfully convenient that, *immediately* following a DLF bombing, mutineers aboard his XOs' flagships would assassinate their commanding officers. Do you believe they could be opportunists, or are we looking at a legitimate conspiracy here?"

Her Majesty was sharp, as was to be expected of the leader of the largest galactic power. Hakar knew that she would be a fearsome enemy if he ever crossed her. He thought for a moment. He had only the barest information pertaining to this tragedy, and Kra'al had not much more. But her instincts felt right. "I don't know if I believe it, Highness, and I doubt the DLF would conduct themselves this way, but I believe we should investigate. Thoroughly."

"I agree. I'm glad Mindor's fleets are far from the Dias Traverse. We couldn't afford to have grieving officers initiating retributive attacks."

Hakar frowned at that. "We may need someone there to keep order?"

"What order?" Kra'al scoffed. "But you're right. I intend to mobilize High Grand Admiral Pirsan's fleet to Iracha. Ezai could spill over to the rest of the Dias any day now." She looked out the windows and gazed out at Sherata's skyline. A cold rain was falling. Usually Kra'al left Tagea in the winter months to go back to her warm homeworld or tour the Coalition. "You mentioned an investigation. I want someone I can trust looking into this." She looked at Hakar pointedly.

"You're sending me to the Traverse?" Hakar asked, perplexed.

"No, you're getting your wish. You go to the Alkyra to help your mercenaries pretend to be sojieri. Your fleets will be coordinating defenses along the Tears. I want you to personally tour some of the key worlds, meet with their leaders, and then set up in the D'zen Gulf."

Hakar approved. He didn't much like the idea of public relations but it was a small price to pay to be close to the action. "Thank you, Your Highness. It would be my honor. And this investigation?"

"You'll be guarding the mouth of the Yangtze, but I want you tapped into every report concerning these attacks. Perhaps there's another angle. I can't believe that this was a coincidence, and I hope you're right that the DLF wasn't behind it."

"I hope so, too," Hakar said, clicking his tongue to signal his emphatic agreement. "I will do the best I can, Your Highness."

"That's all I ask." Kra'al dismissed Hakar. The grand admiral quickened his step and moved through the ranks of bodyguards, wondering how in all the hells of all the faiths he would find out what she wanted to know.

§

The lights were on when Leon opened the door to the apartment. "Rachel?" he called as he unknotted his tie.

There was no response, but he could hear the shower running. He went into the bedroom and undressed, folding and hanging his uniform trousers and jacket in the closet and giving his medals a quick polish with a cloth. He pulled on jeans and a faded blue Empress Kalex University of Voss, Triatha t-shirt from his alma mater. Standing alone, facing the mirror on the bathroom door, his fingers drifted to the base of his skull, caressing the barcode tattoo and the neural interface jack that marked him as just another discarded weapon of the Coalition. A shiver ran down his spine.

Giving the bathroom door a light rap, he entered and got a faceful of steam. "I thought you were spending the day in town."

"I did. You're home late."

Leon glanced at his watch and frowned. "Sorry, I had a lot of prep meetings."

"So you're leaving tomorrow." It wasn't a question. Rachel had made no secret of her bitterness at coming in second to another private war.

Leon pulled aside the shower curtain, and Rachel gave him a perfunctory kiss. He took in her glistening body.

"Eye contact, Mister." Leon looked up and gave her a lopsided grin as she ran her hands through her hair, rinsing out the shampoo. "Is this job going to be dangerous?"

"Possibly, but I doubt it. I think these people are paying for the brand name. The Jackal Pack stripes carry a lot of weight if you're trying to scare the right people."

"And if the people you're trying to scare have never heard of you?"

"We'll make sure they remember." Leon felt himself cringe. He hadn't meant for that to sound like bravado. "A month is a long time, but you'll be fine."

"Of course, I'll be fine, Leon. I'm an adult, I can keep myself occupied. I'm more worried about you."

"I promise I'm only going in an advisory capacity. Did you have dinner?" Leon asked, changing the subject.

"Not yet. I'll be done in a few minutes, but I don't feel like driving all the way back to town. The Desher Vaux is fine," she finished curtly and turned away.

"Okay." Leon stepped out of the bathroom and walked back into the bedroom, noticing a pile of Rachel's clothing and a stack of magazines that were scattered on the duvet. One of the magazines caught his eye: it was the latest copy of the *Coalition Registry of Genetics,* one of the galaxy's premier scientific journals. He picked it up, sat down, and began to read. For a few minutes it was like he had gone back in time.

When he snapped back to reality, Rachel was standing beside him, naked and drying her hair with a towel. "I saw that and thought you'd be interested. I never see you reading that stuff. And … I thought it might help you with the project you're working on." The annoyance had faded from her voice.

"Thank you, baby." Leon smiled tiredly and tossed the journal back onto the bed. "I was in it once. I got credited on a paper by one of my professors."

"Who says you can't be in it again?" She was trying to be supportive, and Leon hated to disagree with her.

He grabbed the journal again and showed her the abstract of the article he had been reading. "This is what I wanted to do. But now

... the field is light-years ahead of where it was. Light-years ahead of me."

"You think you've been out of the game too long." Rachel looked skeptical as she took the journal and leafed through it. It was hard to focus on the conversation with her standing there nude. "I think you could do it. Just the fact that you *understand* what they're talking about...."

"Barely." Leon almost laughed. "I'm pretty far out of date. Honestly, I wouldn't even know where to start. It's like wanting to reenter a room and finding out the doors moved when I wasn't looking." He had started off trying to find something, anything that might give him a clue to deciphering the Abaddon genome, but he had given up, instead leafing through the most recent articles related to his own concentration, xenogenic chromosome therapy and implantation. "Before I bailed, that would have been my doctoral research. You know, I told you I left school to provide for Natille and the others, but the truth was that I was barely good enough to get a passing grade to begin with, and I probably wouldn't have made it through grad school, never mind get a decent job with any reputable lab."

"Tell me about it anyway."

Leon was so touched by her encouragement that he couldn't bear to disappoint her. "All right. You know that we can easily code proteins from other heliconomic species using artificial chromosomes to cure disorders, right? I wanted to find a way to take proteins from spironomic species and translate them into heliconomic species. I got some Terran soil bacteria to take up a gene from a similar organism from Tissan, but I never got them to express it."

"I had a friend who had an artificial Tez'Nar chromosome to treat a metabolic disorder. She had to go in for treatments every few months."

"Sure. There are a lot of cases where another species has a protein that would fix a problem much easier than our own genes. But we've never been able to go across genome types. I remember I took a class once where the professor was comparing a Rukadj protein to a Sheff'an protein that performed the same function. The Sheff'an protein was less than a third the size, was far simpler. But there was no way to get it to code properly in a Rukadj because their genomes didn't read the same way. Polymerase swarms still hadn't been developed, and I never would have thought of them." Talking about it now, Leon couldn't help but wonder what new understanding would come out of the spheronomic genome Moira Traveler had elaborated, assuming her research ever saw the light of day.

"What about the Cincons in the Valinata, though? They're Humans with Rukadj genes."

Leon nodded. "Sure. In their case, the Rukadj genes were directly translated from tubulonomic configuration to heliconomic. And look at how much was lost in translation."

"What happened to them is so sad. My mother always said it was the worst crime ever committed."

"She's not far off the mark," Leon agreed gravely.

"Sorry, I didn't mean to depress you."

"I just remember hearing about the Cincon rebellion. It was one of the reasons I wanted to sign up and fight the Valinata."

"I'm glad it never came to that."

"Now I'll never get the chance. They're all gone."

"Don't think about that," Rachel urged.

Leon lay back on the bed and stared at the ceiling. It was plain, blank, until Rachel's face moved into view. He gave her a wan smile, and the smile widened in surprise as she straddled him.

"Why don't we do a little genetic recombination of our own?" she whispered suggestively, leaning close so her wet hair tickled his face.

"I thought you were on birth control," he said, poking fun at her ridiculous comment. He was excited, though, and she knew it.

Rachel shrugged and winked. When he stirred against her, she feigned surprise. "Wait, what was that? Is your safety off?" She tossed her towel.

Leon forgot all about the journal article and the Valinata.

4: Deployed

Raptor Merikii heaved the barbell onto the rack and sat up, breathing heavily. After a moment's rest, he reached over for his water bottle and gulped its contents in one long swallow. His daggerlike teeth were clearly visible as he caught his breath, his broad jaw hanging open. Several people were watching him. "Can I help anyone?" he asked. They went back to their own workouts.

Jeric was watching him, wide-eyed. "Man, what the fuck do you even want a spotter for? That's a hundred kilos more than I weigh." Raptor towered over him by half a meter, and his long, spine-ridged tail added another meter and a half of pure predator.

The Prross stood and began removing the weights from the barbell, sliding them back onto the rack. "I'm going for a swim. Coming?"

Jeric had nothing else to do, but he didn't particularly want to get his hair wet. "Yeah, okay. I got tired just watching you."

They walked toward the natatorium, past dozens of sojieri in the middle of their morning routines. Jeric stopped to flirt with one of their female comrades who had been watching him from afar. Women always seemed interested in Jeric at first—it was only after they got to know him that things deteriorated. "I thought you were going golfing," Raptor growled when the pilot caught up to him.

Jeric laughed mirthlessly. "What's the point? The general ordered the grounds crews to stop watering because of the drought. The whole course is one big sand trap."

"Thank the goddess no one else has to suffer like you do," Raptor chuckled.

Things had been moving slowly, plenty of time to drink and cool off after that … place they had gone to. Jeric still didn't like to think about what they had seen, and he hadn't even gotten off the ship other than to grab a rock for his collection. Leon and Raptor seemed haunted by it, and Asar had nearly died.

The Jackal Pack gym was refreshingly full of life. It was big, with well-kept equipment and a staff of professional trainers who supplemented the noncommissioned officers for physical training.

Near the entrance to the natatorium, a cluster of Jackals cheered on a group of officers engaged in a push-up contest.

"Go, Trax!" called Jeric as he and Raptor passed by.

Lieutenant Traxus Tachai's auburn fur was matted with sweat, and her tank top was drenched, but she was relentless. Looking at her now, it was hard to believe she was Grand Admiral Hakar's younger sister, let alone the future matriarch of her clan. In anticipation of her mission to Tikal, she had chopped off her Terran revival braid in favor of a severe Mohawk, and she was clearly looking to prove herself to the sojieri whose platoon she would be commanding.

The Tagean physique was often lanky to the point of gauntness, but Traxus's muscles were toned, and she could push herself far beyond the limits of many of her comrades. The members of the Echo Company quick-strikers gave up one by one until only Tom "Gus" Miller remained. The sergeant was a big man with thick arms, but he was only Human. One of his hands slipped out from under him, and he went down hard. He tagged in Lieutenant Anna Tendaji to take his place, and she threw herself down and went at it. Even fresh, she couldn't keep up with Traxus, and finally she, too, gave up. Traxus managed one more triumphant push-up and sat back, exhausted but triumphant, running a hand through her Mohawk. The troops around her went wild.

The pool had plenty of room for Raptor to get in his laps and cool down after lifting. He wanted to be in peak physical condition if there was to be more killing. Their team had been caught off-guard on Korinthe and again on Aethaleia, and he would not let it happen again. Two bad missions in a row was a lot to handle for a team used to perfection, but they would recover as they always did.

Jeric wanted to get in shape, too, but he couldn't seem to muster the willpower. He leaned back against the side of the pool, hooking his elbows over the edge to hold himself up and kicking languidly. "You talk to Vic recently? He's been lying low."

"You could talk to him yourself."

"Right." Leon had walked away from them after Aethaleia, just walked away like they were yesterday's spent bullet casings. The others had turned a blind eye, but Jeric wasn't ready to let it go. "He's been hiding in his apartment with Rachel or behind his office door for the last two weeks. If he's not willing to make some effort himself, I'm not going to do it for him."

Between strokes Raptor said, "I know you're frustrated, Jeric, and you do have a point, but you need to give him a break right now."

"Whatever, man. We're his crew. He can't turn his back on us. This is because of Rachel."

Raptor paused at the other end of the lane with an amused expression on his face. "You do know how you sound, right? All the shit we just went through, all the literal bullets we just dodged, and *she's* the bad influence? You must be joking." Raptor ducked his head underwater and shot over. His tail gave him an added agility in the water, and Jeric had the unsettling feeling that he knew what it would be like to be attacked by a crocodile.

"Look, Rachel is a good woman, and she's good for Leon," Raptor said, standing up in front of Jeric. His chest rose out of the water, glistening as the water poured off him. Unusually for a Prross, he was bereft of tattoos, but his mottled hide was covered with scars, the shadows of bullet wounds and stabbings. The wounds he had suffered at the hands of the Valinata cruiser's security detail were healing, the bruises fading, but he would have a few more scars to add to his inventory. It wasn't the physical scars that worried them all, though: their line of work took a far higher psychological and emotional toll. "Are you going to sit here and begrudge him a little R&R after a mission like that?"

"You know, we all suffered on Aethaleia," Jeric said bitterly.

"Easy for you to say. You were on the *Faithless Bitch*. You were spared the worst of it."

"You seem to be taking it all right."

Raptor scoffed, an angry staccato snarl escaping his throat. "Is that so? Half the time I can't sleep, Jeric. And when I do, I wish I was awake." The jet-black spines that ran in twin rows from the crown of his head to his tail rose and fell in time to his pulse. "Look, I wish Leon were a little more open with us, too, but he can't be expected to take care of us all the time."

"Yes, he *can* be expected to do that. That's why he's the colonel, the guy in charge." Jeric dunked his head under the water, partially to cool off and partially to escape Raptor's judgmental gaze.

How dare he imply that Jeric had had things easy on that mission? He might not have ventured through the deserted streets and fought the deranged scavengers that were all that remained of Aethaleia's population, but he had held his own when they had been captured by the rogue Valinata cruiser. His own nose still bled periodically since his septum was nearly crushed by a VSF marine's rifle, not to mention his exposure to Aethaleia's treacherous atmosphere. All four of the mercenaries who had gone to that wretched place were suffering the aftereffects. Only Leon and Asar had the solace of lovers on which to rely.

When Jeric came back up for air, Raptor was looking at him with placid, knowing eyes. "I know this is hard for you, Shorty. Things are changing fast, and you feel like you might get left behind."

"I *am* getting left behind. He pulled me off the Mekon DaVoi account. He's taking Tamara Kelly and Hifotza. They're glorified shuttle pilots."

"And it's a glorified bus route. You're not missing anything. Clearly, you and Leon still need some time apart. You can use that time to sulk and drink and shoot up, or you can use it to get yourself in order. Maybe clean yourself up and go on a date with Alexis. Whatever you do, stop trying to come between Leon and Rachel. You can remain his friend and earn his respect, or you can become an anchor around his neck and earn his resentment."

"You know," Jeric said without bothering to mask his irritation, "I get pretty sick of your warrior monk act."

Raptor cocked his head as he looked at his friend. "I'm sorry to hear that. I work hard to make it convincing. You could leave, too, you know."

"Maybe if Rachel started sleeping with me, too, I'd consider it. You know, it wasn't as bad when she had the apartment in Tesa."

The Prross ignored the innuendo. "This isn't about Rachel. I don't even think it's really about Leon. But until you figure yourself out, you need to keep your mind on the job."

"Give *me* a break, Raptor. This is more than a job for me. It's the only place I get to fly. No one else would have me."

"That's it, though. You're at home here, and so am I. I sympathize. I know what it's like to not belong, and how empty and alone you felt before you found this place. We chose to give up our homes to be here. Leon's here out of habit, fear of change."

"Yeah? Well, I didn't give up *anything* to come here, Raptor. My life was boring on Shine, and then it was hell until you and Leon pulled me off of Kai-Lun and made me one of you. So forgive me if I'm afraid of change, too. That doesn't mean I don't want the guy to be happy." Jeric was glaring daggers at Raptor although some small part of him felt bad for turning this into an argument. "What about you? Aside from small spaces, what are you afraid of?"

"Don't make fun of me," Raptor said fiercely. "I have my reasons for staying in Jackal Pack, and they have nothing to do with fear. I don't want to die unfulfilled. Do you?" Raptor's words conjured memories of Buzz Parker, and the pair fell silent, with only the muffled noise of the other gym occupants and the closer sound of the water lapping at the sides of the pool to fill the void. Buzz had died unfulfilled, they both knew, and he was far from the only one. There were a lot of empty graves in the grove near the plateau that stood in mute testimony to that fact.

Finally, Jeric broke the silence. "It's just changed so much. You're right, I'm man enough to admit that I feel like I belong here, but I never would have gotten here without you and Leon. Rockmore never would have taken me in, either."

"You're afraid that if Leon leaves, you'll lose your place here? That's crazy, but do you really expect that things will never change?" Raptor prodded softly.

Jeric had no answer to that.

"Nothing escapes change, Jeric. Nothing. Entropy is the fundamental law of the universe. You need to embrace that. Embrace Leon the next time you see him." He looked at Jeric, gauging his mood.

Jeric screwed up his face but managed to hold his tongue. Raptor was right, after all. The big oaf was always right. "It's always about entropy with you. I just feel like … I don't know, like he thinks he's better than me."

"He is."

"I mean because he's educated. He thinks he's better than this life. And like I can't make something of myself." Leon would never come out and say it; it was just his manner, his unconscious belittlement, and it had always infuriated Jeric, especially as he loyally followed in Leon's wake. "So what if I want to drink a little and have some fun? Not everyone has to want to change the world."

Raptor's quiet growl of annoyance was more menacing than he intended. "Don't look at Leon, look in the damn mirror." Wisely, Jeric decided to let it go. Since his hair was already ruined, he joined Raptor in swimming, losing himself in the rhythm, the burn of muscles he didn't ordinarily use.

After a few dozen laps they got out of the pool and dried off. "Come with me," Raptor growled softly, and Jeric followed him back to his quarters, the sun pounding down on them out of a cloudless sky. As members of Jackal Pack's pool of freelance specialists, they weren't part of the legion's rank and file. Consequently, they had no formal positions or regular duties, nor were they required to live on base although both chose to do so. Jeric, as an advisor and advanced instructor for the Pack's combat aerospace wing, chose to remain in the pilots' barracks. Raptor occupied a small cottage abutting the officers' apartments. It was more of a converted storage shed, really, renovated to add a kitchenette and a water closet. He was certainly an odd one, always apart, the only member of his secretive race in Jackal Pack, likely the only one on Eve. It was still weird to think that a Prross was Empress of the Coalition.

As they walked, they talked of the lifting of the contract freeze—this was, of course, the big news on the base—but they didn't talk of the upcoming mission for Mekon DaVoi, Inc. Leon professed to be an objective leader, but if Jeric quarreled with him, he got cut off. How very objective.

They entered Raptor's apartment, and Jeric had to wait while his eyes adjusted to the dark. The main room was small and dim, lit only by a heat lamp beside the bed. Raptor sat down on the mattress and removed his boots. "Food?" he asked distantly.

"Sure." Jeric looked around. He had grown used to Raptor's peculiar lifestyle, but the monastic austerity of the apartment would always puzzle him. Aside from a small shrine in one corner and a banner covered in tribal pictograms, the only decoration was a group photo of Leon, Raptor, Jeric, Buzz Parker, Heidi Eastern, and Traxus.

On the nightstand beside the picture was a small stack of books. Jeric tilted his head to read the titles. "Shakespeare?"

"I figured I'd see what all the fuss was about." Raptor smiled. "I have to say, I like it. Very musical." He rose and went to his kitchenette.

"It's written in iambic pentameter, you know. It's a pattern." Jeric was proud to show off his knowledge—he had not had much education, but his father had insisted he read.

Raptor poked his head into the fridge. "Oh. I guess that's why. He's funny, though."

"Try reading *Macbeth.*"

"Is that funny?"

Jeric smiled. "You might think so." He sat down in the dwelling's only chair and yawned, bored by his minimalistic surroundings. His own quarters in the flight officers' barracks was cramped but would have been manageable under the occupation of a neater tenant. Flight suits were draped over chairs, clothing was scattered over the floor, odors wafted from open food containers to mingle thickly in the air. On a shelf, beneath a poster of a topless and preposterously well-endowed woman with blonde pigtails, he kept a labeled collection of rocks, one from every world he had visited. The collection included one from Aethaleia and another from Kai-Lun where he, Raptor, and Leon had first met. It was messy and it was juvenile but it felt like home. Raptor's apartment felt more like a prison cell.

"What do you want to eat?" Raptor asked as he rummaged.

"Just a beer."

"Really? Already?" The reproach in Raptor's voice was grating.

"A sandwich, then."

Raptor nodded and set about making lunch. Over the sound of his knife on the cutting board, he said, "You have to make your peace with Leon, Jeric."

"I know," Jeric said, mostly to himself.

The knife paused. "What was that?"

"You know what I said," Jeric said sharply. Raptor dropped a sloppily made sandwich onto a plate and thrust it at him. Jeric took it. "Thanks. At least *you've* still got my back."

"Always."

§

In the Jackal Pack headquarters main conference room, the meeting was droning on, and Leon's anxiety was mounting. It was just the usual pre-mission nerves, but for some reason he couldn't focus.

Major Liam Dawson, who would have temporary overall command of Third and Sixth brigades in Leon's absence, was nodding enthusiastically at something Captain Braeburn had said. "Good idea, Kyle. Can you schedule a meeting with Major Da'Cir? I don't see why she wouldn't be open to the idea. Leon, any thoughts? Colonel?"

Leon, caught daydreaming, snapped to attention. "I'm sorry, what was that?"

Liam Dawson frowned, the expression looking unnatural on his windburned but youthful face. "Is everything all right, boss?"

"Yes, carry on." In truth, Leon had been thinking about the strain this month away would put on him and Rachel. Part of him wondered if she would still be here when he returned. No, that was unfair. Rachel had forgiven him for so much, and the trouble she had caused him was nothing compared to what he had wrought on her life—he stopped himself again. "What's the plan, then?"

"Captain Braeburn was suggesting that we approach Colonel Akida's armored units for a skirmish, to test our quick-strike units' ability to neutralize armor at close range."

"That's a good idea," Leon agreed. "Nice thinking, Kyle. It'd be a good opportunity to use that old mining settlement."

"Urban combat simulation? Sure thing, sir."

"And much as we might like to, try to avoid actually destroying any of Colonel Akida's tanks."

"No promises, sir." Braeburn smiled a gap-toothed smile.

"Okay, then. Heidi, what—whoa, I didn't even notice your hair."

Heidi Eastern, Leon's chief of staff and Pack administrator, smiled. Her hair was always brightly colored, but today it was a shade of red so bright it seemed to slide past the visible wavelengths. Her nails, lipstick, and eyeliner matched. "You like it?"

"I feel like I'm looking at a supernova."

"You're saying I'm hot?" Heidi smiled again, radiant and charming. Leon tried hard not to notice the wheelchair in which she had been stuck for four years. She hadn't always been a paraplegic or an administrator in charge of personnel and payroll; once she had been an operator like Leon. Four bullets in the back that had been meant for him had put an end to her field work. So many people had lost something because of him. Some, like Buzz Parker, Tresh, and Jenn Rada, had lost their lives.

"Don't tell Rachel." Leon glanced back at Dawson and Braeburn, caught them rolling their eyes. "Anyway, we're wheels up in a few hours. Any more info on Mekon DaVoi?"

"Nothing you don't already know." Heidi reached forward, passed Leon a sheet of paper. "Everything I dug up corroborates their application. Privately held, incorporated in the Shar'dan so they don't have to file anything or report earnings. Nothing immediately jumps out as suspicious."

"Any products we'd know?" asked Dawson, who had only gotten the high-level overview before.

Heidi wrinkled her nose. "Hard to say. They specialize in high-end research and development, then license their tech to the highest bidder, so they tend to stay behind the scenes. That being said, I think they're on the level: they've got patents in food processing, molecular circuitry, telecom, even stardrive manufacture, and their client list includes some big names. That client list also includes some fairly shady groups and a handful of rogue states, so if they're this worried about keeping their secrets it's probably more than garden variety paranoia."

As Heidi spoke, Leon read over the file again. It was true, they didn't have much more to go on than when he had approved the contract. It sounded like Mekon DaVoi had received credible threats after coming close to a breakthrough on a project and needed some added muscle to supplement their in-house security forces.

"Okay," he said when he was done reading. "Any other business before I prep for launch?"

"Just Major Craf," Heidi said. "There isn't enough in the budget for the dropships."

Major Craf, Leon's brigade S-4 logistics officer, and by extension, the Pack's primary stacker, was a stick in the mud. He was a newcomer, and his can't-be-done attitude was the reason he had not been included in the meeting.

"Work on him until I get back, otherwise I'll deal with him myself. I want those dropships." Leon drummed his fingers on the tabletop and finally stood up. "Well, I'm convinced the battalions are in good hands."

"Yes, sir. Take care of Dyran and Mikaela for me. They won't let you down." Dawson stood, pushed aside his nonregulation mop of red hair, and saluted, along with Braeburn. Leon returned the salutes and shook their hands. "Good luck, sir."

§

"The flowers are beautiful, but it's going to take more than that," Rachel said without even sniffing the bouquet. She put them beside her on the ledge.

Leon sat beside her, dangling his booted feet over the precipice. The two of them were at the edge of the Luxor Plateau upon which the Jackal Pack base was perched, looking out over the open savannah to the north. It was a beautiful view, miles of open land peppered with little oases of trees. It was far removed from Rachel's homeworld of Amalthia, a carefully structured urban paradise. Others called Eve barren, but to Rachel it was still exotic.

"Baby, I'm sorry, but you know I put my name on that mission long before Aethaleia."

"And I'm pretty sure you could have taken your name off of it." Rachel saw the hurt look in his eyes and relented. "I'm not trying to get you to stop now, Leon. I'm trying to make my peace with it, but saying goodbye to you is never going to get easier, especially not after what happened the last time."

"I know. But saying goodbye is as important to me as saying hello. I never want to leave angry."

"That's sweet, but you're the one putting me in this position." Rachel was angry, though she knew Leon's words were genuine. It was hard to stay mad out here with the warm breeze and the handsome man beside her. She picked up the flowers and inhaled their scent. They would be dead long before Leon returned, but she would keep them anyway. "You know you can count on me, Leon. I'm loyal, as loyal as you. I don't want you getting distracted wondering if I'm okay. As much as I hate to say it, when you're on the job, focus on the job. I'll be waiting at the cosmodrome when you get back."

The smile that broke across Leon's face surprised her with its unbridled eagerness. He leaned against her shoulder, and she stroked his hair. She hated to disappoint him, but.... "But...."

"But what?" He straightened up and looked at her, the smile vanishing.

"I'm losing my mind here, Leon. I can't sit here passively, watching the clock tick. I need to *do* something, something that means something. Do you understand?"

"Of course. And I respect that."

"Do you? I know you think of me as this perfect sculpture behind glass sometimes."

"Aren't we modest," Leon said, trying for levity.

She glared at him, but it was a mirthful scowl. "Seriously, though, I know you love me and want to provide for me, but I don't just go into standby mode and power down when you're not around. I don't want to resent you for it, and honestly I want to contribute my fair share."

"Okay," he said warily.

"I feel like I'm coasting here. You pay for everything, and I just lounge around all day and go out to the city for lunch and drinks when my friends call me."

"You could learn to cook," Leon joked.

"You can fuck off with that," Rachael snapped. "Did Jeric feed you that line? I'm not going to play housewife while you go off to war."

"Honey, I was kidding," Leon said. "I'm sorry."

"I forgive you." She drew up her feet and stood. "Have you heard of signal fires?" she asked as Leon got up beside her.

"Sure," he said, frowning as he considered her question. "Like smoke signals, right? People used to light fires on hilltops to warn neighboring villages of danger."

"Well, when I worked for Hyphen Telecom, I managed a project that repurposed infrastructure from an old network that was used for something like that, back during some war five hundred years ago."

"Oh, really?" Leon asked, perking up.

"Yeah. Half of it was scrap, and it was a total write-off, but I learned a lot. Apparently these systems had been attacked repeatedly, so they set up an ansible link to each other. If the signal cut out or one world sent out a warning, all the planets in the network could be alerted in minutes to coordinate their defenses and make themselves less appealing targets." She looked back out over the savannah, imagining it burning. "When you came back from that ... place, I started thinking about it. You're not the only one who's been doing research. The Tears of Alkyra used to have something similar, way back before the Coalition folded them in. They used them to warn each other about marauders and pirates."

"A superluminal tripwire," Leon whispered, impressed. "You should take this to Rockmore," Leon said emphatically.

"Maybe. I need to work on it a little more." She took hold of Leon's hands. Her grip was surprisingly strong. "I know you're trying to protect me, but I know you're not telling me as much as you know. Something is seriously fucked up in the Valinata, and we're right next to it. Every instinct is telling me to run back home, or somewhere else, anywhere but here. I can't do that, though. My home is with you now. But if I'm going to live here, I'm not just going to passively wait for something to happen."

"It's a fantastic idea," Leon said earnestly.

"I'm glad you think so. I'm going to dig into Eve's public archives and see what I can learn about the Alkyra's network infrastructure. And then maybe I'll take it to your boss. Or to the governor."

Leon was looking at her with unabashed admiration. Rachel knew she was smart, and she knew she was driven, but it had been a long time since she had felt like the master of her own destiny. Even leaving Amalthia had sprung from rebellion against her mother rather than her own ambition. Since then she had ricocheted between Leon's gravitational field and that of her family. Maybe this way she could travel alongside the man she loved rather than in his wake.

"I love you," Leon said softly, the words almost lost in the wind.

"I love you, too." Once they had been able to say that without sounding awkward and forced. Maybe someday they would again. Rachel pulled Leon close.

§

"Tikal System reversion estimated in ten minutes," the intercom blared.

Thank God, Leon thought, emerging from the head. It had been a long, rough journey. Because of the Valinata border closing, their dropship had been unable to cut through the ruined kingdom's territory. The alternative route was circuitous and involved a long loop through Aradon Dominion and Shar'dan Confederacy space, with customs stops at each border.

Their transport's long, slim hull left little room for creature comforts, instead jamming the occupants in along two padded benches that ran bow to stern, facing each other. It was built for quick, short-range insertions, not journeys such as this one, and the troops felt every light-year. Leon made his way along the shaking deck, nodding to his people in passing, and strapped himself in between Raptor and Traxus just aft of the bridge hatch. To his right, Raptor sat quietly with his eyes closed, meditating or pretending to sleep. The Prross wore his customary red patent-leather jacket and his battered Hyphen Telecom hat, his head cradled by the deep, cushioned drop seat. To his left, Traxus looked apprehensive but excited, repeatedly checking her gear and looking over to smile at Leon. Though she was more than sixty years old, by Tagean standards she was still young and inexperienced, and sometimes it showed. This was her first field mission as a team leader, her first mission at all in nearly a year, and both Leon and Rockmore had their reservations. After all, she was Grand Admiral Hakar's little sister; she had been entrusted to them. For quite a while she had worn her hair in the Terran Revival fashion, but Leon saw that she had chopped most of it off in preparation for the mission, instead wearing a fierce and functional Mohawk. Her lean, muscled form was restless, and she repeatedly folded her arms, crossed and uncrossed her legs, and rechecked her gear. The Jackal Pack colors, black with red tiger stripes on the left side, looked natural on her. Leon leaned over and put his hand on her shoulder.

"Hey, Trax. It'll be fine."

She smiled tiredly. Her emerald green eyes were full of emotion. "I know," she said in her mother tongue, Tagean Mze, lilting and harsh at the same time. "I ... Leon, I appreciate your standing up for me and getting me this mission. I won't let you down."

"Would you two keep it down?" Raptor growled. "Some of us are trying to sleep here."

Leon laughed. It was doubtful the Prross could even hear them over the roar of the engines. "Did you have a bad dream?" he asked loudly.

"Yes, I dreamed I was sitting next to you on the most boring mission ever conceived."

His tone serious, Leon leaned close to his fearsome comrade. "Would you rather be on a mission to Aethaleia?"

Raptor quieted down after that, shutting his amber eyes.

Across from Leon, against the starboard bulkhead, sat Dyran, a male Tagean with silver-gray fur. One of his ears was missing, and a jagged scar ran the length of his muzzle. Even taller than Traxus, he was folded uncomfortably into his seat, leaning forward, his hands wrapped around the barrel of his autorifle. He was a good sojier and had been for nearly four decades, first as a Unified Commonwealth Authority sniper and then as an instructor at one of their academies. He was one of the Pack's best shots, just a few spots beneath Asar abu Seif, and far more skilled than Leon. It was unlikely that his particular skills would be called upon, but it paid to be prepared. Beside him sat Mikaela Sommers, a former shield who had been discharged after sustaining a disfiguring injury in the line of duty. Her face was a ravaged mess, but her eyes blazed with confidence and determination.

In addition to the specialist team leaders, there were two noncommissioned officers from Echo Company's Third Platoon in the command section, sitting to Sommers's left. Leon did not know them well, but their records spoke for themselves. They had been drawn from Braeburn's quick-strike units, the best of the best when it came to front-line skirmishers and commandos. Like Mikaela and Traxus, both wore their hair in close-cropped Mohawks of the kind Leon had favored during his time in the CRDF. They were young, chiseled, and imposing. Santor was the blond with the crescent-shaped scar on his forehead, and Levy was the slightly slimmer one with the moustache. Both also possessed neural jacks similar to Leon's own and were trained EMMA operators. Farther down the line were their sojieri, three full squads of light infantry, all looking a little seasick, thanks to the turbulent ride.

The dropship shuddered again, and Leon bumped his head on the bar that held him in his seat. It was an old ship, a UCA *Curix*-class insertion vessel converted by the Pack to mount a gravdrive for travel between the stars. All Jackal Pack dropships were designed to operate independently of a mothership, but only about half of them had been constructed that way. The upgrades could be unstable; it was why Leon was so adamant about purchasing new ones.

A loud laugh drew the colonel's attention. Glancing over at Santor and Levy, Leon saw them comparing tattoos. Levy had a naked woman on his right forearm, and was flexing his muscles to make her dance.

The man caught him looking. "Any ink, sir?" he called over the din.

Leon shook his head. "Just the barcode on my neck."

Santor, a former CRDF sojier himself, nodded knowingly as his hand drifted, almost subconsciously, to the base of his own neck. It was a nervous habit among many Coalition veterans.

"That's where you got your MMI?" Levy asked.

"That's right." Leon's neural interface jack, or mind-machine interface, had allowed him to operate an EMMA with the power of thought, merging sojier and armor.

"What was she?"

"An old ML-5587," Leon answered.

"Fire Witch," Santor said, and both he and Levy nodded approvingly. "You must have been a one-man wrecking crew."

Leon wasn't interested in dwelling on that part of his past, so he turned back to Traxus. "Looking forward to seeing Tikal?" he asked her.

"Yes, surprisingly," she replied, "although your brief didn't exactly make it sound like a garden spot."

"No, it didn't. Then again, I wasn't exactly writing a travel brochure."

"I wish I'd known before I packed a surfboard," Traxus said, feigning shock. She quickly turned serious again. "So, are these R&D guys being paranoid, or are we in for a fight?"

"I honestly don't know. I find it hard to believe anyone would commit an act of violence just to get a product to market, but then again we're not in the food service business."

Traxus chuckled at that. "Well, it's a lot of money for moderate risk. Hopefully they'll finish their little sub rosa project ahead of schedule and we can go back to knowing which side the bad guys are on." She grabbed at her gear to keep it from sliding as the dropship jerked again. "Leon, thanks for getting me this command. It means a lot to me. But ... I have to ask, why did you take Jeric off the team?"

This was not an issue Leon wanted to address. He would rather have kept talking shop with Levy and Santor. "Trax, not now."

"No, Leon. Now."

"I'm just not sure he and I should work together right now. His drinking has gotten out of control, and I'm concerned about his reliability."

"This doesn't have anything to do with you two fighting after the last job?"

"Like I said, not now." Leon turned away from her, concentrating on reading over the contract one last time. He and Jeric had hit a number of rough patches in their friendship over the years, but they had always managed to ride them out. Jeric's was a unique personality, and he was not shy about broadcasting his opinion. Leon could have used his support in the wake of Rachel's return, and he hadn't gotten it. Over the years, that selfishness had worn thin.

"You're his best friend," Traxus said, persistent. "You expect him to *not* care that you're thinking of leaving? You're the reason he got off drugs. You're the one who got him into Jackal Pack, got him made advisor to the fighter corps. You think change isn't easy? Imagine being dependent on someone and having them leave."

Almost as soon as the words left Traxus's mouth, she seemed to realize her error.

"When my folks died," Leon began evenly, "I didn't have the opportunity to put up an argument. My life got turned upside-down, and I was the only one who could tip it back over. I'm still working on it. Besides, Jeric's not dependent on me."

"Sure he is." She glanced at Raptor. "So is he, after a fashion. And me."

"Do you think I'm excited about leaving?" Leon tried to keep the bitterness from his voice, but it slipped through his teeth. Sommers and the others were pointedly ignoring the conversation; Leon was a little embarrassed that they were hearing any of this, but he was too annoyed to turn back. He was tired of everyone assuming that he could bear any burden, simply because he was the colonel, that he was above grief, above doubt. "I may not ... love what I do, Trax. But I love all of you. I mean, what exactly am I supposed to do out there?"

"You don't have to do anything."

"You expect me to sit around on my ass and get fat?"

"Try it. You might like it."

Leon snorted. When he realized he was rubbing the scar beneath his right eye, he pulled his hand away irritably. "You know I used to love reading, Trax? Novels, I mean."

She flicked her ears, no.

"Rain, shine, it didn't matter. I could lose myself in a book for a whole day, forget to eat, fall asleep with it open, wake up, and pick up right where I left off. I'd miss class sometimes because of a good book. Once I missed an exam." He frowned. "I don't remember the last time I read a novel. Now the only books I read are finance manuals and books on strategy. And the occasional scientific journal." Although they tended to depress him. "The point is, I can't do that anymore. I have to be doing something, something that matters. If I don't keep moving, I feel like I'm nothing."

Traxus said nothing.

"Reversion commencing," announced the pilot, Tamara Kelly. "All hands brace."

When the dropship slid out of the conduit, it jolted hard, and an alarm blared. The ship began to shudder, just a slight tremor at first. It gradually increased until the deck seemed to undulate beneath their feet. Leon held on, his knuckles white as he gripped the harness bars that pinned him into the seat. *This has never happened before.* Even the most turbulent atmospheric entries under fire rarely felt so hull-shatteringly violent. He wanted to go up to the cockpit and see what was wrong but didn't trust himself not to fall and break his neck.

With no portholes in the troop cabin for them to orient themselves, the effect of the shaking on the passengers was terrifying and nauseating. For a long time, dropships had been referred to as "express coffins," and if something went wrong and the vessel plowed into the earth, the troops inside would certainly be buried quickly. Or cremated, their ashes spread across a thousand miles.

Beside Leon, Traxus's eyes were wide, the whites around her emerald irises seeming to glow. Raptor, too, looked frightened. He was claustrophobic to begin with; sleep was usually his way of coping with dropship travel, but that was no longer an option.

"Everyone hang on!" Leon shouted, unable to muster anything else. Sommers had turned very pale, her eyes squeezed shut. The other troops were likewise fighting off their fears, breathing quickly, panic barely contained beneath the surface, ready at any moment to spill out and overwhelm them. *If we were going to explode, we would have already,* Leon told himself, unconvincingly.

Finally, after what seemed an eternity, the shaking subsided, and the engines resumed their healthy drone. Leon released his harness and stood on shaky legs, making his way to the hatch leading to the bridge. He pushed it open. "You mind telling me what the fuck that was?"

The pilots looked as though they had seen their own ghosts. The Human, Captain Tamara Kelly, was covered in sweat, and her hands trembled. Beside her, the nasal crest of her Sheff'an copilot, Ensign Hifotza, was so inflamed it looked ready to burst. "Gravdrive field destabilized too quickly," answered Kelly, her voice as shaky as her hands. "I thought we were going to lose the starboard engine to the gravitic wave."

"We'll make it?"

"We'll make it. I think we should scrap this heap, though."
There was a note of sadness in her voice. Leon made his way back to
the troop compartment and sat down heavily. Traxus did not press
him further on the issue of Jeric or of retirement.

4: Mekon DaVoi

The clock on the wall said two-thirty. The Jackal Pack detachment would be arriving at Tikal and beginning their descent into the planetary atmosphere any minute now.

Seated in an old leather chair that reminded her of the one in her father's study, Rachel leaned back and cracked her knuckles. The conference room table was strewn with documents and mem screens.

Outside in the hallway business continued as usual, with officers and staff bustling about their business. Jackal Pack's nerve center had always been well appointed, the better to attract high-end clients, but to Rachel the fine edges appeared to be fraying a bit, walls in need of repainting, furniture in need of reupholstering or outright replacement as the styles changed.

It's a corporate security job. He's probably standing in some board room to intimidate clients or something. She could lie to herself all day, but it was a defense of diminishing returns.

"I need a break," Heidi said from across the table, draining her coffee cup. "Lunch?"

Rachel agreed. She wasn't hungry, but she knew she needed to unwind. "I could use some fresh air."

"Why don't you go find us a spot outside? I'll wheel over to the officer's mess and grab sandwiches. Anything you won't eat?"

"Surprise me," Rachel said, smiling. "And thanks."

Before she could rise, there was a gentle knock on the door. "Ladies, how goes the project?" asked General Rockmore genially.

"Well enough, General," Heidi answered. "We've barely scratched the surface, but Rachel was right about there being something here. Some of the old arrays might even work to handle the additional bandwidth we'll need."

"Glad to hear it." The general was worrying at the deep scar in his face with a thick, calloused finger. Rachel found herself repulsed by it, feeling for a moment like one more war-junkie on Rockmore's payroll.

"Actually, I'd like to visit this array in Tesa," Rachel said pointing at a spot on a map of the capital she had unrolled on the table. "It hasn't been used in decades, but the power grid might still be up to it."

Rockmore glanced at the map and frowned. "That's in the Moraj District. I'd prefer it if you didn't venture there. The gangs have been causing trouble out that way again."

"Thanks for the advice, General. We were about to break for lunch, anyway" Rachel said more abruptly than she intended, feeling suddenly claustrophobic.

Rockmore smiled graciously, picking up on her sour mood. He didn't question them further but congratulated them on their progress so far and left.

Wishing that she was back in White Coast on Amalthia, Rachel practically ran down the stairs to the building's main doors. She had begun skipping showers to support the water rationing effort, and though she feared she stank in the office's close quarters, no one seemed to have noticed. The air was hot and dry, Eve's drought still in full force, and Rachel had to shade her eyes against the sun. At least the breeze, while warm, was fresh, carrying only the faintest hint of cordite and smoke from the artillery range where the guns boomed faintly in the distance. She found an unoccupied bench under a tree with yellow leaves and sat in the shade.

Developing the Signal Fire Protocol was no easy feat. Rachel was grateful for Heidi's help and connections in the planetary government. For it to have even the faintest chance, it would need support throughout the Alkyra, first and foremost with the regional trade council on Benez.

From a technical standpoint, it would require incredible amounts of energy and a direct linkage of resonant mass ansibles and comm arrays. For some of the less populated, poorer worlds along the Alkyra, the infrastructure and funding would be hard to come by. A planet like Eve could afford it (barely), but the smaller colonies only used realtime comms in an emergency. A project of this magnitude could bankrupt them within months. Were this a territory of the Coalition or Commonwealth, there would be all sorts of subsidy programs to apply to for grants. As it stood, the Tears of Alkyra were so loosely affiliated that they barely qualified as a federation, more like an opportunistic alliance.

Her head already spinning again, Rachel turned her attention to the courtyard's occupants. Since the contract lock had been lifted, the Jackals seemed to be reenergized, and a positive mood buoyed her spirits. Even if their purpose was mayhem and murder.

She saw Jeric emerging from the pilot's barracks, shirtless, with a towel over his shoulder. He was handsome in his arrogant way, with captivating blue eyes and his usual impeccably styled blonde hair. His body was less toned than Leon's, but his skin had fewer scars. He walked with the sort of self-absorbed condescension Rachel knew all too well from her cohort on Amalthia, but there was something else in Jeric's walk besides put-on confidence: the loose, springy movements of a natural predator.

He saw her and waved. Rachel waved back but made no move to talk to him, and he kept walking. Thirsty and not wanting to wait any longer for Heidi, Rachel stood and walked to the main mess hall south of the administration building to get a cup of Kaf.

When she entered the hall, she was hit with a wall of boisterous sound. The mercenaries were in a singularly jocular mood, and someone threw a muffin that barely missed her as she walked toward the Kaf machines. "Sorry, Miss Case!" the thrower shouted, as insults were hurled in his direction.

Kaf in hand, she walked back outside and spotted Heidi's bright green hair easily. They met at the bench, unwrapping their sandwiches and eating in companionable silence.

"I want to see that old ansible array in the Moraj," Rachel said determinedly.

"You heard the general." Heidi gauged Rachel's reaction and shrugged. "I can arrange an escort if you're really interested in it. I know more than a few people who wouldn't bat an eye at chasing off some hoodlums."

"Thank you. I'll think about it," Rachel said around a mouthful of her sandwich.

Heidi was an anomaly. Though most of the Jackals were ferocious enough, the majority came from planetary or galactic militaries, shield departments, or other private military outfits. Her sunny disposition and brightly dyed hair seemed at odds with her past, and Rachel never would have guessed that she, better than most of the mercenaries, fit the stereotype of an adrenaline junkie fortune hunter. From what Rachel could gather without prying, Heidi was a genuinely violent and amoral person. It was jarring to discover this, but she supposed she shouldn't have been surprised in a place where the main cafeteria had an anti-aircraft cannon mounted on the roof.

They were still eating when Jeric passed by again, his hair wet. He made no indication that he saw Rachel this time

Heidi saw Rachel tense, and she whistled loudly. "Jeric, don't be an asshole."

The pilot diverted course, reluctantly, it seemed.

"Nice morning," he said stiffly.

Rachel nodded. "Did you go for a swim?"

He nodded. "I figured I'd get some laps in while Raptor's not around to hold me underwater. How are you doing?"

"Keeping busy. Heidi and I are working on a project for the general." Somehow, even talking to Jeric was better than being left to her thoughts. Zenna had invited Rachel to stay with her in Tesa, but perversely, the base was starting to feel like home. "Why didn't you go to Tikal?"

A strange expression passed over Jeric's face, and his lip twitched ruefully. "Not my specialty, I guess." He shifted uneasily, kicked at a rock with his sandal. "I should go. I have to brief the next patrol."

Rachel nodded, but once he had turned his back and begun to walk away, an irresistible urge came over her. She and Jeric were hardly friends, but one of them had to end the standoff. "Jeric, we should get dinner."

He turned back. "Maybe. I've got a lot to do today."

"Come on. My treat."

"Okay," he said uncertainly, drawing out the word.

"Eight o'clock?"

He nodded. "Sure."

Heidi winked at Rachel as Jeric walked away. "See? He can be trained."

§

Tikal was far from a paradise, it was true, but it had an odd, ugly charm. Leon watched from the bridge of the dropship as they plunged into the atmosphere. The planet had long been uninhabitable, but the lodes of trykon crystal and other valuable ore were enough to justify the cost of full terraforming, courtesy of Edenbridge Planetary Industries. After fifty-odd years, the air was breathable though faintly scorched and sulphurous, and imported flora and fauna managed to thrive beneath the roiling black clouds and red streaks of lightning. The planet was trapped beneath a blanket of supercharged ion clouds that made travel difficult: the inhabitants were served by a single spaceport equipped with a massive, charged airshield that plowed a clear channel through the disruption. Similar shields existed elsewhere across the world, chasing away the clouds and creating bright pockets of sun-drenched countryside upon which perched defiant settlements.

A population of about six hundred million called Tikal home, the majority of them Humans of Argentinean descent or Verician and Therzhian Borin who didn't mind the darkness. The Borin ran the mining combines and carried out most of the excavation, while the Humans managed the service industries that kept the planet's domestic commerce thriving. Like everything else on the planet, the inhabitants existed in a precise, carefully built equilibrium.

The largest settlement, just south of the spaceport, was home to fifteen million inhabitants. Nueva Formosa was a gleaming tangle of highways and high-rises, bathed in a thick pillar of sunlight that was almost dreamlike in contrast to the shifting thunderheads on all sides. The light appeared to be tinted green due to the impact of the ions against the airshield. Leon noted that although Nueva Formosa was a Spanish name, many of the buildings looked Borin in design, with Borin corporate logos adorning their walls. Looming over the other buildings from a hill near the southern edge of the city was the Mekon DaVoi headquarters, a thick, secure-looking skyscraper that was distinctly utilitarian when compared with some of the whimsical spires around it. Mekon DaVoi was a fairly young company by Borin standards; it was managed by a mixture of off-world investors and a local board of directors.

Leon and his team debarked gratefully after the shaky descent, for the atmospheric entry had brought a new round of hull tremors, and one of the airfoils had actually buckled a few minutes before touchdown. Although they were still reeling from the drop, they surveyed their surroundings with composed professionalism.

To the east and north of the spaceport, Leon could see vast fields of ribbed metal protrusions erupting from the ground. From the brief, he knew that they were ion receptors that collected the energy from the red lightning's static discharge, used in powering the airshields and many of the planet's homes and businesses. Off to the west vast gantries marked the gaping maw of one of the mines.

A Mekon DaVoi representative met them at the main customs station, introducing himself as Oscar Mendoza. *"Bienvenido a Tikal, Colonel."* His Spanish was crisp, aristocratic. "Your people look tired."

"It was an exciting trip," Leon said drily.

During the mission to Korinthe, Leon's team had been forced to go in unprepared when their heavy equipment and his EMMA were held up in customs. Buzz Parker's death had been due at least in part to that. Leon had prepared himself for a similar situation on Tikal, but his concerns were unwarranted: almost magically, Mendoza expedited them through customs, weapons, armor, and all. Leon was puzzled and impressed. Apparently Mekon DaVoi was a big deal here. The customs officers didn't even give the Jackals a second glance.

A gravbus awaited them, with Mekon DaVoi's double-sun logo splashed across the side. Shield escorts stood ready ahead of and behind it, ready to escort the new arrivals through traffic.

Leon took a moment and examined their guide. Oscar Mendoza was a short man with thin, graying hair. A strip of beard descended from his lip, jutting pharaonically from his chin. He wore an expensive, tailored suit, a new Adrevani, Leon saw, and a necklace with two pendants. One was a crucifix, the other a disk in the shape of the galaxy, the core made of bright star-stone, black with gold pinpricks. So he worshiped at the Temple of the Biocosmic, adhering to that odd belief that the universe was an infinite, eternal entity and all the planets and beings throughout it tiny parts of the whole anatomy. The religion had experienced a resurgence in popularity over the last few decades. Even Leon's sister Natille had joined the Temple, and while he himself lacked much in the way of faith, he had to admit that the Biocosmic presented a uniquely attractive idea.

When they were all aboard and the bus had risen on its Rombaldt Radiant Mass antigravity fields, Mendoza turned and favored Leon with a warm smile. "You might as well get the question out of the way." He had clearly seen Leon eyeing his dueling pendants.

"I'm just curious how you can follow two diametrically opposed philosophies."

The man smiled the smile of one who has answered the question many times. "We all serve many masters, Colonel."

Leon favored Mendoza with a smile of his own. "For us it generally comes down to credit rating."

Mendoza's smile broadened. "Well said. My point is that we all move at the whims of others, sometimes voluntarily, sometimes out of convenience, sometimes out of obligation. I serve the Holy Trinity and the Temple, yes. Two doctrines, mutually inflexible. I also serve Mekon DaVoi. Ultimately, I also gladly serve my wife and my children."

Leon nodded. "Well, you've sold me on that."

"It's not for sale," Mendoza said softly. "It just *is*." He had clearly been asked this question many times. Their conversation turned toward other topics. Although he looked stern, with a wind-lined face and hard eyes, he was a friendly host, eagerly pointing out prominent landmarks as they entered the city proper. The other mercenaries filling up the bus were subdued, taking in their new host world.

They were nearly to the city perimeter when Mendoza said, "I heard about your difficult entry into the system. I'm sure it took its toll. You can all get some rest before your briefing. We've arranged quarters for your people at the base of our compound near the main gate. They're not as luxurious as the company apartments off-site, but I hope you understand that we wanted you all close by in the event of trouble."

Leon nodded. "That won't be a problem. Any information you can provide regarding this 'trouble?'"

The man pursed his lips. "I'm sorry, that's just such an unusual question. Most people in our industry tiptoe around the issue. I've never worked with reapers, so please forgive me if I am a little stiff."

Leon flinched at the word. It had been a long time since he had been called a reaper, at least to his face. "We're licensed Ronin, Señor Mendoza. Sanctioned by all major powers."

The man looked embarrassed and a little puzzled. "I am so sorry. I did not realize there was a difference."

"The difference is one of legality," Leon said by way of explanation. From a moral standpoint he supposed the man was right: after all, did some bureaucrat's stamp of approval change the nature of the bullets? It was true the sanctioning system was imperfect, and both its qualification and enforcement differed from kingdom to kingdom, but it kept the mercenaries mostly in check. Didn't it?

Mendoza interrupted his rumination. "I ... don't mean to be rude, Colonel, but you *are* Leon Victor, aren't you?"

"I am."

The man seemed relieved. "We're delighted to host you. I'm sure our security is in the most capable hands. General Rockmore spoke highly of your team. So have a number of your former clients."

"I'm glad to hear it." The gravbus was a fast conveyance, especially with the shields clearing traffic ahead of them, and the rough landscape blurred by. It was a much smoother ride than the dropship had been, and Leon found himself nearly lulled to sleep. He shook off his lethargy when they passed into the sunlight around the city, and it was as though the entire planet had caught fire. In an instant, bright light again flooded the windows, and the ground turned to a lush carpet of green and blue grasses shot through with carefully tended flower beds.

Nueva Formosa was not a large city, and its sensible, grid-like layout provided impressive views down the broad avenues. The convoy turned a corner near the city center, and Leon narrowed his eyes, his interest piqued. Up ahead, the Mekon DaVoi compound glowered at the end of a vast boulevard. There was a high, thick wall around it, almost prisonlike. It wasn't like any corporate headquarters he'd ever seen for, although the skyscraper itself looked ordinary enough, the smaller structures around it looked distinctly fortresslike. Were those guard towers at the corners? "This certainly seems like a secure facility," Leon observed.

"It is. In addition to our regional management team, the bulk of our R&D is here. Our competitors are tenacious, though. Before you ask, those are observation towers, crewed by armed guards. They're just a precaution. The entire compound is also comm-shielded, so we'll have to provide your team with keyed-frequency units."

"Thermal shielded?"

"Some of the critical facilities are."

It was a paranoid approach to doing business, but it was not Leon's place to question the client. "You're the chief of security for Mekon DaVoi, but I'd like to speak to the local shield commander, as well."

"That would also be me," Mendoza said proudly.

That hadn't come up in the file. It was certainly interesting. "Well, then. I'd also like a chance to speak to your director of operations, to ensure that we get full cooperation in assessing areas for improvement. We don't want to be underfoot, but we require a degree of access."

"Your people will have access to our security grid and our personnel although you understand that we have a number of secure areas that will be off-limits to your team."

"That's fine." Leon sat back, felt the vibration of the bus's engine against his spine. "You've had a chance to review the final contract, I hope?"

"I have," Mendoza said. "My employers have a few additions to make, regarding a nondisclosure agreement."

"We guarantee the security of all your company's proprietary information."

"I appreciate that, Colonel, and I believe you. We still need it in writing."

"Will my signature suffice, or do you need the general's?"

"Yours will do. I must also insist that your team turn in any video recording devices."

"It's standard operating procedure for us to wear helmet cameras."

"I'm afraid we can't permit that. There is a great deal of sensitive information in this facility. We can't take any chance of a leak."

"I'm not sure you understand, sir. A primary condition of our sanction is full audio and video. Violating that would expose us to a huge potential liability."

"Please, you don't expect me to believe that Jackal Pack operatives have never overlooked that particular requirement. Some of your most satisfied—and least legal—clients commended your organization's discretion."

Leon frowned. He didn't like that, but it was true: Jackal Pack specialists, including his team, often "forgot to put the batteries in" their recording equipment when taking on jobs that already involved sanction-violating activities. In for a penny, in for a pound. "The liability...."

"Mekon DaVoi will cover any violations and waive all rights in that regard."

Leon hesitated. "I'll need *that* in writing."

As they entered the compound, passing through two sets of armored gates, the mercenaries saw that the air of militarism was more than just window dressing. The smaller, industrial-looking structures of the facility seemed haphazardly strewn about, children's blocks knocked awry. Seeing some of the bunkerlike supercrete blockhouses, Leon wondered just what sort of research was being conducted here. Here and there he spotted men in blue fatigues and black flak vests, assault carbines slung over their shoulders and black helmets on their heads. They looked well drilled, but they were clearly little more than a militia. Mendoza informed him that roughly half of them were full-time Mekon DaVoi employees, while the rest were moonlighting on their days off from the shield precincts in the city. Inside the compound, Leon's comm lost its signal. He switched it off, and Traxus ordered the troops to do the same.

The mercenaries debarked, and Mendoza showed them to the barracks. They had been given a separate wing with plenty of room and a dedicated shower facility. Mendoza pulled Leon aside as the troops picked their bunks and got settled.

"Your team has been inoculated?" Mendoza asked.

Leon tapped the spot on his shoulder where he had been injected with a multitude of vaccines. It was still sore. "We have, and we're aware of the risks." New sanctioned colonies carried mandatory quarantine periods of up to fifteen years. Even after the standard eco-probe and molecular workup to determine habitability, colonies were kept isolated in order to determine the virulence of local pathogens and their effects on livestock, produce, or the colonists themselves. It only took one careless ship's crew to act as a vector for a potentially devastating interplanetary epidemic.

Since its terraforming, Tikal had experienced several setbacks that had extended the quarantine period, mainly involving a species of rapidly adapting fungus that had been discovered in the mines. It was no longer considered dangerous, but it was endemic so the barracks was equipped with foggers, giving the place a nasty chemical smell, and everyone on the planet had to take a daily supplement. As a result, though travel had been open for nearly a decade, the starport remained fairly barren, and planetary entry and exit involved extensive decontamination procedures.

"It's nice to see the Confed observing the quarantine laws," Leon noted.

Mendoza shrugged. "Well, we all saw what happened to the Vali when they ignored them on B'ster." Leon was well aware of the Valinata's notoriously irresponsible colonization policies. The inexplicable calamity that had befallen the entire kingdom was something far more sinister.

Mendoza stood back near the door as Leon turned to his troops. They had gathered around him and Traxus in a half-circle, standing at ease. Traxus cleared her throat. "Okay, everyone, the colonel and I will leave you here to get settled while we get the tour from Señor Mendoza. Until further notice, I'm restricting you all to the company compound, so stay on-site.

"I recommend you take the time to get some sleep before we get to work. The day-night cycle here is thirty-nine hours. That means long shifts. Your team leaders will hand out your assignments. This whole compound is comm shielded, so you'll turn yours in to me to exchange for keyed-frequency units." Leon would have wagered that those would be tapped by their employer, but none of the troops would be dumb enough to take that bet. "Avoid all off-limits areas like they're minefields, and do whatever the staff ask of you. This could be a very cushy job if we play our cards right."

Mikaela Sommers crossed her arms. "Lieutenant, are we cleared for weapons?"

Traxus deferred to Mendoza, who nodded.

Mikaela wasn't finished, though, and she tellingly directed her next question to Leon. "What if they want us guarding multiple sites? We can't possibly take more time on."

This time, however, Mendoza answered without waiting for a cue. "This is the only site on Tikal, and I assure you that our own security team can provide personnel if you need them. The only issue is that they're all locals, and we have no PDF training facilities so they have basic shield tactical training." He turned and left. Was he insulted?

When Leon and Traxus left the platoon, Mendoza was waiting in the hallway, cleaning his fingernails. Leon still couldn't picture him as the security chief, let alone the city's shield-in-chief. He looked more like a jumped-up marketing director. He looked up when they approached. "I apologize, Colonel, Lieutenant, if I was out of line. It's an officer's prerogative to brief her troops."

Traxus shrugged in the Human fashion. "Not a problem. Our people are still just a little jumpy after the ride, that's all."

"We, too, are jumpy. We've been under the guillotine for months now, with nothing but local boys to protect us. I'm not sure how much we can count on them."

"You don't have any other outside talent?" Leon asked.

Mendoza smiled sadly. "You *are* the outside talent, the only ones who would come. My mother and father colonized Tikal as part of Mekon DaVoi's original seed team when the company cofinanced the terraforming. I inherited my position." That explained the tight relations between the civil service and corporate officers. Mendoza looked uncomfortable. "So, the tour. Shall we?"

"Please."

The facility was far from ordinary, but nothing about it struck Leon as especially clandestine. There were duplicate power generators, squat fusion reactors with fat trunks snaking out toward different structures like gleaming metal roots. The office building was the expected maze of cubicles and conference rooms except for a dedicated control center on the top floor where Mendoza and the other higher-ups could monitor all operations as well as a large armory in the basement that included two double-heavy powered infantry units. Leon was given only a quick glimpse into those rooms, but they were clearly well-equipped, if lacking the people to wield that equipment. Leon doubted they were as helpless as Mendoza made them out to be. There was also a private hangar with a number of sleek courier ships and passenger jets. It was when he was shown around the first of the research buildings that Leon realized this was not an average R&D plant. The equipment was state-of-the-art, and most of it was beyond his comprehension. Stranger still was the fact that the controls to the city's airshield were contained in the underground armory.

"What exactly is it that you do here?" Leon asked warily, watching through a thick, shielded window as a pair of technicians in powered isolation suits lifted a heavy, vapor-emitting canister into a larger containment vessel.

"I'm delighted that you take an interest, Colonel. This lab conducts quality assurance testing for a number of our biohazard containment systems. We're even rated for antimatter control," Mendoza bragged. "I admit, most of what we do here is disappointingly mundane. The bulk of our labs are dedicated to refining the texture of synthesized foods produced from raw carbon."

"That's worth killing for," Leon put in, only half-joking.

"Many space travelers would agree, I think." Mendoza made a face. "We're hoping to approximate the texture of muscle fibers found in most natural meats. And, of course, the crispness of fresh fruits and vegetables has always been a challenge. We think that if those two factors can be isolated and improved, the rest of it will fall into place."

"And?" Traxus put in.

"Excuse me?"

"You said, 'the bulk' of your research has to do with food. What about the rest?"

"Of course. Unfortunately, this is where your specialties come in. You see, the rest of our resources are tied up in medical technologies. Our high-profile projects include an alternative to the Generation Five Polymerase Swarm—which we think we have a chance of beating to market—and realtime diagnostic nanomachines fitting the DER-6 criteria for full-spectrum care. Those are a little farther off, but our newest test models are smaller than ever and can fool most white blood cells, avoiding the typical inflammatory responses that usually derail nanotreatments. Our most promising project, however, involves implanted telecommunications modules for search and rescue teams. That way they can communicate with each other more quickly and pick up open comm bands, like distress signals. Especially helpful for large-scale relief efforts."

"You're talking computer-assisted telepathy." Traxus sounded awed.

"That's the rough cut, I suppose. Unfortunately, we've run into the same problems with comm implants as the military has with neurolinked powered armor: rejection in an unfortunately high proportion of otherwise promising candidates. The mind is a very proud organ, Lieutenant, and it hates to be second-guessed. The neural links in armor contain external switches and physical controls which provide a sense of detachment and sovereignty for the user. With a comm implant, there is no such object to focus anxiety, no physical anchor for the sensory supplement. People reject it because, although for all intents and purposes what they perceive could be catalogued as a sixth sense, they know it's a foreign source in their mind."

"Very philosophical," Leon said.

"Not at all. There's a term for it: psychopartitional distortion. Normalized partitioning allows you to suppress painful memories, prioritize tasks, try a dish after getting food poisoning the last time you ate it, ignore pain, that sort of thing. Unfortunately, with a hardwired piece of equipment, shunting mental input can lead to aneurism. For most species, the mind is a private place. We don't like intrusion. The sense of being 'plugged in,' if you'll pardon the pun, to a collective entity, is unnatural."

Leon could clearly remember the sense of disorientation and nausea that had accompanied his early EMMA training. It was not widely known, but many sojieri began to experience hallucinations after using a neural interface for too long, the syndrome even manifesting as schizophrenia or degradation of cognitive function. The Coalition's hospices for overloaded EMMA operators were a quiet testament to the risks, and Leon knew far too many sojieri who had been affected. "So how do you solve this psychopartitional ... distortion, was it?"

Mendoza nodded. "We're looking for a way to tailor an implant to an individual's unique neural pathways, insert it seamlessly into the flow of thought."

"Abstract."

"Somewhat. And it's a surprisingly new approach. You see, most implants simply broadcast at an individual's brain, overloading the normal thought process. I'm sure you understand why that makes perpetually active implants impractical and unsound. We think a phased integration may help with the acclimation."

"But that's not all."

"No, but surely you don't expect me to share all our proprietary information." Mendoza smiled innocently. He seemed like a decent guy although he clearly had his share of secrets. Nowadays Leon couldn't tell if he was just being paranoid, but he wasn't about to trust a man just because he wore a crucifix.

"I guess I don't. But I can see why espionage might be a concern. This seems like something the military would be interested in."

"It is, and the Shar'dan maintain oversight rights over any cybernetic technologies. We haven't declared any of this in the hope of keeping things academic for the time being. This technology, properly applied, has the potential to save lives and lower the barriers between people. Used incorrectly, it could be a terrible weapon or a way of policing people's minds."

"Funny, most worthwhile innovations seem to have that kind of problem. So where's the threat assessment? Rival corporation or activists out to stop bioengineered augmentation?"

"Neither, actually." Mendoza looked uneasy for a moment. "Well, I suppose a rival corporation is indirectly involved. At least, probably. Colonel, are you familiar with the Black Rose Syndicate?"

Leon struggled not to scoff. "I've heard of them. I don't want to alarm you, Señor Mendoza, but I'm sure you know that we've had dealings with a lot of people on the outside of the shield, so I have a fair bit of insight into various cartels and syndicates. That being said, never once have I actually run into this mythical Black Rose. The arms dealing, the drug running, the political manipulation ... they make for a nice conspiracy theory, but in the end, it's too farfetched."

Mendoza blinked. He looked like he had more to say, but he changed course. "Well, Black Rose or no, there's a black market concern operating on Tikal, and they've already successfully raided one of our deliveries. I highly doubt that they have the firepower to try anything here, but we couldn't take that chance."

It made sense now. Leon nodded. "Well, now you can."

§

Jeric ate like a machine thought Rachel as she watched him shovel food into his mouth. Although she had been the one to suggest dinner, she found herself without an appetite. With embarrassment she realized she was nervous, but she was an adult and she would carry on.

"Jeric," she said and immediately knew that her tone was too cold. He looked up, eyes guarded. "We need to talk."

"Really," he said blankly.

"Look, I know we don't exactly get along well—"

"Let's leave it at that, then." Like a nervous animal aware that it is being watched while in a vulnerable state, Jeric returned his attention to the pasta on his plate.

"No, that's not good enough. I love Leon, Jeric. I *love him*." Rachel said it emphatically, hoping she wasn't being too confrontational. "Maybe you don't believe that, but it's true. I'm not out to change him, not in the way you think. And I'm not out to come between the two of you."

"Great. Enjoy your food."

This was harder than she had expected. No one loved facing up to their shortcomings, but Jeric's sarcastic deflection was infuriating. *If Leon had introduced me to Jeric before I got on that ship with them, I might never have left Amalthia,* she thought. "Jeric, I'm serious. Please."

He threw down his fork and stared at her, his cheeks absurdly full of food, tomato sauce smeared on his chin. He looked comically childish, but his eyes were dark and full of disdain. "Fine. You've got a captive audience." He swallowed, sat back, and crossed his arms. Rachel recognized a defensive stance when she saw one.

"Okay...." Embarrassed, she found herself at a loss for words. "We both want Leon to be happy, right?"

"He seemed happy enough before you came into the picture." It was good that Jeric had decided to participate, but his remark stung. Was he right? "Maybe what we do isn't ethical. Shit, I won't defend it. But we do it. And this is Leon's home. You don't understand it, but this is where he belongs."

Jeric had made a mistake; as in a game of chess he had overextended and left himself open to attack. "But he *doesn't* feel that Eve is his home. You know how much it hurts him not to be a Coalition citizen. He was forced into this career."

"And you think that screwing up that career will make his life easier?"

"Maybe not right away. But nothing worth doing is easy."

"Quit reciting General Rockmore's lines."

"What do I have to do to get you on my side?" Rachel asked, exasperated.

"Leave," Jeric snapped loudly, and some of the other patrons in the Desher Vaux pub looked up curiously.

"You know I won't."

"I'm sorry, maybe I'm confused, but didn't you already?" Jeric asked cruelly. There was a hurt undertone in his voice, and Rachel realized for the first time that not all of his anger was self-centered, that some of it was empathy for Leon, one brother looking out for another. It came as a shock to her, and suddenly she wasn't so sure of herself. "The guy broke all his rules for you, aborted a mission because of you, put us all on the back burner."

"I know he's going to propose to me, Jeric. And I'm going to say yes."

"Are you going to mean it?"

Rachel nodded wordlessly, and Jeric cocked his head, considering.

When he spoke again, he was quiet and surprisingly reasonable. "You have to understand something, Rachel. Jackal Pack would keep on going without Leon, but he means a lot to his battalions. Not a lot of officers would die for their sojieri. Not a lot of officers would go to hell and back for us, to protect us, to pull us out of trouble, to get us the best equipment and the best contracts. He's more than a leader to these people. He's a friend and a brother in arms. There are a lot of good officers here, but none like him."

"But why does he have to go on the missions himself?" Rachel asked, angry at the pleading note in her voice.

"Because he *has* to," Jeric said matter-of-factly. "Maybe it's not always the most responsible leadership, but he can't allow anyone to do what he's not willing to do himself. That's why he goes on the toughest missions. People think it's for the hazard pay or because he's some adrenaline junky who can't let anyone else get the glory, but that's what it comes down to. People talk about leading by example, but he lives that rule, so we would follow him *anywhere*. When I met him, I risked my life and spit in the eye of one of the biggest kingpins in the Valinata on his say-so, and I didn't even know his first name. It's like he's got a gravitational pull. Fucking magnets or something."

Rachel was speechless. For a long time she had wondered if Leon was one of those burn-out cases she had heard of, sojieri who couldn't handle life without fire and blood, who were so desensitized to normal life that they actively sought out danger. She had long ago learned that Leon was different, but she had still missed this crucial detail.

Jeric, seeing that his words had had some effect, seemed pacified. "Just ... make a deal with me, would you? If by some miracle you and Leon stay together, you won't try to cut us out of his life, will you?"

"I would never do that," Rachel said quickly, ashamed that that had once been precisely her plan. "You're his friends, you're part of the reason he is who he is. And I know you've saved his life before. You think I could be so ungrateful to you for that?"

Jeric actually seemed flattered. "And people say you're unreasonable." With that first joke, Rachel knew that the healing process had at long last begun. It would take time, and there would be scars, but this was a start.

"Who says that?" she asked pointedly.

"You know ... people." He smiled thinly and picked up his fork. "Mm, I love cold spaghetti."

§

The first week on Tikal passed without incident. Combating boredom was the greatest challenge the team faced as they walked the hallways and courtyards of the compound. The facility was decorated with plants and reflecting pools, and most of the buildings had atriums to let in natural light tinted green by the airshield, but the monotony and the compound's isolation swiftly became grating, claustrophobic. Traxus had elected to keep the platoon close until they better understood their situation, and the troops had no contact with the city outside the walls. While the Mekon DaVoi personnel were polite, they kept to themselves. Some of them ignored the Jackals altogether.

By the ninth day Traxus was almost wishing for a raid by a rival company. The perpetual buzz and crackle of the airshield left her with a perpetual headache. If not for Dyran and two enlisted Tageans in the platoon who shared her plight, she might have thought she was crumbling under the stress. Now she knew why there were so few of her kind on the planet. Combined with the excruciatingly long day-night cycle, the job, boring as it was, was taking its toll.

Leon alone seemed unbothered by the inconvenience of their work and the setting. Traxus had set up the duty shifts so that either she or Leon would always be on the job, bookending their respective shifts by patrolling the grounds together. It gave her the chance to brief him on the day's events and gave him the opportunity to critique her privately. He was almost cheerful as the two of them strolled past labs buzzing with activity even through the night, reenergizing her even during such a routine assignment.

Traxus knew she could be as valuable an asset as Raptor in a firefight. She might not be as uncannily accurate a sharpshooter as Asar or Dyran, but she was ranked in the top ten percent of the Pack in terms of weapons-handling. Still, she could almost hear Leon's voice in her head saying, "The firing range isn't combat."

She was grateful for the command and a proper field mission, but she continued to be annoyed that Leon had tossed her an easy catch in the form of someone else's platoon. Echo Company's Third was competent, even exceptional. The troublemakers had been ironed out, and they were a well-coordinated machine, making Traxus's presence more of a formality than anything else. She wondered if the enlisted men and women resented her for replacing a lieutenant they all knew and respected or if they would give her the benefit of the doubt. Even that was in question, for their good behavior could simply have been out of respect or fear of Leon and his Prross enforcer.

Traxus supposed she should be used to being spoon-fed by Leon and Rockmore. But why? She was a sojier like everyone else in Jackal Pack, regardless of her pedigree. So what if she had been injured on a mission? Who hadn't been? It was part of the job: there were sojieri in the Pack with a dozen scar rings around their arms or legs where cloned scaffolds had been grafted on to replace lost limbs. How was she supposed to step out from under her brother's shadow if he kept looming over her shoulder?

Leon, at least, seemed satisfied with her performance. She had briefed him on the uneventful day, and now they were just chatting as they walked between buildings.

A pair of Mekon DaVoi research scientists spoke in hushed tones beside a Kaf machine, and they broke off their conversation as the two Jackals approached. They nodded terse greetings, waiting until Traxus and Leon were out of earshot to resume their discussion.

"Do you think there's something they're not telling us?" Traxus wondered aloud as they rounded a corner.

"Almost certainly," Leon said remotely.

Traxus glanced down at him. Not for the first time, she found herself mesmerized by the way his eyes seemed to take in everything at once, always roving, never resting. Even knowing what a bundle of nerves he could be, she was often taken in by his air of quiet and occasionally contemplative menace.

He caught her looking at him and flashed her the roguish smile that had convinced her that Jackal Pack was the place for her, even after she had decided it was her brother's idea of a dumping ground to keep her out of trouble. "Can I help you?"

"Just wondering what you're thinking about."

"Rachel," Leon said without hesitation.

"You wish you'd stayed with her." It wasn't a question.

It wasn't often that Leon seemed so genuinely bewildered, and it was painful to watch. "Yeah. No. I don't know. Trax, you know I love her, and you know I love what I do. I'm supposed to be good at making decisions under pressure, but I honestly have no idea how to go forward without regretting one decision or the other."

"Well, you can't just avoid making the call. You can only put it off so long."

"I know, and I want to marry this woman. I honestly do. I'm not stupid enough to think I can just make her accept this life, but I don't want to give it up, either. At least, not right away. It's become a huge part of who I am."

Traxus considered for a moment. If he was genuinely asking for her input, she couldn't simply shoot from the hip. He deserved genuine compassion. "I don't know how many serious relationships you've had," she began, considering his many flings, "but this sounds like the kind of dilemma everyone eventually goes through. You have to preserve who you are and continue to grow as an individual. You also have to respect the relationship. You're part of a couple now, and that's bigger than one person. You owe her, and your relationship, the truth. Don't just draw it out. It'll only make the inevitable hurt more for both of you. If you can't commit to this, don't try."

It was then that Traxus realized Leon had stopped walking a few strides back and was staring at her, dumbfounded.

"I didn't mean to upset you," she said softly.

"You didn't," Leon replied hollowly. "I mean, you're right. I know you're right. I still don't know what to do."

"Yeah, you do." Traxus decided to change the subject. "I was wondering..." she began. She had known Leon for years, but Jeric and Raptor had been with him prior to Jackal Pack. She often felt left out of their stories, their shared past. They rarely talked about it, and many of the records were sealed by one government or another. Like most people, much of her intel on Leon had been churned through the rumor mill a few times. It was strange to be so close to someone and still not truly know them. *That's not quite true: I do know him. Just not all the details of how he got here.* "What was the most boring job you ever took?" she asked innocuously.

Leon's smile broadened. "This one's right up there."

Traxus rolled her eyes and pushed him half-heartedly, causing him to stumble.

"Okay, okay. You ever hear of the clan Kesh… Keshkagan? Keshkajan? I can't remember. They would have been big around the time you came of age and had your debut."

"Doesn't sound familiar," Traxus admitted.

"I figured you might have heard of them since your family is in the tritium mining business."

"They were in the Confed?"

"Yeah."

"Then my family probably wouldn't have dealings with them. We're traditionalists."

"So were they. Anyway, they were a pretty big piece of the action on Lion's Well. They had been in some century-long feud with a rival clan in the industry. Murders, reprisals, sabotage, you get the idea."

Traxus did get the idea: the history of Tagean aristocracy, especially those descended from frontier settlers, was rife with subterfuge and petty warfare.

"The Keshkagan had run out of heirs so they traced every matriarchal line, looking for a suitable woman, until they were forced to settle on Aos, this minor functionary from the next system over. He was a good man, but he was way, *way* out of his depth. He wasn't prepared for that scale of grudge-match. His people hired some private security teams, including Mourning Star. We were attached directly to him for a month while he and his family got settled. He had a young daughter, and she was the real prize. Once she was old enough, she would have inherited the controlling shares." Leon tapped his chin thoughtfully.

"We spent weeks scanning and rescanning their entire mansion for listening devices and bombs, frisking everyone that came through the door, spying on their associates to make sure no one was turning their coat. Then, out of nowhere, the rival clan announces an end to the feud and says they want to form a partnership with some of the other families on the planet. Aos decides that it's a perfect opportunity for new beginnings, that he's the new scion to put their differences behind him. As a show of good faith, he dismissed us all overnight."

Traxus clenched her jaw. She could see where this was going. She had asked Leon about his most boring job. She hadn't meant to bring up old traumas.

"Raptor and I told him he was being naïve, but he didn't like taking advice from a disgraced Human and some Prross outcast, so he threatened to dock our pay. Obviously we backed off."

"What happened?" Traxus asked, fearing she knew.

"What do you think? They held the summit, and the rival clan wiped out his family, including the little girl." Leon's smile had long since vanished.

"What did you do?"

Leon shrugged. "What could we do? I was ready to burn them down, but there was no one left to pay us, and we weren't about to put our necks on the block for someone who was already dead." Traxus could hear the detachment slide into place like armor plating, protecting Leon from the memory of yet another in the series of tragedies that seemed to make up his life story. She thought perhaps he liked it that way.

6: Hostile Takeover

Rachel held the comm away from her ear as her friend Zenna excitedly—and loudly—relayed the tale of her promotion at the hospital. When there was a pause, Rachel interjected, "We have *got* to get drinks to celebrate! Your treat, of course."

Zenna started laughing, but a buzz alerted Rachel to another incoming call. She glanced at the ID and frowned. "Sorry, Zenn, I've got to let you go. I'll call you back as soon as I can, and we'll make plans." She switched channels. It had been a busy day on the comm: first Leon had woken her up after failing to figure out the time difference between their worlds and time zones, then her brother had called to tell her one of their aunts had passed away, then Zenna, and now this. "Hello, this is Rachel."

Heidi sounded chipper on the other end. "Rachel, great news: I got us a meeting with Governor Jurayan and his communications director."

Rachel straightened up. Heidi certainly could be persuasive. "That's fantastic. How did you manage it?"

There was a pause. "Hold off on congratulating me for a second. It's at the end of this month. It was the only window I could get."

"Well, shit. Let's get to work, then. I'll meet you at your office."

After the morning catching up with people, Rachel still needed to get dressed. As she hastily threw on her clothes, she ruminated on the task at hand. She had been no stranger to impending deadlines in her days with Hyphen Telecom. In fact, she had worked for a VP who had relished lopping unfeasible amounts of time off their project timelines, often forcing her and her team to scramble. However, it had been over a year since she had really put her mind to work this way. All that time lounging poolside and being taken out to dinner after dinner had left her feeling like her brain had atrophied. Nothing like pressure to jumpstart it, though.

At least getting back to work had achieved the desired result of shaking off her lethargy and making her feel like a whole person again. Drifting along in pampered stasis might have been fine for her mother and her brother, but it had never suited Rachel. And she had to admit Heidi set a formidable example, a self-taught woman with a mind as finely trained as her body had been when she was still a warrior.

When Rachel reached Heidi's office, she found the mercenary administrator perusing a datasheet on a new exoskeletal assistance device for paralyzed sojieri. Heidi wore a wistful expression as she slid the sheet under a folder and turned to Rachel. Her hair and nails were a matching shade of royal purple that was almost subdued compared to her usual gaudy hues.

"I've always wondered why you don't use prosthetics," Rachel said without meaning to sound like she was prying.

Heidi sighed as she wheeled over to her credenza and poured a glass of Hais for herself and another for Rachel. "I've tried them all, but I'm not compatible with the direct neural link setups. Leon and the general keep insisting that the self-driven predictive units are good, too, but in the end it just never feels right. It feels too much like I'm being walked around instead of doing the walking for myself."

With no frame of reference, Rachel would have felt presumptuous making a suggestion of her own. She took the glass of whisky and took a sip, suppressing her grimace. Ordinarily she didn't touch the stuff, but she could tell the camaraderie meant a lot to Heidi.

"So where do we stand?" she asked, opening her computer on the desk and pulling up the latest cost-benefit analysis. "If hub worlds can afford to both transmit and monitor reception of the poorer planets, we could bypass some of the budgetary concerns."

Heidi tapped her own screen. "That would put a lot more on the shoulders of a few worlds, but it would give everyone access. I like that a hell of a lot better than just restricting the whole model to the six core systems and leaving the others to cross their fingers and pray. Here, look at this."

Rachel opened the model that Heidi had created and now shared with her. It was a painstakingly detailed map of the Tears of Alkyra, accounting for system drift and the newly announced phase change of the Benez system that would temporarily slow travel through the sector. The Alkyra was a small region by most definitions, with only a few dozen habitable worlds scattered throughout it. But its strategic value was obvious even to a civilian like Rachel. "The only problem that I'm seeing with this is that if there's a problem at one of the broadcasting points we're going to have a hard time coordinating with any subordinate worlds that were relying on their feed."

Heidi shrugged and sipped her own whisky. "If there's a problem at one of the broadcasting points, everyone's going to have a hard time. We can still use it to broadcast an alarm, regionwide. To the CRDF and the UCA, too, for that matter."

"And hope that they show up before things get bad." Rachel toyed with the model for a bit while Heidi reviewed their proposal outline. Rockmore came in to check on them and see if they wanted to order lunch before leaving them to work.

Taking a break to stretch sometime later, Rachel walked around Heidi's office, thinking out loud. "On this kind of timetable we don't need the proposal to be airtight. We can present two different options to the governor and his team and workshop their favorite to present to the regional council."

"Well, we can scratch the systemwide initiative. Half the worlds could never afford it, and a lot of them would probably think it's unnecessary anyway."

"Give people a little credit. Everyone knows something went wrong in the Valinata."

Heidi cradled her chin in her hands, looking thoughtful. "I suppose that's true. And if Benez really is traveling out of phase, people are bound to get weird."

"It's a big deal when something like this happens, isn't it?"

"Oh yeah. I was reading up on it: the last time the Alkyra went out of phase, I think Alkyra herself was still walking around. I think most recently it was the Western Reach that broke off from the Yangtze. That was five hundred years ago, and it's just kept drifting. Now it's so hard to get there that half the colonies died off or were abandoned. At times like this people tend to find religion, or at least superstition. I would be surprised if cults didn't start coming out of the woodwork to pray to the conduits for succor or something."

"You're not thinking … mass suicides, are you?" Rachel asked, aghast.

"Who knows? Probably. With things as tense as they are… people are capable of anything."

Not wanting to contemplate such things, Rachel changed course. "Do you even know what it is we're preparing for?"

"No," Heidi admitted, an expression of worry flickering across her features.

"You think the general does?"

"I think he has a pretty good idea. Leon and Akida, too. I don't think he would encourage us to do something like this if it didn't matter. And if the governor has any sense to look around him, he and his cabinet will back it."

"Then let's get back to it." Rachel leaned against the windowsill. "Can you still get me an escort to that old array in the Moraj district?"

"If you think it will help."

§

Leon was brushing his teeth when his right shoulder popped, and he winced in pain. He switched the toothbrush to his other hand while he slowly rotated his right arm, hearing it pop again with each turn. Old injuries had a habit of clamoring for attention at odd times.

He recalled his inspection of the guard battalion and thought they were in decent shape. As a Shar'dan Protectorate world, Tikal could not raise its own standing defense force, and few off-world sojieri would be willing to make the journey, save the Jackals. Mekon DaVoi's men and women could shoot reasonably well, and they had at least skimmed an outline of basic unit tactics. Still, as Leon had long ago learned, there was a very real difference between theory and application in the chaos of battle. With any luck, they could keep their knowledge academic.

He spat into the sink and then washed his face. The cement floor was freezing cold against the bare soles of his feet. When he looked back up into the mirror, he saw dark circles under his eyes, the gift of Tikal's double-length day. At first he had had trouble sleeping without Rachel beside him. As the long days wore on it grew easier, but his dreams had been restless, and their talks had been infrequent and all too brief.

A loud crunch reverberated through the walls, and the mirror shook, Leon's reflection doubling momentarily. Dust flaked from the ceiling, settling in his hair. He regarded his quivering reflection for a moment, the twinned pairs of hooded eyes meeting as though in mutual understanding. Once again, luck had run out.

The siren began blaring a few moments later, long and loud, a call to arms. Leon had already turned, running for the barracks and his gear. Mikaela Sommers had flipped out of her bunk and was already pulling on her black fatigues, her pale skin standing out bright in the harsh fluorescents. The others were likewise getting ready, Traxus groggily shouting encouragement.

"What the fuck was that?" asked Mikaela, her piercing eyes wide, fixed on Leon.

"Sounded like an explosion to me. Maybe a lab accident. Kit up, meet me out front in one minute! They may need help."

The comm crackled. "Colonel! This is Oscar Mendoza. We have a situation at the gates! They came in fast, stealth dropships and landing pods." *So it was no lab accident.*

Leon replied quickly, "On our way." He switched bands. "Levy, Santor! Gates, now!"

"We saw the explosion, Colonel," Levy said. "First gate has been blown. Shaped charge I think. We're heading down now."

Traxus took over from Leon as she pulled on her gear, talking to Levy and Santor to guide their squads and plan the defense.

Leon wrestled with what to do about Traxus as he pulled on his own fatigues. He had never actually expected that they would have to fight. On the one hand, he could keep her here and take control of her command squad himself, but she would never forgive him for that. Or he could let her do the job she had contracted for. He strapped on a flak vest and helmet and donned his gunbelt. "Let's go, now!" Mikaela was already out the door with the command squad, carrying her heavy machine gun. Raptor was right behind her with his Banshee Gatling gun. Dyran was last out, loading a clip into his rifle.

Leon turned to Traxus. "Stay here," he said authoritatively.

"Fuck that," Traxus snapped, checking the spare clips for her Jackhammer autorifle. "You need me, and the platoon is mine."

"No, you stay here. You're exhausted. I'm not letting you into the line of fire."

"I'm *primary*, Leon! We don't have time for this bullshit!" she growled.

He stood there for longer than they could afford before he nodded. "Fine. But you stay by me no matter what." He turned to the door, saw Santor's and Levy's EMMAs standing empty beside it, glimmering darkly in the lights. If they had time, he would order the two to suit up. It might give them the advantage they needed.

Traxus and Leon stormed into the courtyard a few seconds before the inner gate was blown off its track in a shower of metal and concrete, a vast, accusatory finger of smoke and fire stabbing inward. Traxus tapped her comm. "This is Lieutenant Tachai. All units converge on the courtyard. Watch the walls, there may be sappers coming over." Two of the observation towers were already in smoking ruins, and another exploded as they watched.

More and more blue-uniformed guards were storming out of the neighboring barracks buildings and the headquarters building, but they had little cohesion, little direction. They were seeking cover, though, and that was good.

"Set up a base of fire from the HQ steps," Traxus ordered, "and assemble between outbuildings B-4 and B-8, keep them from flanking. Remember, *watch your blind spots!*" Leon had to keep himself from preempting her orders, had to bite his tongue and repress a decade of carefully honed instincts. For better or worse, it would be her show.

When the first elements of the attack emerged from the smoke, the courtyard of the compound became a deafening crossfire with the two groups spraying bullets and energy beams at each other. A bright blue laser carved across the wall of the barracks building behind Leon, leaving a glowing scar in the supercrete.

He blinked, blinded by the indigo afterimage of the beam. "Mendoza, get your dragoons ready. Santor, Levy, get back to the barracks and suit up, now! I want heavy support ASAP!"

"Understood, Colonel," Levy replied, "but we need cover fire to cross the compound."

"You've got it." Traxus conveyed the order, and they returned their attention to the gates, where more and more figures were emerging from the smoke. Leon had trouble making them out in the predawn gloom. They were like wraiths, larger than life, and he abruptly realized that they were looking at EMMA-clad sojieri, dozens of them. Traxus had seen them, too, and called out a warning.

Whoever wants this tech is certainly serious about getting it. Leon aimed his TK-77 proton rifle at one of the approaching forms and fired. The sojier went down in a shower of sparks, armor and circuitry melting.

"Suppressing fire!" he ordered, and Raptor rose from cover, the Banshee spraying a red stream of energy. By the gates, the raiders were scrambling for cover, and Leon called Santor and Levy over. The two big sojieri ran, hunched over, and were nearly across the compound when a yellow beam cut the air between them and shifted left, into Santor. His light armor did nothing to protect against the laser, and it ignited. He sprawled face-down on the concrete, smoking, and Leon's breath caught in his chest.

"Sergeant Santor is down!" shouted one of the enlisted Jackals.

"Stay calm and stay in cover!" Leon ordered, overriding Traxus. She shot him a warning look, but they both knew that now was not the time to squabble over authority. "We need large-caliber rifles down here on the double. Armor-piercing and explosive rounds!"

"It's a shooting gallery down there!" an unfamiliar voice exclaimed over the radio.

To Leon's right, Levy disappeared into the barracks. It was hard for Leon to see if he was hitting anything through the smoke. When his team had arrived, the compound had been littered with stacked cargo crates and parked vehicles that would provide excellent cover for an advancing force. He had convinced Mendoza to remove all those objects, but these troops were smart, bringing their own portable barricades. Unfortunately, the lack of cover was working against the defenders as well as for them. Several guards fell on the steps of the headquarters building, rolling down.

"Colonel, this is Mendoza! We need to get our critical personnel and research out of here!"

"How exactly do you intend to do that?" Leon shouted into his mic as chips of concrete pattered down on him.

"The covered pad on the roof of the building. All troops pull back, there are too many armored troops down there!"

Leon tried to counter the order, but the guards obeyed Mendoza. None waited to begin their withdrawal up the steps. Mendoza's interference cost lives; unprepared, many of them simply turned and ran. More than a few were cut down as they fled. Leon and his platoon found themselves isolated, right in the path of the enemy advance. So much for an orderly withdrawal.

Traxus was on one knee, firing her autorifle, and Leon grabbed her shoulder and pushed her down. "Stay behind cover!" he ordered. "We have to fall back to the main building!" he shouted to his team. "We'll wait for Levy, then fall back by squads. Traxus, *stay on me*." If only Leon had had time to don Santor's EMMA ... but it was too late now.

More and more people were swarming into the courtyard. Now Leon counted at least twenty-five of the hulking, armor-clad warriors in addition to men and women in lighter armor. A dozen or so Mekon DaVoi guards lay crumpled on the ground before the HQ, and Santor's body was smoking in the center of the compound as laser beams and tracer rounds criss-crossed over him. They had only brought down five of the enemy. These troops were shrugging off just about everything that was thrown at them.

When Levy finally emerged from the barracks, he was clad in black-and-red-striped heavy armor with a death's-head helmet. Leon's heart leapt at the sight. Stomping past their position, Levy opened fire, a heavy Cougar assault rifle roaring in his hands. It was powerful enough to punch through EMMA armor and give them a fighting chance until the dragoons arrived.

"Trax, move!" Leon pushed her from cover and started running toward the HQ. The command squad did the same, keeping plenty of space between troops to avoid drawing too much fire. Two of them went down all the same, sprawling on the concrete. Leon half-turned to see if there was any point in going back for them. There wasn't. The imposing edifice loomed before them, thick square columns flanking the main entrance. Five stories up, the columns ended and the office levels began; guards were knocking out the windows to fire down on the advancing intruders, but their small arms were more of a nuisance than a real threat to the EMMAs. Here and there large-caliber rifles were opening fire, as well, with a loud, steady *crack-crack-crack.*

Bright beams of light slashed across Leon's field of vision, and one sliced into the concrete before him, leaving a glowing trail. It seemed to take forever for them to make it across the open ground, but finally Leon, Traxus, and the command squad reached the safety of the thick stone columns. They turned to cover Dyran, Mikaela, and second squad, while Raptor and Levy courageously brought up the rear, laying down a field of fire that kept the enemy in cover as the third squad sprinted the longest distance to cover.

There was a loud groan behind them, and Leon turned to see the stone walls on either side of the main entrance grinding apart like great jaws. He could just discern the silhouettes of gigantic mechanized sojieri within. Finally, Mekon DaVoi's double-heavy infantry dragoons, concealed in that armory beneath the building, were emerging from their slumber. Dwarfing Levy's EMMA, the thirteen-foot-tall armored units stomped out of their hidden lifts and took up positions at the building entrance. They were reminiscent of the cavalrymen of Old Terra, with decorative crests upon their broad, rounded chassis. Armed with railguns and Gatling lasers that were the bigger cousins of Raptor's Banshee, they could easily hold off a force ten times their size. Abruptly the advantage shifted to the defenders, and the intruders scattered again, their advance halting. Nevertheless, they had reached the cover afforded by the outbuildings, and were gradually flanking the entrance.

Nearly deafened by the fire thrown up by the dragoons, Leon listened in as Traxus and Mendoza continued to coordinate the defense. As the sun began to rise, casting its light upon the debris-strewn compound, Leon spotted a pair of dropships outside the gates, disgorging more troops. The advancing force popped smoke grenades to conceal their movement, and the courtyard was once again hidden beneath a swirling pall.

Leon pulled on his Tac-goggles to get a better look at the enemy forces through the smoke, but he found it less than helpful.

Their armor was thermally and electromagnetically shrouded, so all he saw were faint traces of movement. That kind of armor enhancement was not cheap. *Who are these people?*

It wasn't long before the enemy brought down one of the armored dragoons. Rockets streaked out of the smoke, slamming into the hardened armor around the torso. The first two did little more than stagger the ironclad warrior, but the third crashed into the relatively vulnerable join between the left arm mounting the railgun and the torso containing the operator. The arm sheared away, and Leon's team was nearly thrown flat by the concussions of the explosions. Sparking, the dragoon toppled backward, smashing against the stone wall and gouging it. It did not move again.

"Eleven o'clock, by Building Thirty!" Traxus shouted, elbowing Leon. The advancing enemies were protected from the guards on the upper floors by a broad overhang. "Third squad, hit them with grenades!" The Jackals shifted their fire, pelting a group of heavy infantry that were trying to cross the open ground between them and the main building. Levy's troops threw a volley of grenades, and explosions sent shrapnel and concrete chips flying. Armor dented and pierced, the intruders withdrew for the moment.

Without warning, Traxus stopped firing, and Leon glanced over, fearing the worst. But she had not been hit; she was staring, open-mouthed, at their attackers. She put out her hand, pushing Leon's rifle away, and shoved him behind the pillar. "Did you see?" she asked, sounding terrified.

"See what?"

"Their ... colors!"

Leon risked a look out. In the pre-dawn gloom, he honestly hadn't been able to make out much more than vague shapes. Now that the sun was coming up, piercing the clouds through the channel created by the airshield, he saw blue and red armor glinting. *Oh, shit. Shar'dan Republican Guard.*

He shouted into his comm, "Mendoza, those are SRG troops! We have to surrender immediately!"

"Negative, Colonel. Repel them at all costs."

"You don't understand! We *cannot* engage sanctioning government forces!"

"Do it or you'll be dead, Colonel, one way or another."

Leon couldn't think, felt the disorienting effects of panic blurring the edges of his perception. Sanctioned Ronin like Jackal Pack, authorized by governments to operate within their territories, were still considered illegal combatants, and there were almost no grounds for defense if they were captured by a federal branch. Some organizations simply shrugged and went on with their illegal activities and hoped to avoid capture, but Jackal Pack made a policy of not directly engaging any sanctioning military force. And here they had violated that rule, not only in attempting to evade capture but in killing Shar'dan troops.

"Cease fire, cease fire!" Traxus shouted into her comm. "We need to surrender to the SRG units." She did a remarkable job keeping her voice even.

"Are you crazy, Lieutenant?" asked Mikaela Sommers from across the steps, casting an incredulous glance her way. "If we do that, these fuckers will *kill* us!"

Leon gave the double-heavy the order to stand down. He was ignored in turn. They had been betrayed, misled into thinking that the danger was from corporate raiders when in reality it had been from the Shar'dan Confederate *government*. He should have known something was wrong when Mendoza had explained Mekon DaVoi's refusal to declare their projects. And now that bastard was out of Leon's reach at the top of a skyscraper, about to escape.

Why didn't they ask us to surrender? Leon found himself reminded of the mission to Korinthe, when the local government had deliberately initiated a bloodbath, pushing Leon, Raptor, and Buzz Parker into a suite full of drug dealers in the hopes of turning the press of a slaughter to their advantage. Buzz and most of the dealers had been killed. Were they on the receiving end of just such a raid now?

With their comm channel open to Mendoza, Leon had no choice but to switch to Xhosa. Among his team, only Raptor could understand the language, one of many spoken on the African continent of Old Terra. "We have to bring down this heavy and give up."

"Agreed," Raptor replied. The Prross was across the steps, past the downed armored unit, half-hidden by the fire and greasy black smoke. "My Banshee won't penetrate that armor."

"The TK-77 might have a chance at the rear where the pilot's hatch is. You and Levy draw his fire."

"Do our best," Raptor promised curtly.

With fire pouring at their position, shattering the heavy glass doors of the building and smashing pits in the once-glossy marble walls, Leon readied himself, shifting his aim away from the incoming sojieri and toward the big battle suit to his left. The pilot was smart after the felling of his comrade, keeping his bulk behind the relative protection of one of the broad columns, exposing only the suit's arms in order to fire.

Like a startled animal, the dragoon bucked as Raptor and Levy's squad opened fire, slowly turning to face them. Its digitigrade legs ended in three-toed, articulated pads that crunched the stone of the entranceway beneath them, tiles cracking as though they were eggshells.

As the other mercenaries backed away, firing futilely at the lumbering mechanized sojier, Leon slid around its other side, coming in line with the back of the suit. Mendoza was screaming in his ear, declaring the mercenaries enemies. Leon was dimly aware of the other Jackals, firing in all directions as the Mekon DaVoi guards turned on them, but he had eyes only for the hatch: near the top of the rounded torso, it was less than half a meter across, just enough for a sojier to slip in and take the controls. Leon's angle meant that it was unlikely he would hit the pilot directly, but if he could blow open the hatch, the detonations of the destabilizing proton clusters from his TK-77 might be enough to kill or disable the operator and any electronics inside. Seeing the hatch come into view, he shouldered his rifle and began firing. Energy bursts whipped out, slamming against the armor, but like Raptor's and Levy's fire, the blasts dissipated harmlessly against the metal. This unit had apparently been hardened.

"It's not working!" Leon shouted.

"Do something, Colonel!" Levy pleaded.

Leon dropped the rifle, and it swung on its strap, banging into his side. He drew one of his Sprawler pistols and dialed up the output.

Ordinarily the weapon functioned as a powerful kinetic sidearm with a large charge capacity. However, when the power was amplified, its bursts were enough to punch through the heaviest armor plate at short range; Leon just hoped it would work in time. He took aim and fired at about where he thought the operator would be. The Sprawler let out a deafening crack, and he felt the recoil snap up his arm.

The first shot knocked a gaping hole in the rear of the armor, the second blew open the hatch. Leon fired again and again, battering the suit but failing to penetrate to the pilot.

"Colonel!" Levy shouted, desperate, as the railgun came in line with him. The dragoon fired, and the roar of the cannon was deafening. Levy's torso exploded with the force of the impact, and his EMMA crumpled lifelessly to the stone, blood and bone sprayed across the shredded metal. Two more sojieri went down as the mass driver slug fragmented, and a column ten meters behind them shattered.

"*Fuck!* Sommers, grenade that bastard!"

Mikaela Sommers had stabbed a nearby Mekon DaVoi guard; leaving her knife in his chest, she turned away and rose. She pulled a grenade from the webbing on her vest, leapt up onto the ankle of the suit, and lobbed it into the cabin before leaping away. "Cover up!" she shouted, ducking behind a pillar.

Leon tackled Traxus, and the two of them lay prone as the back of the dragoon armor blew off, cracking open like a clam. With fire streaming from the breach, the sparking battlesuit fell forward across its vanquished companion.

"Levy?" he asked, standing up.

Across the flaming wreckage, indistinct through the shimmering heat, Raptor simply shook his head. Leon took a deep, mournful breath. *More of our people down.* They had lost both noncommissioned officers and nearly a third of the platoon. Leon looked down at Traxus, whose hair was full of dust, much of it soot-black. At least, she was unharmed.

They waited for the Shar'dan troops to notice that they had stopped firing, and eventually the incoming fire tapered off, as well. There was still a constant rattle of gunfire as the sojieri continued to trade fire with the guards in the windows above, but for the moment the mercenaries seemed safe. Holding his proton rifle above his head in surrender, Leon came into view. The rest of his people did the same. The last time Leon had come forward in surrender, he had nearly been killed by scavengers on Aethaleia. He desperately hoped that this time would be different.

The Shar'dan troops had closed very quickly, their blue-and-red armor scarred and pitted from bullet impacts. Their guns were trained on the Jackals, unwavering, and when they began to fire, Leon was less than surprised. Once again he tackled Traxus behind one of the stone columns as large-caliber shells chipped away at it. Out of the corner of his eye he saw Sommers get cut down as she reached for her machine gun. Dyran and Raptor managed to get away, although the Prross's jacket had a few new bullet holes in it. Several of Leon's troops were mowed down even as they begged for mercy. Now he only had half the platoon left. He felt sick to his stomach.

"Cease fire! We surrender!" Traxus screamed at the top of her lungs. After a few moments, the firing stopped, and Leon could hear loud voices arguing on the steps.

Crawling forward on his hands and knees, Leon risked another glance out and stopped in his tracks.

More troops had emerged from the smoke, these wearing the black-and-green of the Knights of the Coalition. Leon had once been on the verge of initiation into their order, but that had been a long time ago, before Daltar, before his career was vaporized along with everything else in the city of Misande Dun Rai. Like their Shar'dan colleagues, the knights were armed with heavy Cougar pulse rifles and Domino machineguns, but they also bore their trademark broadshields, battered from absorbing so much fire. Powered broadswords hung at their hips, looking incongruous but no less lethal. Their presence was frighteningly practical: for millennia, warfare had evolved—if it could be called evolution—to the point where an entire conflict could be won or lost in a matter of minutes by the careful application of orbital bombardments or nuclear strikes. To counter such wholesale slaughter, tactics had regressed, with opposing forces closing the distance to prevent such devastating and unstoppable attacks.

The leader of the Knights contingent was arguing vehemently with the head of the Shar'dan Guard. He was a captain, judging from the three pips, like stout spikes, upon his broad shoulder pauldrons.

"We're not here to execute prisoners," the knight said evenly, his voice menacing as it rattled out of the helmet's speakers. With their comms jammed, they were forced to resort to audible communication. "These men came out with their hands raised. Even if they are collaborating with ... what do you call them? Grendel?"

"They killed your troops, too, Captain Tannhauser," the Shar'dan Guard captain replied angrily. "They're just hired guns. What information could they possibly provide that the last group of traitors we came across didn't? Put bullets in their skulls and dump them into the nearest black hole on your way home."

Leon was crawling on his hands and knees toward Mikaela, who was laid out on the ground, breathing heavily, her limbs splayed awkwardly. Her vest was punctured in three places in a neat line rising from below her right breast to her left shoulder. Eyes dulled with pain, she reached for Leon, listlessly taking his hand.

"I can't believe I listened to you," she wheezed.

"Quiet. You're going to be okay." He didn't know if he was lying or not. Blood was pooling beneath her, and a lifetime's worth of murdered friends flashed before Leon's eyes. He turned to the Knights and Republican Guards, unsure if speaking out would get him shot. "We need some help over here!"

The two leaders turned the emotionless fascia of their helmets toward him, and he could feel the disdain. "What makes you think you're eligible?" asked the Shar'dan captain, deadpan. "Ask your Celestials for help."

With his friends peeking out from behind cover, Leon stood, unclasped his gunbelt, and dropped it to the ground. He turned around, full circle, so they could see he was now unarmed, before reaching slowly for the catches of his bulletproof vest and releasing them. As the vest slipped off, the high flak collar opened to reveal his neck.

Understanding, one of the knights approached, rifle slung, and checked Leon's barcode. It had nearly gotten him killed on several occasions, but on others it had saved his life or at least bought him time. Up close, the EMMA-clad sojier loomed over him, and a great, gauntleted hand pulled roughly at Leon's collar. He heard the fabric rip and nearly choked as the front of his collar dug into his throat, but that hardly concerned him at the moment.

There was a pause as the knight read the string of characters etched into Leon's flesh beneath the neural port that had once linked him to an EMMA of his own. "He's an XRK," said the sojier finally, her voice weary.

"Goddammit," sighed the knight captain, exasperated. "Let him go." With the guns of the front rank still pointed at them and the troops in the rear still trading shots with the snipers in the windows, Leon and his team warily descended the steps. "Who the fuck are you? The Mourning Star?"

Leon nodded wordlessly. The captain turned, metal hands on metal hips, unease evident in his posture as he turned first one direction, then another. "What the hell are you doing here?"

"We're contracted," Leon said, trying to sound in control. "You could have at least given us the option to surrender, declared your identities."

"Are you fucking *kidding*?" scoffed the Shar'dan commander. "We've been demanding that Mekon DaVoi stand down for *three days*." Leon's gaze snapped back and upwards to where Mendoza and his cronies had barricaded themselves. No one had mentioned an impending attack or the option to surrender. Leon wanted nothing more than to wrap his hands around Mendoza's throat.

The Shar'dan commander laid a hand on the knight captain's pauldron. "Tannhauser, I want these mercs in *shackles*."

"Just a moment, Rodinne."

"When we agreed to work with your knights, it was with the express agreement that *we* retained operational command."

"Don't forget, they took out that dragoon. The least we can do is let them explain themselves."

"Meanwhile, their clients are digging in."

"They're not, they're leaving," Leon said, hands still raised. "Whatever you came here for will be gone with them."

"We've already commed the local governor to shut down the airshield," Captain Tannhauser said.

"It won't do any good. They've got an override in the armory below."

"Show us," said the knight commander sharply.

"Absolutely not!" the Shar'dan leader declared. "They'll lead us right into an ambush."

In the end, the two leaders came to an agreement, and Leon guided a small detachment of their troops down into the bowels of the Mekon DaVoi headquarters building. The ramp leading down into the armory was silent but for the heavy footfalls of the troops, black stone walls pressing in at them.

"I'd say it's a good bet that they've got what we're here for," muttered one of the troops.

"What is that, exactly?" asked Leon. The sojier behind him shoved him roughly, and he closed his mouth.

"How much farther?" asked the lieutenant in charge of the squad.

"I didn't come this way before, but it can't be too far."

When they reached the armory they found that it was a vast underground warehouse lined with shelves and racks of equipment. "Armory" was a misnomer, for although it had housed the dragoon units and contained a sizeable arsenal, it mostly served as a storage space for spare equipment, including the trucks that had originally been outside. Those trucks had now been moved to form a ragged barricade across the open space, and more than a dozen Mekon DaVoi militia crouched behind them.

The government troops were not stupid, however, and they quickly found cover from which to continue their assault. With the clock ticking, speed was essential, and the Coalition sojieri pushed forward relentlessly, catching the brunt of the incoming fire on their shields. They were a marvel to behold, fearless and unyielding. Leon felt, not for the first time, a pang of regret so strong it nearly overwhelmed him. Right now, though, he had to keep his head clear. Staying in the rear with two guards who laid down supporting fire with heavy machine guns that were deafening in the enclosed space, Leon could only watch. A spent shell casing hit him in the neck and nestled in his collar, burning him until he could shake it loose.

One of the trucks' fuel cells exploded, a great fireball with no place to go but outwards, and it swept over attackers and defenders alike, engulfing them in flames. The Knights emerged from it unscathed, but ten Mekon DaVoi guards lay scorched in its wake, and more were critically injured, calling out for mercy in the fiery afterglow. A stab of remorse coursed through Leon; while he had not known these people well, he had been fighting with them until just a few minutes ago. *Does that make me a turncoat? No, a survivor.*

The rest of the guards fell before the assault in moments, some already stunned by the blast, others dropping their weapons and throwing themselves on the mercy of the Knights. They were only local boys doing their jobs. Those who chose to stand and fight were killed quickly.

And then the backup controls for the airshield stood before them, protected behind a wall of bulletproof glass, the door sealed against unauthorized access. Knight sappers carefully blew the doors off with small charges and then set about shutting off the energy shield that kept the sky above the city free of ion storms. With the shield down, the Mekon DaVoi ships would be unable to lift off.

This done, they returned to the vast, open lobby of the headquarters. It was dominated by a great atrium reaching to the skylights in the roof. It was astonishing how quickly the perpetual ion storms had closed the gap: where bright sunlight had poured in only minutes before, it was now angry and dark, lit only by intermittent flashes of red lightning.

A steady procession of Knights and Shar'dan troops pushed up the sweeping staircases, and the sounds of battle drifted down from the upper levels. Resistance now was light and fading fast. Periodically, one of the interior windows looking out on the atrium would shatter in a spray of tracer fire, and the glass would rain down, glittering and cutting.

The troops were efficient, having clearly prepared this raid well. They had rapidly taken control of the lobby and the lower office levels, setting up a base of operations with a comm amplifier that allowed them to overpower the interference. The wounded had been brought inside and were laid out to one side beneath the overhang at the western edge of the atrium, near an abstract steel-and-trykon statue. Sommers and the wounded Jackals were among them, along with Levy's shredded corpse, still encased in armor.

Leon was put back with his friends, hands tied behind his back, cheek against the cold stone floor. He was angry, angry that they had been misled, angry that they had been used, angry that they had been treated with such contempt by the sojieri who had captured them. *What were they doing here?* he wondered, far from idly. *What were they doing to attract SRG* and *Coalition attention?*

"Colonel, does this mean we don't get paid in full?" asked Dyran quietly from beside Traxus. He, too, was chained, laid out on the open floor.

"Maybe now is not the best time to ask," Leon replied through gritted teeth.

Another group of defeated Mekon DaVoi guards, battered and bruised, were brought unceremoniously downstairs by the new management. They looked as though they had been fighting for a month, not half an hour, and once again Leon was reminded that they were not sojieri, not even shields, but a poor man's militia raised from the low-income Humans and Borin on the planet. It was remarkable they had lasted as long as they had. *They had help—until we betrayed them.*

"Leon, is Mikaela going to be okay?" Traxus asked. There was a peculiar note in her voice sounding afraid and uncertain.

"I don't know, Trax. I think—"

A roar of machine gun fire cut the air and bullets rang out against the floor, sparking off the statue. Instinctively, Leon rolled onto Traxus, praying that he didn't get hit. If he did, the shell would likely penetrate him and hit her anyway.

Beside them there was a bright splash of red, and Dyran began to scream long and loud, howling in pain. Another shell hit so close that Leon felt the air snap as it passed. Though they had been caught off guard, the troops in the lobby quickly recovered and concentrated their fire. Once again the lobby was filled with choking smoke and the roar of gunfire, spent shell casings tumbling through the air. The machine gun fell silent, and so did the guns of the Knights and SRG troops. Once again the only sounds were the gun battles farther up and the moans of the wounded and dying.

Leon rolled off Traxus and looked over at Dyran. He was alive, moving slowly, crying out weakly. His left arm had been shot right through, the fur around the wound slick with dark blood. Leon hadn't realized how bad the injury was until two knights knelt to drag him to their medics and the ragged strips of flesh and tendon let go, the limb tearing free. Still handcuffed to his other wrist, it trailed pitifully behind. Dyran let out one last scream and passed out.

The ranking officers of the Mekon DaVoi operation did not intend to be taken alive. With their means of escape cut off, they detonated the top levels of the tower, and Leon watched them vanish in an expanding sheet of fire. His clients had escaped, after all.

7: Extradition

"I would consider it a personal favor, Marshall." Hakar's voice was controlled, but beneath the surface he was seething, mortified beyond words.

"What you're asking ... it's impossible." High Marshall Dominguez looked sorry, but her stern, lined face betrayed little else. Hakar didn't know her well enough to know how tractable she was. "Perhaps you don't understand: they were complicit in *high treason* against the Shar'dan Confederacy. They are directly responsible for the deaths of a dozen sojieri. If that doesn't move you, recall that two of those casualties were your own knights. I can't just let them go."

"I'm not asking you to let them go, Marshall. I'm asking you to release them into my custody."

"It has not escaped my attention that your sister was among the captured mercenaries as was the Mourning Star. No one in the SRG is suggesting that you or your people had anything to do with this, but it is making a lot of us, including me, very uncomfortable. I'm afraid that releasing any of them, particularly those with ties to the Coalition leadership, would set a dangerous precedent, especially now. Our Justice Department would insist on extradition. We will be conducting a rigorous investigation into the Jackal Pack Mercenary Legion's sanctions and their relationship with your Star Chamber as it is. You're a practical man, I am sure you understand."

"This isn't about family ties or nepotism, Marshall. It's about justice. Those people were duped, and the moment they knew better, they made the right decision."

"To join the winning side? That just makes them opportunists, and traitors twice over."

"They were instrumental in stopping Mekon DaVoi from getting that technology off-world."

"There could have been other shipments before the raid," Dominguez said, unmoved.

Hakar decided it was time to risk it. "You said I'm a practical man, and you're right. I hope you're practical, too. What do I need to do to make this happen?"

Dominguez's tone shifted abruptly. "We want full access to your defense information network, all data culled from your hacks of the Valinata Whispernet, and your consent to place patrol fleets of our own within the Coalition-Shar'dan DMZ." That answer had come awfully fast; she had clearly prepared her shopping list for this little negotiation.

"I can't authorize that."

"You can make it happen, Admiral Hakar. We are allies, after all. If war is coming, we need to meet it as a unified front." Marshall Dominguez looked at him expectantly, her eyes never wavering.

"Any collaboration would have to be a two-way street. We would expect reciprocation. And access to your feeds."

Dominguez nodded. "It sounds to me like we have an agreement. I'll patch you through to your knight commander. I will say, they are every bit the sojieri we were led to expect. You should be proud."

"I am." *But only of them.*

After Captain Tannhauser had made his report, Hakar congratulated him. Tannhauser, who had a record of excellence that was clinical in its spotlessness, looked uneasy despite the praise. "I'd like to speak to Victor," Hakar said.

"And the woman claiming to be your sister, sir?"

"Keep her chained with the others." Traxus had gone far over the line this time, aided and abetted by a man whose loyalty Hakar had thought was unimpeachable.

"I don't understand, Admiral. Is she not your sister?"

"She is. That nets her zero special treatment. Put Victor on, please."

Leon appeared appropriately humiliated and defeated. Once Hakar had thought of him as a son, but he was infuriated to think that this colonel had put his little sister, the future head of his clan, in danger. Not just in danger but in the sights of Coalition Knights. Nevertheless, he kept his tone light.

"What have you gotten yourself into this time?" Hakar asked. "If I didn't know better, I'd think you wanted my attention."

When the reply came back, bounced between relays across the galaxy, Leon's voice was almost squeaky with shame, his normally soft and cool demeanor crumbling. "Hakar, you have to believe me. We had *nothing* to do with what happened down there."

Hakar held up a hand. "I know, son. They wiped most of their comm logs, but we intercepted enough to know that you did the right thing as soon as you knew the truth. Your team were late arrivals, what they did happened while you were still on Aethaleia. You couldn't have had anything to do with it. But dammit, Leon, it looks *bad*. You were never there, do you understand?"

"I ... yes. What exactly did they do?"

"I can't disclose that, not to you. And listen, Leon. After this, I am going to have to seriously reevaluate Traxus's position within the Pack."

"Hakar, you can't just dictate what she does."

"I'm going to pretend you never said that." When the message reached Leon, his face fell, and Hakar felt a sliver of regret creep into his resolve. It vanished quickly; Hakar had buried two brothers, and he did not intend to bury his little sister. "Listen, get back to Eve and stay there for a little while. We're going to wipe the slate clean of Jackal Pack's involvement, and you made the right call helping our people. Without you, those bastards might have gotten away."

"Did this have something to do with Raven Blue?" Leon asked, his eyes sparkling.

"I wouldn't think too much about that if I were you."

"Well, is there any word on the data we recovered from Aethaleia?"

"Negative. I strongly suggest that you abandon this line of questioning if you know what's good for you. Get some rest, Leon, and give my love to Traxus." Hakar turned off the comm and turned to Empress Kra'al, who sat just out of range of the transmitter's camera, stroking her chin with one slender, clawed finger.

"Well, that was certainly embarrassing for you," she said softly—deceptively softly, Hakar suspected; she was angry.

"Colonel Victor is a good man. And his involvement may actually have benefited us, obliquely."

"Maybe, but what was Mekon DaVoi doing out there on Tikal, collaborating with the enemy?" Kra'al shivered from the cool air or the frightening realization that things were getting worse, Hakar wasn't sure. "Could they have had anything to do with Cratos's death? I don't see the connection to the massacre on Ezai."

"It's possible, but I doubt it. These seem like independently operating cells, but I still don't understand how a galactic corporation fits into this. I'm more concerned about their development of comm implants that could tap into our frequencies. They were much farther along than we had expected."

"And what do our friends in the Service have to say about that?"

"They're strangely silent on the whole matter, but their personnel have moved into Mekon DaVoi's Tikal facility for the time being. They'll strip it bare, I'm sure. In the meantime, the Knights are continuing to cooperate with the SRG, preparing more raids against Mekon DaVoi sites. You were right to preapprove the concessions to Marshall Dominguez. How did you know what she was going to ask?"

"It's what you would have asked for. But never mind. You could have fought her a *little* harder on the issue."

"I thought it prudent to be cooperative in this case." Hakar realized he couldn't avoid the issue any longer. He had to know. "Your Highness, how does this affect our planned contract with the Jackals?"

"Are you sure they can be trusted? I mean, this champion of yours was just working with a principal *collaborator*. The last thing I want is to let these people in the door and have them stick a knife in my back when I turn to brew some Kaf."

"They can be trusted. I'd stake my own life on that."

"Well, if you intend to be out there with them, it may come to that. I'm inclined to quash the deal."

Hakar kept the disapproval from his voice. "That's your prerogative, Highness."

"It is, and I'm glad you recognize that. But...." She drew her long, black tongue along her teeth, her golden eyes narrowed in concentration. "But ... Admiral Telec has also vouched for them. After Aethaleia, he seems quite confident in their abilities and their loyalties, if they possess such a quality as loyalty." Kra'al rose from the chair beside Hakar's desk and went to his window. The view was poor when compared to her own. "You should see about transferring to Mindor's office now that it's vacant," she said coldly. "Where do we stand on the investigation?"

"It's slow going, Your Highness. If I had physical access...." Hakar waggled his fingers in the Tagean equivalent of a shrug. "It appears that the site on Ezai may reveal interesting facts. Cratos appears to have been killed well away from the bombsite, gunned down, in fact."

"Really?" Kra'al turned from the window and regarded Hakar. "By whom?"

"The ballistics report hasn't come back," he blurted in exasperation. "We're being forced to review the data not only with our own forensics teams in the CRDF but also forward the information to the Irachan labs. The DLF leadership insists on being kept in the loop, to ensure that we're not trying to pin something on them."

"I feel terrible. These are my people, Hakar," Kra'al mumbled, "but I want them punished. Give me your best guess."

"By the time reinforcements arrived, the DLF and the Irachans had killed about five hundred people between them, and the DLF had wiped out our troops on the ground. We assumed that they also killed Cratos and his retinue, but I have it on good authority that he was killed by rounds fired from a CRDF-issue Cougar assault rifle, possibly by one of his own escort." The news had floored Hakar when he first heard it. Now, however, a disgusting pattern was emerging. "It may have been the commander of the detail, who appears to have died when his suit decompressed after getting hit, also by bullets from a Cougar. The bombing was a diversion, to deflect attention from the real assassin."

Kra'al mulled it over. "But surely the comm logs would reveal evidence of a mutiny."

"That's the thing: the logs were set to wipe automatically by an embedded program. Everything was routed through the command shuttle's relay and recorded there, but there's a half-hour gap between the time they touched down and the time everything went to hell. Anything could have been said."

"Does the embedded program tell us anything?"

"We've got cryptographers working on it, but all I can tell you is that it probably isn't CRDF in origin. Probably."

The empress looked lost, and her voice was subdued. "If this is true, and I'm not yet convinced it is, it would have the added benefit of directing our attention to the Dias Traverse. Find out how this happened, Hakar. What's the connection to Larador and Geran?" If they could find a common thread behind whoever killed Mindor and his executive officers, they could attribute the killings to a concrete faction and move beyond some vast, shadowy conspiracy of traitors. Unfortunately, the only identity they had for certain was that of Vice-Grand Admiral Geran's killer, who had splattered any information across a bulkhead along with her brain and skull. As any student could attest, one point of data was not enough.

"I need time," Hakar confessed. "There may be a connection, or they may be, as you said, opportunists. I don't believe that, though. I believe this may be part of a systematic attempt to remove the military and political leadership of the Coalition, which began with the murder of the Prime Minister." It was a chilling thought.

§

Rachel's first impression of Eve's capital had been one of a ramshackle border town, an impression that had softened only a bit. Despite boasting a population of several million, Tesa was a poor imitation of the clean, high-functioning metropolises she was used to. She had always been advised to stick to certain districts, and she had not had cause or desire to venture beyond them.

The Moraj district along Tesa's southern edge was dominated by boarded-up storefronts and rundown factories operating at a fraction of their former output. The streets were largely deserted and dark; the few streetlamps that still worked illuminated densely packed graffiti on just about every surface. A few groups of sullen-looking youths were perched on the steps of old tenement buildings, guarding their territory.

Surroundings aside, Rachel felt like a VIP, seated in the back seat of the sleek black sedan that wafted quietly through the streets. Beside her sat Lieutenant Tendaji, one of Leon's officers. Rachel barely knew her, but she was polite and professional. Her curly black hair was pulled back in a tight topknot that bloomed out into a wild bush. In the front seats were two of her sojieri. All were wearing civilian clothing, with light body armor beneath, and submachine guns beneath their jackets.

Rachel could tell they would have preferred to go out more heavily armed, but they did not want to draw attention to themselves.

"It's up ahead," Tendaji said, tapping the driver's shoulder as she consulted her mempad.

Rachel had gotten reluctant directions from an officious administrator in the governor's cabinet as well as a warning that the area was not policed nor was the old array fit for visitors. He hadn't come out and explicitly stated that gangs had overrun the array, but from Tendaji's preparations it was a distinct possibility.

With the presentation to the governor looming near, Rachel wasn't about to let this opportunity slip by. There was plenty of data in the old Tesa records, but there was quite a bit that had clearly been lost, particularly with regards to the power grid. It could come in handy.

As the car drew to a stop before the fence that marked off the site, Rachel found herself breathing rapidly, her heartrate picking up. Lieutenant Tendaji and her team were surely used to this sort of thing, but she wasn't, and she didn't want to be. She fiddled with the straps of the bulletproof vest Heidi had insisted she wear.

"Would you prefer to wait in the car with Weaver?" the lieutenant asked softly, keeping any trace of judgment out of her voice.

"No," Rachel said firmly. "I'm not going to learn anything sitting here. I'm ready." She opened her door and stepped into the cool night air.

One of the sojieri stayed with the vehicle, but Lieutenant Tendaji sent the other to scout ahead while she and Rachel followed.

"Thank you again for volunteering to come," Rachel said, looking up at Anna Tendaji.

"Of course," the Jackal replied simply. She kept her hand on the grip of her weapon, scanning the area as they moved along the fence.

"Chain's cut," said the other sojieri when they caught up with him. He toed at a length of thick chain that lay on the ground before the gate. "Recently, I think."

Rachel squinted up at the ansible tower itself, a long, beckoning finger reaching into the darkening sky. It was leaning ever so slightly, a skeletal ruin of its former essential function. It had probably been stripped of just about every useful scrap of material. There appeared to be lights on inside, though. Was a gang using it as a base of operations after all or perhaps just squatters taking shelter?

"Stay behind me," Tendaji said firmly to Rachel as she pushed open the gate.

In the next instant Rachel was blinded as floodlights flared to life in front of them, and a voice crackled over a speaker, "Stop where you are. This area is restricted. Return to your vehicle."

Whoever he was, he didn't speak like a thug. There was power and authority in that voice. Half a dozen figures emerged from the light's corona. They wore civilian attire like the Jackals, and like the Jackals they did not walk like civilians. Unlike the Jackals, they weren't carrying submachine guns but full assault rifles.

These were sojieri but whose?

Every muscle in Rachel's body tensed. She had gotten used to seeing guns after spending so much time among the Jackals, but a frightening electricity seemed to spark in the air as Tendaji and her colleague faced down the team barring their way.

For the briefest moment, Rachel was afraid the lieutenant would draw and fire. As good as they were, she doubted her bodyguards could take out so many heavily armed sojieri. Luckily, Tendaji's assessment of the situation matched her own, and she waved Rachel back toward the gate as she began backing slowly away herself.

"Run along now, before something bad happens," said the leader of the squad mockingly, as his comrades watched them impassively.

"I'm sorry, Miss Case," Tendaji said as they got back in the car. Rachel didn't respond. She was trying to stop her hands from shaking. She would have to find another way.

§

The Tikal team boarded a new ship with a new crew for the solemn ride back to Eve. Every man and woman aboard was keenly aware of what rode in the cargo hold: a dozen coffins, one unused EMMA, and the bloody remains of another, fit only to be cannibalized for scrap.

Traxus sat beside Dyran, keeping him comfortable. His eyes were glassy. He would live and would even be fitted for a scaffold—a genetic blank that would eventually mimic the arm he had lost—but his injuries seemed to go far deeper than the physical. He muttered, often incoherently, sometimes asking after Levy.

Mikaela Sommers lay beside him, unconscious, her chest rising and falling slowly. She was lucky she wasn't dead; her vest had slowed the bullets down, one stopping just short of her heart.

Traxus was glad to have the distraction of tending to the injured. It saved her from having to contemplate her own failure. Hakar, so furious he wouldn't speak to her; Leon, who had selflessly thrown himself on top of her twice to protect her while she had not done anything but passively lie there; the sojieri, for whom she had been responsible, a quarter of them dead and more wounded. Only Leon's quick thinking had saved them, yet Hakar had talked to him as though the colonel had tried to kill Traxus himself. Worst of all, she knew Leon still idolized her brother even after the reprimand, and he always would.

What would General Rockmore have to say? She dreaded touching down on Eve and the debriefing that would follow and wondered if she would ever command or even go on a mission again. Then again, how could their normally thorough client evaluation have missed the fact that Mekon DaVoi was under investigation by the Shar'dan Department of Security *and* the Coalition Ministry of Defense? They were lucky they weren't all dead or hidden away in some deep, dark Confed prison.

"My arm feels funny," Dyran moaned weakly, and Traxus mopped at his face, trying to keep him cool. The fur that covered his face was matted with sweat.

"Shh, Dyran. You're fine." She glanced at Leon and Raptor, sitting at the forward end of the troop compartment and looking like the stoic statues of vengeful demigods. Since boarding the dropship, the colonel had said nothing but had simply sat staring at the dog tags in his hand: LEVY, MOISHE, and SANTOR, CONNOR. They had thirteen more markers to erect in the grove north of the Jackal Pack base, thirteen more funerals, thirteen more families to console. Several of the other wounded were moaning from the back of the passenger cabin. Their comrades did their best to quiet them.

He's going to blame himself for a long time, Traxus thought, looking at Leon, his face drawn and covered in a three-day growth of beard. His eyes were hard chips of flint, his mouth a bloodless line. Raptor, by comparison, seemed unmoved by the whole episode and was reading a book of poetry.

And how do I feel? she asked herself, startled not to find an immediate answer. She did not know the dead well, but she had been on a first name basis with them and had developed a rapport with them over the past weeks. Each of those names had stung as she pulled the bloody dogtags from their still bodies to hand to Leon. It wasn't personal grief she felt but rather a gap in the bench across from her that seemed representative of something greater. As Dyran would continue to feel the ghost of his missing arm until the scaffold was reattached, so would she feel the missing sojieri until she was back on the base, surrounded by the living. This dropship was too much like a tomb, a mausoleum to failure.

Mekon DaVoi would fall: the company's assets would be parceled off, the employees rigorously interrogated by both the Shar'dan and the Coalition, the books and data pored over relentlessly by clinical, trained eyes. The surviving managers would be hunted across the galaxy and arrested.

"My arm feels funny," Dyran said again. "I think it fell asleep. Could I ... have some water?" Traxus quickly obliged him. He drank and fell into an uneasy, fitful sleep.

§

The mood on the base was somber, and Leon's return was once again unheralded. This time Rachel watched as the coffins were unloaded in pairs before Leon and his remaining friends trudged down the ramp. Medics carefully carried Dyran, Mikaela Sommers, and the other wounded to the clinic. It had been a routine mission on paper, yet it had gone so wrong, and they all felt it. "Rolling the bones," the

Jackals called it: sometimes the dice came up a hard eight, and sometimes they rolled into the gutter.

This time General Rockmore did not come to the landing pad, and the remaining officers went directly to his office. Leon barely had time to kiss Rachel before running off. Word had spread that their client had been involved in far shadier dealings than originally expected, and the Coalition and Shar'dan had actually stepped in. The fact that Leon and his team had not only surrendered to government forces (which was a matter of policy and necessary for the mercenaries to retain their sanctions) but had actively assisted those SRG and Knights *against* the client could pose a major problem for the Pack. It set a dangerous precedent that left many of their backers feeling exposed, and they might begin to question Jackal Pack's reliability. That being said, Jackal Pack was incorporated in the Shar'dan for regulatory reasons, and the SRG could have frozen or seized their assets outright if they felt the Pack was culpable. It hadn't been much of a choice.

Rachel tried not to think about that, focusing only on the fact that Leon was home. When she had heard he was returning early, she had raided the base PX for supplies and cracked open a cookbook that had until then been purely decorative. Once Leon had cleaned up and checked on Mikaela Sommers and Dyran in the clinic, he staggered through the apartment door and drew in a deep breath of home cooking.

It might have been better to try something less ambitious, but Rachel figured Leon needed something to eat and what better than one of his favorite dishes? The humble dumpling was the closest thing to a universal dish across cultures and species, and Leon had a particular fondness for Fego Sheff'an-style spicy dumplings. They came out reasonably well, and Leon fell on them voraciously.

Their attempts at normal conversation stalled until Rachel finally ventured, "What happened on Tikal can't...."

"Nothing happened on Tikal." Leon laughed sourly. "I can't ever remember the general telling us to pretend something never happened, but that's what we're going to do."

"I'm sorry about the people you lost." The words sounded hollow to Rachel. You didn't *lose* people in combat. You misused them, and they died because of it.

Leon nodded. He was taking this much better than he had taken Buzz's death, though she knew he must feel the echoes of that tragedy and all those before it. "We were lucky. Sommers and Dyran will be out of action for a while, though."

"What about you?"

"I'm not sure."

Rachel pried open a dumpling and poured in the tangy sauce, spreading it around with her chopsticks. "Can I ask you something?" she said with her mouth full.

"Always," Leon said, surprised by her hesitation. "Is this part of your...." He had almost said "game," she knew. Upon her return to Eve, she had asked him to try a trust exercise with her in which they asked one another questions and had to give honest answers. It had revealed much, but much more was still hidden.

"After Natille's wedding, can we go somewhere?"

"A vacation? Where did you have in mind?" Leon asked, his interest piqued.

"I honestly don't care. We can stay on Terra after the wedding. I'd like to see where you grew up. I just ... don't want to come back here. Not right away."

Leon dabbed his mouth with his napkin and sat back, considering. "I don't see why not. That could be fun. We could at least stay an extra week or two."

Rachel was nearly overcome with joy. She hadn't expected him to agree so readily, but they both needed time away from Jackal Pack. To put things in perspective, at least. She was about to go around the table and kiss him when she saw the trickle of blood on his upper lip. "Sweetie," she said, gesturing at her nose.

Leon quickly held his napkin against his nose to stop the bleeding. The poison of Aethaleia was still with him. "Goddammit," he muttered. "I'm getting old," he said, unable to suppress his disappointment. "I'm falling apart."

"Well, here's to getting old and falling apart." Rachel raised her glass.

§

Life went on, and the Jackals feigned routine, doing their best to pretend the mission had never happened. As always, they gravitated to the Desher Vaux pub in their quiet moments. A few nights later, Raptor finally got Jeric and Leon into the same room where they sat in the pub's darkened interior, their hands wrapped around cold glasses of local beer. Raptor, however, seemed more interested in having an altercation with one of the quartermasters. Leon stared open-mouthed at the big Prross as he returned to their table, carrying a basket of chicken wings, the spoils of victory.

Leon couldn't tell if he wanted to laugh or be angry. "Good god, Raptor, did you have to break Rosie's *arm*?"

Raptor did not look amused as he sat back down. "I didn't mean for that to happen, Leon, but what was I supposed to do? It's not my fault he got drunk and challenged me." He stripped one wing to the bone and reached for another. "I told him it was a little taste of Tikal." At that Leon's good humor iced over.

"Knock that shit off," the colonel said softly but in a tone that brooked no argument.

Raptor sucked the meat off another wing and tossed the bone aside. He gave no indication that he had heard. He glanced at Jeric and snapped his fingers, clicking his claws loudly. "You in there?"

Jeric's attention was fixed on the screen over the bar, where sleek cars tore around and urban track before millions of cheering spectators. It took Leon a moment to realize that it was the Hiraeth Gran Prix, the most prestigious endurance race in the Aradon Dominion. For Jeric it was a bittersweet occasion.

Another Jackal noticed it, as well. "Is your team racing, Flyboy?" the sojieri called good-naturedly.

Leon saw Jeric's fingers tighten around his glass. It was not exactly a secret that Jeric had bought a driver's spot in the race several years ago with a loan from Leon and Raptor. It had been with Prima Madaan, a custom carmaker and one of the few non-aristocrat owned teams trying to break into the circuit. After a record-setting qualifying run, Jeric showed up on race day to be handed a record-setting number of penalties only three hours into the one hundred-hour endurance race. The mortified team manager fired him on the spot.

"Fucking ponces," Jeric muttered, turning away.

"They'll never find anyone as fast as you," Raptor offered by way of consolation.

"So Mikaela's going to be all right?" Jeric asked Leon to change the subject. His bitterness over being left behind during the mission had faded, and he counted himself lucky that he had avoided the disaster on Tikal. "I haven't seen her yet."

"Doc Reonil says she'll be fine. She'll need her left lung swapped out, though. Bullet tore right through it. Dyran's getting himself a new arm, too." Leon took a sip, then a deep swallow, and then a gulp. "They're lucky."

"Poor Levy. He was a good guy. Who was the other one?"

"Santor," Raptor said.

"I didn't know him."

"They were both in the armored quick-strike companies," Leon informed him. "Without Levy, we would have gotten cooked before we ever got to cover."

"Well," Jeric said, leaning back and stretching, "You'll be happy to know that I spotted Asar at the firing range. He seemed a little stiff, and he's off his game a bit, but he's back on his feet."

"Good for him." In fact, Leon was quite relieved. It was nice to have a bit of good news for a change. Asar abu Seif had nearly been killed during the ill-fated mission to the Valinata world of Aethaleia, and he had been recuperating on his homeworld in the company of his wife and newborn daughter. Still, Leon was jealous that Asar had a family to go home to, and part of him resented the sharpshooter for coming back when he could have taken the exit Leon longed for. *If I had that...*. "Listen, guys, I called you here to have a serious talk."

"Yeah, we know you're planning on retiring," Jeric said, rolling his eyes.

Leon wasn't accustomed to struggling for the right words, and he stammered, "Maybe. Not exactly, but ... I always thought I'd be able to go out on a high point, but it's just been one disaster after another." He turned his glass in his hands, looking at his distorted reflection. "Maybe I'm losing my edge."

"Someone's fishing for validation," Raptor murmured, trying to make a joke of it. Leon didn't take it that way, though.

"I really want to make this thing with Rachel work. You both know where she stands. I can't keep up this balancing act. I can't keep going into the field."

"Good for you," Raptor growled good-naturedly. "Leaving the front line doesn't mean leaving entirely, you know."

"Exactly," said Leon, quick to reassure them. "A while back, the general was talking about opening garrisons in other regions to improve our deployment time and coverage. If he does, I might be responsible for one of the pilot outposts. I would want both of you with me."

"I would be honored," Raptor said. Jeric looked thoughtful.

"Thanks. I don't know how likely it actually is, though."

"You sound disappointed at getting edged out," Jeric observed wryly.

Leon shrugged. "I should start acting my rank, at least, and stop micromanaging the officers. And if I'm retiring from the field…." He didn't finish. *There's nothing for me to do but grow old.*

Jeric took a breath. "Look, man, you don't have to tell us stories about how you might take us on to start some new garrison. Rachel and I talked while you were gone, and I think I'm starting to get it."

"Thanks, Jerr. She told me about that." Leon smiled mischievously. "She also told me you got spaghetti sauce in your hair." He couldn't help teasing his friend, just a little.

"She *told* you?" A flush crept up Jeric's neck.

"I wish I could be surprised," Raptor muttered.

Leon held up a hand to end the torment. "Seriously, though, I really appreciate that you sat down with her. I know it couldn't have been easy."

"It wasn't."

"That's why it means a lot. You have to understand, I don't want to pretend none of this ever happened."

"Some of it, maybe," Raptor interjected, raising a clawed finger.

"Some of it," Leon agreed, ignoring the surge of painful memories that threatened to well up. "That doesn't include *you*."

"Listen," Raptor said, his tone shifting abruptly to one of seriousness as he leaned forward in the booth. "I've been meaning to talk about something with you guys, too."

"You start to sound like that, I know I need another drink." Jeric waved to Mara. "Hais, please, on the rocks." The two Humans turned their attention to their brooding companion.

"It's just that after Aethaleia and Tikal it's obvious that there's something big going on, and I mean more than just ... what happened to the Valinata."

"Elaborate," Leon said.

"I know you're obsessed with what we found on Aethaleia, Leon, and you're not the only one. How likely is it that the general was contacted by someone who just *happened* to need Moira Traveler rescued? And Doctor Traveler just *happened* to be a highly placed geneticist researching some mysterious ... thing?"

"This again?" Leon rolled his eyes.

"Come on, that Zoh Hegemony ship that rescued us was on station almost as soon as we were captured. And they just *happened* to be monitoring us. Randomly. You really believe all that?" Raptor was staring daggers at Leon. "I almost guarantee the CRDF was behind it. Maybe not Hakar, but *someone* contacted the general, and judging by the mission profile, they asked for you personally."

"This is ridiculous," Leon sighed.

"Mara! I think I need that Hais now!" Jeric declared, his words slurred.

Raptor turned back to Leon. "I just don't think they're done using you."

Mara the waitress delivered Jeric's drink as well as a bowl of roasted, spiced nuts. Leon ate a handful and glared at Raptor. "That's unlikely. Besides, it's not like I can just ask the general." With that, he drained his glass and stumbled to his feet. Jeric thought he looked uneasy. "We'll talk again in the morning. I have to go...." He trailed off as he headed for the door.

Traxus intercepted him as she walked in, uniform rumpled and dirty. She steered Leon back to the booth and sat down beside him. "Where have you been?" Raptor asked as she sat.

"Training," she said simply. Like many Jackals, she found catharsis in strenuous activity, especially after a rough mission. "So what's the story, guys?"

"Raptor was just regaling us with his conspiracy theories again," Leon said, glancing at his watch.

"Trax, you look like you need a beer," Jeric said, reaching for his wallet. "Mara, a beer for Lieutenant Tachai and another Hais for me, please!"

Mara sauntered over, appraising Jeric coolly. She had long ago caught on to his antics. "Are you sure, Shorty? I just brought you a Hais two minutes ago."

"And I have no idea where it went off to. C'mon, hit me up." She shrugged and walked back to the bar. When Jeric turned back to his friends, he was surprised to see them looking at him with guarded expressions on their faces. He bristled instinctively. "What?"

Quietly, Traxus said, "Maybe you should ease up a little, Jeric. You've been hitting it pretty heavily."

"This *again*?" Jeric scoffed, irate. "I'm not going to take advice about drinking from the three of *you*."

"Jeric, you drink as much as all three of us combined," Raptor insisted calmly.

"Because you're lightweights." He frowned, staring at the empty glasses before him. "You know what? The three of you can fuck off. How is this any of your business?"

"Aside from the fact that we have to rely on you in combat?" mused Leon, trying to keep his voice light.

Jeric wanted to punch him. "Oh, here comes Colonel Victor, pulling rank because he *cares*. When's the last time anyone put me in a position to be relied on?" he blurted, surprising himself.

"We relied on you at Aethaleia, and you let us get captured," Raptor said.

"I *let*...." Jeric's hands clenched into fists. "I am so goddamn tired of you judging me and plotting how to fix me like some broken toy. Do you know how frustrating it is? I've gotten used to not being taken seriously by everyone else around here. But the three of you ... I don't need it."

"Look, Jeric," Traxus tried, "we're all feeling the strain right now."

"Oh, are we? I don't think *we* are. You get to go home and become some posh lady whenever you decide to stop playing sojier. I would trade places with you in a heartbeat, do you understand?" Traxus looked hurt, and her ears flattened. Jeric turned to Leon. "*You* can retire on all those savings you've built up after years of forbidding yourself to have any fun, and go play house with Rachel. And Raptor, you can go scratch little messages to heaven in the dirt."

"Look, we're trying to be your friends here," Leon said, but his temper was peeking through.

"Yeah, well, I came here to forgive *you*, and now I forget why. I don't want your fucking olive branches or peace offerings or whatever. Assholes." Jeric got up and moved to the bar to await his Hais. Infuriatingly, the pub was reasonably empty, and he could still hear them from where he sat, their voices patronizing, full of pity. For him. As though he needed or wanted their pity.

"What do olive branches have to do with anything?" Raptor asked rhetorically.

"We've all got problems," Leon said quietly.

"Well, frankly I'm tired of him dominating the discussion," said Traxus bitterly, glancing his way. "This isn't how I wanted to patch things up. Besides, what does he know about the Tagean matriarchy? Do you think he's ever heard the term 'golden cage?'"

"It's 'gilded,' and probably not," Leon mused. "But you have to understand, Humans hold Tagean culture up almost as an elite caste. You *are* considered the high culture."

"Some high culture. Everything we have is scavenged from the ruins of our ancestors. Do you realize how it feels to rediscover, bit by bit, what they cast away millennia ago? Our sacred relics are their trashed hard drives. And they didn't even tell us *why* before vanishing."

"Do *you* actually know how it feels?" Leon sighed. "Look, Jeric didn't mean to insult any of us—"

Traxus clicked an angry laugh. "Oh, get over yourself, Leon. We don't always need you to act as peacekeeper. You become such a sanctimonious prick when you try to fix everyone's problems." Traxus got up and left, leaving Leon and Raptor facing one another.

"Well? What the hell are you looking at?" Leon finally snapped at his friend.

"I'm just waiting for you to give me some advice, too."

"Fresh out. How about a beer instead?"

"Okay. As we say on Prrastra, the deepest well holds the most water, but it is hardest to fill."

"I'm sure that's relevant somehow."

Mara brought Jeric the Hais and the beer for Traxus. Jeric paid and drank the Hais in one long swallow, then took the beer and walked out into the night. He found Traxus standing on the edge of the pool of light thrown by a street lamp. "Traxus, I'm sorry. Do you want your beer?"

"Why don't you choke on it, Jeric? This was supposed to be a nice night. The four of us haven't been together for a while, and you ruined it. We look out for you, and you throw it in our faces every time." Traxus turned to face him. Her green eyes glinted in the darkness. "One of these days we're going to stop caring enough to try."

Jeric took a swallow of beer to keep from saying something he would regret. When the bottle came away, the words were lying in wait, anyway. "I love how you showing concern involves making me feel like some half-retarded charity case. You're supposed to be my friends." He drained the rest of the beer and threw it in the general direction of a trash can. It missed and crashed against the wall of the PX. Traxus was looking at him, mouth open, when he turned away and walked into the darkness.

§

Rachel watched Leon lurch around the room as he disrobed for bed, noting that he still took time to neatly fold and hang his trousers. Clearly, his evening with the boys had not gone quite as planned. How they managed to keep the stress of their lives from boiling over more often continued to surprise her, but she hated to see him like this. Her inquiries into why he was upset were met with grunts. It was unusual for him to be so curt with her.

He turned to her. "I'm so sorry, I've been so wrapped up in my own bullshit that I haven't even asked about Signal Fire. How is everything going?"

Glancing at the couch and coffee table, both covered in printouts and memscreens, Rachel couldn't help laughing. "Let's just say I see how you got so invested in the research you were working on. I just realized it looks like a bomb went off in here."

"It's not so bad. It's going well, though?"

"So far. We have a meeting with the governor's team tomorrow morning to pitch it." She decided to omit the close call with the sojieri at the old array site. No sense worrying him unnecessarily.

"I had no idea," Leon said, alert enough to sound embarrassed.

In fact, Rachel had told him over the comm while he was still on Tikal, but she didn't care at the moment. Honestly, she was more concerned that Leon had nearly been blown to pieces by the Coalition Royal Defense Forces, the Shar'dan Republican Guard, and his client all in one morning. "It's okay. Heidi has been stellar, though. I never realized how smart she is."

"She hides it well," Leon agreed with a chuckle. At least he was cheering up a little.

Rachel threw a pillow at him. "Don't be an asshole."

Leon flopped into the bed beside her and threw an arm over her shoulders. "Were you still planning to look for work in Tesa after?" he mumbled into her hair. With the capital city less than an hour by gravcar, it would be an easy commute. "I know this isn't Amalthia, but there are opportunities here, too. Not many, but—"

"I don't expect Eve to be Amalthia, Leon. You need to quit worrying that that's what's going to bore me. I'm here for you, the planet is just window dressing. You get that, right?"

"I do. I also know that you like to keep busy," he said, slurring his words. "You wouldn't be satisfied sitting around here or just relaxing by the pool."

"You're right. I will start looking, but I've got plenty to keep me occupied until after your sister's wedding." Leon's kid sister Natille was getting married in just a few months, and going as Leon's date made Rachel feel oddly uncomfortable, and she wasn't sure why. *The engagement ring is in this room right now*, she reminded herself.

She would be as patient as she needed to be; she had seen too many friends press the issue of marriage with their lovers, and it was a bad omen if both parties weren't ready.

"Can you turn off the light?" Rachel asked Leon, but he was already asleep.

§

The morning dawned cold and foggy, the perfect sort of morning to stay in bed, but Rachel was up before dawn. Her meeting with the governor's team occupied her thoughts, waking and sleeping, and the thought that she might be able to contribute something real, something more valuable than a better entertainment network for the super-rich, filled her with pride.

Leon was tangled in the sheets, his loud snores the soundtrack to Rachel's prep work as she read over the finer points of the presentation. She wanted not only to know the facts and figures but also to understand their context. Selling herself on it was the most important part of selling it to the governor.

Her comm buzzed on the coffee table and she grabbed it. She wasn't surprised Heidi couldn't sleep, either. "Good morning. Ready for our big moment?"

"They cancelled the meeting," Heidi said without preamble.

"What the hell?" Rachel blurted, and Leon's snore caught. He rolled over, muttering. "Did they say why?"

"No, I just got some bloody voicemail thanking us for our hard efforts and saying they would consider our proposal."

Rachel clenched her fist. She had sent over an outline of the plan a few days earlier, to spark some interest. She knew the governor and his people were busy, especially these days, but she thought the proposal warranted more than such a summary dismissal.

"I'm sorry, Rachel, I know you poured your heart and soul into this thing. Hopefully, they at least request the rest of the data."

Rachel wasn't sure what came over her in that moment, but she was shaking her head. "No," she said forcefully. "We're going there."

"Yeah?" Heidi asked, sounding energized. "Great. I'll drive."

Ten minutes later their Hyena plowed through the fog, the ungainly military truck rolling loudly along the highway between the Jackal Pack base and the capital city of Tesa. Ahead of them, the city's lights twinkled through the haze, pretending to be a larger metropolis than it was.

Rachel and Heidi barely talked. It was too easy to become negative at a time like this, and if they were going to invade the governor's office first thing in the morning, the last thing they needed was to be antagonistic, as well. Neither did they rehearse their presentation in their heads. The facts and figures could be pored over later. For now they needed passion, enough to convince the officials who governed Eve's population of outcasts that their cause was in the whole world's best interests. Not just the world, but the whole godforsaken Tears of Alkyra.

Both women wore simple attire without adornment, and Heidi's hair and nails were an almost somber shade of cobalt. Their color would probably appeal to the Rukadj governor. Even the Hyena was a civilian model, without armor plating or handrails along the exterior. Most importantly, its paint job was a dark blue, without Jackal Pack's signature red tiger stripes. They were here as experts, not mercenaries.

Traffic was light, and it wasn't long before they found themselves barreling down the Kingsway, the broad avenue that marked the birthplace of Tesa and Eve's colonization. At the far end loomed the governor's palace, a building hardly deserving of the term. Perhaps it had been a majestic edifice in its day, but now it was dwarfed on all sides by corporate offices, unscrupulous banking headquarters, one giant, gaudy, holographic billboard, and the Palace of Luck, the planet's premier casino. Rachel had always been surprised that more people weren't outraged by the fact that the Jurayan clan and the planetary banks were the casino's principal investors, but she supposed gambling was responsible for half of Eve's tourism and a large proportion of the planetary economy.

In contrast to the buildings around it, the governor's palace looked squat, hunkering defensively into itself, with oddly small, squinting windows and stonework that looked somehow wrinkled with age.

As they were pulling into a parking deck down the block, Heidi broke the silence. "I was going to wear those prosthetics today, but they didn't arrive in time," she said bitterly. "I wanted to stand in front of this man and show him the way."

Rachel glanced over in time to see Heidi wipe away a tear, but that was the only emotion on the beautiful young woman's face. "Honey, you don't need to stand for him."

"It was for me."

The governor never saw them coming. A sympathetic aide gave in to their demands and led them to a plush office overlooking the Kingsway. Their interruption of the governor's morning briefing did not go unremarked.

"Normally, persistence is a quality I welcome," Governor Jurayan said, rising. Even annoyed, he observed decorum, and his polite if icy reaction kept the rest of his attendants from jeering. "I can give you ten minutes."

As the room emptied, Rachel took a moment to appraise the man she had only ever seen on the news. The tall, blue-skinned Rukadj wore a finely tailored suit. He extended his right hand in the Human fashion, and Rachel took it, dipping her head to show respect. Governor Jurayan Myton cut a dashing figure, and he traced his lineage back to the first settlers of the Alkyra. The Jurayan family name seemed to be emblazoned on half the buildings on Eve. Though the planet was predominantly settled by Sheff'an and Humans, the Alkyra trade route itself had been a Rukadj stronghold for thousands of years, and they still represented a slim majority of the sector's population.

In appearance Rukadj and Humans looked very similar, enough so that members of the other sentient races often confused them. Rukadj skin color ranged from pale blue to nearly purple, and downy beds of feather-like fronds used for homeostasis and nonverbal communication crowned their heads. Their resemblance to Humans was uncanny, made even stranger because their faces were not naturally expressive. For someone trained to read Rukadj body language, their fronds said volumes that their faces did not. Having grown up on Amalthia, which had a substantial Rukadj population, Rachel was better versed in their languages than most people and could also pick up on many of their nonverbal cues. Judging by the faint flutter of the governor's fronds, he was agitated but hiding it well.

Governor Jurayan, for his part, seemed to have studied Human customs and made an effort to supplement his natural body language with approximations of Human facial expressions. Because they were rehearsed and deliberate, they came off somewhat delayed and a little eerie. Still, Rachel was impressed.

"Miss Eastern, Miss Case, I'm sure you realized I canceled this morning's meeting," he clicked in his native tongue, speaking slowly for their benefit. "Still, it is a pleasure." He spoke Bosoch, a Rukadj tongue that had a murmuring, musical quality to it, punctuated by rapid trills.

"We do appreciate your willingness to meet with us anyway, especially after we barged in like that," Rachel said, hoping politeness would appeal to his sense of etiquette.

"It's not as though your request was frivolous," the governor admitted. "Please, join me." He waved Rachel to the couch against the near wall, and moved a chair out of the way so Heidi could join them before sitting across from them. "Ordinarily I would pour you Huus but we don't have time for the finer things. So, what can I do for you ladies?"

"With your permission, and with respect to your time, I'll get right to the point," Heidi said. "Signal Fire was a sound idea, and we thought it warranted a proper evaluation."

"I agreed to look over your outline, which I did. It was inspired."

"But you're passing?" Rachel blurted out. "I don't understand."

Jurayan's face and fronds were still. "I don't mean to sound rude, but I do not feel that I owe you an explanation."

"With all due respect, governor, there is a lot going on that you may not be aware of."

Jurayan's lips split in an approximation of a grin, but it came off as very insincere. Of course, that may have been the intent. "With all due respect, I am not a fool, and there may be quite a bit *you* are not aware of."

"Perhaps we should call General Rockmore," Heidi said, fishing her comm out of her bag.

The governor held up a hand and sighed. "That won't be necessary. As I said, the idea is inspired."

"Then will you at least look over the proposal in full?" Rachel asked, offering him a datakey.

"That won't be necessary."

"Governor, won't you at least look at it?" she pleaded, lowering her hand only a little bit.

Jurayan clasped his hands and deliberated for a moment. "As I said," he repeated for emphasis, "the idea is inspired. I mentioned as much to the Coalition Regional Base, who promptly hacked your network and took everything they thought looked interesting."

Rachel gasped, and Heidi's jaw clenched. She never would have imagined such a thing happening, but hearing it didn't surprise Rachel as much as she wanted it to. Perhaps she was becoming jaded.

Difficult as it was, she focused on what the governor was saying. "The good news is that the Coalition will be adopting your initiative throughout the Alkyra, with far more funding and resources than the trade council could have hoped to allocate."

It confirmed two things: their proposal was sound, and things were bad enough that the Coalition would clandestinely seize control of this operation and directly interfere in Alkyran affairs with the quiet consent of the regional leaders. Having this information, even if only indirectly hinted at, made Rachel queasy.

She didn't know what to say, but Heidi's mouth was still closed firmly, so she managed, "I suppose we should be grateful our efforts didn't go unnoticed."

"Why the subterfuge?" Heidi asked, regaining her composure.

Jurayan clicked rapidly, which Rachel recognized as laughter. "You think I had a choice? At least, I convinced the CRDF agents that your people would eventually find out, either from me or from your network security team. So they've authorized me to hire you both as consultants, with ten thousand talon retainers. More than that, you perceived a real, viable opportunity that my own communications directors and those of the other Alkyran worlds failed to see or recognize. I've accepted Director Terkir's resignation for his refusal to acknowledge your proposal's merit, and that's going to open a few spots in the office. I hope you'll both keep that in mind. My people will be in touch if the Coalition needs anything further, and your funds have been wired to the Jackal Pack finance office. Now, I believe our ten minutes are up."

After Governor Jurayan had seen them to the lift and the doors had closed, Rachel looked down at Heidi. "What the hell just happened?"

Heidi looked as shocked as Rachel felt. "I think old Jurayan just offered us a job."

§

There had been a time, early in Hakar's career, when standing in one of the palace's main communication centers would have been a thrill. This was the Coalition's nerve center, pulsing with information in and out, the whole of the galaxy laid open to those with the right security clearance.

That time had been a long time ago, and lately the information coming in had only made Hakar sick to his stomach, as though it were spreading some infection. It came in dark, it went out darker.

At the moment, though, he tuned out the thrum of running the Coalition and focused on a live feed of the closed session of Parliament where Empress Kra'al was pleading her case.

Hakar felt like a voyeur, watching as the junior ministers' reactions shifted from shock to anger at having been left in the dark. Finally they accepted the situation, shepherded along by the senior ministers who had done a stunning job of putting aside their party differences, speeding up a process which otherwise might have taken months that they did not have. It might have been the most productive two hours in the history of the Coalition government or perhaps any government ever. It was a tragedy that it was in service of so loathsome a decision.

There were objections, vocal and not without cause. Privately Hakar believed wholeheartedly in what they were doing, terrifying though it was. Still, he was glad of the dissent. When people looked back on this moment, these objectors would be proof that Kra'al had not been an autocrat steamrolling the opposition. And their voices would hopefully continue to moderate the actions to come.

Gradually he became aware that the communication center's eternal buzz had subsided as even the operators and supervisors stopped their work to observe this momentous occasion. Who knew what critical processes galaxy-wide were going off the rails while they took it in.

I'm at the front of a runaway train, Hakar mused darkly. Finally the matter was put to a vote, the declaration of war carrying with a substantial majority, and the motion to grant emergency funding and mobilization to the Star Chamber carried, as well.

Hakar's comm chirped at him, a quiet authorization. He turned away to begin the war.

§

Jon Rockmore sipped at his Kaf and turned the page. Since lifting the contract freeze, he had been deluged with applications from prospective clients and his own officers. It was just as well: the only way to avoid dwelling on the Tikal disaster was to work and keep working. He knew he should penalize Leon, keep him at arm's length. The fact was that Victor's heart was no longer in this, not the way it had been. In Rockmore's estimation, a person who couldn't be counted on to stay generally didn't deserve much in the way of emotional investment. Leon wasn't like other people, though, and certainly he was not like other mercenaries. He had long ago earned Rockmore's trust and more than a little reciprocal devotion. If his time in the Pack was indeed drawing to a close, Rockmore couldn't allow himself to be embittered. It certainly wasn't what he had planned for his protégé, but Leon had made Jackal Pack a great deal of money over the years, and like any thoroughbred, he deserved to be put out to pasture once his race was run.

He would deal with that thorny issue later. It was dark outside, and Rockmore knew he should turn in. The day had been long and hot, and he wasn't a young man anymore. His inquiries to the Coalition Regional Base had been dodged for the fourth time. He supposed he should have been angrier that they had hacked into the Jackal Pack network and stolen the Signal Fire proposal, but as long as some good came of it, he could live with it. He had long since grown out of any naïve hope that privacy mattered, especially when it came to the Coalition government. They could claim they were no longer interfering in Alkyran affairs and that the regional base was in the process of shutdown and withdrawal; for once the petty subterfuge was a boon.

Beyond that, the constant churn of running a corporation yielded a startling amount of bureaucracy. The planetary transportation director had called to insist on more stringent protocols on flight paths and training maneuvers, citing complaints from commercial liners that Rockmore's black-and-red fighters were getting too close. Debt collection agencies were still scratching at the door, sniffing after assets they could seize as collateral. With the border practically on fire, he was amazed that people could still care about interest rates and appeasing spoiled corporate agents.

He poured himself a cup of fresh Kaf. It burned his tongue on the first sip, and he put the drink down while he kept reading until his irritation got the better of him. He shut off the mem screen and pushed aside the paperwork, taking a moment to gaze at the picture of his wife and distracting himself from his fury at Leon, Hakar, and everyone else involved in the mission gone south.

Rockmore's right hand moved unconsciously to his left ring finger, stroking the pale gold wedding band there. It was because of Theresa that he had left active service and started Jackal Pack as a place where professional warfare could be turned into a lucrative business. Because he had been a pirate-hunter himself, he had seen a path to harness and focus otherwise vicious people, to turn them into sojieri of the highest caliber. It had worked far better than anyone had expected.

Theresa had never approved, but she had believed in him, and so she had lent her considerable wealth to the endeavor, helping Rockmore build his military for hire. Over the years, Jackal Pack had gone from a band of a few dozen disillusioned veterans and fortune hunters on a rusty frigate to a veritable army with a rock-solid reputation and an asset-to-liability ratio that would do many major corporations proud. His commanders all had military experience. Some, like his seconds in command, were unparalleled officers whose careers had taken unfortunate nosedives. Rockmore didn't care. The Pack was better off with them, and while they occasionally—frequently even—butted heads, a little competition was healthy. That was especially true in a profession where the reward for complacency was often death. He was sad Theresa had never had the chance to meet Leon or Irún. She would have liked them, despite their flaws.

Many had argued that the Pack was simply a way of shoveling sugar over shit, hiding brutality behind a mask of professionalism and good conduct. Others had said that codes of conduct limited the Pack's effectiveness and its profitability. The legion's leader, however, saw the Pack's narrow spectrum of specialization as its primary differentiation from the competition. He didn't think of the Pack as a group of sojieri for hire. He thought of it as a force for good, though their way of doing good could be a bit indirect. Perhaps it was romantic and a little naïve, but as long as he had a say in it, the Pack would continue to do business this way, even if it meant disqualifying the occasional hundred-million-talon contract.

Rockmore's and the Pack's longevity was proof of the experiment's success. They were known across the kingdoms as reliable, dedicated, efficient, and worth the price tag. Rockmore felt just as much pride at this desk as during his tenure as a Unified Commonwealth Authority general. He had done the nearly impossible and brought together some of the finest, most dangerous military specialists available; people who had once been enemies now worked together, across all borders and ideologies. And now it was all in jeopardy because of the actions of the team on Tikal. Rockmore had trouble finding fault with his people since he couldn't say he would have done it any differently; he hoped the trouble would pass, but he suspected that the fallout would be far-reaching.

It could have all been different, he thought. Fate had a strange way of weaving its different strands into an unexpected whole. Setbacks like the Mekon DaVoi job were an unfortunate but unavoidable part of their business model. Rockmore was secretly pleased that Leon had not grown so jaded as to be able to shrug off the losses. It was one of the reasons that he was such a good officer, despite his unpredictability and tendency to cause nearly as many problems as he solved.

Rockmore's reverie was interrupted by a loud beep from his comm. He answered it. "Priority signal from Tagea, General. It's Grand Admiral Hakar."

Rockmore frowned, allowing himself a moment of naked puzzlement in the privacy of his darkened office. "Put him through." Hopefully, the admiral was calling to apologize for the inconvenience this bullshit on the border had caused them all. Somehow he doubted it.

The tiny screen on the comm unit flickered to life, and Hakar's face appeared. He looked stricken, more upset than Rockmore had seen him in a long time. "General Rockmore. We need to talk."

"If this is about Leon and Traxus, I've already taken steps—"

When Hakar interrupted him, Rockmore realized it was a realtime ansible call, and he fell silent. "It's nothing to do with that, Jon. It's happening."

Second Movement:
Sweet Sorrow

8: Payday

Rachel was shaking Leon, and he awoke with a start, disoriented and reaching for a weapon. He didn't know where or when he was, just that Rachel was in danger. His heartbeat thundering in his ears, he braced himself as the bedroom swam into focus. He could see the clock beside the bed. It was too early for breakfast, far too early for sex.

"Wake up, Leon, wake up!" whispered Rachel urgently. "Heidi just called. They're on their way."

"Who's on the way?" Leon mumbled, rubbing his eyes.

"The general and Akida."

"Now?"

"*Now.*"

Trying to focus, Leon flung himself out of bed and set about getting dressed. Hastily Rachel pulled on one of his t-shirts just as a knock sounded at the door. She glared back at him as she went to open it.

His first coherent thought was that she had made a good point when suggesting they upgrade to a larger apartment, with a bedroom separate from the main living quarters.

The door opened. Silhouetted in the glow of the streetlamp were Rockmore and Akida. They made their apologies and entered. How early was it? Leon wondered. A glance at the clock, still fuzzy in his vision, was enough to tell him.

And yet, tired as he was, he could see that there was something wildly kinetic about the two other officers, as though they couldn't stand still.

Leon was too exhausted and too used to military barracks to feel self-conscious about his nudity as he pulled on fresh boxers and an undershirt, but he gave Rachel an apologetic look. She stood stiffly by the kitchenette.

"Good morning," Leon stammered.

"You're almost as slow as I am, these days," Rockmore said with a rueful smile.

"Are you hung over?" Akida asked, incredulous.

Not bothering to answer that last barb, Leon buttoned his shirt and tucked it into his trousers. "These meetings seem to be getting earlier," he quipped.

Rockmore handed him a thermos full of steaming Kaf once he was mostly dressed. "You're going to need this. Irún, the news, please."

Akida turned on the screen facing the bed and found a news channel. It wasn't hard, since every channel save the silent Valinata bands seemed to be broadcasting the same press conference: Empress Kra'al stood solemnly before a purple backdrop emblazoned with the Coalition's symbol of unity: the double-pronged Rienda in silver surrounded by eleven starbursts representing the charter species. "... have to acknowledge that a state of war exists between the Coalition and this aggressor," she intoned. Leon stared, dumbfounded.

The members of parliament shown on-screen listened attentively, but a current of shock ran through them that mirrored Leon's own reaction. Kra'al's voice was a low rumble, full of latent energy, but she was composed, poised. "The loss of life in the Valinata is catastrophic. It cannot be overstated, nor can the loss of our own loyal Fifth Fleet. If any good can be said to have come of this, it is that we now understand the true cost of isolationism in this dark time. Mistakes have been made in the past, but we must look now to our future. Our intent is to bring this conflict to a swift and peaceful conclusion. It is clear to us that in order to do so we must wield the full might of the Coalition Royal Defense Forces and do so wisely. I want to thank the members of parliament for their quick, multipartisan authorization for rapid deployment and full funding." The Prross leader drew a deep breath, her golden eyes molten, haunted. "Our petty squabbles and selfish agendas must be put away for the sake of the war effort. To that end we are offering long-term asylum to all Valinata refugees until such time as their homes can be liberated and resettled. Please join me in wishing our fleets and troops a speedy and victorious journey as we turn our eyes to the Outbound Arc...." Pundits started talking over the recording, analyzing Her Majesty's words, and Akida turned off the screen.

"What the fuck..." was all Leon could manage, his knuckles white as he gripped the thermos.

"She wasn't kidding about the funding. Parliament has just injected quadrillions of talons into the CRDF's discretionary budgets, and Grand Admiral Hakar has a job for us." The general was pointedly not looking at Rachel. Akida was looking around the apartment with curiosity; it was the first time he had entered it in all the years since Leon had joined the Pack, and he seemed surprised that it was decorated with even a modicum of taste. "The Coalition is officially at war as of four days ago, and we are lucky enough to be in the line of fire."

Leon was still too tired and too hung over to process what was happening as he tried to don his jacket while juggling the Kaf. It took him two tries at the jacket before he remembered that the red tiger stripes were supposed to be on the left. "So it's finally happening," he mumbled. "Do we have any more information on who we're facing? That speech was pretty damn vague."

The sadness on Rockmore's face, which Leon had first taken to be exhaustion, surprised him. "I think you know who we're facing, son. Hakar's given me nothing concrete yet, but I'm told a dossier is on its way. The news about the Fifth Fleet is concerning, though."

"Is that Flora Rodriguex's fleet?" Leon was stunned. He had never met Rodriguex but he had known her by reputation and she was an able combat commander, hardly the sort to sink her whole fleet or stroll blindly into an ambush. *CRN battle fleets don't just get wiped out. Are the things from Aethaleia back?* "When did this happen?"

"Be prepared for another surprise. Her entire battle group was annihilated before your team even headed to Tikal. The CRDF has been sitting on the information while they moved assets into position."

"That was almost three weeks ago. Where the hell are these assets you're talking about?" This was like a bad dream. Leon could barely keep the facts straight.

"The CRDF has been swarming the Arc, trying to pick up the pieces. Grand Admiral Cratos Mindor's fleets are now in the area, and more are on the way."

"We have it on Hakar's authority that Mindor has been killed, though," Akida put in. When Leon's jaw dropped, he snapped, "Looks like your CRDF got caught with their pants down."

Leon's retort was cut short. "Gentlemen, please!" Rockmore exclaimed, exasperated. "We need to get going and get the troops mobilized. Hakar's command flotilla is leaving Tagea already. We should expect them in a week, barring trouble."

"*Hakar* is coming out here?" Leon asked dumbly. He felt like his mind was working in slow motion. Why did this news fill him with terror?

"Daddy's coming to rescue you," Akida muttered angrily.

"Not now, Irún. Gentlemen, let's leave Miss Case in peace." Leon gave Rachel a quick kiss goodbye as she turned the screen back on to watch the news.

Outside in the chill morning air, the general waved Akida onward. "Leon, I need a moment with you."

"Sir?" Leon rubbed his eyes. He still felt half-asleep, but the thought of a mission from the Coalition, a chance to prove he still had what it took, was invigorating. All his resolutions to retire, to phase out, to scale back, were forgotten in an instant.

The general waited until Akida had gone into the courtyard. The two officers stood bathed in the light from one of the nearby streetlamps. "I know what you're thinking, son. Hakar's leading the task force himself, but...." Rockmore looked down. It wasn't like him to fumble for words. Leon frowned, perplexed.

"I've been ordered to keep you on the base for the duration of the contract." The general said it quickly, to get it over with, but the words still hit Leon hard.

"I don't understand, General," Leon said, but it was a lie. He understood all too well. *Exile doesn't end.*

"Apparently, senior members of the parliament got hold of the contract, saw your name in the fine print, and decided to show it around. After Daltar, and now with your involvement in the Tikal incident ... it's a miracle we still have a deal. I'm sorry, Leon, but you're hardly loved by any of the major parties." Rockmore scratched at his beard for a moment, buying time. He was kind enough not to mention that most of the parliament probably still thought of Leon as a butcher. Leon wasn't in a mood to say anything; he felt sick to his stomach. "Look, Leon. Hakar went to bat for you on this one, you can count on that. He knows as well as I do that there isn't a finer sojier or a better officer for this job. But you have to understand this is a political move, not a logical one. Leon?"

Leon was lost in thought, his fists clenched. After all this time, hadn't he served his penance? "General, I—I want in on this mission."

"I know, son. It's not up to me, and in this case it's not even up to Hakar. One of the stipulations of Parliament releasing the funds was that no private contractors operate without their oversight, and your name was mentioned in the rider specifically. There's absolutely no leeway on this one."

"Are you asking me to resign?" Leon asked, the knot in his stomach tightening.

"Absolutely not. There's no one I'd rather have in the field than you. But if war is really coming, there's no one I'd rather have guarding our home." Rockmore's voice hardened. "It's time to stop wishing and move on. You've got a place here. Your crew can come or stay as they please, but Traxus is going to be attached to Hakar directly. I'm not sure how much say I'll have in the matter. Leon, *listen.*" The colonel was staring into space, pondering.

"I'm listening," Leon said firmly, snapping back to the present.

"For all intents and purposes, you'll be acting president of Jackal Pack. You run the show: logistics, finances, recruitment ... most importantly, I need you to coordinate all our activity along the Alkyra. You'll have a full regiment in addition to the base garrison company."

"What about my brigades?"

Now Rockmore looked embarrassed. "Akida will absorb the Third, and I'll take the Sixth, with Major Kir commanding."

"And Dawson? Three is his."

"And it will be, again. I'm planning on making him acting commander in your absence, if you think he's up to it. First, I have a job for him: you're not going to recruit a whole new brigade overnight. We're going to need subcontractors. I trust his judgment in the field but he's never really mastered contracts, not the way you or Irún have. I'm putting him in charge of setting up a deal with a naval patrol outfit. See how he does, then send him out to me." Rockmore could tell the idea didn't sit well with Leon. "You've done a fine job with all your units, Leon. They'll make you proud.

"I understand that you're angry, believe me I do. But you can look at this another way: which second chance means more to you? The one Rachel Case is offering you or the one you *think* you *could* have with the CRDF?" Rockmore took hold of Leon's shoulders, and Leon realized he was looking into the face of the man who had adopted him as a son. "Your staying here may be exactly what you need. But you have to come to grips with life as it is, not as you wanted it to be."

"You're right, sir. Of course, you're right." *I've been chasing after expired dreams. Rachel* does *mean more to me than getting a Coalition knighthood. Besides, being in charge of the Pack won't be so bad. Paying job, quiet, Rachel and I can spend all day in Tesa or Las Serras.* He told himself that this was a blessing in disguise. Somehow the bitterness lingered.

"When I started the Pack, I didn't know if it would work out. It was an experiment. But you and Irún, you've validated my life's work. You're a fine sojier, as fine as any I've ever known. And right now I need your help getting this army on its feet."

§

It took until the sun came up to get the thousands of Jackal Pack troops on their feet, but when daylight broke across the courtyard it fell upon a shimmering sea of black and red. Gathering the entirety of their force for an announcement was unheard of, and all the brigades together barely fit into the parade grounds.

Word of Kra'al's declaration of war had spread like wildfire, and there was a dark thrill in the air, carried on the excited murmur of the troops. This was what they trained for, what they waited for.

A stage had been rolled out of storage and set before the headquarters, looking out over the sojieri. Leon stood to General Rockmore's left, opposite Akida. Around the general were arrayed the rest of the top officers and administrators.

The first to catch his eye was Commander Louis Irakundu-Tshomane, CO of the *Star Wolf*, standing sternly with his broad arms crossed over his even broader chest. He had skin the color of coffee and was large for a Human in every dimension; it was he who had taught Leon and his friends to speak Xhosa. Making him look small by comparison was Morai, the leader of Leon's shock troops. An enormous, scarred Vodroshoyan with a broken horn and bristling hair blacker than his Jackal Pack uniform, he cut an imposing figure. Akida's seconds stood with him, Major Da'Cir whispering into his ear as he nodded. She looked uneasy.

With Leon were Belladonna Kir and Liam Dawson, his loyal executive officers. Leon's other majors, Dennic and Brydock, were off by themselves, talking quietly. Captain Kyle Braeburn looked like he was struggling to stay awake.

"Good morning, everyone," Rockmore said into the microphone, his gravelly voice carried over the courtyard by loudspeakers. The crews of his orbiting fleet listened in via comm transmission. "Ordinarily I would have your officers brief you, but this is bigger than protocol and I want you all to hear it from me. I'm sure by now the news of Empress Kra'al's announcement has spread: the Coalition is at war. While this is grim news, I'm pleased to announce that Jackal Pack has been offered an exclusive contract by the CRDF."

No one spoke, no one moved. A gust of wind through the courtyard was the only sound.

"We are still working out pay details and timelines but this is an extended, full deployment. The entire legion will be going up, including all ground and naval assets." He paused for effect. "I will be going into the field with you." A ragged cheer of approval went up from the assembled battalions.

Rockmore smiled and gestured for silence. "I have asked Colonel Victor to remain behind as acting president of the corporation as well as the commander of Eve's defenses. I know many of you have husbands, wives, or families here, and we can all take comfort that he'll be watching over them. Anyone that dares to strike at Eve while we're in the field will be running into a brick wall. The colonel here would obviously much prefer to be in the field with us, but he has graciously agreed to protect our home." Leon smiled as enthusiastically as he could manage. It was a gracious way to spin his expulsion, but he wondered how long Rockmore's version of things would last before the truth came out. "I've also given him a target of twenty percent growth in recruitment for the next quarter. As for his brigades, Colonel Akida will take command of the Sixth, and I will personally oversee the Third." If that news shocked anyone, they were too professional or too tired to show it. There were even a few scattered cheers, which made Leon feel like a hypocrite considering he was so seriously considering leaving the Pack.

"We light the engines in one week. I know that's not a lot of time, but we will be ready. We will be linking up with the Coalition's Second Fleet and the Seventh Royal Line. Your COs will brief you further, but for now, every single one of your accounts has received ten minutes free ansible time, and travel vouchers for those of you with families here, should you wish to relocate them. I know you're all going to make me proud out there, and make us all a lot of money. None of us would ever wish for war, but if war has come we will fight it better than anyone.

"The Coalition's enemy—*our* enemy—is out for blood. I aim to drown them in it. In Spite of All!"

The Jackal Pack motto was echoed back at Rockmore followed with a chorus of "*Oohrah, Oohrah, Oohrah!*" Fifty thousand voices, fifty thousand fists pumping in the air. Fifty thousand warriors itching for battle.

As the troops dispersed, voices raised in excitement, energized despite the early hour, many of the officers turned to one another, shaking hands enthusiastically. This was a momentous day. Jackal Pack's sojieri of fortune were poised on the leading edge of the Alkyra, hurtling toward destiny. For Leon it was a bittersweet occasion, but he kept up his encouraging smile and embraced Irakundu-Tshomane as the big captain let out a booming laugh at his own joke, something about mushroom clouds.

Rumors were already spreading: how much they would be paid, how much autonomy they would have, who would get the choicest missions. Many of them turned to Leon for his perspective, not realizing that he had nothing to offer and wouldn't have divulged it even if he did.

"… in the ballpark of seventy million a month," suggested one of Akida's captains.

"That's some ballpark," replied Braeburn, their rivalry forgotten in the rush. "Forget ballparks, we can buy our own league for that!"

Leon chuckled, leaving them to their fantasies. He came face to face with Akida, the other colonel's expression unreadable.

"He did that well," Akida said.

"You mean burying me? Thanks a lot," Leon replied, letting his smile slip.

"Come on, no one wants to bury you," Akida said, sounding weary of the years of their rivalry. "Believe me, I wish I could say I would have done things differently on Tikal, but I don't know that I would have."

"Tikal? Haven't you heard? We were never there."

Akida cracked a smile. "I must be mistaken, then. Listen, I'll try to do right by your people out there. I promise."

"I know. And I appreciate it. I have to check in with some of them." Leon turned away, discomfited. He wanted to find Akida's sympathy grating, but in fact he was grateful.

Raptor and Traxus were waiting with some of Leon's other specialists beside the stage. He hadn't spotted them within the vast legion, and his heart leapt to see them now.

At least until Traxus fixed him with an accusatory look. "The Second Battle Fleet? That's my brother's fleet. You could have warned me." Behind her, Raptor gave Leon an apologetic shrug and mouthed *sorry*.

"I didn't find out until early this morning," Leon assured her. "Not that it matters."

"I suppose not. I'm out of action again, I'm guessing."

A knowing half-smile crept across Leon's face. "Actually, I've asked the general to attach you to his command battalion. You might not be on the front line but it'll be good experience."

"Assuming Hakar allows it," Traxus said bitterly. "I'm sorry, I know I should thank you. I just don't like being stage-managed. I'm a sojieri."

"Yes, you are," Leon said emphatically. "That's why you're going to war. I'm a liability, and that's why I'm staying."

Realization dawned on Traxus. "I didn't realize that. I'm so sorry."

"Nothing to be done about it now," Leon said with a defeated shrug.

"Well, the general got one thing right," Raptor declared. "You'll pulverize anyone that dares to dip into this system."

"I'll do my best," Leon promised. "Either of you see Jeric in the crowd?"

"No," Traxus answered. "I messaged him earlier to make sure he wasn't sleeping in. I never heard back. He's probably nursing a hangover."

"When isn't he?" Leon sighed, exasperated. "Well, I hope he at least listened in." Glancing past his friends, Leon saw more of his specialists queueing up to speak with him. He clapped Raptor on the shoulder and gave Traxus a quick hug. "I have to get moving, but let's talk later."

§

With the announcement of a new war, Leon had vanished, sucked into the machinery, just another line of code in a program with a singular purpose. The rude awakening had jarred Rachel more than she realized, and she had grudgingly risen with the sun. Somehow she couldn't bear to do her regular morning workout on a base full of sojieri getting ready for battle, so she busied herself writing and rewriting a letter home. Her gaze kept returning to the locked closet near the bed where Leon kept whatever gear wasn't stored in the armory. Soon it would stand empty.

She avoided watching the news feeds until her curiosity became unbearable. As expected, the airwaves were crowded with commentators and self-proclaimed experts trying to put their stamp on this momentous turn of events as though that somehow gave them some measure of control. Living among the Jackals had refined her ability to detect bullshit, and she found herself worried by how little substance was distilled from the great volume of words being volleyed about. They didn't know anything, did they? Maybe it was her proximity to the Valinata that heightened her awareness, or perhaps it was because half the people she knew would be taking up arms as part of the conflict, but Rachel was terrified. Annoyed by the complete absence of meaningful information, she went to take a shower, though she left the news on with the volume turned up so she could hear anything important.

When she got out, she sat down to watch despite herself. Finally, a report came on Shar'dan Broadcasting Network Six that told her something real: the SRG was mobilizing and stood ready to support their allies in the CRDF. That news did nothing to lighten her mood but struggling to bear witness was still better than sticking her head in the sand and waiting to get kicked in the ass, so she sat on the bed in her robe and painted her toenails while the galaxy fell apart around her.

The anchor remained appropriately somber as she pivoted to the next story: "The Coalition is still reeling after the private funeral held for Prime Minister Adam Somerset in the wake of his unexpected death, and many wonder how he would have addressed the looming prospect of war. The Prime Minister, who was always a friend to the Shar'dan despite his family having fled Confederate territory after the political reconstruction, suffered a stroke while working on his address for the upcoming Terran Economic Summit. Sources close to the prime minister said he was exhausted following a five-month tour of key Coalition and Unified Commonwealth agricultural worlds and had been consulting a physician for stress. Although several strong candidates have emerged in the Coalition parliament, the ruling body is expected to choose a successor from Prime Minister Somerset's own Legacy Party. Empress Kra'al's popularity has waned in recent months, but the prime minister's poll rankings remained consistently high up until his death, with more than half of surveyed citizens expressing satisfaction with his performance and policies.

"The Prime Minister's ashes will be interred in the Vault of Honor on Tagea. Some politicians are calling this premature and even inappropriate as the Vault of Honor has typically been reserved for those diplomats, rulers, and sojieri who have fallen in service to the Coalition. Whatever the case, the prime minister was a voice of reason and will be greatly missed, especially as the situation on the Coalition-Valinata border continues to escalate.

"In related news, the contract for diplomatic flagship is up for bids after the *Royal Dawn* failed to pass several criteria during a safety inspection. The storied ship will be launched into the Tagean star in honor of her accomplishments, despite calls from many aerospace museums to host an exhibit. A number of leading starship manufacturers are bidding on the new contract, including Hairon-Kam Shipyards and Starfield Aerospace. Sources in the diplomatic corps have hinted that the Coalition may be considering a military shipyard in response to recent events. They insist that the ship's tradition of flying weaponless will be preserved although the defense ministry has declined comment."

Rachel chewed her lip as the story about Somerset repeated, featuring a montage of images and clips of the late prime minister, his posthumous highlight reel. She saw him in parliament, meeting the press, meeting foreign dignitaries, out among the people, at home with his family. A candid image of him sitting deep in thought at his desk struck her as particularly sad. He had had an honest face, lined and solemn but with a mirthful glint in his eyes. She had always thought of Somerset as earnest and dedicated, but her family had always seen him as a naïve idealist who wasn't cut out for political office. It was a typical reaction for citizens of the Unified Commonwealth, who liked their leaders witty and nimble. Either way, she suspected his absence would be very much felt as the Coalition continued to grind toward war.

A knock at the door startled her; when she opened it, there was an envelope on the doorstep, partially tucked under the doormat. Rachel made no move to pick it up right away, instead searching the courtyard for the messenger. She saw no one. A bitter sigh escaped her.

This had happened once before, and she felt the bile rising in her throat as she remembered reading the fateful words that had sent her careening back to the Commonwealth, away from Leon, nearly for good.

A faint breeze rustled the dry leaves in the courtyard and tugged at the corner of the envelope. Reluctantly, Rachel crouched and plucked it off the ground. She went back inside, slamming the door behind her. Safe in the darkness of the apartment, she turned off the news feed and sat at the little table in the kitchenette, the envelope before her. Like last time, there was nothing written on it. It didn't matter. She knew it was for her.

After a delay that felt like hours even though the clock on the wall said it had only been five minutes, Rachel thumbed open the flap of the envelope and pulled out a disposable mem screen. Leon's face was staring back at her, though not as she had ever seen him. The face was younger, unscarred, clean-shaven. His eyes were cold, his mouth partially open as though he was about to speak. It must have been taken years ago. Beside his photo was another, that of a bald man with a facial tattoo that crept across his scalp. His expression was blank, his one good eye contemptuous. Rachel realized they were both mugshots, Leon's probably taken after his arrest nearly a decade ago.

The other photo and the story, however, were much more recent. "BLOOD MONEY: TWO SIDES OF THE SAME COIN" read the headline. Comprehension dawned as she scanned it, and her eyes blurred with tears of anger, revulsion, and disappointment. Words swam before her: The Hotel Thescalon on Korinthe ... botched interdiction ... murder. Rachel had known about the disastrous job; after all, Leon's friend Buzz Parker had lost his life in that hotel just before her return to Eve. Somehow, she had managed to avoid the details or their implications. The temperature in the room seemed to drop as she reread the article again and again. No matter what, it always ended the same way.

Rachel didn't want to be horrified, but she was. The whole galaxy was teetering on the brink of war, yet her whole world had drawn into itself, leaving only her and the monster she loved. She stood shakily, got dressed, and fled the apartment into the sunlight.

9: Confessional

The machine had started winding up and there was no stopping it. The Jackal Pack administration building was a hornet's nest of activity, with administration staff and officers scrambling as they tried to figure out how to coordinate the whole strength of the mercenary legion.

Never before had all fifty thousand troops deployed together, and they had little practice in mobilizing the huge number of autonomous combat teams and freelance specialists alongside the conventional infantry and armored companies. They had been drilling for some time, but they had to get it right to appear credible in the eyes of the CRDF, especially given the intense scrutiny to which they would be subjected. It would hardly be fitting for their troop carriers to crash into one another upon launch.

Leon attended briefing after briefing, planning meetings blurring into budgetary breakdowns that gave way to ordnance inventories. Rockmore made a show of handing over the reins to him and Heidi, but it felt hollow. Leon Victor was in the eye of this hurricane, strangely untouched but in some ways wishing it could sweep him along with it. He was a man without a purpose at the moment, yet he had the opportunity to observe.

Ducking into his office for a breather between meetings, Leon took stock of his new lot. He loosened his tie and sat down at his desk, letting the sun warm his back through the window. The ever-increasing pile of newly acquired administrative work would keep, for a little while at least. The drone of voices through the open door was somehow soothing.

His comm buzzed, and he quickly answered upon seeing his youngest sister's ID on the screen. Natille Victor's soft, olive-skinned features appeared before him, her face framed by thick waves of dark hair. "Thank God you picked up!" she blurted. "Do you know how much I had to bid on a realtime tunnel? Usually the Eve bands are cheap, but all of a sudden it's a hotspot." Her green eyes narrowed. "We heard the news. Is it as bad as it sounds? The news reports here

make it seem like just some border skirmish, but Kra'al's speech....
Are you in danger?"

"I don't know much yet, sis, and I can't even tell you that, but
you know the Coalition is sending ships out here. We're as prepared
as anyone could be. I'm going to be busy, but—"

"What does that mean? Are you still coming home? The
wedding is—"

"I don't know," Leon repeated firmly. "I'm going to do my
best. As soon as I know more, I'll tell you." He lightened his tone;
after all, she was his baby sister, and she had paid a lot of money to
talk to him. "Tell me, how's everything at home? I could use a
distraction right about now. How's work? How are things coming for
the wedding?"

Natille looked at him with suspicion; she knew his evasive
tactics well. "That's all fine. We had another one of the old pump
stations fail under Crossing, so I've got my team working on a
proposal to replace them all outright. I just hope we don't get
underbid by those bastards at Edenbridge again. As for the wedding,
Naomi is being a bitch, as usual. Everything has to be just so. It's like
she wants a do-over for her own wedding." She hesitated. "You
should know, Alex is staying with us for a couple of days."

"What? *Why*?" Alex, the older of Leon's two younger brothers,
had been born with a learning disability, but he had lived on his own
for years.

"He had a confrontation with some customer at the market. The
guy shouted at him, and Alex got startled and pushed him. He fell and
bruised his ass or something, and now he's talking about suing the
market. They know Alex isn't at fault, but they had to suspend him
while they look into it. Naomi is trying to shut the whole thing down,
but she'll wipe the floor with the guy if he pushes it to court."

Leon blew out a sigh. "Dammit. I've told you all, Alex doesn't
have to work. If this is about money—"

"It isn't. You can't throw money at all your problems, Leon!
Alex *likes* working at the market. He likes the people, usually. This
just needs time. You can't shelter him from the world, even if he
wanted you to, which he doesn't."

Forcing himself to calm down, Leon tried again. "You're right. Listen...." He trailed off as he saw Major Belladonna Kir appear in his doorway, tapping her watch. He held up an index finger and nodded. "Listen, Natille, I have to go, but I need to ask you something. I need to talk to Rachel first, obviously, but I don't want her here if things heat up."

"Of course, she can stay with us," Natille said, preempting his question. "It would be fun to have her here. Maybe she can help me control Naomi." Her tone was only half-joking.

"Thank you," Leon breathed. "Let's talk later."

"Fine, you call. *You* can pay for the realtime connection."

"Deal. I'll call back as soon as I can. If Alex is there, maybe I can talk to him, give him some encouragement, you know?"

"That would be good. He misses you almost as much as I do. Be safe, Leon. We love you."

"Love you, too." He hung up and rose from his desk, regarding Major Kir. She did not look happy.

"Major. What am I late for now?"

"You and Heidi were supposed to walk through KIA benefits with me. I've been waiting in the east conference room for the last ten minutes. I hate to be short, but it's not like we have a ton of slack time today."

"You're right, I'm sorry. She wasn't next door?"

Major Kir shook her head. "Her assistant said she took a call and headed toward the visitor lounges." She hooked a thumb over her shoulder and led the way. Belladonna Kir was short, wiry, and always looked disappointed. She was also an exceptional combat commander, coming from a distinguished career as a planetary defense force marine for the planet Cerdora in the Commonwealth. The fringe of an elaborate tattoo crept up her neck past her shirt collar like ivy climbing the side of a building.

Leon followed Major Kir back into the hall and they set off toward the comfortable meeting rooms where they usually put visiting VIPs. "If she's not available we'll have to reschedule. I'm no good at that stuff without her. Is the general joining?"

"I doubt it. I saw him meeting with Captain Irakundu-Tshomane and Liam. Something about subcontracting private pickets to guard our airspace while *Star Wolf* is gone. It's just you, me, and Heidi as far as I know." Leon was fine with Rockmore and Dawson focusing on the pickets: he was being left with a sizeable complement of troops, but they did not include aerospace assets. Privateers would be a welcome addition.

"Do you mind if I call Rachel? I haven't had a chance to talk to her since this whole circus kicked off." Kir shook her head, and Leon dialed Rachel.

They turned a corner and Leon frowned as he heard a familiar comm chime from behind one of the closed doors. He knocked and entered.

It took him a moment to register everything, and he immediately regretted intruding. Rachel was seated on one of the leather couches, facing Heidi. Heidi was in her chair, holding one of Rachel's hands while Leon's lover looked down at the beeping comm in her other hand. She looked as though she had been crying.

"Baby, are you okay?" Leon asked tenderly, ending the call and pocketing his comm. When Rachel didn't look up, he tried for levity. "If you're going to cheat on me with Heidi, at least I know you have good taste."

The scathing look Heidi shot Leon killed his half-formed smile. She blushed, her cheeks matching her pink hair.

Rachel stood, ramrod straight, and stared Leon down. Though she was shorter than him and wearing only a tank top, shorts, and sandals that showed her half-painted toenails, she was intimidating. Leon had faced warlords, elite sojieri, notorious criminal empires, and the monsters of Aethaleia, yet somehow, they all paled in comparison to the venom in her eyes. "You're an idiot," she said, pushing past him and the dumbfounded Belladonna Kir.

"Jesus, I wasn't serious," he mumbled, embarrassed. His brow creased in confusion.

"Come here," Heidi said sweetly, and Leon walked over to her, glancing over his shoulder. He was torn between his need to go after Rachel and his duty to keep things moving here.

Leon turned back to Heidi. "What was—" he began, when she reached up and punched him in the face.

Shocked, Leon reached up and felt his split lip, tasted the blood. "What the fuck was that for?"

"Because she would never do that, even though you deserved it."

"Dammit Heidi, I was *joking*."

"You think she's upset about *that*?" Heidi asked, groaning in exasperation. "Admittedly, you picked a hell of a time to try to be funny." She tossed him a disposable mem. He fumbled and dropped it, then knelt to pick it up, frowning. His frown deepened as he scanned it, his lip forgotten as blood dribbled into his beard. A picture of a young, idealistic fool stared back at him, cold surprise in his eyes. It took Leon a moment to recognize himself in the photo that had once momentarily graced the airwaves and made him a pariah.

"Why would you show her this?" he asked Heidi, his voice hitching.

"You think I...?" Heidi was offended, and her eyes narrowed to angry slits. "That is none of my business. It's between you and Rachel. Evidently someone else around here feels differently." She reached back to the end table beside the couch for a tissue and dabbed at Leon's mouth. He jerked away, then gave her a conciliatory look. He took the tissue to wipe off the blood himself.

"You need to go to her and fix this now before it becomes a real problem," Heidi commanded. "That woman doesn't know where to turn right now or who to trust. You fuck this up, I guarantee that you lose her. And no, I won't be there for you." She sat there watching Leon, and her eyes were as cold as her voice was devoid of mirth. He was reminded that once she had been a killer without parallel, savage and ruthless. But never totally heartless. "You're right, Heidi. Thanks. I'm ... sorry about—"

"Are you fucking stupid, Leon? Don't waste time apologizing to *me*. Go after Rachel, you big, dumb asshole." Leon nodded and crumpled the mem, along with the pictures of Marcus Keegan and a naïve sojier who had aimed for glory and only managed to ruin his own life after ending so many others.

"Bella, I'm sorry," he said to Major Kir as he slipped past her. She looked annoyed and faintly embarrassed.

"It's fine," she said tonelessly. "Heidi and I can handle this, I think. Good luck."

He caught up to Rachel in the lobby. She didn't run away, but she didn't slow down for him, either. "Please, Rachel, I'm begging you, let me explain."

"Are you sure you can spare the time?" she replied icily.

Leon decided to push past that. "Look, baby, you deserve the truth. You once asked me if there were times I had ever enjoyed killing. Well, that was one of them."

Rachel didn't even look at him. "*That* is all you've got?" She picked up her pace, striding through the headquarters' front doors and into sunlight.

"You shouldn't have had to read—"

"Are you really about to tell me that I shouldn't have read that? Think real carefully before you do."

What could he say to make this right? Probably nothing, he realized.

"You know," Rachel mused, "it's not that they came to our home in the middle of the night and woke us up like that. It's not even that you got a hard-on like a teenager seeing his first pair of tits when you heard there was a war on." She turned toward the apartment they shared. "Somehow, it's not even that after all this time I'm surprised when I read about how you murdered someone. It's that this is your world, and no matter what you say, I'm starting to wonder if you can ever really put it behind you."

Could he blame her? He had been so excited by the prospect of a CRDF contract that he had been blind to her feelings. More than that, he was afraid she might be right.

"Is that who you are? And who am I? Am I supposed to go into cold storage while you fight this war? I'm starting to lose myself in this, and the fact that it takes a story like that to really wake me back up scares me."

Leon wasn't used to being rendered speechless, and it infuriated him.

Still, Rachel was at least a little sympathetic. "I don't know, maybe you think I'm being selfish for throwing this at you now, with everything else that's going on. Hell, maybe I am. That doesn't change the fact that I love you, and I want to see you do something better with your life. I know you're at home here, and I've tried to adapt, too. Every time I think I get a handle on it, it reaches out and slaps me in the face. It's not *normal*."

"And that's what you want? Normal?" Leon didn't mean for the question to sound accusatory but it was too late to take it back.

"I don't know. I want to know I'm with a good man. Most of the time I'm sure you are."

"Not all the time, though."

"No," Rachel said after a pause. "Not all the time. I swear I am trying to make my peace with what you do, but you just got back and now you're going to take off again. Who knows what will happen?"

"You've got it all wrong, Rachel," said Leon quietly. "I'm not going anywhere." Rachel finally looked at him, brow furrowing as she searched his face. She paused in the courtyard, her arms crossed, waiting for him to continue. "I'm the one going into storage. The Coalition made that one of the conditions of the contract. Can I explain?"

"You've got five minutes."

"It'll take longer than that." Intrigued, she followed him, an arm's length of distrust between them.

"What happened to your lip?"

"Heidi hit me."

"Good."

They left the base behind, moving toward the edge of the plateau past the headquarters building and officers' apartments. The wind whipped around them, and Rachel pulled her hair back to keep it from blowing into her eyes. Leon began to pull on his sunglasses, not just to protect his eyes against the dust but to protect him from having to make eye contact. When he saw Rachel braving the wind, he tucked them back into his breast pocket.

The small park overlooking the northern savannah was deserted, and they made their way to one of the vacant benches with a view of the windswept plains.

Leon was still trying to figure out what to say when Rachel asked, "What happened to you, Leon? How did you get this way?" There was no malice in her voice, just puzzlement. "And I don't mean

Marcus Keegan. Heidi told me it was a setup. She told me all the details about the Korinthe job that the news left out. It's fucked up, I'll grant you that. I'm not sure you should have gotten away with murder but I can admit I'm glad you did." He could feel her eyes on him, but he stared ahead at the golden grass far below. "I mean it, though. What happened to you? You have to tell me eventually."

She was right. He did. And if not now, he might never work up the courage again. "What I'm going to tell you is bad. You might … not look at me the same way again."

"If you don't tell me, I know I won't."

There would be no going back if he told her. Once she knew, she might only ever think of him as a monster—if she thought of him again at all. "It's a matter of public record. You could have found out any time you wanted."

Rachel's voice was unsympathetic. "Whatever it is, I want to hear it from you."

Leon supposed this was his chance to preserve a shred of his integrity. "You've heard of Daltar."

"It's a planet, right?"

"Yeah. I was there for a year and a half. I've been trying to move on for ten years since, but no one will let me." His sigh was lost on the wind. "Fuck it, maybe I won't let myself." He licked his swollen lip.

"Just start at the beginning."

"Well, for starters I never planned to be a career sojier," he began reluctantly. "I was going to see my brother and sisters through college and then get out once they were on their feet. I should have left when Naomi got her law degree and took over the family debt, but by then I was good at it." Thinking back, it was almost funny: Leon had not signed up out of some lofty ideal like patriotism or even to chase thrills but for a paycheck, plain and simple. Maybe that should have been a clue to what was to come. "My first tour was with the Terran Legion on Auriga. It was supposed to be a simple territorial patrol, but we got ambushed by rebels. My unit got stranded during the withdrawal and we were stuck there for almost a month, evading enemy patrols, before we got pulled out.

"I must have made a good impression because they promoted me and offered me a spot in officer candidate training. It was like being back at school, almost. That was when they placed me with Special Projects labs. I guess I could have finished out my tour there, but I was not cut out for that sort of shit. And honestly, I felt guilty working in those nice clean labs after my friends died on Auriga."

"I'm sorry, Leon. So, you stayed for them?"

It was hard to tell, now. Was it for their memory? Or by then was it for the thrill, after all? "Maybe at first. But after a while I was really proud of it. I had new friends, a new family, a purpose. It's a cliché, maybe, but it's true what they say about brotherhood and loyalty among sojieri. I signed up for another tour as soon as I could." Leon had been surprised to find within himself such fervent devotion to his comrades. That and his inexplicable knack for turning disaster into success that had brought him to the attention of one of Hakar's field commanders, and eventually the grand admiral himself.

It was Hakar who pulled him out of the infantry and made him a captain in his elite Information Operations, Reconnaissance, and Strategic Intervention Regulatory Activities Detachment. In IORSIRAD, Leon's skills were honed to perfection, and his determination and leadership, tested, but he had triumphed against all odds, often with little to no support in battles about which the public would never know. A classified mission on Heavenfall had sealed his fate: before he knew it, he was a colonel, and his trajectory suggested he could even make vice grand admiral, or perhaps join the Star Chamber itself.

"I'd never even heard of Daltar before Hakar sent me there, even though the fighting had been going on since before I was born. I was a colonel for less than a year before I got the assignment." If resolving a territorial dispute between the Coalition colonists and the indigenous Daltari had seemed like an odd assignment for a special forces detachment, Leon had not thought to question it. Hakar had asked him personally to lead the campaign; how could he refuse the man who had made his career? Most of his troops had thought of it as a vacation, light duty to reward them for a series of unrelenting campaigns.

Leon should have known immediately that things were not right on Daltar. For centuries, the Daltari had remained isolated from their neighbors to the extent that their languages were not even part of the FLASH battery that allowed other species to understand one another. Even those Daltari who lived and worked among the colonists kept themselves—and were kept—apart. The rift had filled with suspicion and eventually outright animosity. Leon spent a great deal of time studying their history and culture and insisted his officers do the same. He was startled by cultural norms that included ritual combat, caste divisions, and a great deal of xenophobia. Nevertheless, his mandate was to end the conflict peacefully and equitably, and he believed in that mission.

Hostilities had originally erupted decades earlier when a Coalition-sponsored archaeological report inadvertently revealed that the massive Daltari ancestral tombs and subterranean cities contained rich deposits of trykon crystal and even rarer trykon-sigma that was critical in gravdrive and hypercomm ansible manufacture. Coalition interests in the region spiked, and local militias, spurred on by corporate interests, began evicting Daltari tribes and seizing their land almost overnight. The natives responded by sabotaging supply lines and kidnapping miners for ransom. While the corporations withdrew to figure out how to get rid of the indigenous obstacles, the local situation escalated.

Leon and his people had traveled the edge and fought along it for years. In fact, life in IORSIRAD was a whistle-stop tour of worlds on the verge of defection or outright rebellion, and they had faced insurgents, marauders, and traitors. Leon had sworn to uphold the Coalition and protect the emperor and his interests. He may not have thought much of the man himself, but he trusted Grand Admiral Hakar and the majority of the Coalition's leaders. While he often lamented the circumstances that forced him into conflict with his enemies, he never doubted his mission.

Compared to many of their theaters of operation, Daltar was civilized and densely settled. However, the unique and poorly understood indigenous population made it seem alien and somehow primitive, even threatening. The prevailing attitude that no one outside the Daltar system cared what happened there only enhanced the sense of isolation. The hardened troops of IORSIRAD had the feeling that they had finally wandered beyond the edge of the map.

Daltari customs being as inhospitable as they were, what little the colonists knew of their armor-plated neighbors was filtered through the planetary government's Ministry of Indigenous Affairs, a political group with a commercial agenda. When the Daltari fought back against the colonists infringing on their territory, MoIA did their best to paint the attacks as a savage uprising, even terrorism. Those Daltari allied with the colonists saw an opportunity to seize land and power from their rivals and were only too content to help perpetuate the lies. "They told us we could trust them and arm them against the other Daltari. They claimed to have sighted mass graves, and they had us running all over the DMZ looking for them while they looted. That's what I walked into," Leon said with a bitter laugh. Rachel was listening intently, her eyes locked on him.

"Emperor Telemon's cabinet caught wind of the situation, and Uncle Franz himself called for economic sanctions against the Daltari resistance. Of course, that didn't stop them. Ever since, I've tried to look at it from their perspective, and it must have been terrifying to stare down an empire to make their demands heard, especially when most of the galaxy didn't even know they existed, or care."

Two Jackal Pack officers walked by, cups of Kaf in hand. "Colonel," they said cordially.

Leon waved absently, then folded his hands in his lap.

Rachel cleared her throat. "You were saying?"

"Daltar's Coalition-sponsored PDF troops were the muscle. They had been tangling with the Daltari for years by the time we touched down. They were undisciplined and they were excessive, burning homes and dynamiting underground crypts to get their point across. Their Daltari auxiliaries were just as bad, using the conflict to improve their own clans' holdings, no matter what it took. Hakar was eager to get us in there before either side graduated to outright atrocities."

Twelve companies of hardened, intelligent sojieri had landed on Daltari soil, hoping not to be the prelude to a larger invasion. Leon and IORSIRAD's fearsome reputation had preceded them: as soon as they arrived, all hostile action ceased while the Daltari withdrew to assess this new variable. To prove their peaceful intentions, IORSIRAD brought no battle fleet, only Leon's flagship, *Calypso*. Although Leon was given operational command, Emperor Telemon had a man on the ground already: a senior advisor to oversee the PDF troops by the name of General Ellis Heron. Heron had a reputation for objectivity and a long list of successes both diplomatic and martial under his belt.

Heron and his people had been in-country long enough to have close connections among the government and the PDF, who all insisted that the Daltari were at fault. Determined to protect Coalition colonial interests from a race that had refused to even ratify the Coalition Charter and uninterested in the Daltari side of the story, Heron had gradually succumbed to the pressure of his hosts and began to advocate direct action.

What had started as a collaborative partnership didn't take long to dissolve when Leon questioned Heron's unilateral approach and refusal to meet with Daltari leaders. Uncontaminated by exposure to the colonial bias, Leon defied Heron and redirected PDF efforts, even going so far as to reach out to the Daltari and attempt a meeting. That was enough to set in motion the chain of events that would define Leon's whole life and end so many others.

Now all but ostracized from the allied command and excluded from much of their decision-making, Leon made an enemy not just of the man he had been sent to help, but of much of the local leadership. Thinking himself above playing politics, he withdrew from that theater and set up his base of operations on the edge of Daltari territory, trying to act as a buffer. That suited Heron just fine. "That was my first mistake," Leon admitted. "My second was thinking I was still one of the troops."

"It must have been hard to command your friends," Rachel observed, "when they still saw you as one of them."

"They were professionals, and they followed their orders. It was me. I was promoted too quickly. I was so worried that they might resent my success, and so preoccupied with not letting it go to my head, that I spent way more time trying to maintain those relationships than I should have. And honestly, command is lonely, especially when you've alienated yourself from the people who are supposed to be your peers. I was starved for friendship. It's stupid but it's the truth.

"I lost the high-level view. I kept forgetting to command them. At heart, I was a sergeant with a colonel's crowned falcon on my shoulders. Sometimes I wonder what Hakar saw in me, but I do know that even if no one anticipated how bad Daltar could get, they should have seen that it required a more experienced commander. I took too long to learn how to maneuver."

The campaign dragged on for months. The troops, used to rapid, decisive action, grew frustrated, and their frustration curled in unexpected directions. Recon units from Heron's advisory group were folded into Leon's companies, bringing their cynicism and bigotry with them. It wasn't long before some of Leon's officers and their sojieri had bought into the local propaganda. Like any population, Leon's forces were made up of individuals who formed their own opinions, their own factions. He failed to see the schism until it was too late, until his troops were turning on each other. His rivalry with Heron fueled the fire, and his own authority began to crumble little by little. He was left commanding a force in disarray, too wrapped up in keeping friends to see how many enemies he was creating.

Realization came, and Leon might have been able to reassert control and bring the rogue elements back into the fold, but the Daltari chose that moment to escalate from ambushing patrols and raiding outposts to full-scale assaults. While poorly trained, they were fearsome, four-armed fighters, covered in thick exoskeletons that could stop a bullet, and they were well equipped. Nothing was ever proven, but Leon was certain that they were supplied by the Valinata Space Force whose own designs on the trykon-sigma deposits were obvious.

Peace was slipping through Leon's fingers as he tried to balance a measured response with an unyielding defense. The xenophobic but understandably paranoid Daltari would never trust an overture that came from their Coalition oppressors, and even the Coalition-sponsored colonists and their PDF resented the intervening IORSIRAD troops. Leon and his companies were caught between cultures, without reinforcements, on a world at the edge of civilization. Too proud and foolish to ask for additional resources and unable to go on the offensive, Leon ordered his troops to fortify what settlements remained, and they began seizing PDF armor and artillery, frequently at gunpoint. The Daltari did not see the dissent within the Coalition ranks as an opportunity to make peace. Instead, perhaps justifiably, they exploited it to drive deeper into colonial territory.

"How did you ever delude yourselves into thinking that the Daltari would see special forces troops on their own soil as anything but a threat?"

Leon was caught off-guard by that, and he stammered before replying. "It seems obvious now," he admitted. "For all I know that was Telemon's plan all along. General Heron and the local brass were never able to establish a dialogue with the Daltari natives because they never really tried. The Daltari pushed us back, chipping away until there wasn't much left. The PDF was only ever nominally under my control. When they broke, they broke hard. Some elements went renegade and there weren't enough of us to stop them. They declared total war on the Daltari and got themselves annihilated in the process but not before slaughtering civilians and bringing down the wrath of the whole Daltari army, which was getting bigger every day while ours was getting smaller."

Leon paused and looked up sharply. "You know, I could get thrown in the Vault just for telling you this. My freedom and immunity were contingent on my discretion. I signed enough confidentiality agreements to circle the Tagean equator."

"Then why are you telling me?" Rachel asked, her expression open, unguarded. "Not just because I asked you to."

"No, because I can't keep it from you anymore. I can't ask you to love me, to give me chance after chance, under false pretenses. And … I guess I'd rather risk prison than that at this point. It took me a while to figure that out."

Leon was startled when Rachel touched his knee gently.

He looked at her hand a moment before continuing. "I only knew Heron by reputation before Daltar. I don't know what happened to him, but the man I found on Daltar wasn't the same man everyone told me about. Once the rest of the PDF buckled, he began initiating an endgame protocol. That's what we called a last resort countermeasure, to hit the enemy hard enough to make them back off, or at least do as much damage as possible before you're overrun. I thought he was out of his mind, and I had no idea what kind of counterattack he was planning, so I took my most loyal sojieri and relieved him of command. I had to put a gun to his head when he wouldn't stand down."

"It seems like everything you did was at gunpoint."

"It was a war. My war. Heron was out of control at that point, wanted to fight to the last man, make some last stand that would get him in the history books with a nice rack of posthumous medals. If I had left it up to him the only difference would have been an even higher death toll. I still can't believe the colonists could think the Daltari were somehow monsters, even after living side by side for so long … if there's anything, any sick lesson to be learned from this disaster, it's that ignorance is poison. It's the worst weapon the weak-willed have in their arsenal, and it works very, very well." He swallowed. "That, and the nukes."

"Nukes? I don't get it. Why would you even have nuclear weapons on a peacekeeping mission?" Rachel asked suspiciously. It was a question that had been asked thousands of times, in front of military tribunals, cameras, and parliamentary committees.

Leon blinked. "It sounds crazy, but it was standard procedure. The *Calypso* had a set of support satellites that included antimatter and nuclear warheads. They were meant to be used against enemy ships to clear an exit vector and buy us time in the event of retreat."

"The Daltari had a navy?"

"Not much of one. They weren't much for space travel. Even so, they did manage to bring down *Calypso* and half my satellites, but not before I finally had the sense to call for reinforcements to pacify the Daltari and the colonial troops. Still, with *Calypso* out of the picture, the Daltari pressed the attack." Leon was nearly overwhelmed by the memory of the night when the native forces had struck his headquarters, killing half the command company before they were driven off. He could still smell the smoke, still hear the rain drumming off his armor as those powerful, glistening, armored warriors rushed the hill in the face of machinegun fire. Part of him would always be on that hill, with his back to the mountains.

He had never realized how much the Coalition's vast, seemingly invincible army was feared by the galaxy. Nor had he realized he would have to watch his own people as carefully as their adversaries. He had grown so confident in the troops of IORSIRAD; after all, they were among the most highly trained in the galaxy. Still, he had taken their morale and their morality for granted, and his guard had dropped. He had never stopped to consider that they were people, with all the strengths and weaknesses that entailed. Leon's own moral certainty following the brutal but necessary actions he had taken on Heavenfall should have been warning sign enough. He should have recognized it. For a man who had borne witness against and meted out justice to fellow sojieri who had lost control, naiveté was a poor excuse. The court-martial convened in Daltar's aftermath had agreed.

Leon paused again, searching his memories and his feelings. He should have been tearful, breathless. Instead, the years had left him numb.

"That's not all," Rachel said insistently, watching him expectantly.

"No." Still thinking how to proceed, Leon bit his lip, and it started bleeding again. "I did what I was ordered to do."

Rachel's eyes narrowed almost imperceptibly, and that told him all he needed to know. He rushed to explain. "Everyone else had collapsed around us, just turned and bolted. They left their own people. *We* held the line. We never faltered. When all else failed, my orders were to protect the people of the Coalition. I followed them. Too well.

"There was nothing between the Daltari and the capital of Misande Dun Rai but a few hundred troops in some stolen tanks, so we evacuated the city while two companies held the outskirts. By the time the Daltari finally broke through, the eastern half of the city was a pile of rubble. It wasn't enough."

Unsure of how to explain what had happened next, Leon stalled for time. Hatred had colored the gazes of so many people when they looked at him. His own sister Naomi had waited less than a day after the news hit before going to the courthouse to change her name and the names of their siblings. Only Natille had changed hers back to Victor when she got the opportunity. His shame was public record, his painful failure a footnote in history textbooks and at military academies. To the Daltari, he would always be The Enemy. What was the point of hiding it?

"I might have thrown myself on the mercy of the Daltari, anything for a cease-fire, but for that, I needed to communicate with them. General Heron had no authority, not after I put him in chains, but he was my only link to the MoIA people and their Daltari allies. So I went to him for help. I went to him for translators." Leon turned away from Rachel, staring out at the savannah far below them. The wind sent ripples through the peaceful, golden grass sea.

"I listened to Heron's people. I had tried to learn what I could about the Daltari, study their languages, but I barely understood any of the chatter over the radio. I had no clue the translators didn't even speak the same dialect as the people they were talking to. The Daltari were never unified, and the ones working with us saw an opportunity for favored trade status and a way to remove their enemies. They told me that the army occupying the city was going to annihilate us and everyone we had been sent to protect.

"So I used my last resort, the endgame protocol Heron had tried to start. I turned the satellites on the capital and launched the entire atomic arsenal. Misande Dun Rai was gone, the whole city. It took a hundred years to build that city. It fell to the Daltari in a hundred days, and I vaporized it in five minutes. The surviving Daltari surrendered to us without another shot fired, and we sat staring at each other over the wreckage until the Coalition relief fleet arrived."

"That's it?" Rachel asked, aghast, her words nearly carried away on the wind.

"Hardly," Leon said, turning to meet her shocked gaze.

"Leon, how could you? How could you do that?"

"It was frighteningly easy. I just gave the order, and some lieutenant called it in. Standard operating procedure did the rest. It's crazy, we keep telling ourselves how far we've come, how advanced we are compared to the generations that ruined Terra and fought the Dawn Wars, but it never struck anyone in our 'enlightened' government as irresponsible to put that kind of destructive power in the hands of some twenty-seven-year-old colonel. Even if I was some kind of prodigy, that didn't mean I wasn't still practically a kid. Most people don't even realize that my decision to launch the atom bombs was one of the few I made that the investigation declared as justified, with the proviso that I was acting on rotten intelligence."

"That doesn't excuse anything," Rachel said. Her voice was cold, but her eyes flashed with anger. Her hands gripped her knees tightly.

"The Casino Protocol was set to run when certain parameters were met. They were met."

"You can't be so cruel. That's a pathetic copout and you know it."

"You're right," Leon agreed, deflated. "I was scared, Rachel, we all were. Maybe if it had just been us, my troops, we could have retreated, hidden in the mountains until help arrived to sort it out, evaded like I did on Auriga. Or maybe I would have surrendered. Hell, maybe I would have done the same thing, we'll never know. It wasn't just us, though: I was trying to protect hundreds of thousands of civilians, and when that army started rolling toward us, I had no way left to stop them. I still couldn't figure out how they were fielding so many troops," he said through gritted teeth.

"They weren't all sojieri," Rachel guessed.

"We travelled light, but for the Daltari, it was more like a migration. There were two billion of them worldwide. The 'army' pursuing us was about five million strong. They figured we would never flatten our own capital, so they moved their civilians into the city for shelter. Either the recon units I sent out couldn't tell the difference between combatants and civilians, or they didn't care." It was a chilling thought, and Leon was afraid he knew the answer.

"Two hundred thousand died in the blasts, and half a million more died from radiation poisoning later. The Daltari physiology couldn't even begin to process it." Leon took a deep breath and forced himself to give voice to his crimes. "I wiped out six entire clans, generations of them. They were just … gone." He opened his hands, and there was nothing in them.

"All because of a mistranslation," Rachel said softly.

"A lie!" Leon answered forcefully. "Lies on top of lies. That motherfucker, Telemon, said the Daltari were an embarrassment to the modern galaxy. He couldn't have cared less if they were wiped out.

He just didn't want it done so theatrically. They sent us as peacekeepers, but they never wanted us to keep the peace. They fully expected that relations between the allies would deteriorate until we were at each other's throats, and that I would lose control of the situation. I was a scapegoat, made to order." Leon forced himself to sit back down, but he couldn't look at Rachel anymore, and the serene vista brought no solace.

His voice dropped. "Heron's people were so proud of their trick," Leon said bitterly. "When I figured it out, it was too late to stop it, but I couldn't look away. You go blind when an atom bomb goes off in your face, but for that split second before I lost my sight, it was the most beautiful thing I'd ever seen. I knew how a god must feel, this intense pride and incredible self-loathing all at the same time. The trace image was seared into my retinas for days: a city being erased, along with all the people in it. That was all I saw, day and night. By the time I could see again, I was in shackles."

"I can't even imagine," Rachel said numbly, but Leon could tell she was holding back. Was this therapeutic for her? It certainly didn't feel that way for Leon. Still, if he was going to open his heart to her, there was no room for half-measures. "Were you exonerated? I mean, you said you didn't know."

"Yeah, great. I launched weapons of mass destruction at a civilian population *accidentally*. I think that makes it worse."

"Well, I'd rather be incompetent than a monster, wouldn't you?"

He shrugged resignedly. "Even the Daltari tribunal conceded that point after they finally got their independence, after Kra'al came to power and most of the colonists were removed or bolted. After they had tried and executed the other Daltari who had supported the occupation. I don't blame them for that, but I wouldn't exactly call it the dawn of a golden age."

Rachel kicked at a loose rock, and it rolled toward the edge of the plateau and tumbled over. Leon watched it go. "I lost so many friends there, and for what? Brick Stern, Kal Navez, Andrea Brody, that kid Tristan...." Leon's fist clenched as he stopped himself from reaching for the engraved IORSIRAD switchblade in his pocket, a commemoration he no longer deserved.

"You're glad they didn't live to see you do it." Rachel said it bluntly, a statement rather than a question.

"Maybe. Even the ones who survived might as well be dead to me. Hell, I'm sure they think I should have died there, too. Afterwards, no one would touch me. Hakar *tried* to help: he actually arrived in the Daltar system after another Coalition relief fleet. He intimidated them into turning me over to his custody, but the administration sent some Falcon Regulators to reclaim me and gagged Hakar before he could sink his own career. Uncle Franz and his cabinet still thought that if he hung it all around my neck they could protect themselves, so they pulled out all the stops: they stripped me of my rank in front of cameras, broke my officer's saber. It wasn't enough to deflect the investigation into his involvement or stop the backlash. When the Ministry of Justice demanded that I be put on public trial instead of a quiet court martial behind closed doors, the cabinet was afraid of what I might say under oath. The way it was supposed to happen, they could have passed me off as a rogue psychopath out to rack up a body count and lock me away.

"With the nukes involved, everything went under the microscope. I might have executed the MoIA translators and PDF officers who set the damn thing up, but when my second in command relieved me she kept them on ice. They caved and testified, and the CRDF Regulators found out about Heron's actions and his messages back and forth to the emperor. When the investigative commission came back and corroborated my version of events, the noose tightened, and they knew they couldn't throw me under the wheels without some of the blame spilling on them." A bitter smile tugged at the corners of Leon's mouth. "What they never knew was that I probably would have kept their secrets if they had ordered me to. I was an obedient little war criminal." He was no longer so naïve, but the cost of that lesson was tragically, absurdly high.

In response to the disaster, the Coalition Articles of War were rewritten, and the grand fleets were ordered to recall their special operations detachments for judiciary review. The units that had acted autonomously for so long, without oversight or accountability, finally came under scrutiny. Many were disbanded or reorganized, but no more courts-martial were convened.

"They offered me amnesty and exile in exchange for keeping my mouth shut about Heron and the colonial authority atrocities. I got off light, and by the time they realized that letting me go wasn't going to save them, I was already in the Shar'dan, replacing my blood with alcohol. They couldn't extradite me to testify and save them, so Telemon and everyone else who wanted a massacre got the spotlight turned on them instead.

"The final nail in the coffin was a letter from one of the emperor's senior advisors to one of the Star Chamber admirals. It quoted Telemon saying something like 'Let nature take its course. Evolution and the Coalition are done with them.' I don't remember all the details of the plan, but you have to understand that the Daltari were vulnerable to bacteria that are endemic to Humans, Tageans, and Sheff'an after centuries of comingling. They needed monthly doses of antibiotics that could only be manufactured off-world, or they got these horrible infections in their joints that eventually led to organ failure. I doubt it was Telemon's idea, but he apparently signed off on a plan to distribute placebo antibiotics to the Daltari and let them succumb. Somehow the bastard was offered clemency for stepping down, and he's probably living out his life in some nice manse somewhere in the Shar'dan himself." The bitter smile returned. "The defense Hakar used to keep me away from a firing squad was that you don't punish the attack dog that follows its master's orders."

"You shoot it," Rachel blurted out.

Leon laughed hollowly. "That's exactly what I thought. The fact was they thought of me as a weapon. I killed what I was aimed at, and I did as I was bid." The smile shattered. "How could they not punish me? I've passed judgment on so many people less guilty than I am, and yet I go on. Why?" He looked into Rachel's eyes and saw uncertainty staring back at him. "I never thought about killing myself. I chose order. I do have a moral compass."

"I know, Leon, and I know you try to be a good man, but sometimes there's a difference between trying and actually being one. Your compass doesn't always point in one direction. The needle moves, especially when there's a lot of money involved, and you've made a fortune doing … *this*. A *good* man would stop killing."

Leon said nothing.

"You're just willing to take that guilt on your conscience? You're willing to do terrible things to stop terrible people? How does that math work?"

Leon stopped to think. He wasn't actually sure. He cleared his throat. "I'm not weighing karma or the effect my actions will have on my immortal soul, if that's what you're asking. When I see rabid attack dogs hurting people, I don't feel bad for putting them down."

The look Rachel was giving him was hard to read, but it seemed to be a mixture of revulsion and ... something else. Pity, maybe? He would settle for pity. "Why don't you tell people? If more people knew...."

"I can't," Leon said. "I told you, I swore an oath. It's the one thing I've got left. Years back, some people from a bipartisan veterans' reconciliation group came to see me, to ask if I would come to Daltar and speak at some memorial dedication. I actually thought they were assassins at first." He laughed humorlessly. "I couldn't even tell them why I wouldn't speak to them. Besides, it's not like my side of the story really exonerates me."

"But you're out, and Telemon's going to be imprisoned on his little world until the stars burn out. You don't owe him anything."

"It's not him," Leon said dismissively. "I was finished, and so was he, but there were people I served with who would have been ruined, like Hakar. He was a good man, and the Coalition needed good people, especially then. I made a choice when I stayed silent. It had to stop with me. It wasn't about my own personal sense of justice. It was the only good thing I could make of that whole catastrophe."

A long moment of silence passed between them, with only the wind whispering between them. "I realize I sound like I'm trying to put the blame on other people. I'm not. I gave the orders, and I was so arrogant I was blind to the facts on the ground. It's almost funny, I was never naïve enough to think that it was always about good versus bad, and I even recognized that in IORSIRAD I would have to do things that called that into question, that challenged my morality. Still, I *did* think I was smart enough to always know where I stood in relation to that line, and that at least I would be able to make an informed decision. It happened so gradually, so insidiously, and I wound up on the wrong side of history because I wasn't paying attention."

"That's when you became the Mourning Star."

"Essentially. When I went into the Shar'dan, I was in a dark place. I was questioning everything I ever believed in, from the sojieri I had trusted to the politicians I had served, to my own basic decency. It's not like I thought Telemon was fundamentally a good man, but I thought the checks and balances were enough, and to have the whole system turned upside down basically wrecked my whole worldview.

"They labeled me a monster, and I guess I played to type. If the elected officials of the Coalition could misuse sojieri so badly, what was the point in trying to be discerning? I was good at war, so I just kept doing it. I took jobs from some pretty unpleasant people, at the start. The kind of people who saw my reputation and my actions as something to be harnessed. I let the lines get real blurry. Believe it or not, when I met Raptor and Jeric on Kai Lun, we basically saved each other. They reminded me what it meant to fight *for* something."

"I believe it. About Raptor, at least." Rachel was quiet for a long time. "I don't know what to say, Leon. I know what it took for you to tell me this, but I need time to think."

Leon's rueful half-smile twitched, struggling to gain a foothold on his face before it was routed again. "Take all the time you need. If Eve is in danger, I don't want you anywhere near this hellstorm when it breaks."

"What are you saying?" Rachel leaned away, looking betrayed. "You want me off Eve? And where am I supposed to go, exactly?"

"You don't want to go home?"

She crossed her arms. "When are you going to get it through your thick skull? This *is* my home now. With you, for better or worse."

Leon drew a deep breath, stunned by her statement. He had not expected such a vote of confidence after the things he had told her. He struggled to maintain his composure as he said, "You could go to Terra. My sisters would be honored. If you don't mind helping with wedding preparations, that is."

"I'll think about it," Rachel said. "I don't want to leave you." Her mouth set in a grim line as she thought, and Leon waited, giving her a moment. Finally she looked him in the eye and said, "Well, what does all this mean for you?" She put her elbows on her knees and rested her chin on her palms, staring into space. "Heidi told me you're the president of the corporation now."

"Acting president," Leon clarified.

"I know the idea of settling down is abstract for you, Leon, but at some point it won't be. What if we had a child? Would you really want me dealing with that alone?"

Leon's brow knitted in thought.

"Have you never considered that? You've had other girlfriends, surely that's come up."

"They've been in this line of work, or else they haven't stuck around long enough for it to come up," Leon said uneasily. He wondered if she knew her words carried a dangerous weight.

"So? What does that mean for us? You're never going to kill your way to redemption, you must see that. Retire."

"I don't like ultimatums, Rachel," Leon began, holding up his hands so she would withhold her objections. "You're right, though. You're always right. I think it's time to move on. This morning proved to me that no matter what I do and how much I want it, the Coalition will never have me back, and Rockmore can't give me what I want, no matter how much he wants to." Verbalizing what he had been thinking was painful, but it felt like a valve had been opened somewhere to let off excess pressure. "I'll resign my field commission, but it will have to be after things settle down."

"When is that?"

"Rockmore and Akida are both going into the field. Liam Dawson and Belladonna Kir will take over for me, but that transition will take time. You know I can't just leave them, Rachel, especially not at a time like this."

"I understand, Leon. I really do." Was that relief in Rachel's voice? He could hardly blame her: she had spent the better part of their relationship trying to save him from himself. "I know this has been a huge chapter in your life, and you can't just walk away. I know you don't work like that. The fact that you care enough to stay on and help them after being frozen out is one of the reasons I love you. You're not just thinking of yourself, and I don't think you ever have."

She took a deep breath and brushed away a tear that was threatening to spill down her cheek. "I wonder if you're even doing this for yourself or just for me. But … if you're doing it for me, I hope someday you decide it's what you want, too."

"It is what I want," Leon said firmly.

"In that case … I have something to tell you," Rachel said. Her hand drifted to her belly, and Leon's mind began to race. Was she pregnant? Was he going to be a father?

But she only smoothed her shirt and wrung her hands. "I've known the truth about Daltar for a while."

It was like being punched in the throat. Leon couldn't breathe, couldn't think. "How long have—"

"Months."

Suddenly it all made sense, in a way. He felt claustrophobic despite the wide-open landscape and the cool wind. She had been remarkably calm while he told her about the events on Daltar. "Is that why you left?" he gasped. "I don't—"

"It is why I left. I came back to get your side of the story."

"I don't understand," Leon said, frowning. "You let me lie to you for months and dodge the issue. Why didn't you say something?"

"It had to be on your terms, Leon. If I demanded it, you might have reacted defensively, tried to gloss over details, even lied. You would have hated me for it, and I might have hated you more."

"No, I—"

She held up a hand. "Yes, Leon, but I believe everything you told me. And no, it doesn't make your actions any less terrible. But I understand them now. When I went back to Amalthia I couldn't stop trying to reconcile the man I know with the monster I read about. The road to hell really is paved with good intentions."

"I still don't get it. What made you decide to look into it?" As far as he knew, Rachel had never dug into his past before, though it must have pained her, especially considering how easy it would be to do. Leon had assumed it was because she knew ignorance was bliss and didn't want to dispel the illusion. She had found out, though, and had kept her knowledge from him. Because she wanted it from his lips, he reminded himself. Still, her deception threw his own back at him, amplified a hundredfold.

"I didn't look into it, Leon. I knew you would eventually need to tell me what your deal was, because deep down you're a decent, honest person." She snorted a bitter laugh. "Believe it or not, finding out the way I did, going away, gave me time to prepare myself."

"Then how?" Heidi's words came back to him, suddenly relevant. *It's between you and Rachel. Evidently someone else around here feels differently.* "Someone sent it to you. Your mother?"

"I thought so, but she swears she had nothing to do with it. She wanted me to learn my lesson the hard way, I guess. Charming, I know." Rachel pointed back toward the apartments. "This morning I found a mem slipped under the door with the article about Korinthe. It happened once before. It was morning, and you were at a meeting in the city. There was a knock at the door and an envelope on the step. I packed my bags and tricked one of the off-duty guards into taking me to the cosmodrome without telling you. I reread that article a hundred times. It didn't have many details, just enough to make me wish you were dead." She looked sorry for saying that, but Leon couldn't fault her honesty.

"After I got home, I dug up everything I could. It was all I could think about." Her voice was manic, her eyes almost wild. "I was obsessed. I hated you, Leon. I thought I was going to need therapy. It was like I had just escaped a kidnapper. I read and read, watched old news reports from the Coalition, Commonwealth, even the Valinata. Some of them painted you as a madman, others just made you sound incompetent."

Leon was about to object, but Rachel gave him a look that stopped the words in his throat. "I know you, and I know that's not who you are. So I started to think, if they were wrong about those details, what else might they be wrong about? I love you, and I thought you deserved a chance to explain it to me."

Leon cringed. That was what he had done to her. He had brought her to Eve under false pretenses, gotten her to fall in love under a blanket of lies. Did she still feel that way about him? He had managed to delude himself, believing that not telling her somehow absolved him of guilt, that what she didn't know wouldn't hurt her and couldn't hurt him. It had been childish self-deception. So who had done this to him? Who among his comrades hated him so much they would try to sabotage him this way, not once but twice? Why did so many names come to mind?

"What does it matter? I love you, and I know you. More than that, I trust you. We have our work cut out for us, but that's a good starting point. Don't be afraid of the truth."

"Who was it?"

"I don't know, Leon, I swear. I never tried to find out. What good would it do? Obviously, whoever it was didn't want any credit, they just wanted us apart."

Leon rose from the bench as he put the pieces together in his mind. Someone had tried to ruin the best thing in his life, and the way they went about it was so underhanded and vicious…. There were many cunning minds in the Pack, but he could think of only one who would lie in wait and conduct such a surgical, psychological strike.

"Leon, what's the point? Don't do this!" Rachel exclaimed as Leon started back toward the compound. There was fear in her voice. Did she think he was going to kill someone? "The point is, they were wrong about you. That's why I came back. Don't prove *me* wrong."

"Are you coming or staying?" Leon asked over his shoulder without breaking stride. He spoke into his comm. "I'm looking for Colonel Akida." His eyes narrowed at the response, and he changed direction. *Convenient*. He reached the officers' apartments, stalking across the courtyard to a dwelling much like his own.

Rachel hurried after him, begging him to stop, to turn back. His stomach was coiled with rage, and he couldn't meet her imploring gaze. Reaching Akida's door, he hammered on it with his fist again and again.

When Akida opened it, he was clad only in a towel, his hair wet. His eyes narrowed when he saw Leon. "What is it? Is everything all right? I just stopped in for a shower."

"You motherfucker," Leon spat. "Are you really so miserable that you have to try and fuck up my life for sport?"

"No," Akida said simply. His eyes searched Leon, and they gradually moved to Rachel, standing behind him. "What are you talking about?"

"You can cut the bullshit. I know you slipped Rachel an article about Daltar to scare her off. And when it didn't work, you decided to try again with Keegan on Korinthe. Did you fail to read them yourself when you decided to fuck with me? Didn't you notice what they said about me?"

"Leon!" Rachel exclaimed. "Stop it!"

"Was that a threat, Victor?" Akida asked snidely. He crossed his arms and leaned against the doorframe. "I'm going to let you keep making a fool of yourself on my doorstep because maybe if you continue to marginalize yourself we can get this organization back on track." He narrowed his eyes. "Are you so arrogant you think I would concoct some elaborate scheme to hurt your feelings just because I don't like you? Believe it or not, I have better things to do, like keeping my battalions under control. It seems to me that you are on the verge of retirement, which is perfectly fine with me. Why would I want to screw up the relationship that's slowly pulling you away from the Pack?"

"Why wouldn't you?"

"Because interfering in your love life does not interest me. Your little universe is not my business, it's not my place ... and it's not my problem. So fuck off." Akida straightened up, and his eyes went cold, blank. "People like us can't have conventional relationships."

"You can't have conventional relationships because you're an asshole."

"I'm glad you can think clearly enough to insult me. Are you sure you're not the asshole here, Victor?" Akida cracked his neck. He was putting on a good show of acting casual, but Leon's mind was clearing, and he realized he had hurt the man. "Look, I'm sorry that you've got a bad case of survivor's guilt mixed with your malignant hero syndrome, but somehow you've found the one woman in the galaxy who can stand you despite that. I'd spend more time focusing on that part." He stepped back and made to shut the door.

"Wait," Leon said urgently. "I ... I'm sorry I flew off the handle. Do you have any idea who did this?" It couldn't be said of Akida that he didn't keep himself well informed. Leon suspected he spied on everyone in the Pack to keep in practice.

Akida paused. "Like I said, it's not my problem. You're a smart man, Victor, despite the way you act. If I were you, I'd spend a little more time getting my house in order and less looking for enemies outside of it. Now I'm going to get dressed so I can go to Tesa to deal with an actual crisis." Akida shut the door, leaving Leon standing there looking at his nameplate. Rachel was still behind him, but she said nothing. Wordlessly they turned around and walked to their apartment. Maybe Akida was right. Maybe he shouldn't focus on the fact that someone was out to undermine him and spoil his relationship but on the fact that Rachel was sticking with him despite that. He reached out blindly and took her hand, giving it a squeeze. She squeezed back.

10: Outbound

In the space over Tagea, the expeditionary force was awake, stretching like a predator awaking in its den. From the bridge of his command ship, *Condor*, Grand Admiral Hakar watched the fleets converging. His huge Empress Kalex-class cruiser dominated the formation, two and a half kilometers from her circular bank of primary engines at the stern to her hawk's beak of a bow. She was a two-hundred-gun flagship, designed to be a self-sufficient fighting force. A full dozen of her guns were nuclear dispersion cannons capable of annihilating an army on the ground or another ship in a single broadside. Her decks housed battalions of marines and in her hangars roosted an entire combat aerospace wing. Crewed by a force large enough to populate a small town, she was rivaled in size only by the prodigious troop carriers housing the infantry and vehicles of CRAG, the Coalition Royal Army Ground.

Circling Tagea now were the ships of the Second, Twelfth, and Thirty-second Grand Fleets, tracing their history all the way back to the once-proud Seventh Royal Line. Second Fleet spilled across thousands of cubic kilometers of space, a glittering horde. But for all that, the fleet was not as grand as it had once been, hardly as regal. Long ago it had been the spearhead of the royal battle line of the Tagean Dominion, but now it was only one of dozens of enormous armadas grinding space between the stars. Centuries and budget cuts had reduced the line from thousands of battleships to mere hundreds. At least, it was easier to keep track of everyone.

The Twelfth and Thirty-second fleets, under Vice-Grand Admiral Shra and Vice-Grand Admiral Shekint Veraxus, respectively, were approaching from port, cruising slowly around the horizon of Tagea. Made up of medium assault ships, fighter carriers, and heavy missile platforms, Shra's fleet was the ideal fast-attack force, designed for deep incursions and hard strikes. It was that fleet that would set up shop at the mouth of the Alkyra, in the Ilieth system. Shra's flagship, *Antares*, a swift and maneuverable vessel despite her ungainly, slightly chunky design, led the smaller armada. Stretching out in a ragged cloud, Veraxus's troop carriers and heavy destroyers passed by on their own trajectory. Beneath the mating flotillas, cities glittered like gems set into the surface of the Tagean throneworld, peaceful, sleeping.

As Veraxus's and Shra's fleets made for open space and the major conduits that would take them to the Outbound Arc, Second Fleet's ships slowly and systematically fell into place behind *Condor*. Soon a long conical formation of ships stretched astern, battleships and destroyers along the flanks, the more vulnerable carriers and tenders protected within. The ships came about in perfect synchronization, their flight computers linked, pointing their bows toward the first of their stops on the way to the Outbound Arc. It was a multileg journey, one which required absolute precision to bring so many ships to the right place at the right time.

The officer of the deck approached, waiting uneasily while Hakar's bodyguards frisked him. Hakar didn't show it, but it made him nearly as uncomfortable. He was used to having an aide at his side, but tensions were running high since the assassinations, and all flag officers had been assigned a permanent security detail.

Clearing his throat, the deck officer tried valiantly to appear unruffled. "Admiral Hakar, I've been notified that Commander Metha and his unit have boarded."

Hakar nodded approvingly. "That's everyone, then." He was eager to see Jow Metha again. He felt a little regretful that he was pulling the commander and his vanguard units off one patrol only to throw them into a warzone.

Hakar turned to Commodore François Tarot, commander of the *Condor*. "Commodore, everything running as expected?"

The aging Human officer nodded curtly, his bald head shining in the bright lights of the bridge. Tarot had served under Hakar for years, and he was too much of a professional to show any bitterness at being reduced to second fiddle, but it couldn't have been easy. "Yes, Admiral. We had trouble with capacity when the navigational computers linked, but it's all been smoothed out." He had been hunched over the chief tactical officer's screen, but he straightened up now. "I'm still not confident in the new sensor calibrations. They feel rushed. And linking the ships' arrays could backfire."

"Plenty of time to fine-tune them once we establish ourselves in the D'zen Gulf." Hakar forced a benign smile. The upgrades *had* been rushed. Still, while François Tarot was a renowned officer, he was a Luddite at heart and his distrust of Special Projects was legendary. If he had had his way, they all would have returned to the ancient days of navigating by the stars. That didn't make Tarot any less right: until Special Projects had more data and could produce actual prototypes, all the alterations had been made based on pure guesswork and what little information had been gleaned from the so far disastrous encounters with Raven Blue. They might be good enough to improve scanning resolution ... or they might make matters worse. Until first contact, they could only speculate. All ships in the fleet would have their sensor systems linked into a soft array in the hope that while a single ship could only chase intermittent ghost contacts, multiple ships working in concert could triangulate the enemy more reliably.

The ships' navigation systems were likewise linked, at least for the transitions to the gravity conduits. Computer autoplotting ensured orderly and collision-free entry and exit: History was littered with tales of formidable fleets reduced to crumpled wrecks when reversions went wrong.

Because the ships could not enter conduits while in close proximity to sizeable gravity fields such as those generated by planets or stars, they made for open space above the solar plane. It took hours before Veraxus's fleet jumped, vanishing in a series of flashes. Shra's fleet was not far behind. Once Second Fleet had gone far enough, an announcement was made, alerting all hands. The officers took their seats and strapped in. The myriad sounds of a ship under full steam were drowned out by the scream of the gravdrive as it sucked enough power to create an envelope of gravitational energy around *Condor*. There was a flash of stars shifting, and the ship jerked, wrenching Hakar in his seat and sending a forgotten drink thermos to crash against the aft bulkhead. The stars stretched into streaks of white light and then disappeared, hidden by the purple maelstrom of the conduit. A low roar like flooding water could be heard beyond the bulkheads.

Hakar lost himself in the indigo vortex as he always did, mesmerized. Purple had been chosen as the Coalition color to symbolize the joining of so many worlds by these mysterious gaps in reality. The conduits were the gravitic bridges between cosmic bodies, vital to transit and communications. When they were first discovered, the conduits were perceived as nothing but wormholes, but scientists had made startling discoveries when attempting to transmit through them. More than simply holes in reality through which matter could drain, they were essential to the structure and motion of the galaxy. Between two given celestial bodies, the channels were tight, focused, channeling energy and gravitically enveloped matter. As they neared their endpoints, however, the flow weakened and slowed, the result of gravitational baffling caused by the other moving bodies in proximity to the star, including its planets. There the conduits destabilized, widening like river deltas, and matter and energy spilled out. Skilled flight crews could maintain the gravitational envelope long enough to penetrate deep into a system. A fundamental shift in understanding had come when it was discovered that energy flowed through the conduits, energy found nowhere else in existence, superluminal particles and waves that proved the age-old theories of faster-than-light tachyons. Twinned masses laced with these tachyon-like particles, when activated in resonance, could trigger whiplashes of energy through conduits, allowing for the transmission of coherent data. More than just wormholes, the conduits were arteries of energy that maintained the galaxy's interdependent fractal structure, the so-called sacred geometry of the stars.

Trying to comprehend these concepts could drive a mind to distraction, but that was just what Hakar needed. He had always known impatience when he had a job to do, and this mission was no different; his stomach was doing flips, though he knew part of it was the reduced gravity. The deck of *Condor*, like the deck of any modern ship, was laced with particularly dense masses which generated localized gravitational fields when subjected to a current. Known as Rombaldt Radiant Masses, in sufficient concentration these fragments of matter could generate nearly normal gravity based on the Terran/Tagean standard. They drew substantial power, however, and when in conduit most ships reduced the currents to maintain a tolerable fifty percent field. That was part of it, he knew, but he also knew himself well enough to recognize the familiar charge of excitement. It had been a long time since he had been on active duty.

With the Fifth Fleet pulverized, the Outbound Arc was up for grabs. Since the last battered survivors of the Talriis massacre had limped back into friendly space behind the cover of Admirals Daris and Najo, Raven Blue had made no move to invade further. It was as though the enemy was daring them to retaliate. And retaliate they would, to what end Hakar did not know. With a sigh, he turned to Tarot. "I'd forgotten how true the cliché is. Waiting is the hardest part."

The commodore favored him with a tight-lipped smile. "It's going to be a long wait, Admiral." The smile faded. "Not long enough, though."

The whole journey would take a little less than two weeks, the first leg traveling along the super-conduit known as the Crown Road. From there they would transfer to the Yangtze Tradeway and then to the final stretch along the Tears of Alkyra itself. Twenty days from the throneworld to the contested edge of their kingdom.

Hakar would hold *Condor*'s crew to that schedule. They were skilled, among the best in the Coalition Royal Navy. The officers and enlisted who served throughout the rest of the fleet were well trained, drilled, and prepared. Drilling and training were not the same as winning or surviving. He trusted in all of them, would have to. Other men and women would deal with the details of this war: as a grand admiral, Hakar was expected to advise and observe, commanding from on high. He was notoriously disobedient in that regard, but still he understood that the tactical decisions would be made by his subordinates. Commodore Tarot commanded the naval forces, while General Arkady Romanov, a Zoh Hegemony-born Coalition Royal Army Ground officer of high regard, oversaw the ground troops. Romanov was aboard his own carrier, tending to his tanks. Hakar's responsibility was grand strategy, hence the "grand" in his rank. He was expected to command an entire theater of operations, tending the menagerie to plot the outcome of a campaign that would dwarf any planetary war.

Deep down, Hakar supposed that he had never been fully tested in that arena. In his lifetime there had been only a handful of wars, the majority involving a few worlds or a sector. This … this was something different, something apocalyptic. Four grand admirals were storming the Arc: Daris and Najo were fortifying the region around the Calama conduits while Winters rushed into the Amanra Crescent to hold the Gates of the Arc. That made Hakar's fleets the first line of defense on any remaining likely attack route. *Have I forgotten Rodriguex? She was the first line of defense.*

Once Hakar's fleets secured the Alkyra, Romanov's CRAG forces, composed of two full armies accompanied by armor and artillery support, would begin the process of turning each world into a citadel. Knowing that others would be in direct control of his fleets, Hakar felt bereft of his command already. He had to make do and yet, with all this weighing on him, he felt a small sense of triumph: to be back among the stars, to make good his escape from behind a desk. All it had taken was a war.

§

Jeric sipped at the cold beer quietly. The Desher Vaux was unusually empty. He was still hung over from the night before, but only one thing silenced the screams in his head, screams that would escape the cage of his teeth if he didn't plug it with a bottle. After all, he had discovered that the best cure for a hangover was simply to keep right on drinking.

"What's the matter with you?" growled Raptor, falling wearily into the seat across from the pilot. "Quit drinking or no doctor will be able to salvage that liver. I swear by the Goddess Above that you Humans are the stupidest fucking species in this universe."

"We're going into action, and the booze is going to be hard to come by. Besides, Leon isn't going to be around to make me behave," he said bitterly.

"Leon's got his own problems. Belladonna's in charge now. She's never going to clear you for duty if she sees you this drunk. Is that what you want? To be sidelined like Leon?"

Jeric put the bottle down. It missed the coaster and hit the scuffed tabletop with a loud *thunk*. "What armchair psychology book have you been reading? This wasn't what I had in mind when I wanted Leon to get a taste of his own medicine." Raptor frowned, annoyed, and Jeric tipped the bottle toward him in a gesture of concession.

The Prross grabbed the bottle away from Jeric and chugged the remainder of the dark ale. He slammed the empty bottle down on the table, almost hard enough to break it.

"Look, Raptor, that was *my* beer, I wasn't offering it to you. More importantly, I just think it's a bad time for the Pack to take anything on faith, even from the CRDF. And I think Leon picked a bad time to give his notice. People here rely on him, and not just us."

"You are aware it wasn't all his decision, right? He would be right there with us if he could be."

"I know it's his decision to abandon us for Rachel."

"You throw the word 'abandon' in there like you have some serious childhood issues. But who's the one who packed up and left the farm as soon as he could? You are. And as far as I know, you've never been back."

"I send my family money. That's all they actually want," Jeric said resentfully.

"That is as sad a statement as I've ever heard." Raptor gestured for two more beers, and Mara brought them over. The Prross raised his glass in salute. "To your family." He guzzled half the bottle.

Jeric's mouth twitched in an angry spasm, but he drank, too.

Raptor's dorsal spines rose and fell, pressing against the lining of his jacket. "Do you remember Lieutenant Kreuz?"

"The guy with the shoe fetish?"

Raptor hesitated, frowning. "You remember the strangest things."

Jeric sipped his beer. "The man had, like, seventy-five pairs of shoes. I'm supposed to forget that? Rockmore gave them all away when he died."

"Fine, whatever. He was burned out after those fights on Polis, and his heart wasn't in it, but he went into the field anyway. He didn't take Dyran's offer to go in his place, and he didn't look at the intel Heidi gave him on the raiders. So when his people stumbled into the first ambush point, he froze up, and when he should have pulled back, he tried to push through. One distracted jackass gets killed, fine, he had it coming. Kreuz got his whole squad wiped out because he didn't know when enough was enough."

"A good officer should be able to separate his feelings from the situation."

"Officers are still people, Jeric. Even Leon. He cares a lot; part of the reason he's such a good field commander is because he takes everything personally."

"Yeah, and it's the reason why he's such a mess, too."

"I admit it's a two-edged sword, and that's exactly my point: he shouldn't be in charge if he can't focus. He's been here most of a decade. Maybe it's time to move on."

"Is that what you think happened on Korinthe? He couldn't focus?" Jeric had not been on the mission, but their friend Buzz Parker had died in a hotel room, drowning in his own blood because Leon had been stubborn and tired. No, that was unfair. Jeric had forced himself to sit through some of the footage from the helmet cameras; Buzz had been stubborn and tired, too, and he had been careless.

Raptor did not answer right away. "It's a moot point anyway: General Rockmore makes the decisions, and he made this one."

"You mean Traxus's brother makes the decisions, and Rockmore tells us what they are."

"In this case, yes." Raptor sat back, his claws tapping a rhythm against the side of the beer bottle. "I love Leon like a brother, but *he* is *not* Jackal Pack. We'll stay, and we'll do our jobs."

Akida entered the pub and saw them. The sunlight coming in through the north-facing doorway was proof that it was too early to be in there. Somehow he managed to look totally at ease, even now, with the base a hurricane around him and the galaxy hurtling toward war.

"I'm surprised you two aren't with Victor," he said under his breath.

The two looked up, expressions guarded. "He's got his hands full," answered Raptor carefully.

"I'm glad the two of you are coming with us." Akida paused. "For the record, I wish he were, too." That was probably very hard for him to admit. "It's too bad someone's fucking with him at a time like this." He turned away, gathered the officers he was looking for, and led them out without another look at Jeric or Raptor.

The two turned to each other, eyes wide with surprise. "Well, how about that shit?" asked Jeric, stunned. "If I didn't know better, I'd say he was going to miss Leon."

"Don't kid yourself. Everything he just did was perfectly calculated." Raptor was frowning. "And what did he mean about someone fucking with Leon?"

Jeric's eyes were now following the tapping of Raptor's claws. "I think everyone's a little wound up over this. It doesn't help that we don't know who we'll be fighting or for how long. He probably meant the whole getting left behind thing."

Raptor stood up; Jeric got unsteadily to his feet, too. "Maybe. By the way, thanks for the beer."

"Fine, fine." The pilot fumbled in his pocket and tossed some cash on the table. Brent and Mara were no longer serving on credit since they didn't know who would be coming back alive to settle up. "Shall we?"

"Yeah. We don't want to be late for the war."

§

"I'm sure this won't last long," Leon said unconvincingly. "Maybe a couple of months at the most. Coalition High Command is probably overreacting." He knew it sounded hollow, but he had to put on a brave face. He doubted the CRDF was jumping at shadows, and even if they were, sometimes the shadows jumped back. If this Raven Blue had demolished an entire CRDF battle fleet, not to mention the Valinata Space Force, then they were nothing to be trifled with. He had *seen* Aethaleia, *smelled* the death as he walked through a graveyard masquerading as a city.

"I can't just wait on Terra forever," Rachel declared, squeezing Leon's hand. Her voice was authoritative. "It's not like I can just go home this time, either. When I told them I was coming back here, to you...." Had her relationship with him strained her family ties that much? Leon felt ashamed. "I'd rather stay here, with you. I may not be a sojier, Leon, but I love you, and if you're in the line of fire, that's where I want to be, too. You wouldn't leave me, would you? How can I do the same?"

Leon understood, and that sentiment was nearly enough to undo his resolve. "It's not that simple. I can't just let you—"

"You can't *let* me?" The determination in her voice gave Leon pause. "I'm not one of your sojieri, Leon."

"You know I would never give you an order, Rachel, but I can't be worrying about your safety the whole time. I have work to do, and it isn't like before."

"Don't buy into your own legend, Leon. You're not invincible."

"Don't think about that." Leon's mind drifted to the day he had stepped off the shuttle on Triatha to begin college. He had been so excited to be somewhere new, meet people whose topics of conversation went beyond Terran renovation and shared poverty. Naturally that excitement had turned to homesickness, and being light-years from home was far more trying than he had expected. His parents had been unable to afford realtime ansible calls to speak to him, let alone visit or book a flight home for him. In nearly four years he only set foot on Terra twice, and the second occasion had been the funeral. He had never even received his diploma. He felt almost as isolated now. *I don't want Rachel to go, but what choice do I have?* "Listen, honey, I know I'm not invincible. I'm not even going to war right now. And if I was, you still can't dwell on all the possibilities, even the probabilities, of failure. If you do that, you've lost before you begin. I have to stay positive, and you should, too."

"You think I haven't been paying attention to what's going on? The Valinata is gone, Leon. Gone. Billions of people vanished. Their navy, their army, smashed without anyone knowing. And so what if it took a year? A day, a week, a year, a decade...." Rachel's sadness was turning to anger. "I'm savvy enough to see that a force that could do that will go through the Alkyra and Jackal Pack like they weren't even there."

"Oh, they'll know we're here," Leon said, but he knew she was right. Some fundamental piece of machinery inside him had broken, was running in reverse. The thrill had vanished, replaced with a deep longing for quiet, for her. If he never saw another dead body again, it would be too soon. He didn't get to articulate any of this, though; his comm beeped, and he was almost grateful for the interruption so he could gather his thoughts.

"Leon, it's Rockmore." Leon frowned, so much left unsaid, and he could see that Rachel took it as procrastination. But something in Rockmore's leaden voice indicated that he would do well to pay attention.

"Go ahead, sir."

"One of our Shar'dan backers just pulled out: Trank Holdings."

"Did they give a reason?" Leon asked glumly. It was hardly a surprise; they had been expecting some level of fallout from their investors, at least initially. After all, who wanted to put their money in an organization that was likely to get pulverized shortly?

"They cited financial stability as a key factor. It's not all bad, though: applications are up."

"We've got a lot of morons eager to get killed. Any with military background?"

"Quite a few reservists from the UCA and even some Aradon Dominion guards who don't want to sit on the sidelines. I'm forwarding them all to you and Heidi. I want fast turnaround."

"You got it. Thanks for the update, sir." Rockmore hung up, and Leon turned back to Rachel. He could see she wasn't done.

Leon found himself feeling unimaginably small in the face of the situation. Eve was just one tiny planet in a sector on the verge of becoming a war zone. With that feeling came the realization that the company of troops he was being left with would be useless in the face of any serious offense. The Coalition Regional Base had a garrison, but Leon didn't know their full capabilities; in any case, he doubted they would make much of a difference.

Rachel sensed his unease. "Well?"

"You trust me?"

Rachel hesitated. "I do," she said guardedly.

"Then trust me. I want you off this planet as soon as possible. I'm going to see about getting you a ticket, all right? Please, no more argument. Passage off-world might suddenly be at a premium. Anyone with common sense is going to run."

Leon was grateful when Rachel nodded acquiescence. "Okay, Leon, okay. Are *you* all right?"

He tried to say yes, but the word caught in his throat. If a fight came to Eve, they would be outnumbered and outgunned.

"Leon? Give me something." Rachel put her hand on his arm.

"You're right, Rachel. You're absolutely right. About all of it. And if this godforsaken war could have waited a couple of months, it might not have been our problem. But you know I can't just run, right? Not now."

"I know, Leon." There was something hard and flinty in Rachel's eyes, but she understood duty and loyalty. "This isn't just you being melodramatic. They need you right now. Just don't forget that I need you, too." She withdrew her hand, frowning. "Don't take this the wrong way, but Jackal Pack *can* replace you if you die. I can't."

Somehow, that actually made Leon feel better. "Raptor says everything changes, but I'm watching the same mistakes piling up, just on a larger scale."

"Not your mistakes this time," Rachel said encouragingly.

"No...."

"I'll tell you something, Leon," she said suddenly and aggressively. "If I'm going to let you push me off-world, we're going to make the most of the time we have together."

"No arguments from me." He managed a smile.

11: Waking Giants

Time seemed to speed up as the date of Second Fleet's arrival loomed nearer, and then, seemingly without warning, it ran out. Only a day before Hakar's arrival, Leon found himself standing on the main parade ground, staring up at the sky and a little black smudge above the clouds. He knew that up close the *Star Wolf* looked almost factory-like, with boxy substations and towering gun emplacements, frighteningly utilitarian. But in low geostationary orbit she looked like a twinkling star, perhaps slightly larger than the others burning light-years away. In the light of day she was just a speck among the clouds. Leon shaded his eyes. He couldn't even see their other ships. "Our fleet isn't going to be enough."

Jeric grunted his agreement. Jackal Pack could deploy as many ships as a typical PDF, most of them light corvette-class cruisers. The troop carriers were much larger, and while they had never been filled to capacity, they were capable of carrying nearly all the legion's troops, armor, and fighter complements. However, their role was primarily intimidation, and aside from *Star Wolf,* few were capable of standing up to an actual naval attack force. The Fifth Battle Fleet had been such a fleet, and it had been crushed by this mysterious adversary. It was a sobering thought.

Nearby a pair of sojieri were running a crate toward the back of a truck, its engine idling, belching smoke. One stumbled in his haste, and they both went down. The case hit the ground but did not open. Their lieutenant rebuked them from the bed of the truck, voice hoarse, undoubtedly having spent the morning yelling. The men scrambled to pick up the case and load it. Leon and Jeric watched quietly. The excitement, anxiety, and sense of purpose were palpable all over the base as a steady line of trucks, loaded with equipment, made its way down the winding road that fed into Tesa's main highway system. Leon longed for that same sense of purpose, but he had to keep reminding himself that he had a role in all this and, more importantly, a goal beyond it.

"I still can't believe they're leaving you here, Vic," Jeric said after a few minutes.

Leon managed a smile. "It's okay, bud. I still don't believe it myself." He returned his gaze to the tiny spot that was all they could see of the enormous Jackal Pack cruiser, drifting far above them. "Rachel's leaving. I'll be alone here."

"It's all for the best," Jeric said, putting his hand on Leon's shoulder. "You all right with it?"

"I have to be," Leon said, shrugging. What was the point in fighting it? "At least, she'll be safer that way."

Out of his peripheral vision, Leon could see Jeric nodding. "That's a good way to look at it, man."

A young-looking Terran lieutenant with her hair shaved into a Mohawk approached from the direction of the main mess hall. Leon turned to her as she drew up and saluted. Her insignia identified her as being from Third Brigade. "Colonel, sir."

Leon returned the salute. "At ease, Lieutenant. What can I do for you?"

"Sir, we know you're busy, but we've got half the brigade packed in the mess, and … it would be an honor if you'd join us for lunch, to see us off."

"I appreciate that, Lieutenant Hansen. Of course, I can spare a few minutes for my troops." In truth, it was a major ego boost right when he needed it most. He followed her toward the mess hall. "Jeric, you coming?"

"I won't turn down free chow," the pilot said, strolling alongside him.

When they reached the doorway, Lieutenant Hansen whistled loudly. The roar of chairs and benches scraping against the floor was deafening as nearly three thousand sojieri got to their feet, raising glasses. Leon was greeted with toasts in dozens of languages. It was nearly enough to bring tears to his eyes. He smiled and accepted a drink from Mikaela Sommers, who was looking pale and thin, her own Mohawk grown shaggy. It was good to see her moving about, and Leon put his arm gently around her shoulders as he raised his own glass to the troops.

"Thanks, everyone," he shouted to be heard over the shifting sojieri. "This means a lot to me, and you all know how much I wish I was going out there with you. The hardest order I have ever had to follow is to wait here while my people go into battle without me. Watch each other's backs, take care of those CRDF punks, and always give better than you get. In spite of all!" There was a cheer throughout the hall, and the troops drank.

Leon watched them joking and guzzling beer and wondered how many of these faces he would ever see again.

He was reminded of something Rachel had said to him that morning. Naturally, it had come up in the course of an argument.

"What would you kill for?" she had asked him out of the blue while they ate breakfast. "If you weren't a mercenary or a sojier, I mean. What would it take to drive you to violence?"

His first instinct had been to laugh and evade the question with a joke that would only have irritated her. But Leon had learned when to take her seriously. She often had a point, even if she came around to it obliquely. He had put down his spoon, let his cereal get soggy while he thought. "I suppose I would kill for you," he said, dead serious. "If you were in danger."

She had nodded, accepting this. He couldn't say whether or not she believed it.

"What about you?" he had asked her, hoping her response would be at least somewhat in accordance with his own.

"That's just it, Leon. I don't think I could kill for anything. I know maybe that seems weird to you. It seems weird to me, too. But I honestly think that if I were faced with the choice of pulling a trigger or being killed myself, I couldn't do it. I couldn't take a life, not even one I thought deserved to be taken. I'm not wired that way."

Leon had forgotten all about his breakfast at that point. Once he had been exactly the same way, and part of him wished he had stayed that way, ignorant, at least, of his true capability, his capacity for murder. Better never to know the answer to such a question, certainly better not to have answered it so many times he had lost count. How could one lose count of such a tally? *Take a life*, as she had said. Some of those lives had deserved to be taken, Leon firmly believed. Even Rachel acknowledged the possibility that a person could deserve to die. But many of them had been people like himself, doing a job, possibly with families to go back to. Once, after a battle, he had found an enemy sojier's wallet, complete with cash and someone's business card. People carried the strangest things with them into a fight. Also in the wallet had been a family photo: a plain but kind-looking wife and three plump, smiling children, posing proudly for their uniformed husband and father. Leon couldn't have said whether there was a family resemblance because the man had been hit by an explosive round and was no longer recognizable. But surely he had deserved the chance to see those children again.

"I'm glad you're not wired that way," Leon had said, meaning every word of it. "Could you … ever forget what I've done?"

"No, but I can try to forgive it," she had answered, smiling.

"Come on, Colonel," Mikaela said, her voice thin and reedy. "The food isn't that bad." She limped toward a table. Leon realized he was still standing in the doorway. He laughed and followed her into the mess, sipping thoughtfully at his beer.

§

The mercenaries had eaten quickly and moved on to their other duties: with the Pack mobilizing its full strength for the first time, the cafeterias were working on overdrive. There was barely room to breathe and certainly no time to waste. Most people would have had difficulty eating before such a grand undertaking, but the Jackals forced their anxiety behind a mask of bravado, feasting heartily.

Part way through lunch, a call had come through from the arsenal, so Leon found himself walking alone down the dirt road leading from the main compound toward the armories. The repurposed hangar known as the Cradle loomed over the rest of the compound. It was left over from when Rockmore had first purchased the plateau and its resident fueling station. That hangar was Leon's destination, but his first stop was the quartermaster's depot. Considering that quartermasters and logistics officers were responsible for keeping the Pack's stores, ordnance, and supplies organized, the cluttered mess of their main office always came as a shock.

Captain Denny Rosenthal was cheerful despite the gel brace encircling his forearm. He seemed to relish life as a stacker as well as his duties as one of the Pack's armorers, never running short of good humor regardless of the time or weight of his workload. "How are you, Colonel?"

"Good, Rosie. How's the arm?"

Rosenthal looked down at the brace as if seeing it for the first time. "Much better, thanks. Tell Merikii there are no hard feelings. And remind me never to challenge him to an arm-wrestling match again."

Leon remembered the sickening snap and the way Rosie's eyes had gone wide, though he hadn't screamed. For Raptor, it had been near effortless. "Hey, I warned you. You probably should have just given him that chicken wing." Leon stepped back as two more armorers walked briskly past. "So, how is life under Major Craf?"

Rosenthal winked. The new brigade S-4, Major Craf, was very good at his job and was therefore a pain in everyone's ass. "So, what brings you to our neck of the woods, sir?"

"Apparently the Behemoth is acting up, but I figured I'd stop by you first and see about getting some ammo. Something for the TK-77. I need some penetrative power after the fight on Tikal. What'll punch through dragoon armor?"

"You *do* hunt big game. So does that mean you're deploying, after all? I bet you're excited to run with the CRDF again."

"Apparently the feeling's not mutual. You heard right: I'm staying here."

"So what's the ammunition for? You just like to make a statement? You know, Colonel, the base pulse is plenty for neutralizing soft targets. It'll cut right through flak armor and whoever's beneath it. But...." Rosie turned to his computer and punched in a query. "I can get you power packs for vehicle-mounted YQ3s. They'll be costly, and you'll need adapters to plug them into your proton rifle. You should also know that these are hard to find. The CRDF has been tightening restrictions on high-explosive energy pulsers. Of course, whatever you hit is going to feel it." Rosie printed out requisition forms and had Leon sign them.

"Thanks, Rosie. I owe you."

"You're going to have a real bad day when I finally invoice you."

"I know it. Is Vandestan in the Cradle?"

"Yup."

Leon walked back out into the sunshine and turned down the path that led to the enormous hangar. The big motorized doors, sixty meters tall, stood open. He walked through, pausing for a moment as his eyes adjusted to the dim lighting. The air inside was cool except for the venting fans of a large humming generator which blew a steady, warm breeze past the door.

Leon spotted a fighter hung nose-down from a rack on one high wall, its engine cowlings open and one wing missing. Three tanks in various stages of disassembly hunkered in shadow. They looked menacing waiting there in the half-light, and the hot air from the generator's cooling fans made it seem almost as though they were breathing. To the far right lurked three colossi, iron gods in a rusting temple. Leon looked up at them and marveled as he always did.

"Colonel Victor! Thanks for coming so quickly. Sorry to interrupt your lunch," called a voice from above. Chief Karoo Vandestan was a thin but unusually short Tez'Nar with grease-stained yellow plumage and a long groove in his silvery beak, the relic of an old injury. Like many Tez'Nar, his eyes were sensitive to light, and even in this half-dark he wore tinted welding goggles.

The hangar thrummed with activity as technicians moved through the dark labyrinth of machinery and clambered over the scaffolds that surrounded the giants. Vandestan descended a ladder to stand before the colonel.

Leon finally wrested his gaze from the enormous warbots. "What's the problem with our girl?"

"She locked down her authorization registry and won't accept anyone's ID but yours, apparently. Let me hit the lights." Vandestan walked to a nearby control panel and flipped a switch. The hangar and the towering service bays were bathed in a soft white glow. Suddenly the hangar was heaven, not hell, and the fighter swinging on its chains was not a giant bat but a sleeping angel.

Leon turned back to the service bays, looming half-cylinders lined with gantries and winches. Once, mechanae had occupied all six bays; now only three remained. Two of Jackal Pack's robotic titans were rusting in a river on some jungle planet whose name Leon had forgotten, likely overgrown by vines and serving as a habitat for the local wildlife. A third had been sold back to the Commonwealth as for spare parts. It was unlikely those bays would ever be filled again: the mechanae had been rendered largely obsolete by the advent of the nuclear dispersion cannon, which could fell one with a single, well-placed shot. Leon suspected that someday the remaining robots would be sold off, as well. For now, the Coalition was moderately interested in their applications as tools of urban pacification and had ordered them dusted off. It was a testament to Rockmore's pack rat mentality that the legion had clung to them this long despite receiving almost no return on the investments for a long time.

Jackal Pack's great war machines had been deployed only a handful of times, but they had certainly made an impression. Leon would never forget the sight of them lumbering through city streets, crushing pavement beneath their feet. There was no denying their awesome power or the terror they could inspire. Their applications were limited, but within their narrow range of utility, they could be incredibly effective. Leon had spent time working with them, learning to deploy them like any other resource, adding them to his catalogue of tactical assets. As a result, they had been attached to his Third Brigade, made his responsibility. They were no longer as impressive as they had once been, but they were an unusual sight on the battlefield. Few militaries trained to counter mechanae, giving the Jackals an edge on the rare occasions when they needed to use them.

The mechanae were machines, programmed and soulless, and yet there was a subtle facsimile of life that Leon found endearing. He respected his mechanae as more than just weapons. The two nearest to the doors were huge and terrifying. The Manticore and the Scorpion, they were called, and each was formidable in its own right. The Manticore was a long-range support model, designed to deliver heavy ordnance to targets in the rear of enemy lines, thereby disrupting their supply lines. An array of siege mortars grafted onto its back gave the odd impression that the mechana was carrying an enormous pipe organ. Eerily animalistic due to a forward-canted body mounted on birdlike legs, the Manticore could move fast over flat terrain but was at a loss among crags or swamps. This was where the Scorpion, a converted agricultural mechana, came in handy. Built low to the ground, with six articulated legs, the Scorpion could scramble quickly over difficult terrain that would have stymied the other two. The mechana was painted an eye-straining hot-rod red that the Pack techs proudly maintained.

The third bay from the right was occupied by the Behemoth, a robotic warrior which reached nearly to the metallic curve of the ceiling even when hunched. "Behemoth #7742" was stamped on the few remaining original armor plates. Leon had always thought of Behemoth as a "she," due to a vaguely feminine vocal emulator. By far the largest of the three mechanae—far larger, in fact, than any mechana Leon had ever seen—she was humanoid in shape and built like a battleship, with a dull gray and rust-brown finish.

The details of how she had come into the general's possession were known to only a few Jackals, yet the tale had achieved near mythic status among the mercenaries. After a decades-long civil war on the planet L'kellentris, revolutionaries had taken over. As often happens, the revolutionaries became petty tyrants in their own right. Having shelled the planetary capital into oblivion, they built a new city that was to be the shining jewel of their world. They called it Sakura.

On a world bankrupted by war, such an expenditure was not just ostentatious but cruelly irresponsible, inflaming a new rebellion. L'kellentris had been shipping in ice from a cracking operation in a neighboring system, ostensibly to provide potable water for the dispossessed. One such freighter was discovered to be carrying a weapons shipment in addition to the ice. Jackal Pack was contracted to ensure that cargo could not be used against the rebels.

After a risky boarding operation, Leon and his team prepared to scuttle the ship. Thinking it might be to their advantage to steal the cargo for themselves, they scanned the immense block of ice and found what looked like a ship buried deep within it, with a faint reactor signature. Curiosity got the better of Leon, and he ordered them to cut through to it. The mechana they found was surely centuries old, though somehow still functional. When the machine rebooted, it imprinted on Leon, for lack of a better term.

Now, she was one of the most visible symbols of Jackal Pack's military might. Her paint was scratched, and her metallic skin was dented and scarred from battles that had taken place before anyone on the base had been born. Someone had tried to paint red Jackal Pack stripes up her left side but had given up at the knee. Nevertheless, she was fearsome sight and always would be.

The Behemoth's skull-like head had a menacing, grinning quality, and Leon found himself vaguely anxious as he looked up at that dark visage. Mechanae, especially those war machines like Behemoth, had been designed to inspire terror by their mere presence on the field of battle. Hardly practical, prone to malfunction, and almost impossible to maintain properly, they had nevertheless been manufactured in many variants for centuries. Once they had formed the core of armored units, having the advantage of mobility across varying types of terrain which might be impassable for conventional tanks. Thus, they provided heavy fire support platforms for assaults and even functioned as enormous infantry squadrons for attacks on fortified positions where the loss of life would otherwise have been too great.

More heavily armed than the largest beachhead tank, the enormous mechana could take on an entire armored company, and Jackal Pack had installed some even deadlier upgrades. She was armed with self-reloading missile racks, hullbreaker cannons, large-caliber Gatling guns, and her own deadly body. Her hands, each capable of palming a tank and peeling apart its armor, hung slackly at her sides. Leon doubted a rail gun existed that could punch through her armor. Yet apparent invulnerability was not actual invulnerability, Leon knew, and she had once nearly been destroyed by enterprising sappers in the city of Sakura, after he had turned her against the despot who had originally purchased her.

Vandestan led Leon to one of the lifts that would take them to the uppermost level of the gantries, near the Behemoth's head. From there they could access her command interface. As they rose jerkily past the catwalks, Leon fought off a sudden wave of vertigo. At last they reached the top and walked out onto the catwalk that extended over the shoulder of the great robot. Vandestan moved with accustomed grace, but Leon was nervous, feeling the walkway sway with each step. Behemoth's head was like a bunker, and Leon reached up to steady himself against her cold, metal chin. There was a panel underneath that provided access to her central processing matrix, and

Vandestan opened it. "Try booting up the Behemoth again," he clicked into his comm.

A moment later Behemoth rumbled beneath them. Leon grabbed the handrail of the catwalk as the war machine shifted, her shoulder creaking against the metal deck beneath them. Indicator lights began to glow as she took in her surroundings. For a moment Leon was afraid that she would begin to move and he would lose his footing and plummet to a gruesome end on the oil-stained concrete floor below. "Hey," he said quickly, to get her attention. "I'm up here, so don't start dancing."

The massive head turned. Her main sensor array, two horizontal, deep-socketed rows of scanning devices mounted one atop the other and protected behind specially designed transparent armor, glowed a pale yellow in the half-light. "Imprint recognized: Victor, Leon," droned the loud, metallic voice. The effect was even more unsettling due to her vocal emulator's odd, disjointed modulation.

"Had yourself a nice, long nap, I see," Leon said.

"Interrogative: time since last activation."

"One Coalition year plus three months, give or take a few days," Leon said, after a prompt from Vandestan. "Run basic diagnostic panel."

There was a rapid clicking. "Power plant ... optimal. Sensors ... optimal. Heat sinks ... optimal. Actuation ... nominal. Weapons systems ... optimal. Interrogative: lubrication available."

"If you play your cards right," Leon quipped. The mechana gave no sign of having heard him. Over her many decades of operation, Behemoth seemed to have developed programming quirks that nearly approximated a personality. One of those quirks was ignoring Leon's jokes.

"Everything's in the green, Colonel," Vandestan said. "Or yellow, I should say."

"Yellow is mellow," Leon muttered. Wherever Behemoth had been constructed, yellow had signified optimal function. It had taken them years to figure that out.

"This is where we ran into trouble before. For some reason, she won't recognize any authority besides yours. Did you modify her the last time out?"

"No, and I wouldn't even know how to begin. Did you try asking her?"

"She won't respond beyond booting up. This is the farthest we've gotten. My fault for leaving it until the last minute."

"Okay, Behemoth, I've got an upload for you. Ordinarily, I'd buy you dinner first. I need you to modify your authorization registry to accept any of the following Jackal Pack or Coalition IDs."

The control panel indicators brightened, revealing archaic symbols that Leon could not interpret. It took a moment for Behemoth's ancient but effective security protocols to move aside for the program, but once they did, Vandestan was able to modify the registry. As Leon and the tech waited, they listened to her internal machinery humming and clicking. There were occasional knocks inside, but Leon attributed them to her reactor powering up after being dormant for such a long time. She had functioned without incident for so long—a miracle by the standards of mechanae—that all the techs were afraid of what they might find if they opened her up. A few of them had hinted at self-repairing systems; Behemoth herself could not remember.

Once the changes were made, Vandestan closed the panel. "All set. Sleep tight," Leon said, rapping his knuckles on Behemoth's metal skull, and the mechana powered down.

"Thanks for the assist, Colonel. We may need you on hand when we have to disassemble her for transport, but in the meantime I'll try and figure out why she decided to play hard to get with the rest of us."

Leon laughed agreeably, tempered by the pang of realizing that Behemoth, like the rest of the Third and Sixth brigades, had just been taken from him, her loyalty changed with the press of a button.

12: Final Preparations

There was little to do during the journey to Eve, and as it neared its end, Hakar found himself growing more and more anxious. *Condor* ran smoothly under Commodore Tarot's command, giving Hakar the opportunity to pore over the data Telec's people had compiled for him regarding the extermination of the Ninth Royal Line's senior command structure. Grand Admiral Mindor was hardly a close friend, but Hakar had known him for decades, and an attack on one grand admiral was an attack on them all. Coupled with the gruesome slaying of the prime minister, it was clear that Raven Blue was not above basic terrorism, no matter how theatrical it might seem.

It was almost impossible to believe that the assassins had not been working together, but there was no indication of any communication between them via email, comm, or any other form of communication that the Coalition's intelligence services could identify. Hakar had to admit that the connection probably wasn't there. So why did he persist? Because, unlikely as it was that they had worked together, it was far more unlikely that they had operated independently. Until the murders of Admirals Larador and Geran, the assumption had been made that Mindor's assassination was connected not to Raven Blue but to the unrest in the Dias Traverse. Somehow, Raven Blue had gotten to them. What else could have caused them to turn on their commanders like that?

In the VIP stateroom just below the bridge, Hakar forced himself to go through the data on the assassins one more time. They were from different worlds. They had never served in the same fleet, let alone aboard the same ship. Tracking their network activity and travel movements since joining the Coalition Royal Navy, there was no indication that they had ever belonged to the same political parties, ideological groups, or even social clubs. He had ruled out racial motivation, as well: aside from a single disciplinary citation in the file of Vice-Grand Admiral Geran's assassin, Ensign Lydia Gillette, there was no evidence of even a single drunken slur being uttered by one of the killers.

Maybe he was just pulling an unconnected thread. Hakar rolled up the mempad and tossed it across the desk. He pushed the office chair back in its track. It had been too long since he had been aboard a warship, and he had forgotten what it was like to have all the furniture bolted to the deck. He rose and walked to the cabin's large porthole. The purple tempest of the conduit was hypnotic, but he was uninterested, staring instead into his violet-tinted reflection.

"I can't tell if I'm doing the right thing anymore. My son is growing up without me. My sister will probably resent me for the rest of my life. What's more important: duty or family?"

By the hatch a shadow stirred, rising from a chair and detaching itself from the greater darkness. "It's not my place to say, sir." Commander Jow Metha was Sheff'an, with charcoal-gray scales. He lacked the characteristic nasal crest of his species, his snout adorned instead by a row of stubby, black spines.

"I wouldn't have asked if I didn't want your opinion, Jow." Hakar glanced away from the porthole. Metha's black eyes were two pools of space reflecting the conduit, and they blinked uncertainly. The still warrior made no other movement.

It was a loaded question. Hakar knew that Metha was born on a world where the crestless and the gray-skinned—stoneskins, they were called in the mines—were spat upon. And he was born both crestless and a stoneskin, abandoned by his birth parents to toil away the long years of his life. For all Jow Metha knew, his own mother and father had whipped him, never knowing or caring that he was their child. It was a terrible way to grow up. No matter how far he might climb by dint of his keen intelligence and seemingly infinite resolve, the unfocused hatred born of his oppression would never leave the young Sheff'an, although Hakar had taught him how to hone it, how to use it.

"Family is a sort of duty, sir," Metha said uncertainly. "One without the other is meaningless." For a man with no family, that was an ironic statement.

Hakar snorted. His son barely knew him, his wife had grown accustomed to his absence, his sister resented him, even Leon likely despised him now. And perhaps he deserved it: his conscience gnawed at him daily. Someday he would have to decide if trading family for duty was worth it. For now, he could put off the decision a little longer.

He left his stateroom and returned to the bridge where he belonged. Metha followed, softly closing the hatch behind them.

§

The population of the Valinata refugee tent city, ignored and abandoned by Eve's authorities, continued to grow every day. The CRDF seemed to have given up policing them or trying to extract information. None of these traumatized shells of people had anything useful to tell.

Eve's shields had likewise stopped patrolling the perimeter of the sprawling shanty town, and the food relief trucks simply dumped their goods and left, no longer bothering to oversee equitable distribution. Many of the refugees had turned to the Vugu for supplies. Galactic nomads with a penchant for scrounging, the Vugu were no more welcome on Eve than the Valinata refugees, and many "civilized" people viewed the vagabonds as a nuisance.

At the moment the tent city was in shadow: Jackal Pack's heavy carriers loomed over the cosmodrome's other tenants. Chaos erupted when they landed, but there was nothing the Pack could do to keep the thruster wash from blowing away many of the tents and the refugees' belongings. Hundreds of the Vali watched glumly, covered in dust, as the Legion's vehicles crawled by. Tanks, armored personnel carriers, support trucks, artillery platforms, and the seemingly endless swarm of boxy Hyenas were being packed into the huge ships on rotating racks that moved like some Olympian rotisserie. The two carriers fitted for troops were warmed up on the landing pads, enormous and irregular crystalline shapes built of interlocking and overlapping armored plates. The ships were perched on landing skids that, despite having the girth of ancient trees, looked ready to buckle under the incredible weight.

Jeric surveyed the hulking vessels, hands on hips. "I guess this is it," he said mostly to himself. Even after years with the Pack, years of flying ships through crowded space lanes, the sight of such marvels of engineering still filled him with awe. He hadn't even seen a ship up close until he was twelve years old, and he had lived on a ranch where none of the buildings were higher than a single story. These carriers—

large but by no means unusually so—dwarfed the cosmodrome's control tower. Even lying at rest they were magnificent, relics of an expansionist empire, a time when entire armies were flung from star to star. Now such ships were reminders of bygone eras, maintained nevertheless from habit. The ground crews were like ants scuttling over their hulls and making final preparations, checking the heat-ablative plating and weapon port seals before the flight crews took over for the most dangerous and precarious part of the trip: the ascent back into the atmosphere. "It'll feel good to be back at the stick in a battle instead of a patrol." For him, the killing was only a byproduct of combat flight, which brought with it a thrill unlike any drug he had ever ingested or injected. He considered himself an authority on this matter.

Traxus was beside him, her red-gold fur rippling in the warm breeze. She nodded solemnly. "*You* get to fight. I'm sick of being so pampered, Jeric. Seriously. You know Leon *sat* on me on Tikal when things got rough? Like I was some fat VIP."

Jeric kept his eyes on the ships, hardly in the mood to face her ire again. "Would you rather have ended up like Dyran? Or Levy and Santor? At least he *tried* to get *you* some action. I just got left here." He paused, frowning. "As far as I'm concerned, it's your right to get your ass shot off. But your brother's running this show, and you're an idiot if you think he's going to let you get near a real fight."

"But my brother's allowed to come under fire?" she asked, indignant. "He's the worst offender I know of where following his own rules is concerned!"

"That's different. He's a sojier ..." replied the pilot, his voice dropping to nothing as he realized what he had said. *My track record recently has not been good.*

It was too late, though; the damage was done. "What am *I*?" demanded the Tagean, cuffing Jeric on the shoulder. "I work hard, I train hard, and I'm a good officer, as good as any in the Pack."

Jeric had no ready response to that. The best he could do was, "You don't have the experience."

"I should have, by now!" she exclaimed. "Every time I take a platoon on maneuvers I get the best results consistently. But the minute something went wrong in the field, Leon took over without a second thought. He trusts you and Raptor. He should trust me. I'm just as good."

"As good as Buzz?" asked Leon, coming up behind them. His voice was low, almost deadpan. He was unshaven, and his eyes had bags under them. He had been working harder than anyone on base as though trying to brand an indelible mark on the troops who would soon be leaving him behind.

Traxus looked down, but she nodded, nevertheless. "Yes. As good as Buzz." She rounded on the colonel. "Better than most."

"Jenn said the same thing, once," responded Leon quietly. He glanced away for a moment, and both Jeric and Traxus remembered Leon's stories of a woman named Jenn Rada, a woman who had fought with him and died beside him before the rest of them had ever known him. His thoughts often returned to her: the first sacrifice in his long lineage of martyred friends. A flush crept up Jeric's cheeks, and he saw Traxus looking ashamed, as well. "But we're not talking about Jenn," Leon continued. "We're talking about you ... and you're practically royalty."

"If this were Tagea, Hakar would have to listen to *me*." After all, Traxus bore the Tachai surname, and Hakar did not.

"But this isn't Tagea, Trax," Leon said gently.

Jeric nodded emphatically. "We almost lost you on Mar Sai. If your brother had found out how close we came, he'd have had us all taken before a firing squad. Not you, just us. Remember, you're a merc. You do what the *client* wants you to do. And this time, the client is your brother."

"Shit, Jeric, that actually made sense," Leon said, and the ghost of a smile slipped across his face and vanished again.

§

Condor jolted hard as she dropped out of the conduit on the outskirts of the Eve system. For a few brief seconds, she had the empty vacuum to herself, peaceful and still. After the circus of the Tagean home system and the hub systems they had stopped in along the way, Hakar was stunned, and he stood blinking at the vast emptiness. All too soon the space above the solar plane was crowded with ships, spilling out of the conduit in a series of bright flashes until there were nearly a hundred of them. The fleet assembled in a holding pattern while *Condor* moved deeper into the system.

It felt good to be aboard a ship again instead of trapped within the maze of the ministry. The ship's vibration seemed to pool at Hakar's feet and course through his body, energy fusing him to the vessel. The sensation intensified when the Rombaldt Radiant Masses powered back up, and he grew heavier, rooted firmly to the deck. It was hard to remain aloof from the activity, though; he wanted to walk around, look over the bridge crew's shoulders, chat with the officers. No, he had to advise, serve as the chief diplomat, grease the wheels of government for the fleet to roll smoothly over. He had never thought he would become an admiral emeritus. When had it happened? When had his warranty expired? *While you were filling out forms, old boy.*

On the comm he was all smiles. "General Rockmore. Get the door, if you'd be so kind."

Rockmore's response came back in real time, no more waiting while signals bounced through the universe. "Grand Admiral, it's good to see you and hear you loud and clear. I only wish it were under better circumstances. We've got our bags packed."

"I'm glad to hear it. We're regrouping with the rest of the fleet at the mouth of the Yangtze in two days, before Benez passes out of phase with the rest of the Alkyra. We've cleared cargo bays to accept a regiment's worth of your materiel."

Rockmore looked concerned. "Running on empty? I thought you were supposed to be reinforcing the Alkyra."

"What can I say? Recruitment isn't what it used to be, and tanks are expensive." Hakar was trying to keep the mood light, but Rockmore wasn't fooled. The empress didn't think the Alkyra was worth reinforcing fully, and much of the Star Chamber seemed to agree. Hakar could have wasted time arguing; instead, he would take the few assets he had and use them. He didn't know if they could repel an invasion, but perhaps they could slow one down.

The mercenary general coughed into his hand. Hakar hadn't seen Rockmore in person in years, but he had watched him age via comm signal for some time. Were they really getting this old? "I have to ask, Hakar. Is this show of force your oh-so-subtle way of getting

Eve to realize what it's missing? Governor Jurayan isn't stupid, you know."

"Truth?" Hakar inclined his head. "Even if Benez goes out of phase and the Alkyra breaks in half, these systems would be right in the crossfire. I don't have time for subtlety. Do you think your governor is smart enough to figure *that* out?" He hadn't meant to snap, but there it was.

"You make a compelling point. What's your ETA?"

"Once they clear the traffic lanes for us, ten, eleven hours."

"See you then."

"Hakar out." Rockmore's image disappeared. Hakar took a moment to marvel again at how space travel had changed. He couldn't believe it had once taken years to traverse a single solar system prior to the development of modern aggregate propulsion systems. *But maybe warfare wouldn't be so easy if it was still that way.* Turning to Tarot, he cleared his throat. "Commodore, commence planetary landing maneuvers. I also need a line to Shra."

Tarot turned to the rest of the crew. "Helm, skids on designated coordinates. Comms, secure line to *Antares*. And prepare an inspection with the commander at the Falcon outpost."

Hakar moved to the secure comm bay. Shra was waiting for him on screen, stoic. Had Hakar been so full of piss and vinegar when he was only a hundred and ten years old? His red-furred executive officer had no shortage of confidence and was all the more insufferable because he had the skills to back it up. And yet Hakar couldn't shake the irrational fear that Shra, experienced leader though he was, could meet the same fate as Flora Rodriguex.

Shra's report did little to reassure him. In the short time since their fleets had entered the Alkyra, Shra had already skirted three systems near Ilieth. In most cases, their defenses were barely sufficient to chase off the occasional marauder. As a trade region, the Alkyra's security depended more on the goodwill of its neighbors, the Coalition and the Valinata, whose interests in the sector would deter most attackers, including each other. The Alkyra was worth more intact and flourishing than subjugated. Hakar suspected that Raven Blue didn't care about market incentives.

He understood why Kra'al and the administration wanted to leave the Alkyra a tempting target. If the enemy tied up resources occupying that sector, it would leave fewer of those hideous black ships free to invade the Coalition interior. The fallacy of that logic was obvious at a single glance: they had already completely conquered the Valinata and they were still hungry.

§

Eve was awash with excitement, and Coalition flags hung from windows for the first time since Leon had been on the world. So close to the Valinata, with so many citizens of nowhere, the planet was hardly a bastion of patriotism. Leon knew that many of Jackal Pack's officers had remarked on the stupidity of bringing a ship as large as *Condor* into the atmosphere and attempting to land her. Atmospheric entry and exit were stressful on any vessel, with friction and wind damage capable of shearing off comm antennae or throwing a ship off course. Those problems increased a thousandfold for a ship with such an ungainly profile. Planetfall could crush the skids like toothpicks if the ship came in too quickly, or she could crash altogether if the braking thrusters and repulsion coils failed to fire at precisely the right moment. Ideally, the ship would achieve neutral buoyancy, thanks to the Rombaldt antigrav systems, but there was always the possibility of disaster. Better not to contemplate the odds, especially when standing in her swiftly growing shadow.

Yet Leon had to hand it to Hakar and Strategic High Command. Accountants may have been running everything—as he supposed they fundamentally always had—but they knew how to spark a little confidence on a world that might otherwise have been on the verge of panic due to its proximity to a warzone. Landing a ship such as *Condor*, an old symbol of the CRN's power and majesty and a storied vessel with a storied commander on board, was just the ticket. It wasn't every day that a two-and-a-half-kilometer command cruiser lumbered out of the sky and landed at the civilian cosmodrome, almost within spitting distance of Tesa. It might just be worth the risk to shore up morale in the sector and convince these people they weren't being abandoned.

They'd be in for a show the next day when every ship in the Jackal Pack fleet took off after the cruiser, heading for space. All those flags that had suddenly appeared in windows and over doorways would be flapping in the thruster wash. The news of Hakar's public relations tour masquerading as a real security operation had been kept "secret," leaked just in time to create a fervor and spark that old patriotic zeal across the whole sector. Or was it a security operation disguised as a public relations tour?

Jeric and Leon were among those clustered at the edge of the plateau, watching the huge ship drift to earth like a fallen moon. The long, sleek, gray vessel descended slowly, ponderously. With a sudden roar and a blast of fire and smoke, her braking thrusters fired one last time, and she settled on the ground with surprising grace.

Rockmore and Akida would be on hand to welcome Hakar alongside the commanders of the Coalition regional base, so Leon had been left in charge of the base. With most of the personnel outside watching, he saw no reason not to join the festivities, though seeing *Condor* again had whipped up a storm of conflicting emotions in Leon: awe, nostalgia, fear, envy, anger at being left behind. *I stood on that bridge twice. The first time I was a hero. The second, I was a prisoner.* He decided he was fine with being asked to stay on the base. He was still annoyed by the way people kept tiptoeing around the issue, as though he had just been left by a long-term lover who showed up at the same party.

"Big mother, ain't she?" Jeric watched as the ship, still adjusting, continued to hiss and roar. *Condor* towered over the other ships cluttering the tarmac, even the Pack carriers, spouting steam and smoke in jets from vents along the hull. She looked like a mythical dragon in the midst of a helpless village, villainous rather than heroic. In short, she was the ideal command ship for instilling fear and awe. Even from so many kilometers away, the sound of her descent had been loud, frightening. "That flight crew has some guts." Jeric's tone was unabashedly admiring.

Leon nodded. "Makes the *Star Wolf* look like a daysailer." Indeed, had the Jackal Pack cruiser been lined up beside *Condor,* she would have measured less than half the length of the Royal Navy command ship, with barely a third as many decks.

"So that's Hakar's ship?" asked Traxus, joining them. There was a queer note of disdain in her voice which Leon did not care to analyze.

"Yep," replied Jeric. "Gotta be nice in there. The CRDF has got the cash to deck their ships out in goddamn leather and gold if they want to. Not like the Valinata or the Confed."

"I don't know," Leon said, remembering days aboard Coalition ships younger than *Condor* which had their fair share of problems. Nostalgia was great for propaganda, but it hardly made sense on a practical level. This ship wasn't even the original *Condor*, but she was still old. "Telemon increased defense spending, but somehow I doubt they used it on five-star hotel treatment for the crew. Who knows, though?"

"Full gravity, full larders," Jeric continued, thinking about how much Raptor would like real meat in place of the synthesized carbon-yeast cubes served on most long-haul ships. "Game rooms, rec areas, waterparks, the list goes on."

Now Leon had to laugh. "Buddy, she's a warship, not a pleasure cruiser. They don't have any swimming pools."

The pilot considered this. "Yeah, that might get a little messy in battle. Still … we're gonna be riding in style."

Traxus sighed. "Seriously, Jeric?" She turned to Leon. "You know, there aren't going to be very many people left once the troops are gone."

"Yeah," Leon agreed. "I'll be pretty lonely without you all here. I guess I'll catch up on my reading."

Traxus put her arm around his shoulder. She knew it was a brave front, knew how much he hated being left behind. They all knew, but Traxus wouldn't pretend not to see it. "Dawson'll still be here. So will Dyran and Sommers. And don't forget about Heidi."

"Yeah, hard to forget about Heidi. But I'm going to miss you. Not you, Jerr."

"Aw, sure you will," said Jeric, not at all insulted. "We'll be back before you know it."

"Please, take your time," Leon retorted. "Seriously, though, a five-year contract? That's a lot of time for the Pack to stay in the field. Maybe once we get some more troops, we can have standard tour rotations." He paused, trying to picture a Jackal Pack twice as large as the one Rockmore ran now. "We've never tried that before."

"We won't need to, either. We'll end this quickly." Jeric jammed his hands in his pockets decisively. "I just wish we knew who they are and how many of them we'll have to kill before they break."

There was nothing to say to that, so they looked at the jagged bulk of *Condor*. Would that ship lead them to the answers?

There was a flash over the capital, followed by a loud crack. More flashes and booms followed. Involuntarily, reflexively, hands moved toward sidearms. A moment's consideration revealed the blasts to be nothing more than a welcoming fireworks display.

Jeric gave a disappointed little sigh. "Dumbasses blew their loads in the middle of the day."

Traxus smiled. "It's the thought that counts. Not too much call for celebration on this rock, anyway. They must be out of practice."

§

Lying in bed, his arms wrapped around Rachel's bare shoulders, Leon could almost convince himself that things were the same, perhaps even the way he wanted them.

Rachel sighed in his embrace and rested her head in the crook of his arm, looking up at him. Her eyes caught the moonlight streaming through the window, the tears trapped in her eyes throwing the light back, refracting a pattern of priceless crystal thrown upon an unyielding floor. The two lovers looked at each other wordlessly, listening as the Jackals continued to load the ships, the sound of departing transport trucks filling the night air. Someone was shouting orders, oblivious to the hour.

More than anything, Leon wanted Rachel to think that this separation was a small thing. Like an idiot, he had scared her with talk of danger on Eve and scared himself, too. He tried hard to act casual, yawning and rubbing his chin against the top of her head, scratching her with his beard in the way she found so playfully annoying. "I won't lie and say that there's no risk, Rachel. I only intend for it to be a little while, and then we'll be together again. But just in case...."

Rachel pulled away and sat up. One of the Sisters, Eve's nighttime moons, hung large beyond the window, silhouetting her curves. "Don't. Please. I'm worried enough as it is."

Leon ran his hand through her hair, twining his fingers in it. "Don't worry too much. Instead, think about what you want to do afterward. I'll keep out of trouble."

"I'm not worried about you getting in trouble, Leon. *Killed* is what I would like you to avoid."

"Like the plague," he said seriously.

She looked away into the night, and her voice was husky as she said, "I don't want you to get a taste for war again, Leon. I don't want you to fall back in love with the CRDF."

"I don't think you have to worry about that," he said blithely, but even as he tasted the words, he knew they might be lies. "That would be some unrequited love there."

Did Rachel deserve better? Almost certainly. But she had decided that Leon was worth saving; that was a lot to live up to. Once Leon had been able to tell himself that she was a spoiled rich girl slumming it with dangerous mercs so that she could top her friends when they told stories of their exploits. She would tell them how she had tamed the savage beast. And so Leon had tried to remain aloof even as he knew he was falling in love with her. His determination had crumbled quickly, and he was happy it had. They meant more to each other than they had wanted to admit, and Rachel was certainly no spoiled rich girl. There was a sharp, curious mind behind that picture-perfect face, a desire to know the universe beyond what had been handed to her. She was one of a kind, and Leon wanted to become the man she insisted he be.

"I'm serious about retiring, Rachel. I'm getting old, and the last few jobs haven't gone the way I thought they would."

In the dark he couldn't see her expression, but he heard her snort. "You expect me to believe that in all the years you've fought, you intend to quit now just because you had some unexpected problems? After you told me about Daltar? How dumb do you think I am?"

Leon couldn't help smiling. "I don't think you're dumb, Rachel. It's just that I used to find reasons for going on in the face of defeat. Now ... it just doesn't seem worth it. I kept thinking that I would go on one last job, and it would be such a resounding success, with such a fat payout, that I'd feel satisfied. That's not going to happen."

"There's never a big enough payout, is there? Never a big enough rush?" Rachel asked. "You always think that the next time will be different." She was perceptive, or maybe she understood that drive, that addiction to success.

"That's right," Leon said softly. "You keep your head down long enough, you forget to look up, forget that the rest of the galaxy moves at different speeds." He lay back, his hands clasped behind his head. "Not everyone mourns dead friends for a living."

Rachel lay back down beside him, her arm thrown over his chest, her face pressed into the hollow of his neck. Slowly she fell asleep, her eyes fluttering closed against his skin.

Leon meant what he'd said. What he had left unsaid was how difficult it would be to actually cut the ties that bound him to Jackal Pack like thick and tangled roots. It was all well and good to talk of retiring, but he wasn't some enlisted sojier whose duties could be filled as ably by the next man or woman in line. He was an executive officer of the Pack, commanding thousands of troops. Dawson and Kir were exceptional officers, but the transfer of command would still be messy. At a time of crisis such as this one, the task would be doubly difficult. Yet many seemed to think he was a pariah among the people who fought with him and a liability to the Pack as a whole. Leaving him behind made sense, but how long would they leave him in command? Besides, if anything *were* to go wrong on Eve, how long could their defenses hold out? Would Rachel think it was funny that he might be safer as part of the task force? He doubted it.

Careful not to disturb her, Leon slipped out of her embrace and went to the window. The savannah was bathed in the light thrown by the spotlights and headlights of the trucks, a playground for shadows. He couldn't see *Condor* from his window, but he could *sense* the great ship as though it exerted a gravitational pull of its own. In spite of Rachel's dreaming, naked beauty, he felt himself drawn toward *Condor* and the fractured promises of glory she carried.

13: Departure Terminal

The last of Jackal Pack's vehicles, troops, and equipment were bound for *Condor*'s bays, winding around the other ships in an impenetrable tangle. It was a hodgepodge of Hyenas, light tanks, armored personnel carriers, and anti-aircraft platforms, everything that hadn't fit aboard the Pack's carriers, everything Rockmore had been prepared to leave behind.

From the rear passenger seat of his own Hyena, Leon waved to the occasional friend and returned salutes from the troops. His driver, a Niaotl named Corporal Celen, was doing her best to keep to their timetable, threading her way carefully through the long column of vehicles. "We're almost there, Colonel," she promised.

As they neared the head of the column, beneath the great edifice of the *Condor*, Leon couldn't help but drink in every detail. For better or worse, his world was pivoting on a fulcrum, a revolving door closing one path only to open another behind him. It meant reversing direction, losing momentum. But it also meant a new adventure. Leon wasn't sorry he had waited with Rachel; he wanted to spend every possible moment with her, but he needed to acknowledge those who had kept him alive for so long, as well. They had done some terrible things together, but they had done good, as well, and it had been worth it. *Just like it was worth radiation poisoning that almost killed me, to stand on the cliff while my atom bombs went off? What, did I feel some connection to all those people we incinerated? I'm lucky the medics were able to salvage me. There's no treatment for disintegration.*

He caught sight of a family making their way across the tarmac toward a battered planet-hopper that looked overfull already, not to mention overdue for an inspection. They were towing mismatched luggage, and an elderly grandmother was doing her best to placate children whining about the friends they were leaving behind. He saw harried port workers trying to figure out how to direct fuel trucks through the snarl of traffic, arguing with Coalition military police and a sergeant with a beer gut, whose dark purple flak vest was unbuckled against the morning heat.

Two Valinata refugees were working on a couple of gravbikes, eying the Jackal Pack and Coalition troops with caution. Had they stolen that yellow-and-black racing bike that looked like a hornet? Who cared at this point? More refugees were playing cards in the shadow of an old freighter that didn't look like it would ever fly again, and yet they were selling tickets offworld to their fellow exiles.

Suddenly Leon was in shadow, having passed beneath the overhang of *Condor*'s enormous prow, an artificial cliff face blotting out the sun. The steel mountain looked as though it had erupted from the landscape to tower over everything, including the Jackal Pack carriers that had previously seemed so huge. She was at once graceful and ungainly, built on aerodynamic lines but far too large to be genuinely maneuverable in any atmosphere. Above all, she was an imposing reminder of what the Coalition was capable of if she decided to curl her greedy fingers into a fist.

Celen parked the Hyena out of the way, and Leon hopped out. The air was hot and dusty and full of exhaust. He was nearly overcome by a wave of nostalgia, sorrow, and hope, with no idea of how to process it all. Beyond the shadow of *Condor*, he could see the heat rising off the tarmac in shimmering waves as the sunlight blazed off the hulls of the ships. He came upon Rockmore and Irakundu-Tshomane talking with a pair of CRDF naval officers at the base of one of the great flagship's embarkation ramps. Overhead a crane was lifting a skid bearing a cargo truck into a bay, handling the thirty-meter vehicle like a child's toy. It withdrew like the arm of a giant metal spider, taking its prey into its lair. Within the dark cavern of the bay, Leon knew, the crane would deposit the vehicle in a gantry which would slide upwards to make room for the next load. Racks upon racks of them lined the bulkheads to save space. In *Condor*'s heyday, her ground forces had been enough to capture a whole world.

Still looking up at the underside of the ship, bristling with weaponry, all of it scorched and blackened by the friction of the atmospheric descent, Leon approached the general. He couldn't shake the sight of it: it was like looking up at a city suspended above him. His cynicism was chased away by an unfamiliar sense of wonder. *She's magnificent.*

While Rockmore spoke with the CRDF officers, Captain Irakundu-Tshomane approached Leon, beaming. "Colonel."

"*Molo,* Captain. *Unjani?*"

Impossibly, the big captain's smile broadened. "Ah, Colonel, your accent is getting better. I don't know about you, but I'm excited to get under way. It's been too many years since I watched another ship break apart in front of me."

Leon smiled politely. Irakundu-Tshomane was a good guy to get a beer with, but he was at heart a miscreant and a pirate, which was part of the reason his career in the Coalition Royal Navy had stalled and crashed. He seemed to enjoy carnage and watching the frozen corpses of enemy crewmen smacking up against the portholes of his bridge. Still he knew every man and woman under his command, and every rivet and circuit of his dreadnought.

"Colonel Victor." Rockmore smiled and put his arm around the younger man's shoulders. "I wish you were coming with us. Hakar's on the bridge, if you want to see him."

Leon hesitated. He did want to see the grand admiral, his old teacher, his old friend. At the same time, he still felt the sting of abandonment, and however irrationally, he blamed Hakar for the decision. The memory of Daltar felt fresh, an old wound reopened. Seeing Hakar, listening to him try and rationalize the situation, might do nothing more than rub salt in it. "That's all right, sir. I'll stay out of his way. I just wanted to wish you good luck. The base is in good hands."

"I never doubted it for a minute, Leon. But don't miss this chance to shake the man's hand. Who knows when you'll get another?"

"How was the press conference?" Leon asked, evading. Rockmore and Akida had been asked to join Hakar in the capital for a tour and a brief statement to the people of Eve. Leon had been pointedly not offered a similar invitation.

Rockmore grimaced. "Fluffy. Hakar and the governor held hands and talked about unity while the rest of his generals and admirals stood there looking serious. There were some inspiring soundbites, though. So, did you see Miss Case off?"

"Not yet, sir. Her flight doesn't leave until after the fleet has cleared the system." Leon smiled in spite of himself, excited at the prospect of spending a little more time with her. "I told her. About Daltar, I mean."

Another officer had approached with a clipboard, so Rockmore, signing a form, didn't see the smile and only heard the words. "It's never a good idea to part ways upset, son."

When the general looked up, Leon was still smiling. "To tell you the truth, I think it'll be okay." The smile cracked a little, his lips drooping. "I mean, I'm scared shitless, sir, but I think we're going to work it out."

"Good for you, son. Good luck."

Leon glanced at a small cluster of black cars near the base of the landing skid, flying Eve's standard, five moons encircling a mountain with a tree growing inside it. A lift was built into the landing strut, the door flanked by a squad of sojieri. "Is that the governor's motorcade?"

Rockmore rolled his eyes. "Old Jurayan wanted to come for a meet and greet after selling us down the river. Hakar's giving him the tour right now, I imagine. The governor couldn't have been more predictable, with all that talk of reciprocity. He's a decent man, but he's still a politician."

"I can't believe he hasn't said anything to stop this exodus," Leon said. He waved a hand at all the liners and hastily converted cargo barges that were filling up with inhabitants of Eve, all looking for the quickest passage off the planet and out of the Tears.

"That's because he knows how hopeless it would be if the planet came under attack. I wouldn't be too surprised if he tried to hitch a ride out of here when *Condor* leaves."

"You're not doing a lot to reassure me, sir," Leon said, trying to mask his real concern with a laugh.

"Leon, look at that ship up there. Hakar and his fleet are a much more tempting target. He's splitting up to make the individual task forces seem vulnerable, but they're all going to be no more than a few hours from each other. And if this enemy is as ambitious as they seem, they'll be going after big game. After Rodriguex and Mindor's people, the only way to satisfy their appetite will be to scratch another grand admiral off the board."

"So Hakar's trying to lure them away?"

"What would you do if innocent people were in danger?" Rockmore asked pointedly. "What *have* you done when the chips were down? Draw fire."

It was a risky plan but a noble one, Leon had to admit. Hopefully, it would prove unnecessary.

Akida had arrived a minute before, remaining silent the entire time, only his eyebrows rising little by little in consternation. "So you told Rachel the truth, huh? I hope you get a lucky roll there."

"Yeah, listen, Irún, about before—"

"Don't bother, Victor. It's not important. I would have reacted the same way."

"No, you would have kept your cool."

"Probably, but that's not the point. You're smart to get her off-world, and hopefully you get the opportunity to join her soon. You're not all bad: you're a good commander, and you run a hell of a show. I'll try and do your troops proud."

It was nice to hear the sentiment directly from Akida, and Leon was embarrassed to find himself a little choked up. "They're in good hands with you. Try not to get killed out there."

"Top of my agenda," Akida said, cracking what might have been a smile. "Take care of the base. One more thing, if I could have a word with you."

Curious, Leon nodded, and the colonels moved to stand apart while Rockmore returned his attention to the Coalition naval officers. They didn't have to whisper to avoid being heard; in fact, they had to raise their voices as a crane swung another truck over their heads. "What's up?"

"I've been … seeing someone in Tesa for a while now. One of the Vali refugees."

Leon suddenly understood Akida's frequent trips to the capital. He understood all too well, but he couldn't help poking a little fun. "Oh yeah? What's his name?"

"Max," Akida replied without a trace of mirth.

Leon felt as though he had swallowed his boot along with his leg up to the knee. Stammering, backpedaling, he realized he had made himself look like a fool. "Shit, man, I never knew. I'm sorry. I didn't mean to be insensitive."

The laugh that erupted from Akida's mouth was unexpected, to say the least. "I don't think I've ever seen you so taken by surprise. But I appreciate the apology." Akida's smile faded. "Listen, if you could do me a favor and look him up if things go … badly, I'd appreciate it. I left his information with Heidi."

"Yeah, sure thing. Again, man, I'm sorry."

"It's all right. Just think before you talk next time. You're starting to sound like that asshole Jeric." Akida extended his hand, and Leon shook it firmly. Then the other man vanished up the ramp, leaving Leon feeling like a backwater moron. He supposed a little embarrassment was better than a split lip any day; Akida had been so forgiving lately, and Leon had done nothing but antagonize him at every turn. What *had* he turned into? Slowly he walked back toward Rockmore.

"Ah, General, where can I find my team? I was hoping to have a word with them." *Just in case you never see them again, you mean?* Leon ignored that thought.

"Raptor's already on board. I've attached him to one of the quick-strike teams under Akida. I'll call him down, but I need all hands accounted for. Especially Jackal Pack personnel, the way I hear it. They don't exactly want us wandering off."

"I understand." *So they'll pay us to do their dirty work, but God forbid they trust us.* "What about Jeric and Traxus?"

A panicked expression appeared on Rockmore's face and was gone in an instant. "I cannot believe they didn't tell you. You're not the only one who's hesitant to talk to Hakar. Traxus has taken a leave of absence from the Pack." He gave Leon a pointed look. "Indefinite," he added for emphasis.

"Wait, what happened?" Traxus had seemed resigned to a rear-echelon posting. Leon wasn't sure what shocked him more: her sudden about-face or the fact that she hadn't spoken to him about it.

"I wish she would reconsider, but it may be for the best. I was tempted to try and talk her out of it, but Hakar told me to stand down."

"He can't tell you how to run the Pack, sir."

"For the amount of money he's getting us, if he wanted us to fight in yellow sundresses, I would encourage you to go try some on. He's the client, and he wants Traxus out of the way. She's headed to Tagea. I also downgraded Jeric's sanction, and I've taken him off active duty so he can get her there safely. They're cleared to leave once the fleet exits the system. They've got my command cutter for transport."

"She's going to Tagea to consult with the matriarch, isn't she?"

"I expect so, but if she thinks her clan will be able to influence Hakar, she's in for a surprise. He's a modern Tagean, and he's in the running for high grand admiral." Rockmore scratched idly at the gruesome scar on his cheek and sighed. "It's just as well. Maybe you don't agree with it, Leon, but I know you want her out of trouble as much as I do. Anyway, I'll call Raptor down. Five minutes. Goodbye, Leon, and good luck."

"You, too, sir. Good luck." They shook hands, Rockmore looking diminished as he moved off to speak with a member of the port authority, pulling out his comm as he did so.

Leon waited by the side of the ramp while the vehicles continued loading, scooped up in the *Condor*'s indifferent embrace. The sound of engines and machinery was a near-deafening roar made louder by the echoes off the hulls of nearby ships. It was really happening. They were going to war. *Without me*, Leon reminded himself. *I trained for just this moment, kept my knives sharpened, honed on the bones of the fallen, and for what? For nothing.*

A few moments later, a big hand clamped down on his shoulder. "You wanted to see me?"

Leon turned, a lopsided grin settling on his face. "Hey. You gonna leave without saying goodbye?"

"That was the plan." He could play the stoic badass all he wanted, but Leon knew the big Prross was upset. Although Raptor did not often show his feelings openly, Leon had long ago learned to pick up on his friend's nonverbal cues. Behind his put-on grin, Raptor looked uncertain, perhaps even afraid. The smell of his cinnamon gum was strong enough to overpower the acrid tang of fuel and smoke.

Somehow Leon wasn't in the mood for macho jocularity, not today, not on the eve of war. "Listen, man. I'm sorry I'm not going with you. It would make me feel a lot better if you would promise me something."

Raptor instantly sobered up, and the gum shot out of his mouth, a red wad on the tarmac. He, too, could easily read his friend, tell what he was thinking. "Anything, Vic."

"Take care of yourself. Don't do anything stupid, chasing after glory."

The Prross's lips parted over his serrated teeth. "That's a promise I can keep. I'm not interested in being a hero. Take care of yourself, too. From what they're saying, this could become the front line at any moment. And the general said that there are reports of traitors all over the place. Keep your eyes open, hand on your gun. Especially with all these Valinata loyalists on Eve." The Prross pulled Leon close in a hug that threatened to bruise his ribs. Then he pulled away and looked around as though afraid someone would see, but everyone was busy and the display of emotion had gone unnoticed.

"You've seen what these things can do, Raptor. We don't have the luxury of blissful ignorance."

"No, we don't. I suspect we won't have the luxury of mercy, either."

Leon found it hard to meet the Prross's eyes. Finally he forced himself to look up, locking onto those placid amber eyes set in a savage visage. "This may get bad, Raptor. If it does, I want you to know you've been a brother to me, closer than blood."

"Likewise, Leon. I have to go. There's much to do. Don't worry, I'll bring you a souvenir from the trenches." The Prross bowed slightly and turned, his tail swaying behind him as he stalked up the ramp. He paused, came back down. "Will you, ah, be here when we come back?" he asked. For a moment, just a moment, his hard eyes softened. Most would have missed it; Leon didn't.

"Probably not."

"Good. You can't wash out your past, but you can start living a real life to be proud of. Send me a postcard from wherever you end up. Let me know if it gets boring, and I'll come blow something up."

"You'll always be welcome." The two warriors regarded each other intently for a moment as the chaos of mobilization roared around them, then the Prross turned once more and walked away.

Leon was dialing Traxus to find out where she and Jeric were when a familiar voice called out, "Got any room in your receiving line for me?"

Jaw agape, Leon raised his head and looked up the ramp. Although he looked small walking down that broad metal expanse, surrounded by military vehicles, Hakar seemed to dominate the landscape. Fanned out behind him, a squad of bodyguards looked on impassively, and above him his great arrowheaded ship pointed the way to war.

"Sir!" Leon said, unashamed by the affection in his own voice. "It's good to see you." His resentment seemed to fade at glimpsing the man he had admired for so long. He couldn't resist a little teasing, though. "Are you sure you should be seen consorting with undesirable elements like me?" *Do I salute? Shake his hand? Give him the middle finger?*

Hakar decided for him, bending to embrace Leon as he reached the foot of the ramp.

"Fuck 'em. Did you really think I was going to leave without seeing you?" The old Tagean's voice was cordial, but there was something guarded in his burning coal eyes. Nevertheless, Leon was touched by the gesture.

"Forgive me, but aren't you supposed to be meeting with the governor?"

"He and Commodore Tarot are getting to know each other. I told him something came up. I'm too old to waste time with wondering if I'm doing the right thing. It's been a long time, Leon."

"Yes, it has, sir." Leon and Hakar had spoken via comm a handful of times in the last few years, but it had been some time since they had met in person. It was a moment that he should have been looking forward to. Instead of elation, though, he felt a peculiar mix of apprehension and outright anger. There was some joy to be sure, but seeing his old mentor and commander under these circumstances was more than a little trying.

Clearly, Hakar sensed it, too. "I'll cut right to the chase, Leon. I'm sorry about how all this was handled. You know I wish it could be different. It's almost funny that I have enough power at my disposal to change the course of history but I can't get my friend a job."

Look at how hard I'm laughing, Leon thought, but he only nodded. "I know, sir, and I appreciate you saying so. Doesn't make it any easier, though."

"No, I don't suppose it does," Hakar conceded. "I have to come clean, Leon. I have an ulterior motive for wanting to speak with you, beyond seeing you." He stepped closer. "I understand Traxus is taking leave."

"I just found out about it myself." Leon shrugged helplessly. "I suppose I can try and comm her."

"Thank you." Hakar waited while Leon tried Traxus's comm.

"I don't need a lecture right now, Leon," Traxus said as soon as she picked up.

Leon smiled thinly. "I wasn't planning on giving you one, Lieutenant Tachai. Where are you and Jeric?"

"He's filing our flight plan. I'm in the main food court."

"Great. Meet me by the arrival gates, under that weird blue thing."

"I like that statue," Traxus snapped. "I'll see you there."

"What weird blue thing?" Hakar asked as they set out.

"A sculpture someone paid way too much for. You'll see," Leon said, rolling his eyes.

Corporal Celen drove them back to the terminal, giving Leon and Hakar a chance to catch up while Hakar's guards followed in a pair of Coalition Hyenas. They were taking no chances, something about security threats to high-ranking CRDF officers.

Their conversation was disappointingly mundane, never straying far beyond superficial pleasantries, but Leon could hardly blame Hakar for being distracted, and he himself was still too bitter to truly open up. When the two of them reached the infamous sculpture, Traxus saw them coming. She was standing beneath the preposterous, artistically bankrupt piece of corporate art, an azure blob that hung over the terminal and looked more like an amoeba than whatever graceful beast it was supposed to represent. She didn't leave, but her expression and her narrowed green eyes betrayed her anger.

She and Hakar embraced in a perfunctory manner. "Hello, brother," she said. She looked around as his bodyguards encircled them, preventing anyone else from getting close. "Well, this is intimate."

"Traxus. I like the haircut," Hakar said in a futile attempt to lighten the mood. "I know you're upset, but it's still good to see you. Are you really going home?"

"I am. I doubt they'll be any more helpful than you are, but I could use the change of scenery."

Hakar looked hurt. "Try to see things from my perspective."

"I have. I do. Maybe you could try and do the same."

Profoundly uncomfortable, Leon watched the icy exchange, wishing he were just about anywhere else.

"Please, Traxus. I don't want to fight."

"Then you picked the wrong line of work," Traxus said forcefully.

"Trax, come on," Leon pleaded, hating to interject. People were looking at them. Even with all the men and women in uniform crowding the spaceport, Hakar stood out, and Leon was a minor celebrity himself. The last thing they needed right now was to cause a scene.

"Life is too short for this," Hakar pleaded. "We're going to war, and if experience has taught me anything, it's not to miss a chance."

Traxus said nothing at first. Leon could tell she realized Hakar was right, but she was too proud to come out and admit it. It was a measure of her youth and inexperience.

"I'm just so frustrated," Traxus blurted after a few seconds of tense silence. "I work so hard, and I'm good at this. I'm not here to rebel. I'm here to be a sojier. The one person in the universe who should understand that better than anyone is so unsupportive it makes me want to scream."

Her brother's eyes seemed to dim a little, as though the fire and the fight had gone out of them. "That's not how it is, and I think you know that. But I have a duty to you and to our clan, just as I have a duty to the Coalition. I can't be worrying about you, not with things as they are."

Leon heard his own words in Hakar's, and he sympathized. Traxus, on the other hand, was livid. "That's just great," she said. "I'll sit in a trophy case until it's time to trot out and bless the moon festival or whatever other bullshit formal events I'm supposed to go to."

"Like it or not, Traxus, you are the future of our clan," Hakar reminded her. "I supported you when you wanted to go out and travel the galaxy when everyone else still thought you should be learning etiquette and politics. I even supported you coming here, but I could never live with myself if I didn't try to protect you. You may be our matriarch someday, but more than that you are my baby sister, and I love you."

It was a beautiful sentiment, but it didn't quite have the intended effect. Traxus's lip twitched and she looked to be on the verge of another angry retort when the fight went out of her.

"I love you too, Hakar. I just want the honor of fighting beside my people. And I promise you, I will." She embraced him, more tightly this time. "Ancients watch over you," she said emphatically.

"Ancestors guide you," Hakar said in return. When they finally released each other, Hakar clasped Leon's hand in his own, looking down warmly at his former protégé. "Good luck, Leon. Until next time."

"You, too, Admiral."

Hakar smiled sadly before he turned away and vanished into the crowd.

Once he was gone, Traxus cuffed Leon on the shoulder hard enough that it hurt. "I'm not mad at you, but that was stupid. What did you think that would accomplish?"

§

With all flight clearances on hold until the CRDF fleet left the system, there was nothing to do but sit and watch the ships depart from the comfort of the Princess Alkyra Skybar and Grille. The weather had turned gray at the last moment, and people were hoping for rain. A thin blanket of clouds had rolled in from the northwest, cottony and dry. The sun had disappeared from sight as had the ships in orbit. Nevertheless, all eyes were on the sky.

Just think, this is the last time we'll sit down like this together, Leon thought. It was an awful feeling, but the sorry trio in the booth overlooking the tarmac refused to bow to it. Traxus made no more mention of her departure or the fact that it might be permanent, but Jeric was animated, unable to hide his own eagerness to embark on the journey ahead. He even seemed to have made peace with staying sober before the flight, though he kept sipping at his soda as though praying it would be distilled into hard liquor on its way through the straw.

The roar of the departing flagship and its attendant carriers filled the air, and the restaurant's bay windows rattled with the force. Outside, across the landing field, *Condor* rose into the sky on pillars of fire, paving a black highway of billowing smoke into the upper atmosphere. The carriers followed. The Pack's fighters and the smaller shuttles ferrying officers back to their ships leapt into the air like startled birds, forming a ragged honor guard. The sky was ablaze, smoke and dust covering the landing field and obscuring hundreds of other vessels like a shroud. Then, as quickly as it had crescendoed, the roar faded and the ships disappeared into the clouds.

Leon stirred his drink, the clinking ice cubes barely audible after the cacophony. "Shit. I forgot how a ship like that would sound this close."

"Yeah." Jeric looked content, almost postcoital. "Gotta love that power." He took a slow sip of his cola.

"So this is how it starts. Eve is emptying out." Traxus took a sip of Hais and looked around the Princess Alkyra. The rooftop restaurant could seat hundreds, and it was typically filled to capacity. Now their only company was a few depressed-looking barflies and a handful of exhausted families, most likely the unfortunate few who had been bumped off their flights. Devoid of its usual colorful clientele, the place looked rundown, a cheap food court. Outside, the first civilian liner limped into the dusk, a poor imitation of the great warships.

Jeric drained the soda and gestured for another. Usually it was difficult to get a waiter's attention in this place; it was telling that he was served almost immediately. "There are still a lot of people staying."

"A lot of stubborn people. But what do you expect? It's home." Leon sympathized with them. "Imagine what it must have been like during the Dawn Wars."

"What do you mean?" Sometimes it seemed as though Jeric thought less clearly when he was sober.

"I just mean, most of the galaxy was at war. Planets changed hands two or three times a year. People learned to live with it then. Otherwise what's the solution? Live on ships like nomads, running from trouble? The galaxy should be past this kind of war, but maybe we're not. They *should* be worried with the whole Valinata gone dark." Leon played with his napkin, ripping off strips and balling them up. "Maybe we're the stupid ones, for digging in here and waiting."

Jeric sucked thoughtfully on an ice cube. "Someone has to stay. We can't just give them whatever they want."

"I agree," Leon said. "But Alkyra's value was as a trade hub between the Coalition and the Valinata. With one side gone, what's the incentive to protect us? Now we're nothing but a buffer zone between the Coalition and the enemy."

"Exactly. So, they'll defend it, won't they?" Jeric said, sounding only half-convinced himself. "I just wish you had more troops. The Coalition garrison here doesn't exactly inspire confidence."

Traxus clicked her tongue. "Jeric, those are Falcon Guard infantry. They don't get that bird without knowing how to shoot. Best of the best, right?" Truthfully, Traxus worried she was being naïve. Every child knew of the brave and formidable Falcon Guard, but she was a sojier herself now and she doubted they could be that much more ferocious than any other military unit. More likely it was a precisely cultivated myth, complete with ritual and pantomime and admittedly impressive suits of ancient armor. She made a face and changed the subject. "It's hard to leave, and I have somewhere to go. Think about how it must be for those people who have only ever known Eve."

The late afternoon sun appeared from behind the clouds just long enough to remind them it was still there and long enough to dispel any hope of rain.

"Hey," Traxus said, perking up. "At least property prices have probably bottomed out."

Leon snorted a bitter laugh. "Yeah, I could probably get that apartment for twenty talons at this point."

Jeric looked puzzled. "What apartment?"

"Rachel and I were looking at places a while back. She and Trax found this great place right in downtown Tesa."

"You should have seen it, Jeric," Traxus put in.

"When was this? I guess you guys decided to leave me out of the loop again." The pilot sounded annoyed, and he stared down at the tabletop, frowning. "Come on, Vic. This shit's in your blood. You're infected like the rest of us. You expect me to believe you can just move down the street and leave it all behind?" When he looked up, he cracked a conspiratorial smile, secure in his assumptions.

Traxus pursed her lips but said nothing. She knew what was in Leon's heart, and she knew Jeric was just refusing to see the truth.

"We'll see," Leon said, in no mood to argue before they said their goodbyes. "Look, wherever I end up, I'll always be a friend to the Pack, and to you." He could see that Jeric was getting worked up, so he offered him a compromise. "Besides, you know I've still got a few shots left in the clip."

"Probably blanks, you impotent prick." Jeric laughed long and hard. "Admit it, you walked into that one, all right! Traxus, can you believe this guy? He—" Jeric broke off, staring over Leon's shoulder as though he had seen a ghost. Startled, Leon turned in his seat, and he broke into a smile.

He waved, catching Rachel's attention. She had a little pink backpack slung over her shoulder that looked like something a teenager would wear. It was surprisingly uncharacteristic of her, given her usual chic accessories, but she had told Leon it was her lucky travel bag. The rest of her things were in suitcases aboard a waiting starliner, minus a pile of clothing she had decided to leave on Leon's bed to remind him of her while they were apart.

She sat down beside Leon and opened a menu. "Hi, guys. I'm going to miss you.… Jeric, are you okay?"

"Where the hell did you *come* from?" asked Jeric, staring at her.

"What?" she said, laughing. "I was just registering with customs."

"I thought you were gone already. Like a week ago." There was open hostility in Jeric's voice, and Leon was shocked.

"Man, what's your problem?" he asked. "You really didn't know she was still here?"

"I—" Jeric broke off, flustered. All three of them were looking at him now. "What about the other day, when you said you would have to be okay with her leaving, because at least she would be safer?"

"Right, because I'm sending her away," Leon said slowly, patiently. "Until things calm down." Something was not right about this. "Jeric, why are you sweating?"

"You're … still together?" Jeric pushed his glass away, drumming his fingers on the table as he looked from Leon to Rachel. "I can't do this anymore, Vic. Rachel, I thought you would take the hint, but you're as dense as you are unwanted."

"Jeric, what the hell, man!" Leon blurted.

Jeric ignored Leon. "I'm the one who left the articles," he said, inclining his head to her, as though in repentance.

"What the *fuck*," Leon whispered, feeling his whole world grind to a halt around him. The galaxy was on the brink of war, he was being abandoned, and his friends were going off into almost certain danger, but at least he had felt secure in their love and loyalty. This, this was too much to process. "Jeric, *why?*"

"I don't have to explain myself to you," Jeric bit back, scowling. His hands had balled into fists.

Leon stood up fast, his chair scraping against the floor as it slid back. "How could you do this?"

Traxus held up her hands, gesturing for calm. Eyes were turning toward the source of the commotion. "I didn't know about this, Leon. I didn't *know*."

"Trax, this has got nothing to do with you. It's between me and my *friend* here." Leon turned his gaze back to Jeric. His stomach was a cold pit of rage, and he felt like he was going to vomit. "You had better start explaining right now."

"I've got nothing to say to you," Jeric said. He stood up, too. Though he barely came up to Leon's chest, he looked ready to fight.

The waiter came over, looking equal parts embarrassed and terrified as he confronted the two mercenaries. "I'm sorry, gentlemen, you can't do this here."

Leon shook his head. "No, of course not. I'm very sorry." He looked at Jeric, but the pilot was walking away toward the double doors that led out to the terrace on the main terminal's roof. Leon strode after him, with Rachel and Traxus scrambling to catch up.

"Jeric! Jeric!" Leon hollered. "Jeric, *get back here!*" Crazily, he found himself wanting to draw his Sprawler. He had never felt so betrayed, not after Daltar, not being left behind by the general.

"Fuck you, Leon. Fuck you!" Jeric stopped, though, and turned. "Like I said, I don't have to explain myself to you."

"Then explain yourself to *me*," Rachel said, putting a restraining hand on Leon's arm. Her eyes were frightened, but more than that, she looked sad. Above them the smoke contrails were dissipating, merging with the clouds. It was as though *Condor* had never been there.

Jeric looked as though he might say something insulting, and Leon was ready to punch him in the mouth. To his surprise, the pilot sighed, deflated. "You deserved to know." He looked at his friend. "She deserved to know, Leon."

"Yeah, Jeric, she did, but don't try and convince me you were doing this out of the goodness of your heart. It was none of your goddamn business. Why did you have to do this to *me*? You weren't trying to make me come clean, you were trying to scare her away."

"And?" Jeric spat. "Look at you, Leon! You've got a perfect life. You've got troops who worship you, you've got a family, you've got money to retire.... What do I have? I have *nothing!*" To Leon's surprise, Jeric was on the verge of tears. "You don't deserve someone so perfect! You lied to get her and you lied to keep her."

He had never known Jeric could be so jealous, but all Leon could hear was "perfect life," and it infuriated him. "What about my life is perfect, you little shit?"

"Oh, don't give me your martyr's story, Leon. You put yourself on that cross, and every time someone tries to pull you down, you climb back up. Never forget that."

Leon couldn't even respond. His patience was gone. He couldn't believe Jeric was doing this and had tried so hard to ruin his relationship with Rachel, possibly the first truly good thing to happen to him since his life had gone careening off on an unplanned tangent.

"You got an education, so you could have been a doctor or something, and then you could have been a grand admiral, and then you could have been leader of the Pack. But none of it has ever been good enough for you. You need to have people relying on you. And as soon as they do, you leave them in the dirt. That's the whole story of your life, Leon." Jeric's face was red, and the veins stood out in his neck. "Well, guess what, asshole? *I'm* leaving before *you* can abandon *me*. Have a nice fucking life, you bastard." The calm coldness with which he spat out the words staggered Leon. Turning on his heel, Jeric stormed off across the roof, pushing his way through the ranks of empty chairs.

Leon stood there, his mouth hanging open. "What did I ever do to him?" he wondered aloud. "That ungrateful little motherfucker. I could kill him."

"*Leon!*" Rachel gasped, and he turned to look at her. Her brows were knitted with concern, and he realized that while most people might say "I could kill him" idly, from someone like him the threat was genuine, and terrible. "Think about what Jeric is going through. He's lonely, and he's scared, and—"

"If I have to listen to *you* defend him, I might throw up."

Rachel frowned. "You can't let this ruin everything."

"You're right. That's just what he would want."

"That's not what I mean, Leon. He's your friend. He's one of your best friends. You've been through so *much* together, you can't let this be what tears you apart."

Leon forced himself to stop, to think, and finally, to calm down. Rachel was right, of course, but the betrayal had cut right through him. How was he supposed to forgive Jeric? Jeric, who had tried to undermine Leon's relationship with Rachel not once, but *twice*, and had pretended nothing was amiss the whole time? His feigned ignorance and his petty subterfuge were sickening, especially from a so-called friend.

Traxus approached, looking wary. "Leon, I'm sorry about all this. I had no idea, I swear. I don't know what's going through his head."

He's lucky it isn't a bullet, Leon thought, but he composed himself. "Never mind, Trax. Rachel's right, I can't let this sour everything. After all, I'm saying goodbye to you, too." He pulled her close in a hug. "I'll try to make it to your pad before you leave tomorrow. Just keep him out of my sight." Before he released her, he said, "I'm glad you said goodbye to Hakar."

"I am, too," Traxus admitted. "If I don't see you again, though, take care of yourself, Leon, and take care of Rachel. I love you."

"I love you, too, Trax." Leon gave her a kiss on her furry cheek. "And you be careful. Take care of that little shit, too." He turned away so Traxus wouldn't see him crying.

She and Rachel exchanged hugs, and Traxus returned to the Skybar to pay the bill. So much for a going-away lunch.

§

The next day dawned cool and windy, with a palpable tension in the air. There was a new undercurrent of genuine fear in peoples' eyes now that the Coalition fleet and most of Jackal Pack were gone.

Leon grabbed coffee with Major Liam Dawson and Commander Stark, the head of the recently arrived privateer picket fleet. He didn't like the look of the man, but he had ships, and desperate times called for desperate measures. At least, until they could hire on some more guns. From there, Dawson returned to the Jackal Pack base. Leon should have joined him, but Rachel was still waiting for her liner to leave. Flight traffic was completely snarled in the wake of the Coalition fleet's visit. Leon wanted to spend every second he could with her.

The departure terminal was a barely navigable sea of frightened people, some trying to bribe their way aboard ships already full to capacity. Leon's Jackal Pack credentials were enough to get him and Rachel through security and to her gate. A family of Sheff'an got up to talk to customs officials, and Leon and Rachel settled into their vacant seats. His comm beeped.

"Colonel Victor, you have a comm from Terra. Your sister." Liam Dawson's voice was all but drowned out in Leon's ear. The major was back in the comm center on the Luxor Plateau, monitoring traffic.

"Gotcha, thanks. Tell her I'll call back in an hour."

"Sure thing, Colonel. See you when you get back."

Leon turned back to Rachel. She was teary-eyed, kicking at the floor nervously until the toe of her shoe pried up a loose edge of the frayed carpeting.

"Honey, are you gonna be okay?" he asked. She hadn't said anything since she had handed her identification papers and ticket to the customs guards.

"Do you think it's possible?" she asked absently. Leon wasn't sure what she meant until he followed her gaze and his eyes settled on the wrinkled cover of a magazine left on the floor beside the couch. Printed in garish letters was the headline: "CAJA-DUUN SIGHTED ON COMMONWEALTH-VALINATA BORDER, INVESTIGATION ONGOING."

Leon smiled sadly. "It would be nice to think they're still out there, somewhere." Every few years, someone claimed to have seen a member of the lost species of the Caja-Duun. They had gone extinct centuries before Leon was born, and he wasn't even sure what they looked like, just that they had been hideously ugly by Human standards. They had been the first spacefaring race Humanity had encountered among the stars, welcoming them into the greater universe.

They were voyagers, a species bent on exploring the galaxy and discovering new species. That had been their downfall, as millennia of colonization caused irreparable genetic drift in their vulnerable spironomic genome. Birthrates dwindled in history's greatest genocrash, and one by one their colonies winked out. The end for the Caja-Duun had come gradually, and they went extinct gracefully, spending their last centuries leaving an indelible legacy of art, science, and exploration. They mapped vast swaths of conduits, catalogued proto-Tagean ruins, and even turned the surface of their own homeworld into a vast, glowing shrine. As a child, Leon dreamed of meeting the Caja-Duun, of being taken from the dreary streets of Crossing on Terra and indoctrinated into their secrets. It had been a long time since he had believed that any of them had survived, but it would have been nice to think there were still good things to discover in the infinite darkness. Leon feared he knew better.

When Leon looked back at Rachel, she smiled shyly. "I just don't want to go. I was never very good at saying goodbye. It's why I didn't say it the last time I left." She looked accusingly through the glass of the terminal's floor-to-ceiling windows at the place that had been occupied by the towering Coalition command ship. It had looked out of place when it arrived, but now that it was gone, the tarmac seemed empty, the land around it bland and featureless. One could almost imagine the pull of a vacuum in its place, drawing everything inexorably toward it.

Leon smiled back at Rachel. "Hopefully we don't have to practice that too often. Can I get you anything from the snack cart?"

"No, I'm okay. I'll eat on the ship. I'm sorry about Jeric, Leon. But there's good news."

Leon glanced at the clock on the wall above the gate. It was fast. "I'm dying to hear it."

"Yes, he tried to get rid of me, and I'm not sure his heart was in the right place—"

"Yup, good news all around."

Rachel sighed, exasperated. "Leon, you're smart, and you're quick, but sometimes you need to wait for people to finish what they're saying."

Leon's face reddened. She was right, of course. "I'm sorry, hon, please continue."

"All his scheming and tricks had the opposite effect. They proved how much I love you, and how much I want to be with you. And you know what else? They got you to open up to me. No secrets, right?"

"No secrets." Maybe it *was* time; after all, if not now, he might not have another chance. "Rachel, this is hardly the most romantic moment, but if we have to be apart I want—"

Her smile was warm as she put a hand on his, squeezing his fingers. "It isn't, Leon. I know what you're going to say, and you know what I'm going to say. Leave it until I get back. Something to look forward to."

He looked at the floor, simultaneously disappointed and relieved. He didn't think Rachel expected some grand, poetic proposal of marriage, but he did want to give her the moment she deserved. "I can live with that."

Rachel nodded and clasped her hands between her knees. They sat in silence for a few minutes, and then she said, "So, Colonel, what are our chances?"

"I don't know, Rachel." Leon looked around at the other occupants of the spaceport terminal. Most of them were families, clustered around mountains of luggage, parents herding tired children while barely able to stay on their own feet. It was an orderly exodus, at least. People kept glancing at Leon. Did they see his Jackal Pack stripes and think of him as a savior, or was he somehow to blame for all of this?

"They all look so afraid," Rachel said. "Somehow I'm past that. I think I've spent too much time around you people."

"Whatever this is, it won't take long. Grand Admiral Hakar knows what he's doing, always has. He and General Rockmore know how to make war."

"That's what I'm worried about. I know you can't just resign, but I'm glad you're taking the right steps. I was hoping you'd meet me halfway."

"I'd like to meet you all the way. You know, I was talking to Raptor—"

"You talk to *Raptor* about this?"

"You know how supportive he's been. He suggested that if I do this, I may not be able to wipe the slate clean, but I can do my best to start living a life that I can be proud of. He's not big on bullshit." Leon leaned over and put his arm around Rachel, accidentally knocking her backpack to the floor. "Sorry," he said awkwardly.

Rachel reached over to pick it up. "Start living," she echoed. "Good sentiment."

"Yeah. You understand I need time."

"Of course, Leon."

"I've been living in this haze for years. The only time things are clear is in the middle of a gunfight. Baby, this kind of lifestyle has its own momentum. Believe it or not, moral complexity aside, it's *simple*. Running the brigades involves a lot of minutiae, but it all boils down to the contract. There's no time to contemplate the ethics of things when you're fighting to stay alive, fighting to *win*." Unconsciously, Leon's hand drifted up to stroke the scar on his cheekbone. "Now I'm trying to figure out how I fit into the rest of the world."

"You sound like a different person."

"Do I?" He shrugged. "I see my friends getting ready for war, and part of me wants to run off with them and fight, you have no idea how much. But the other part...." Leon paused as a Tez'Nar family walked by, the father and mother towing heavy, wheeled trunks upon which their three kids were perched. "The other part is terrified that I'll have to bury them, too, and that I'll be left alone. Of course, I'd still have my family, but there's a line drawn between us now, and I don't know that it could ever be erased. I started to wonder how they all feel about this. Then I started to wonder how Buzz's family must feel. Their son didn't die for a cause. He died because I aimed him and he missed the target. If I ever saw them, I wouldn't know what to say."

Rachel pulled her backpack into her lap so a rather stout Borin could take the seat beside her. "You're serious, aren't you?"

Leon looked at the thick-necked Borin beside them, but he was speaking loudly into his comm, heedless of his surroundings. "Yeah. I am." The boarding call crackled over the PA, and Leon looked up, stricken. "Time to go," he said, rising.

Rachel stood, as well, and placed her hands on Leon's shoulders in an oddly protective way. "You're a good man, Leon. I've always known that, or I would never have come to Eve with you in the first place. It's like fighting alcoholism, though: you have to work at it every day or it's easy to relapse."

That bit of wisdom cut him to the core. In this vast galaxy, how many people would have given Leon so many chances? A handful, perhaps. If it took him the rest of his life, he would dedicate himself to earning her trust and the opportunity she had given him. He didn't want to spoil the moment so, as much as it pained him, he said nothing.

"Maybe my mother was wrong about you," Rachel said quietly. She kissed Leon on the cheek. The Borin beside them snuffled in irritation and spoke louder into his comm.

Leon took Rachel's hand and squeezed it. "You really do need to get on that liner," he insisted.

"I know. I just want to take one last look at you."

"It's not the last look. I'll see you on Terra as soon as I can. There's nothing to be afraid of."

"Everyone is afraid of something."

"Now you're starting to sound like Raptor," Leon said with a chuckle. The laugh was forced, though; he didn't know if he'd ever speak with Raptor again. The Jackals and their CRDF counterparts had left Eve for uncertain fates, and yet they had done so knowingly and without complaint. Looking around at the civilians in the terminal, Leon could see that, although they were frightened, their fates were hopefully not so uncertain. They were going to safety, to stay with relatives until trouble passed. Hopefully they would look back on this time as an unplanned vacation and laugh. That was unless they returned to piles of rubble where their homes had been.

Rachel was looking toward the boarding ramp as the last of the passengers boarded, the terminal emptying just like the rest of Eve. They were alone among the cracked, vinyl-covered benches and dirty windows. The liner outside had lit its engines and was thrumming beside the building, connected by an umbilical jetway. Relieved families were visible in its yellow-lit portholes, settling their children into comfortable seats, stowing their luggage. Somewhere near the bow there was a first-class berth waiting for Rachel. She gave Leon a big smile, courage flashing in his face. He smiled back, a pleasant shiver running down his spine.

There was nothing more to say. Leon kissed her, tentatively. She returned the kiss passionately, and the seconds ticked on before they pulled apart. Leon didn't let go of her hand right away. Finally she tugged a little, her fingers gradually slipping from his grip.

She shouldered her backpack and brushed her hair out of her eyes, sweeping aside tears, too. Leon lost himself in those eyes all over again, terrified that she was leaving, perhaps forever. She turned and started walking.

"Wait, Rachel," Leon blurted. "You asked what I think our chances are. I think they're good."

She gave him a half-smile strangely like his own. "It was a trick question, Leon. I don't gamble." She jogged back, planted another kiss on his lips, and then she was gone down the jetway, pink backpack bouncing, as the ship outside roared, warming up.

§

The D'zen Gulf was just that: a gulf, an empty sector of space without even a customs station to process traffic. With no habitable planets or Deep stations in the area, in ages past the Gulf had served a number of raider lords as a hunting ground. Thousands of ships had been waylaid while they shifted conduits on the journey from the Tears of Alkyra to the Yangtze Tradeway. Those ages were long gone, however, and the only things waiting to ambush the Second Fleet were floating debris and blinking relay satellites.

That would have to change, Hakar reflected, as he stood before one of the panoramic portholes on the bridge of *Condor*, with Jow Metha standing silently to his right. They would need defensive emplacements, a fleet, and possibly a dedicated tending station. Mine clouds, autonomous sentry satellites, and drones ... it would cost trillions, but that was far cheaper than losing it.

Commodore Tarot approached, making notes on his personal mem. "Admiral, cosmographics has the workup you requested."

"Excellent. Have them transfer it to my stateroom." Hakar hoped he was being paranoid, that Mindor's assassination was a fluke, but he couldn't afford to ignore a single possibility. Once-loyal sojieri had murdered their officers, had committed grievous acts of terrorism. It had the Star Chamber and their subordinates looking over their shoulders. Hakar found that he was more keenly aware of the movements of the officers and enlisted around him. But if the officers didn't trust their subordinates, how could the troops trust them in return?

"What's the status of our deployment?" asked Hakar, trying to distract himself.

Tarot entered a command into his mem. A holographic display lit up nearby, and Hakar turned from the window. General Rockmore rose from one of the observer jumpseats at the rear of the bridge and joined them.

Hakar smiled at the mercenary commander. "General Rockmore, have you met Commander Jow Metha?"

"I haven't," Rockmore said neutrally, "but your reputation precedes you, Commander." He extended his right hand.

"As does yours, General," Metha said, blinking in confusion until he remembered the Human custom of shaking hands. Belatedly he gripped Rockmore's hand and gave it a quick, perfunctory pump. The officers turned to the hologram.

The Alkyra appeared as a network of conduits and major nodes representing the inhabited systems. In this simplified diagram it was a dog-legged path with a number of diverging tracks that led to other minor tradeways and systems. The systems in direct contact with the Valinata border were blinking. Shra's fleet was located at the zenith, closest to the edge of the galactic plane, at a deep-space colony array. Veraxus, too, had deployed her forces throughout the Alkyra behind the lines, to be deployed as needed. Within days they would begin securing the most vital worlds, namely, those agricultural and industrial hubs most valuable to a war effort. Jackal Pack's Commander Irakundu-Tshomane had taken *Star Wolf* and its fleet to the Ufonis System.

Each system node was labeled by name with the strength and composition of its defenses. All were inadequate. Eve's defense consisted solely of the Coalition garrison, a mere regiment of light infantry and armor, and the Jackal Pack reserve. The early warning system provided some reassurance to the inhabitants, but it was hardly a deterrent to attack.

Eve had long ago vanished behind *Condor,* but Hakar felt his thoughts returning there again and again, especially as he looked out at the ugly void and the artificial nebulas of trash creating a dull brown haze off to starboard. He had never visited Eve before, but he saw the appeal. It was warm and pleasant, unruly enough to appeal to the adventurous and just civilized enough to remain more or less politically stable. If not for the dust that had coated his fur almost as soon as he stepped off the ship, he would have found it beautiful. Its rolling plains and tenacious plant life had a provincial charm. He only wished that Traxus and Leon Victor could see past their resentment. Then again, he was protecting them in a way. With any luck they would live long enough to see the wisdom in his actions, and then perhaps they would show a little gratitude.

Was it so wrong of him to look out for his little sister? She had always been his favorite, always followed along behind him when he visited home. He supposed he shouldn't have been surprised that she would follow in his footsteps when it came to her career. Now the two of them were virtually outcasts in their own home. That should have brought them closer, but it had only driven them farther apart.

Somehow, Leon's avoidance stung more. He had asked Rockmore to pass along an invitation, but the colonel had been "too busy." What could Hakar do but smile knowingly. At least he had taken matters into his own hands. He returned his attention to the matter at hand.

"We're going to need more," Tarot was saying, looking at the display. His bald pate was shiny with sweat despite the cool air on the bridge. "Will High Command grant us reinforcements?"

Rockmore drew in a breath as though to speak, then seemed to remember that his place here was tenuous. Even though he was now a mercenary and the head of his own private army, military discipline was still deeply ingrained. Hakar turned to regard him.

Rockmore went ahead. "You can fortify all you want, but you can never win a defensive war. At some point you have to attack."

Tarot looked annoyed but held his tongue. Hakar was angry but mainly because Rockmore was right. "We've got to operate on the assumption that defenses will deter attack and make an offensive unnecessary." Hakar lowered his voice. "I just wish I could rely on the local PDFs. Nothing I've seen has inspired confidence."

"They know the region," Rockmore said, trying to sound reassuring. "Hopefully, they can tie up any attack long enough for your forces to get there."

"Perhaps," Hakar said. "That reminds me...." He turned back to Tarot. "Commodore, are our comms plugged directly into Signal Fire?"

"Not at the moment." Tarot moved off to speak with the comm officers.

"Fulltime ansible current will be expensive," Rockmore observed.

"We put the system in place to use it. It could make all the difference. And I've got a hunch I'm not inclined to distrust."

Rockmore eyed him curiously. "A hunch, eh? Should I be worried?"

"Probably nothing more than an old sojier's memories, Jon. But I'd feel better knowing for sure."

The two stood in silence for a few moments, old friends and even older enemies, looking past their ghostly reflections into a silent, forbidding starfield. Behind them Metha was like a statue carved from obsidian. *Condor* seemed to be drifting peacefully, but in reality they were moving at a solid clip, just over two thousand kilometers per hour. Beyond the glass, fighters patrolled, pinpoints of light swirling aimlessly.

Hakar had always found the steady thrum of the engines comforting, but now there seemed to be an ominous undertone to it all, a baritone chorus calling out to him to stop, take care.

"Is it true the enemy field mechanae?" Rockmore asked under his breath.

"Now where did you hear a classified thing like that?" Hakar asked in return, though he was sure he knew the answer.

"Let's just say Leon believes very strongly in full disclosure these days."

Hakar should have known. He couldn't bring himself to be angry. "We have gotten some disturbing reports, but Leon's is the first one I really trusted. We'll be going up against some heavy armor, all right."

"Good to know. Leon's quick-strike units have trained specifically to bring down heavy armor." Rockmore looked at Hakar placidly. "If you have any other helpful information, I recommend sharing it sooner rather than later."

"It's a shame about Leon," Hakar said, to ease the tension. It had the opposite effect.

"Is it?" the mercenary leader replied, his voice laced with bitterness.

"Yes. He's a good officer. He would have been a great help, but High Command wouldn't budge. It's all politics these days, Jon."

"Yeah. You seem to have taken to it better than you realize."

Hakar bristled, and he saw Metha's reflection cock its head toward Rockmore. "Jow, why don't you go below and see to your troops?" The slate-gray Sheff'an nodded once and withdrew. Hakar kept his voice down as he turned back to Rockmore. It would be better not to set a bad example before the crew this early on. "What exactly is that supposed to mean?"

Rockmore, too, knew better than to make a scene. Already distrustful, all CRDF hands would be keeping a close eye on their rough new comrades. "What do I mean?" The general discreetly pointed at the Coalition double prong emblazoned on Hakar's cap. The icon appeared all over CRDF uniforms and hardware, a constant reminder. The Tagean Rienda symbolized honor and valor, the highest Tagean virtues. Legend had it that the first Queen Mother had sewn it on her young son's banners to remind him what their people held sacred above all else. That son had gone on to win the Dawn Wars and found the empire that had united more than a third of the known galaxy. "What does that mean to you, Hakar?"

That pricked the grand admiral's pride. "Honor and valor, Jon? It means I serve my kingdom bravely and unswervingly. Sometimes that means sacrifice. Why, what does it mean to you?" His tone not so subtly implied *to a mercenary who sells his causes for cash*?

"To me? Honor means knowing the right thing and taking it to heart. And valor means *doing* that right thing, no matter how much it scares the shit out of you, how hard you have to fight for it. You sold Leon out. Twice. That man would capture the galaxy for you if you gave him the job. All this time and he still looks up to you, won't tolerate a word against you. But you … you put politics before honor or valor this time, Hakar. You made it about PR."

"Don't pretend PR isn't at the front of your mind at every turn, Jon. Especially after public fuckups like Korinthe. Or Tikal, if we had ever let the word get out."

Rockmore's gaze turned cold. "I couldn't tell him I thought this was all bullshit. It would have been meaningless coming from me. But you could have made a little more effort." With that, the general's lips sealed, a thin, bloodless line. He stared stonily at the void, and the grand admiral decided not to argue. After all, Rockmore wasn't wrong.

It was then that Tarot returned, saving them from further confrontation. It didn't seem possible, but the commodore looked even sweatier and more nervous than he had a few minutes ago. "Admiral, we've established the uplink with the Alkyra. We're cycling our own ansible, but we'll be able to hold it for a few hours at a time. Warrant Officer Kisuuj is the best ansible operator I've ever known. He'll make sure we do a periodic check-in."

"Good enough for me," Hakar said. "If there's a beep out of place, I want to hear about it." Tarot nodded.

Hakar was tempted to leave Rockmore by the porthole, hands clenched white-knuckled behind his back. He couldn't do it, though, and he walked up behind his friend and put a hand on the general's shoulder. "It wasn't up to me, Jon. If it had been, things would be very different. Trust me."

Rockmore wasn't startled, having seen Hakar approach in the reflection on the glass. "We're mercs, Hakar, or had you forgotten? Trust doesn't enter into the equation. I don't really suppose it matters now, anyway. I don't think Leon will be a Jackal much longer."

Hakar controlled his voice as he said, "Of course, it's up to you to run the Pack as you see fit." He couldn't quite keep the bitterness out of his voice.

Rockmore snorted a mirthless laugh. "You think it's my call? Leon can be tough to handle, and he does cause plenty of trouble, but he makes us a lot of money, and I'm as loyal to him as he is to me. I wish it could be different."

That was a puzzling remark, but Hakar didn't have a chance to pursue the point. Tarot's voice blared over the PA, overloud and underconfident. "All hands to action stations, all hands to action stations. Shift to conduit will commence in five minutes. Resistance expected on arrival."

"Now what the fuck is going on?" Rockmore said, instantly on alert.

Tarot huffed over to them to explain. "Admiral, we have a report of Raven Blue contacts at Dobrian. They're glassing the planet. We're the only fleet in range. I made the call."

Hakar nodded dumbly before he could find his voice. "Very good, Commodore." So it would begin in earnest.

The gravdrive began to howl from its lair within the depths of the ship, and Hakar moved to one of the observers' jumpseats along the rear bulkhead of the bridge. He strapped himself in securely; Rockmore, sitting beside him without a word, did the same. Despite being the ranking officer and commander of the fleet, Hakar had refused to displace Commodore Tarot from the command station, preferring instead to maintain his position as advisor. He just hoped the good commodore was up to the task.

With such a small force at his disposal and his actions seemingly hemmed in on all sides by political considerations, Hakar wasn't sure how he was supposed to stem this tide. As the ship began to vibrate, straddling the surreal barriers between space and time, Hakar struggled to put a name to what was bothering him, but the source of his distress eluded him, settling like a coiled snake in his belly. When the countdown finished, the ship jolted, the blackness outside flashing into a brilliant cyclone.

Third Movement:

Sic Transit Gloria Mundi

14: Downfall, Leviathan

Breathing heavily, Jeric half-carried the crate up the shuttle ramp, the sweat on his forehead attracting a thick coat of dust. He had never realized that dried and canned foodstuffs could be so heavy. He would rather have brought liquor, knowing that the penalty for touching the general's onboard stash would be floating home without a space suit. He supposed there were worse fates than sobriety and heaved again. The crate moved another few inches, scraping up the ramp. He adjusted his grip and hoisted, lifting it clear. He tottered up the ramp with the load digging into his thighs.

He secured the crate and planted his palms on its sun-warmed surface, standing in the darkness of the cargo hold. He had made a mess of things, but he didn't want to think about that right now. How could Leon hold this against him? After all, it was Leon who had lied to Rachel. Besides, if those two idiots did stay together, then Jeric could be sure he would be forgiven in time. He had done what he had done to keep things the way they were, the way they were supposed to be. Murder and mayhem aside, these had been the best years of his life. Was it really so strange that he would want to preserve that? He was too old to start over, and he wouldn't even know where to begin.

When he emerged into the sunlight, he found a Hyena parked nearby and Leon standing at the foot of the ramp, looking grim. Jeric wiped his sleeve across his forehead and put his hands on his hips. He stared down at Leon until the colonel blinked and looked away. "I'm here for Traxus," he said tonelessly.

"She's on the flight deck," Jeric said, standing aside.

Leon was halfway up when he stopped and locked eyes with Jeric again. "I don't want it to end this way, Jeric."

"I don't, either, but you didn't leave me much of a choice."

The muscles in Leon's neck tightened, and Jeric braced himself. "We've been friends for seven years, and we've been through a lot of shit. That's the only reason you're not spitting out your teeth right now. If...." Leon trailed off. "Keep her safe," he said through gritted teeth.

"Man, I'm just the chauffeur. She's the ranking officer, I go where she says."

"Leon," said Traxus, appearing in the hatchway. "I'm glad you came."

Leon turned his angry gaze away from Jeric. "I couldn't let you leave without saying a proper goodbye, Trax." He took a few steps up the ramp to embrace her.

To their joint surprise, Traxus backed away. "Say it to him, too, Leon. We're not going to see each other for a while, maybe never again. You'll regret it forever if you don't patch this up." She turned to Jeric. "And you. You should fall on your knees and beg Leon for forgiveness."

"You're one to talk about forgiveness, Trax," Jeric blurted out.

"What's that supposed to mean?" she asked pointedly. Jeric said nothing, merely jammed his hands in his pockets. "I'm a big girl, you know. I can handle it."

"Your brother doesn't want you in harm's way is what this asshole is trying to say," Leon said softly. "You should give Hakar a break." Jeric couldn't believe Leon was agreeing with him. A little over an hour ago, it had seemed as though he might shoot Jeric.

Traxus's flustered sigh sounded like a low warning growl in the back of her throat, and Leon's eyebrows shot up. Jeric, trying to avoid her wrath this time, kept his gaze on the colonel. "Leon, you're the last person on Eve who should talk to me about this," she said, quiet and angry.

Leon took a step back. "Trax, take it easy. You said it yourself—we may never see each other again."

She took a deep breath and leaned against one of the ramp's hydraulic struts, her bristled hair flattening as she forced herself to relax. "I know, sorry. I realized it as soon as *Condor* launched. I may never see my brother again, either, and spent my opportunity taking cheap potshots. I never met Kezt or Send, but I know Hakar loved them, and I know he doesn't want me to follow them. It's just going so fast, and I have no idea what's going to happen." Jeric had never heard Traxus utter the names of her deceased brothers, but from what Leon had told him, Hakar had mourned them for a century.

Jeric's thoughts turned not to his own family but to Leon and what he had done to the man who had dragged him out of the clutches of poverty, drugs, and death again and again. At the time it had seemed so right. After all, he was telling Rachel the truth. The question was why? Was he really so selfish that he couldn't stand to see Leon happy and moving on with his life? The realization that that might be at least partly true was like a kick in the balls. Unable to face either Traxus or Leon, he looked up at the general's cutter. A flat and boxy system-hopper, it had once been a splendid vessel, but its angles looked tired and it needed a touch-up.

All around them, port workers and ship crews worked to ready their vessels. Those people unlucky enough to have been caught in the open when the fleet had taken off had a distinctly sandblasted look about them.

Leon coughed and held a hand in front of his mouth as dust, now carried by the breeze, continued to billow around them, a gauzy layer between them and the afternoon sky. Traxus's fur was quickly becoming coated. "This is just great," she said, trying in vain to dust herself off. She busied herself moving the last of the crates into the shuttle while her friends stood in angry silence.

Jeric glanced back at Leon and was surprised to see him looking unguarded, defeated. It was enough to put a knife of guilt through Jeric's heart. Leon had never been left behind, never been passed over, and yet now he was shelved like a broken tool Rockmore was too lazy to fix and too sentimental to throw away. *Maybe now he knows how I feel all the time*. Still, it felt like a personal insult to all of those who called him friend or leader or both. And Jeric had only made it worse. "Leon ... I *am* sorry. I ... didn't mean for it to go that way."

Almost instantly, Leon's face hardened, his eyes going cold as though steel blast shutters had closed over them. "The retard act isn't going to cut it, not this time."

As always, Leon had gone for Jeric's intelligence, never knowing how deeply such words cut, and the pilot felt a scream rising in his throat.

"Dammit, both of you," Traxus grunted as she moved past them. "Enough."

The explosion was distant, a resounding blast that echoed toward them off the hulls of the ships. A sinister orange glow flickered off the hulls of the vessels west of them. The Jackals turned around, open-mouthed, stunned more than afraid. Past the main administration buildings and the control tower, the port's main comm array was collapsing into a rising ball of fire. Metal pillars a foot thick crumpled like foil. The once proud structure groaned as its top hundred meters sheared away, twisting into the flame.

All three of them were reaching for their sidearms. "The hell?" Leon blurted as he looked around frantically. Had one of those dilapidated Vali freighters crashed? Or was it something more sinister? "You two have got to get out of here now!" he ordered, waving them up the ramp.

"What about you?" Traxus shouted. In the distance they could already hear the wails of sirens. All around them, people had stopped what they were doing to look at the fire and smoke. Port workers were shouting into their comms, trying to get answers.

"I've got to get back to the base and find out what's going on."

"Maybe we should stay and lend a hand," she insisted as she scrambled down the ramp for the last crate.

Leon watched her descend the ramp. "No. I want you both out of here."

"You don't have to tell me twice," Jeric agreed, his heart hammering in his chest.

Turning to Jeric, Leon gave his friend a look bereft of animosity, full of fear and uncertainty. There was another distant boom, the unmistakable sound of a second explosion. "My place is here, Jeric. Listen, take care of Traxus … and take care of yourself." He stuck out his hand. Jeric reached out and took it.

§

Whatever Jeric was going to say was lost in fire as the world split apart, his hand torn from Leon's grip. The ramp lifted up from beneath them, and Leon was thrown onto his back, tumbling, as it sailed over him, cartwheeling across the sky. Flame chased it, and then Leon was somehow facing the tarmac again, his legs above him. His hands came up to protect his face as he came down again, hard. He rolled a few meters as debris rained down around him.

When Leon finally raised his head, he saw that he had come to a stop near a fuel line hookup, nearly fifteen meters away from the shuttle. How was that possible? Leon knew that the explosion had been near them, but when he turned his head, he saw that it was the general's shuttle that had blown up. It took what seemed like an eternity for this fact to sink in. When it did, Leon tried to get to his feet, but his legs buckled and slid out from under him.

An aerofoil from the shuttle slammed down against the hull of a nearby light freighter, and its bow skid buckled, the ship listing away. Leon renewed his efforts to rise, but his limbs refused to respond.

Where were Jeric and Traxus? Through the smoke Leon could see people staggering away, some grievously injured. There were dead bodies sprawled nearby, but none he recognized. He pulled himself forward, hands scrabbling at the dusty tarmac. Fire tickled the light freighter's dented hull, and Leon could feel the heat on his face. His left side had scraped the ground badly, and his jacket and shirt were shredded, gravel caked into his raw flesh. Every part of him ached.

Where are they? As he rolled over, nearly blinded by agony and smoke, Leon saw Traxus sprawled facedown ten meters away, a blackened engine cowling rocking beside her. Had it hit her? Leon had to go to her. He couldn't see Jeric, but as he started crawling toward Traxus, he saw something on the ground nearby. It was part of a hand.

Amid the flames, a familiar shape was writhing on the ground, clutching at a bloody wrist. Jeric wasn't screaming: he wasn't making any noise at all. His eyes were squeezed shut, tears pouring down his blackened cheeks. Ghostly gray dancers of smoke rose off his jacket.

Leon managed to get himself upright, his hands pressed to the sides of his head to try and silence the ringing in his ears. They came away bloody. Was he deaf? The general's shuttle was gone; a burnt-out frame, burst open like the petals of some metal flower, was all that remained. Someone had tried to kill them and very nearly succeeded. *Keegan*, Leon thought. It had to have been some associate of Marcus Keegan, whose last words had been a threat against Leon's life.

He couldn't dwell on that now, though. He had to get to his friends. Traxus was moving feebly, spitting blood onto the tarmac. She looked at Leon through glassy eyes and said something.

"What?" he hollered back.

She frowned, then pointed to her own nose. Leon understood; reaching gingerly up to his own face, he grimaced. His nose was a swollen bundle of agony. The angle of the bridge told him all he needed to know. It was as broken as a nose could get, and the blood gushing down his face tasted salty in his mouth.

They stumbled over to Jeric, who was smacking the back of his head against the rubble-strewn ground. "Jeric!" Leon yelled, his voice muffled in his own head. "Are you okay?"

"Fuck!" the pilot screamed at the top of his lungs, red spittle spraying from his mouth. Leon couldn't hear that, either, but he didn't need to be a lip reader to figure it out. Jeric's jacket was still smoking.

People were approaching through the haze of heat and smoke, port workers and the crews of neighboring ships. Many were wounded themselves. Leon gestured to Jeric, and one of the port workers tied his belt around the ruin of the injured pilot's hand while he screamed. Leon was grateful he could barely hear the shrieking.

He slumped against a shipping container while he waited for help to arrive. Wiping at the blood on his face, he tried to make sense of what had just happened. It was a jumble, made worse by the throbbing, spiky agony in his head. As near as he could tell, through some dark miracle, the ramp had actually shielded them from the worst of the blast as it tipped up and over them. Otherwise, they would have been incinerated. If it was a bomb, it was unlikely that it had been inside the vessel. More likely it was attached to the underside. Port workers gently laid more bodies in the shelter of the container. They were not moving.

There was a piece of bright yellow metal, strangely familiar, lodged inches deep into the surface of the container, blown there by the blast. They had been attacked, of that he had no doubt. But were the explosions related? He didn't see how it could be a coincidence. He had little experience with bombers, but he knew that many of them liked to watch their handiwork, falling in love with the patterns of destruction, the fountains of fire, smoke, and wreckage.

Leon saw frightened faces all around him as people gathered in worried knots, staring at the destroyed shuttle and the burning spaceport beyond it. They were all waiting for instructions, for some authority to tell them what to do, where to go.

The port workers brought Jeric over, keeping his arm elevated. A piece of burning debris had sliced cleanly through his right hand, partially cauterizing it. All that remained of the hand were the thumb and forefinger, twitching feebly. Traxus stumbled over and sat beside Jeric, holding him upright. She said something to Leon, sleepily. She probably had a concussion. They all probably had concussions.

Movement at the periphery of the crowd caught Leon's eye. Someone was moving among the landing struts of a nearby ship. Unlike the other onlookers, this individual wasn't looking at the smoke, the fire, or the racing emergency vehicles. He seemed to be staring in shock at Leon and his companions.

When the man caught Leon looking at him, his eyes widened and he bolted. All Leon wanted to do was lie down and take a nap; the tarmac looked so inviting. Instead, he found his muscles propelled to action, lifting him off the ground. Then his legs were pumping away unsteadily as he gave chase. Somehow he was certain, *dead* certain, that this man had something to do with the explosion.

"*Leon*! Where are you going?" Traxus shouted. She sounded far, far away. Too far to stop him.

The man kept running, easily outdistancing Leon. There were several service vehicles idling nearby, abandoned by workers responding to the blast. The man jumped into one, and Leon watched the truck recede into the distance, weaving between ships.

Staggering to his Hyena, Leon slumped into the passenger's seat, bleeding all over the interior. His face fell as he saw Corporal Celen. A piece of shrapnel had penetrated the windshield and hit her in the throat. Her fur glistened, matted with blood, and her eyes were still.

"I'm sorry," he said as he unceremoniously dumped her onto the tarmac, groaning with the effort. He climbed into the blood-slick driver's seat. He reached into his pocket: his comm was mercifully intact.

There were people lying on the ground, some badly injured, bones protruding, flesh seared, eyes searching sightlessly for loved ones. At least a dozen were dead or mortally wounded, and Leon felt his blood boiling as surely as if he had been seared in the flames of the explosion.

He started the Hyena, and it surged forward as he slammed his foot down on the accelerator. Its response was sluggish, and he wondered if it had been damaged in the explosion, too. His only consolation was that it was still faster than the old Shibui service truck he was chasing.

Barely avoiding a parked shuttle, Leon forced himself to slow down. He knew his reflexes were slowed, that his perception was clouded. Still, that man was his only chance to get answers: after all, why would he run unless that bomb was his baby? Letting him escape was not an option. *Time to do something reckless.*

As he made his way across the tarmac, Leon saw emergency vehicles darting all over the place, unsure to which disaster they should respond first. People were running for cover in every direction, hysterical, getting in the way. Whoever he was, the terrorist had succeeded: they were all afraid. So was Leon for that matter. He kept his eyes on the speeder ahead.

For a moment the gleaming spires of Tesa were visible through the tangle of ships. There were columns of smoke rising from the city. Leon's foot came off the accelerator for a second. These weren't isolated attacks. War had come.

§

As the world stopped spinning, Jeric realized Leon had gone. Traxus was struggling to her feet, a strip of fabric from the lining of her jacket wrapped around her head to stop the bleeding. She had wrapped another tightly around Jeric's hand. She was still calling after Leon as she staggered forward.

Jeric looked down at what was left of his hand and almost threw up. Someone had cinched a belt around his wrist, and the remaining thumb and forefinger were turning purple. How the hell was he supposed to fly with three of his fingers missing? He undid the belt.

"Don't do that, sir!" cried a man kneeling beside him. Jeric could barely hear him. "You're in shock!"

"Gotta ... get to work," Jeric mumbled, throwing the belt aside. He pushed himself upright against the shipping crate and used it to steady himself as he stood. His vision swam again, and he promptly vomited all over the port worker who had been helping him. "Sorry," he said and tottered after Traxus.

She was arguing with another port worker who was blocking the door to his vehicle. As Jeric walked up, Traxus lost her patience, pulled her pistol, and aimed it at the man's chest. His hands came up and he backed away. Jeric moved around to the driver's side and pawed at the door.

"What do you think you're doing?" Traxus yelled louder than necessary due to her own hearing loss. "You're wounded."

Jeric looked again at the ruin of his hand and relinquished the driver's seat. In a few moments they were headed after Leon. Jeric's comm was smashed, but Traxus's still worked, and she called Leon repeatedly. There was no answer.

As he contemplated the blood seeping through the stiff, burned tissue where his fingers and most of his palm had been sliced away, Jeric tried to think through his shock. Of course, he realized what had happened, what Leon must have guessed, too. Someone had set off a bomb. Two, in fact, and maybe more. Most of the planet's communications had been routed through that comm tower. Not only that, they had survived an assassination attempt. Who knew what else had been done? The smoke over Tesa told Jeric all he needed to know. All of this ran through his head in a matter of seconds. One look at Traxus, and he knew that she had reached the same conclusion. The would-be assassins were out there.

§

As Leon's hearing returned, he became aware of a desperate voice yelling over the Hyena's speakers.

"Victor here," he shouted.

"Leon? It's Heidi. Everything's going to hell over here! We just lost the long-comm link with the port! The Hyphen Telecom arrays in Tesa, Denshire, and Kell's River are down, too! I've been trying to send out a priority signal, bounce it off the relays, but there's no telling if it's working or not." She sounded frantic and rightly so. "What's going on there? Are you okay?"

"Heidi, someone just blew up the general's shuttle. They wanted him on it!"

"Casualties?"

"Plenty, but we're okay! What else can you tell me?"

At first Leon didn't hear her reply. Between the rush of the wind around him and the ringing in his ears that sounded like church bells pealing over a choir of cicadas, he was still half-deaf. "Repeat that last!"

"I said most of the Tesa shield precincts have been hit, and the governor's building is gone, too!"

Leon's lip curled in fury, but he couldn't process all that now. The terrorists had hit them, hard. What did that say about their security, that within hours of the fleet leaving, Eve was under attack? It was less and less likely that this had anything to do with him, Keegan, and the bloodbath on Korinthe. "I think I may have a lead on the fucker responsible. I'll update you as soon as I have more information."

"Wait, Leon, that's not all." Heidi hesitated, clearly afraid. "We're getting some weird fucking signals on our scanners."

"Weird fucking signals like what?"

"Like something's out there. But there are no transponders, nothing we can lock onto. Our sensors are all messed up, but we should have been able to pick something out by now. I'm bringing the skybeam online."

This was disturbing news indeed. Eve was a nice soft target right about now. "Keep me posted, Heidi. You and Dawson do what you have to do."

The chase continued on almost languidly, roaming through the kilometers of parked ships, some leaping into the air to try and flee. Leon felt himself going into a trancelike state as he evaded obstacles, many of which were fleeing people. He knew he was concussed, that the trance was nothing but his senses dulling as he fought to remain conscious. And though a small part of him screamed warnings to stay alert, he felt himself sliding into a blissful stupor. He forced himself to keep on going; that was what he had always done.

It was only when a thought of Rachel flitted through his mind that his vision seemed to clear, the haze of lethargy replaced with the cold lucidity of rage.

§

It was stunning how quickly order could disintegrate, how quickly people could abandon any semblance of rational thought. Cargo trucks had been abandoned, crates spilling across the tarmac. Luggage was strewn everywhere, forgotten, and people were looting ships or trying to force their way aboard. Ensconced in the relative safety of the port authority gravcar, Traxus felt detached. She just wished she could see out of her right eye. It was hard enough driving through this chaos without compromised depth perception.

Beside her, Jeric was cradling his arm. "I can't believe it," he moaned. "I'm all natural. I never … I never lost anything before. I … what am I supposed to do?"

He was succumbing to shock, Traxus knew. And how could he not? Despite the wound being mostly cauterized by the heat of the debris that had cut through his hand, he had lost a lot of blood. His hair was also matted with blood from a blow to the head.

They were lucky, though. They could have—*should* have— been dead. Whoever had set off those explosions had done an incredible job of sowing panic, but their timing was a little bit off.

"How am I supposed to fly like this?" Jeric groaned, writhing in his seat.

"Jeric, can we not do this now?" Traxus asked, searching for Leon's vehicle. Where had he gone?

He turned his head to look at her, his eyes unfocused. "Traxus, my fucking *hand* is gone."

"Look in the glove box. Maybe there are some painkillers."

Jeric rummaged through the console and storage compartments around the cabins. He suddenly stopped. "Even if I find a bottle, how am I supposed to *open it*?" he shouted at her, bloody spittle flying. Then he started laughing disjointedly.

"Seriously, Jeric, sit back and shut up. We've got to find Leon. He may need backup."

"He always needs backup." Jeric jerked in his seat and threw up into the footwell. "I think I need a … hospital."

"Soon, buddy. We need to…." She trailed off as the flames of another explosion rose over Tesa, visible in the rearview mirror. She felt woozy and not just from her injuries. She tried Leon's comm again, but the channel was busy.

"Why? Why would they do this?" Jeric mumbled, squeezing his eyes shut.

"Jeric, I don't know why some fucker blew up the comm tower or tried to kill the general. But if we find him, we'll ask." Traxus wiped at the blood running through her fur and over her eyes. The makeshift bandage was soaked. "Ah, I can't see shit, Jeric. Any ideas?"

Jeric planted his good hand on the dashboard and looked around. "It's a mess out there," he said, voice grave. "But I think I see dust that way." He pointed off to the right. "Is that west?"

Traxus fumbled for her comm. This time there was an answer. "Leon, are you headed west?"

"Tesa's behind me," came the disconnected reply. Clearly, Leon was as disoriented as they were.

"Okay, good. Leon, what are you doing?"

"We have to do something. There's no PDF. *We're the PDF.* We're it!" There was a frenzied edge to Leon's voice.

"You have a lead?"

"Closing in. I need you to go to the terminal and find out if the BI for Epsilon Merentis took off!"

"We're coming for you, Leon. You need backup."

"*No!*" he screamed. "Go to the terminal, Goddammit, make sure Rachel got out!"

Traxus was shocked by the rage and terror in Leon's voice. "Keep your head clear, Leon. You're all we've got, and you're responsible for the defense of this entire planet. We're coming after you, and we'll go back for her as soon as we can."

Jeric looked as though he was about to say something but stopped as an unusual and highly alarming sound reached their ears. Traxus's foot came off the accelerator, and the two of them listened, open-mouthed. There was no mistaking that double-voiced banshee wail. It was the distinctive, high-low scream of an air-raid siren.

§

At first Leon hadn't believed he was hearing the siren, assuming it was just the ringing in his ears. But as he drove past more and more people looking upwards, he realized it was real. Still, he had no choice but to keep his eyes on the tarmac. His only chance was to catch up to the bomber before he made it to the open road. That meant driving more recklessly than usual and with a concussion, as well. He was going to feel awfully stupid if he was chasing down some innocent civilian. Somehow, he doubted that was the case.

"Leon! Colonel!" It was Heidi again, buzzing in his ear. How long had she been calling his name? "Leon, do you read me?"

"Heidi, what's wrong? Anything to do with this air raid siren I'm hearing?"

"So the port spotted it, too? We've picked up a large number of inbound contacts. No hails, no transponders. They're coming down all over the place. We've got thirty over Tesa, more than a dozen over the port, a couple near North Bay, even Las Serras has incoming. There are more entering orbit."

"It's not Hakar's fleet?" Leon had been hopeful, but he felt that hope crumbling.

"No. I'm sorry. We've got a visual from our orbital sats. Like nothing I've ever seen before."

"What about the corporate pickets?"

"They moved to engage. As soon as the first few were destroyed, the rest of the cowards ran."

Leon felt the air go out of him. "Time on targets?"

"Like I said, they're coming down fast and hard all around you. Ten minutes tops. We'll keep hailing them. It looks like the Falcons out west sent some of their fighters to intercept."

The realization dawned on Leon that, while he was the ranking officer on the planet and therefore in charge of its defense, he was hardly in a fit state to make strategic command decisions. And yet, he had seen Aethaleia. He had seen what these things could do. There were millions of people on Eve, and whether they liked it or not, they were depending on Leon and his Jackals. He *had* to get back to the base, but first he had to get the son of a bitch in the vehicle ahead of him. And he had to make sure Rachel had escaped. His duty to the Pack and to the planet paled in comparison to his duty to her.

"Heidi, buy time. Bring them down."

"The skybeam is powered up, I'll give them the greenlight."

"I'm sorry I'm not there."

"I'm not."

"Well, just hang on. I'll get back as soon as I can."

There was a pause, and Leon thought he heard Heidi sniffle. "Don't, Leon. They're going to come down on us once we start shooting. Get clear. I...." She hesitated. "Good luck."

"Good luck, Heidi," Leon said sadly, wondering what she had chosen to leave unsaid.

The Mark VII Orbital Cannon Platform, manufactured by defense contractor Light-Arm, was a heavy weapons system designed for defense against invasion. Like most of the Pack's heavy ordnance, it had been purchased secondhand, specifically from a decommissioned Valinata forward base the Commonwealth had captured years ago. While not as energy-efficient or focused as newer Coalition models, it was more than capable of hitting targets in high orbit and knocking them out of the sky. They had never used it. *Time to get some return on the investment.*

Movement in the heavens caused Leon to take his eyes off the other car for just a moment. There was something black below the clouds besides the smoke, coming down fast, just as Heidi had said.

One word blinked on and off insistently in Leon's head: *Monster.*

Far, far above, dropping through the atmosphere, was a long, black shape unlike any ship Leon had ever seen. *It can't fucking be....*

Another one appeared, low enough that it drifted through the column of smoke rising off the comm tower. It was hundreds of meters long, Leon guessed, black and glistening as though it were wet. *No. Not possible.*

Yes. Possible and real. An organic ship. There's your Raven Blue.

Leon stared at it for long moments, mesmerized, as three more erupted from the clouds, dropping rapidly, leaving distrails through the vapor. They were moving, parts of them were moving, wiggling rapidly as the things descended. If he hadn't known better, hadn't known how impossible it was, he would have said they were appendages, curled black tentacles. Now he became aware of a low sound, a mournful moaning that filled the sky. Was it somehow coming from those things?

The traitor. Have to get answers. Leon gunned the throttle, too fast and too carelessly. He pulled over hard, clipping a shipping crate. The sound of scraping metal made his teeth grate as he left a streak of paint on the crate, but he knew he was lucky. A little farther over and he would have *been* the paint. The panic on the ground had intensified as people fled at the sight of the descending vessels, and more ships were taking off whether they were fully prepped or not. His target vanished in the dust of departing vessels.

Up above a loud crackling drowned out even the ringing in Leon's ears. A wide blue beam tore through the sky, north to south, from the Jackal Pack base. *That would be the skybeam,* Leon thought, craning his neck to see through the gravcar's windshield. The focused channel of energy ripped into one of the black shapes, bisecting it neatly. Raining flaming debris, the thing in the sky listed and fell in pieces. The beam left a trace image in Leon's vision, tattooed across the clouds.

Another ray of alien blue light, almost incandescent in its intensity, lashed out across the sky and disappeared into the clouds. There was an accompanying flash somewhere far up, but Leon couldn't see what it had hit. The two trace images left a lopsided V across his field of vision, and he blinked rapidly, trying to dispel it.

He caught sight of his quarry again. They were nearly to the outskirts of the port now, and Leon was still gaining, but he would soon lose his advantage. Even so, in the savannah there was nowhere to hide and not enough speed to get away. The other car was less than twenty meters ahead, slowing to thread its way between ships. Leon wasn't about to slow down, and he kept the throttle wide open.

"What are those things?" Traxus asked, sounding dazed herself. Leon wondered how long she had been talking to him over the comm.

"I wish I knew, Trax. Something else." They sure as shit weren't Valinata.

"That was our skybeam, wasn't it?"

"Heidi is knocking as many of those things out of the sky as she can."

"I've never seen anything like them, Leon!"

"Neither have I."

"We should get back to the base to help!"

"As soon as this is done."

"Well, let's get him, then." The comm clicked off.

The whole sky was lighting up now, the steady blasts of the skybeam mixed with green flashes from the descending ships as they fired on the fleeing civilian vessels. A freighter burned as it sank back toward the tarmac only a few kilometers away. Squads of fighters flashed by overhead, gray and navy blue with silver feathers painted on the undersides of the wings. Falcon Guard. The sight of them buoyed Leon's spirits, but only for a moment.

He couldn't keep his mind off Rachel. She had to have gotten clear. Her ship would have left when the attack started. She was safe and sound and oblivious in her first-class berth, well on her way to the stopover on Epsilon Merentis. She would hear the news there, and she would worry about him. But she would be safe.

Another blue beam arced across the sky, much lower this time. The air all around Leon grew hot with bled-off energy, and the Hyena's instruments went momentarily haywire. One of those terrifying black forms, less than a kilometer off the ground, blew apart, the beam carving through it from stern to bow. The destroyed hulk smashed nose-first into the ground, engulfed in a massive fireball that blossomed outward, consuming everything around it.

Now or never, champ. Leon took a deep breath and gunned the accelerator. The car fishtailed as it leapt forward, the engine straining to put every last bit of speed through the wheels. The bumper of the gravcar grew larger in Leon's field of vision. Too late, he realized he hadn't buckled his safety harness.

§

The forest of landing gear came to an abrupt end as Traxus and Jeric reached the edge of the tarmac, and she looked around to get her bearings. She tapped the brakes, and the forward gravcoils flared, kicking up a new cloud of dust as they slowed the vehicle.

"There he is ...wait, where's the other car?" Jeric asked.

"What? Where are you looking?"

Jeric pointed weakly, and Traxus followed with her good eye. There was something odd about the vehicle off to their left. For starters, it was drifting aimlessly. It took her a moment to realize that it wasn't a single vehicle, but two practically welded together by a collision. It looked like the rear half of a wheeled Hyena had been sloppily grafted onto the front of a run-down Shibui gravcar.

"Oh, no. Jeric, Leon *rammed* him."

"That fucking lunatic. Get us over there."

Traxus hit the accelerator, and the gravcoils pulsed, pushing them forward. Leon's car had slammed into the bomber's vehicle so hard that it had ridden up the trunk and embedded its hood in the passenger cabin. As they came closer, the gravcoils of the lead car failed, and both vehicles thudded to the ground.

"Oh, my God! *Leon!*" screamed Traxus, opening her door and jumping out. Jeric followed, stumbling out and squinting in the sunlight. Traxus had her sidearm out, safety off, as she ran toward the twisted mating of cars.

Jeric drew his sidearm, as well, although at this point Traxus wondered how useful he would be. He staggered along in her loping wake, trying not to drop his weapon. Coming around the side of Leon's car, they checked the driver's seat, but the vehicle was empty, the door hanging open. So was the car he had been pursuing.

"Looking for us?" shouted a slurred voice. Their heads snapped back toward the port over which another enigmatic black form descended unopposed, looking like a shadow lurking in the back of a dream. Emerging from a stand of bushes and silhouetted against the horrifying backdrop was a Human man, his right arm bloodied and hanging limply at his side. Beside him Leon lay twisted in the dirt, face up, eyes closed. In his uninjured hand, the man held one of Leon's Sprawlers, aiming it directly at the colonel's head.

It looked as though Leon had crawled away from the wreck, disoriented, and had been caught by his prey. His nose was pouring blood, and his left eye was swollen shut. He struggled upright, looking incredulously at the bomber standing over him.

"Throw the guns in the dirt," said the man, knowing they could never bring their weapons to bear before he shot their friend. He, too, was obviously badly injured, but he still had the upper hand. Jeric and Traxus dropped their sidearms and stood there, helpless. Traxus looked the bastard over. His accent pegged him as a Valinata refugee. His clothes had once been fairly nice, but the last few months had clearly not smiled on him. While his hands were dirty, they were soft. It was hard to tell with his face grimy and contorted in pain, but he looked about forty, ginger-haired. He didn't look the part.

"All right," the bomber said, gesturing with the gun. "Pick up your friend, and let's go back to the port." When they made no move to comply, he moved the barrel closer to Leon's head. "Or I can shoot you all right here."

"What the fuck would you want to do that for?" asked Jeric. *Are the Valinata making a move, too? Is he a Vali spy?* Traxus wondered. "We're being attacked here!"

"I know. Right on schedule." He said it uneasily. So this fucker had knowingly helped pave the way for this hellish invasion force?

"Wha—" Jeric stopped himself and looked again at the descending absurdities and their slick-looking appendages. There were many of them in the sky now, and several had already landed. Blue beams flashed across the sky from the Pack base one after another, and three more of the vessels were falling to earth around the plateau. "You work for *those* things? What the hell is this?"

"What does it look like? This is the invasion. The Celestials are here to liberate you." Something about the way the man said it lacked conviction, as though he were reading lines he didn't like. "I'm just one of the many people tasked with clearing the way. With your general out of it, this will be much easier, for everyone."

In spite of everything, Traxus looked smug. "I've got news for you, asshole, the general wasn't on the ship or even on the planet. He left with those Coalition ships. Nice try."

"What are you talking about?" The man looked at Leon. "Who are you?" Clearly, he was unfamiliar with rank insignia and the Pack's command staff.

"Not the general." said Jeric. "No one was on that ship, nothing but a lot of freeze-dried ice cream and my favorite jacket."

The man fumbled about for a bit, considering. "It doesn't matter," he declared, clearly unconvinced. "If he's not here, he might as well be dead. This planet belongs to them now." He gestured with his stolen gun. "Now move it."

Leon, sitting broken on the ground, still had enough fight left in him to pull his other Sprawler from its holster. He was slow, and if the traitor had been paying attention, he would have seen it, but their enemy's attention was focused on Jeric and Traxus. He felt the pressure of the barrel against his stomach and looked down. "What the—"

"We're not going anywhere," croaked the colonel. He looked at his friends, grimacing. "You idiots, he couldn't have fired the Sprawler anyway. It's keyed to my biometrics."

Jeric and Traxus took a moment to pick up their sidearms, abashed. They aimed them at the man, who pulled the trigger angrily. When it didn't fire, he reluctantly tossed the big pistol into the dirt. Leon's eyes were angry slits, blood and fury pouring out of them. "You fucker," he whispered. "I should have known."

The man took a close look at Leon now.

"I should have recognized the pieces of that Torsion GT bike," Leon said angrily. "That was your bomb, wasn't it? Think you're pretty slick, do you?" Even if the Vali refugees hadn't made much of an impression, the yellow and black racing bike they had been working on had been distinctive. Even Leon, who knew little about gravbikes, had recognized it.

"It was a shame I had to wreck that beauty." The man's eyes narrowed. "This doesn't change anything," he insisted. "They're already here, and there's nothing you can do." He nodded at Leon's battered uniform. "Whoever you are, you look like an important Jackal. You'll make a good hostage." He swallowed. "Oh. Here they come now."

Back in the direction of the port they could see a cluster of large, black creatures chasing civilians and port workers. Heading right for them.

The things that had come off those monstrous ships were huge, nearly eight feet tall. Even so, they looked light, airy. They walked on four spindly legs with a dreamlike swaying motion, like long beach grass in an ocean breeze. At the join of the legs, a long, hunched, skeletal torso sprang upwards. Traxus could see a multitude of dangerous-looking limbs, moving rhythmically. *Choreography?* she wondered, dazed.

It wasn't immediately obvious to Traxus whether the things coming toward them were sojieri or animals of some kind. She couldn't see any uniform markings although their armor appeared to be engraved with symbols. The only weapons she saw were long, curved swords which she belatedly realized were forelimbs. *What the hell are these things?* They moved with clear intelligence and purpose. *Not animals. Troops.* Sojieri of a species she had never seen before.

The bomber was talking again. "If you're lucky, they'll put you to work, like me. If you're not, you'll be recycled." Traxus didn't relish the thought of being pressed into the service of these things, but it sounded preferable to being "recycled."

"You had best … shut your fucking mouth before I shoot you in it," Leon croaked.

The man said no more, holding his wounded arm and his tongue.

The creatures' armor wasn't strictly black, Traxus realized, more of a midnight blue with an oily sheen. They looked almost liquid, the way they moved, the way the light from the burning ships played off their armor.

A few meters away they paused, fanning out with that peculiar, synchronized movement. Through expressive yellow eyes they regarded the four injured people, their mandibles clicking quietly.

Traxus had never seen anything like them. Elegant and horrifying at the same time, they almost defied description. Still too shocked to process, she noted their superficial resemblance to the invertebrate H'vir, but that was as far as she got. The galaxy was a big place, but it had been a long time since anyone had encountered a new sentient species. Traxus knew that that was exactly what she was seeing.

They began talking all at once, and Traxus shrank back from the noise. As those things she now knew to be ships had landed, a loud, low moan had echoed across the port. These creatures were chattering in a high-pitched tone, using rapid clicks of their mandibles and uttering squeals that sounded unpleasantly like children's laughter. It took her a moment to realize she didn't understand any of it, not a sound.

All her life she had taken language comprehension for granted. Like every registered child raised in the greater powers, she had been imprinted through the FLASH program. And right now none of it mattered, its utility undone by their inability to communicate with the things standing before them.

The word "alien" had never meant anything to her, not really, but now, standing before lifeforms with no discernible emotions, no comprehensible speech, she understood it and grew cold. *Alien.* The towering warriors were all over the port now; the sounds of sirens and gunfire were gradually dying down as the port security force succumbed. Scores of survivors were being led away under guard. The burning hulk of a passenger liner was crashing to earth a few kilometers out, over the savannah. Traxus hoped Leon couldn't see it.

She and Jeric had long since shifted their aim from the terrorist to the creatures, but there were almost a dozen of them, and she could tell they were fast. They looked uniquely evolved for war. Leon, meanwhile, had his back to the enemy and kept his gun on the saboteur. He looked nervous; he kept trying to glance over his shoulder, but his injuries kept him from moving well enough to see them.

The aliens squealed again, an earsplitting sound that made Traxus wince. This time the vocalization carried a distinct overtone of menace. The saboteur began talking again, his voice full of terror and reverence. "Masters! My name is Porter! I am one of your people, and I've captured these three sojieri. They can give us information about the base, tell us how to conquer it!"

The creatures tilted their heads quizzically, almost as one. They squealed in chorus even louder. One took a step forward, the ends of its legs like barbed chair legs jabbing into the dusty ground. Traxus slowly drew a bead on its head. She wondered how tough their armor was.

The saboteur—Porter he had called himself—looked confused and even more frightened. "I don't understand you, Masters. If you'll just bring me back, I can explain everyth—"

The creature closest to Porter flicked one of its swordlike limbs with hypnotic fluidity and savage grace, and the man fell to the ground, his chest slashed open and his right arm amputated neatly a few inches above the elbow. He shrieked, stump flailing and gushing blood as he kicked in the dirt. Traxus ignored him; she couldn't care less what happened to the bastard. It was then that the things turned their attention to her and Jeric, emitting a symphonic chirp.

"Jeric, we have to drop these things. Can you shoot?"

"I guess I'll have to...." said the pilot, voice tremulous. He was trying to aim one-handed, his fingers sticky with his own blood.

Leon was struggling on the ground, trying to turn. "How many are there, guys?" he asked weakly.

"Eight." Traxus swallowed hard. There was no way she and Jeric could get them all, not in time. The blood rushing in her ears sounded like an engine approaching.

And now the saboteur was moving again, crawling pathetically away from the confrontation, back toward the wrecked gravcars. His gaze was fixed on the creatures with fear, anger, and disgust writ large upon his features.

The aliens kept shrieking at them, coming slowly closer. The lead creature was right behind Leon and looked ready to strike. Traxus was having trouble controlling her breathing. "Don't move," she ordered firmly. "Halt or I *will* fire." She wondered if it understood.

Either it didn't, or it chose to ignore her. In a flash it darted at Leon, limbs glinting. Traxus and Jeric both opened fire with their pistols. Bullets sparked off the blue-black armor, but some broke through. Black spurts of blood jetted out of the alien as it jerked under the force of each impact. It collapsed to the ground near Leon, quivering, after Traxus managed to put a bullet through one of its eyes.

With a roar very unlike their previous squeaks, the rest of the creatures changed their stance. Traxus shifted her aim again, trying to remember how many bullets she had left in the clip. Before she could fire, however, all hell broke loose. Tracer fire snapped overhead, large-caliber shells thudding into the dirt and punching through the enemy sojieri. Limbs were shorn off and armor plates shattered. Black blood sprayed out, and the seven remaining invaders fell in a heap.

Traxus was panting. She turned around slowly, wondering what new horror she might face.

Two dusty Hyena trucks had stopped behind them, the barrels of their mounted guns smoking. In the chaos Traxus had mistaken the sound of their engines for her own pounding heart. She had never been happier to see the ugly, utilitarian vehicles before. These bore Coalition Falcon Guard markings and sported heavier armor than the ones the Pack owned.

Behind the Hyenas idled a pair of light tanks, their turrets panning back and forth, back and forth. Beyond them were two trucks, disgorging squads of Falcon troops. The Falcon Guard had a fierce reputation, and made a religion out of war, but all Traxus saw was a platoon of sojieri just as terrified as she was.

"Nobody move!" The speaker was a sojier standing in the top hatch of one of the Hyenas. He was holding the firing grips to the roof-mounted Domino heavy machine gun. Two more sojieri had exited the vehicle and taken cover behind the doors, their autorifles trained on the mercenaries and Porter, who had frozen, his remaining arm raised in surrender.

Traxus pointed to the Jackal Pack crest on her burnt uniform sleeve. "We're Jackal Pack!"

"I don't give a fuck who you are! Drop your weapons and lock your hands behind your heads!" The man's voice teetered on the edge of panic, but he obviously knew what he was doing. All the sojieri were clad in Falcon Guard uniforms, blue on gray, and the vehicles all bore Falcon insignia in addition to the Coalition Rienda. What were they doing out here, caught in the open? Supporting those fighters as they fought their losing battle over the cosmodrome and Tesa?

Obediently, the three survivors and their treacherous quarry did as they were told. The two sojieri left the cover of the doors, ran over, and collected the weapons. "Sergeant!" called one of them, "We've got wounded!"

Some of the civilians that had made it beyond the boundaries of the port were flocking toward the Coalition vehicles, looking for salvation. They seemed stunned by the reception they received. The sergeant fired over their heads and screamed for them to lie in the dirt. Terrified and confused, they did so.

As the sojieri moved over to cover the prisoners, Traxus found herself staring down the barrel of a Jackhammer autorifle. A little less than a meter long and weighing a mere four kilograms, the JK126 "Jackhammer," built by Light-Arm and embossed with the familiar flexed metal arm, was an old and reliable piece of war machinery. A single shell from that rifle at this range would punch through Traxus's chest and out her back. Best not to tempt its frightened-looking owner.

The man in the turret was looking in the direction of the cosmodrome, assessing the situation. A platoon of infantry with two Hyenas and two scout tanks weren't enough to do more than annoy the invaders and get destroyed. He turned back to the sojieri on the ground. "All right. Get those four into the back. Tie their hands. I'll radio the commander."

Another voice came from inside the Hyena as the driver's door opened. "Sarge, what about the rest of them? We can't just leave them!"

"What do you recommend we do with them, Bracx? You going to give up your seat?"

"We've got the trucks."

The sergeant glared at his driver. "There are close to a hundred people over there, kid. We can't take them." He pointed at Traxus and her companions. "Those four look like they might know what the fuck is happening here, so they go back with us."

One of the troops from the trucks approached. Her rifle was slung despite their proximity to danger. "Sarge, give them our spots. We'll make it back to the base on foot."

"Absolutely not, Croyer. We all go back together."

"Sergeant, we'll recon the area and report back. But you've got to get moving. It looks like we drew attention." The sojier pointed with one hand while unlimbering her weapon with the other. There were more creatures sprinting toward them, and a number of objects in the sky that seemed to be getting closer.

"Sergeant, we can't just leave them here," pleaded the driver again.

The sergeant mulled this over while contemplating the approaching enemy forces. "Goddammit, all right. Croyer, get the people into the trucks. Take all the ammo and equipment you can carry, and stay the fuck out of sight." He looked at Traxus and the other wounded. "Pavel, Koshe, get those motherfuckers into the Hyena and tie them down. I'm radioing the commander."

The sojieri began herding people toward the trucks while their comrades pulled supplies from the troop compartments. They clearly hadn't intended to be out for long, and Traxus felt a pang of sympathy. The troops were terrified, but none of them raised a word of protest at being left behind. They were Falcons, all right.

A minute passed as the sergeant called back to his base for instructions. This little group of cowboys had probably been on patrol and gotten diverted to assess the situation once the bombs went off. As he grew more and more flustered, Traxus got the impression that no one was answering. Was it possible the base had been overrun? Were they going to be driving into another trap?

"We got incoming!" shouted one of the sojieri, dropping to one knee and taking aim. "Drone fighters!"

"Shit!" The sergeant dropped the comm mike and grabbed the controls to the heavy gun. He panned it upward, and Traxus's gaze turned with it. The last of the Falcon fighters had fallen, and now there were several sleek, dartlike craft swooping toward them. They were small for fighters, but they were at high altitude, coming down fast.

The sojieri piled Leon and Porter into the third, rearmost row of seats in the lead Hyena before gesturing to Traxus and Jeric to get into the second row, as well. They did so without argument, but it was difficult with their wrists bound by trap-cuffs, strips of wire that tightened the more the wearer struggled. As the roar of the machine gun started up again, the sojieri crammed themselves in, one to each pair of prisoners, and the vehicles took off, skidding around in the dirt and fleeing west. The last Traxus saw of Croyer and the other sojieri was them sprinting off into the brush, fading from view as the sun began its descent toward the horizon.

There was a loud shriek overhead that seemed to pour through the open hatch and windows of the Hyena as the invading fighters made their first pass. The sergeant in the hatch kept shooting.

The fighters wheeled in the sky, coming around for another pass. Traxus was acutely aware of how slow their own ground vehicles were moving by comparison and of the two trucks loaded with frightened civilians. On the second pass, streams of greenish fire poured down all around them, scorching the earth around the convoy. The light tanks were slow to turn around, and one of them was immolated in a flurry of blasts, its magazine igniting and setting off a deadly fireworks display as rounds cooked off and punched through its thin armored skin from inside.

The other Hyena was blown apart, as well, when a lucky shot sank through the gunner's hatch. The man at the machine gun was incinerated in the emerald inferno as the fireball ate through him and detonated. A tire bounced out of the explosion and past Traxus's window. One of the fighters banked, and for just a moment she got a clear look at it. It was smooth, shaped like an arrowhead, its surface glossy. Traxus saw no insignia, but she did glimpse what looked like appendages, tendrils that seemed to somehow assist in propulsion or direction, whirling and pulsing behind it. They circled like sharks, now passing the Hyena, now coming back to fire again.

"Get us the hell out of here!" shouted the sergeant from above, between bursts from the Domino. The sojieri in the back of the Hyena leaned out the windows, firing. All around them was the sound of gunfire, excruciatingly loud in the metal confines of the vehicle. Off to the left, the remaining tank was struggling to keep up with them as it bounced over small mounds and plowed through brush, the light cannon on its turret facing behind them, firing off rounds with a steady clockwork booming. *When did we lose the road?*

The trucks weren't nearly as capable off-road as the Hyena or the tank, and the drivers were swerving to avoid hillocks and rocks. It must have been hell for the civilians crammed aboard with no room to move, being thrown around like cargo. Outside an enemy fighter burst into flames and plowed into the ground, throwing up a fountain of dirt. Rocks and debris peppered the Hyena. Traxus knew that there were forty kilometers or so between the cosmodrome and the

Coalition base. Even with their all-terrain suspension, the vehicles would only be able to manage about thirty-five kilometers an hour. They weren't going to last long enough to cover the distance.

"We have to get to the base," cried Leon weakly. Traxus twisted so she could put her hand comfortingly on his shoulder. He winced.

"Just hang on, Leon," she said softly. "We've got to get to safety."

"Oh God, what about Rachel?" Leon moaned.

"She's long gone, Leon. She's safe." Traxus tried to sound convincing, but she didn't believe it herself. She had seen that liner crash to earth, wreathed in fire. She didn't know that it had been Rachel's ship, but she didn't know that it hadn't been, either.

"Turn around!" shouted the colonel from the back seat, his voice a queer mixture of authority and anguish. "I have to get to the Jackal Pack base!"

The sojier up in the front passenger seat looked over his shoulder. "Shut up, you!" he barked, his voice cracking like a teenager's. Below his helmet's reflective visor his lip trembled.

Traxus bit her own lip nervously. Behind them the skybeam was still firing blasts into the heavens, steadily, desperately. Wrecks were plummeting out of the sky, and the clouds were full of fire. Who knew how many more ships were out there or how many had already landed? Traxus couldn't help but marvel at the coordination of this attack. She was willing to bet anything the Coalition fleet was in a conduit now, unaware of the situation and unable to help, getting farther and farther away. They had managed to hit Tesa and the port and who knew how many other towns, meaning that the Signal Fire pulse should have tripped, alerting neighboring systems. They had also tried to decapitate Jackal Pack, and while the saboteur didn't know the difference between Rockmore and Leon, he also didn't know how close he had come. After all, Leon was the ranking officer on the planet. Traxus frowned, wondering how many more infiltrators were on Eve. She doubted Porter had acted alone. And what had he said? *One of the many*, she recalled with a shudder. Were there any among the troops left in the Jackal Pack base? Jackals came and went as they pleased for the most part. If the enemy knew about Rockmore's personal shuttle, it was a good bet.

"Oh, *no!*" someone yelled, and everything flared bright for a searing, white-hot instant. Traxus shut her eyes, waiting for the crash, for death, but oblivion never came. Slowly she opened her eyes. Smoke filled the cabin of the Hyena and streamed from the windows, but the driver had managed to keep the vehicle steady. Up in the turret, the sergeant was slumped over. One of his troops pulled him into the cabin on top of Jeric.

"Sarge?" cried the sojier whose nametag read PAVEL, T. "Sergeant Brandt! Kevin, can you hear me?" He reached forward to check for a pulse. "Dammit!" Traxus looked at the man who had cut down the creatures, saving them. He had taken the brunt of the blast, the front of his uniform and his chest a black, charred mess. The smell was almost unbearable, overcooked meat and burnt plastic.

"Where the fuck are *our* drone fighters? We need air support *now!*" the sojier in the passenger seat screamed into the comm. He looked at Traxus and Jeric over his shoulder and shifted position. "Don't fucking move," he said menacingly. He trained his rifle on them, and Traxus had no doubt in her mind that he would fill them—and the back of the vehicle—with holes if they did anything.

The sojieri hanging out the rear doors kept firing their autorifles, but Traxus doubted they would do much good against those fast-moving fighters. The standard-issue Jackhammer was fantastic as an infantry weapon: light, accurate, and easy to maintain. But while its ammunition was perfect for punching through flak armor on, say, a sojier a few hundred meters away, it wouldn't do much good against vehicle armor, certainly not at these ranges.

The tank was falling even farther behind, and a shot of the greenish energy rocked it hard. Traxus thought for a moment that it was wrecked, but it kept moving, plowing through the plume of smoke, a black scorch mark scarring the right flank.

Traxus had to act fast. The heavy gun on the roof of the Hyena was hanging to one side, but it looked functional. That would work as an anti-vehicle weapon but not without someone to fire it. She moved toward it.

"What are you doing?" demanded the sojier in the passenger seat. "Don't move, or I'll empty this clip into you and your friends." He turned to the driver. "We should have left them, Omar."

The driver ignored him.

Traxus put up her hands placatingly, showing him the tight wire. "Listen, sojier, I—"

"Shut up," said the man, jabbing the rifle at her. If the bayonet had been extended, it would have gone into her heart.

Leon was demanding to be taken to the base again, and Jeric was nervously trying to silence him before he attracted too much attention. The traitor had smartly chosen to remain silent, focusing instead on the missing length of his arm, gradually growing paler as his blood drained onto the floormats, despite a hastily applied tourniquet.

"Listen to me," said Traxus, sharply. An order. That got the man's attention, at least. "My name is Traxus Tachai. I'm a lieutenant with Jackal Pack. See the stripes?"

The man said nothing, but she could tell she didn't have much time to convince him. "Grand Admiral Hakar is my brother."

"Aw, shut up, lady. Before I shoot you."

The driver turned in his seat, and Traxus was worried he was going to flip the vehicle. "Did she just say—holy shit, it *is* her."

"Dammit, Omar, you believe this bitch?"

The driver glared at the man. He hooked a thumb at Traxus. "You never knew the grand admiral's sister is a Jackal? That's her!"

The gun aimed at Traxus's face lowered a little. "Omar, you better know what you're talking about."

"Swear to God, man. What do I stand to gain by lying?" The driver named Omar kept on driving. His surprisingly calm voice brought a marked sureality to the situation.

"Sorry, miss." The sojier seemed reluctant to admit wrongdoing but even more reluctant to shove a gun in the face of the grand admiral's kin.

Traxus tried to smile politely. "No time for apologies, just cut me loose. I'm good on a gun. If you let me up in that turret, you won't be sorry."

The man stammered. "I, ah, I—fuck it." Now he flipped a catch on the grip of his autorifle, and the bayonet slid out of its storage slot beneath the barrel. He quickly cut the ties that bound her.

Wasting no time, Traxus pushed around Jeric and the acridly stinking corpse of the sergeant, pulling herself up through the hatch. She burned her hands on the still-hot circular rim of the turret hatch but paid the pain no mind. The wind whipped through her fur as she peered over the back of the vehicle. Incoming fire was pouring down like rain, burning the ground all around them. Behind them a wake of flaming green patches stretched across the savannah, bright in the gathering twilight.

The tank's light cannon fired off a good shot, a direct hit to one of the pursuing enemy vehicles. The arrowhead vanished in flame.

Traxus grabbed the handgrips to the gun and pulled it around, her fear gone now that she was no longer a helpless bystander. She checked the ammo drum, still half-full, and opened fire. Her innate sense of balance had always made her a sure shot in the turret of a moving vehicle, a fact which made her as proud as it made her angry to have been squandered as a combat asset.

Focusing on one of the flying objects, she squeezed the trigger, the gun bucking as she led the target out. The Hyena pulled to one side, but she anticipated the move, managed to keep pouring fire on the enemy vehicle. Within seconds it succumbed to her sustained battery and burst into flames, careening into the brush, end over end.

Orienting herself, Traxus looked back over her shoulder, toward the front of the Hyena. Dry scrubland vanished underneath its front bumper and came out from beneath the rear end, bushes whipsawing in the truck's wake. The grassland savannah of Eve stretched to the horizon in every direction, ordinarily serene and welcoming but now bleak and hopeless. The crags of Las Serras da Estrela were visible to the southwest, and beyond them lay the depleted wastes of Eve's strip-mined southern hemisphere. The port was quickly vanishing behind them to the northeast, marked only by pillars of smoke. They were alone with the enemy. How far had they come? Hardly far enough.

Traxus turned back to the far more important task of shooting down the things that were chasing them. Another one found itself in her crosshairs, and she let loose. Her fire was right on target, chewing up its left flank. The dart wobbled in mid-air and flipped upside down into the dirt, plowing up soil and plants, its pointed nose suddenly a giant garden spade.

"Good shooting, Trax!" shouted Jeric from below. Too soon, as a blast slammed into the side of the Hyena, knocking Traxus back into the cabin. The left rear door tore off, and the sojier who had been firing out the window went with it, kicking. The tangle of metal and man tumbled along the ground, receding quickly.

"*No!*" shouted one of the other troops. They couldn't stop, and they couldn't go back. The man was dead one way or the other.

Traxus pulled herself upright, but before she could take control of the gun, one of the trucks behind them was hit. It jackknifed, tipping over onto its roof. Another blast turned it into an inferno. She knew she couldn't actually hear the screams of the trapped refugees, but she could imagine them clearly enough. There was no time to mourn: she gritted her teeth and kept firing while the remaining Coalition vehicles continued their desperate retreat through the long grass and the gathering night.

15: Invasion

The road to Dobrian left Hakar with time to ponder all his frayed, dead ends. In the quiet of his stateroom he blew out a defeated sigh. His quarters were luxurious by the standards of a warship. In fact, they were nicer than his apartment on Tagea, and he felt oddly pampered, as well as disconnected from the rest of the ship thanks to the sound-proofing. Thousands of people were stationed aboard *Condor*, and their presence could be felt everywhere from the engine rooms to the maintenance subdecks, everywhere except here. He pushed his chair back in its track and looked up at the bulkhead above him. The featureless plush paneling—sound-dampening and heat-insulating—held no clues.

He had traced every conduit leading to Ezai back two or three systems, but there had been no unusual reports. Honestly, he hadn't expected any magically convenient coincidences. Still, it made no sense. The conspirators came from different worlds, different military academies, different ideologies. Unless three different treasons somehow coincided, there was a common factor of which Hakar was as yet unaware.

On impulse he brought up Sergeant Munroe's file and the file of Geran's assassin, Lydia Gillette. They still didn't know which of Vice-Grand Admiral Larador's people had turned on him, blowing up the entire bridge tower. Sixty officers and enlisted had died in the blast, and any one of them could have been responsible.

Intelligence had run every possible comparison test. Hundreds of trained statisticians, intelligence analysts, and behavioral psychologists had pored over the data and found nothing. What did he expect to accomplish?

Idly he expanded the timeline of the search parameters. It was ridiculous, frankly, and he wasn't surprised when the computer returned no matches. Both Gillette and Munroe were Human; the search had already scanned for links between them as far back as their eighteenth birthdays, any farther would be stretching plausibility. Would they have been planning this deceit as far back as their childhoods? It was laughable.

Unfortunately, no one had addressed the obvious: perhaps they had never met and never even knew about one another. If they had been recruited as sleeper cells to carry out some enemy's bidding, all they would have in common was an unidentified handler. Not even the logic engines on Triatha would be able to map the linkages between so many people, no matter how invasive the Coalition's tracking practices might be.

Hakar wondered if the autopsies had been conducted. While the causes of death left no room for uncertainty, perhaps toxicology would reveal something. What the grand admiral found surprised him: There had been autopsies, but their findings were sealed at the highest security level. Irritated, he posed a query to the network. The automated reply from the intelligence service systems controller was instantaneous and ominous.

ERROR 22Y//REPORT OF CASUALTY: [GILLETTE, LYDIA E.] CLASSIFIED

ERROR 22Y//REPORT OF CASUALTY: [MUNROE, SIMON J.] CLASSIFIED

ERROR 03G//REPORT OF CASUALTY: [ASSET LOST//TIGER FLOWER] RECORD CORRUPTED

Hakar blinked at the third entry, his throat tight. Why was that there? Was it a mistake? He entered another query, and the error messages disappeared completely, replaced by an assurance that the Service would retrieve the records for him.

Hakar stared at the screen for a long time, hoping futilely that more information would present itself. That third entry was still etched in his mind. It had to be an error. Had to be. Shaken, unable to concentrate any longer, he rose, stretched, and walked toward the hatch.

§

Jon Rockmore stood with his nose almost touching the curved bow-facing porthole of the bridge. As always, he was mesmerized by the vortex of the conduit; its infinite, shifting patterns sometimes created nearly recognizable dreamscapes the same way lightning might reveal darkened countryside in sun-like clarity for the barest instant. Before him the long, pointed hull of the *Condor* stretched like a gleaming headland over a stormy and violet sea. Barely four inches of polycrystal stood between Rockmore and an oblivion so infinite and incomprehensible that it was hard to look at. But look he did. Men and women had gone mad staring into the conduits, seeing shapes and forms writhing in the gloom that could not possibly exist. Myths had sprung up in the early days of interstellar travel to explain the fates of vanished ships and fleets. It was a testament to the conduits' mystery that those campfire tales still persisted.

Was it calling to him? That deep subconscious whisper, seeming to come from a shadowy figure lurking just behind him, made Rockmore shudder. Though he was a man of broad vision, he was not prone to wild imaginings. He didn't believe in the sinuous wraiths coursing through the universe's arcane hallways. He had imagined that voice, and as soon as he decided that, it went silent. All he could hear was the faint crackle of the comms officer's station and the quiet clicking of the bridge crew's computers, their muffled coughs and sighs, and the endless, throbbing hum of the ship.

The crew was operating with a quiet, restless energy, those not on active duty trying in vain to rest. Rockmore felt sleep's call, as well, but there was no chance of that, he knew. The enemy had stolen the march on them, to use an ancient phrase. Dobrian was behind the lines and should have been well out of the way of Raven Blue's advance. Rockmore had brushed up on the sector's history: the planet boasted a few cities and some modest agricultural export centers, but it lay at the end of a string of conduits, leading nowhere. This was obviously a lure, and no one could fail to see it.

Still, Hakar's goodwill tour of the Outbound Arc would fail miserably if they let Raven Blue raze a world under their watch without retaliating. So they had reassigned half of Hakar's fleet, more than enough to annihilate the token force they were told to expect. The whole situation made the hairs on the general's neck stand on end.

The tour would continue after the token victory, though Commodore Tarot had resolved not to land the great warship again. The grand admiral would inspect planetary defense forces and review troops, no doubt approvingly and with inspiring words to set them on.

Waiting for Dobrian to appear, Rockmore was beginning to remember all the reasons he had left the Unified Commonwealth

Authority. No one did anything without an ulterior motive, every move politically calculated. It was troubling that a man as straightforward as Hakar was so caught up in the machinations. And all the flag-waving and rousing speeches were covering up the fact that, even with Hakar's fleet in the area and more on the way, the Alkyra and the surrounding regions were woefully underdefended.

Then again, it wasn't Rockmore's place to question the client. He scratched idly at the old scar along his jaw. Orders were orders, after all, even for a mercenary, and even those in the highest ranks occasionally had to follow them. Without discipline and obedience, an army was nothing more than a collection of violent men and women. Still, Rockmore's principal obligation was to his own troops, and he wouldn't see them misused.

"Admiral on the bridge!" the officer of the deck announced, jumping to his feet as Hakar strode through the blast doors. The rest of the crew likewise rose, saluting. Rockmore, out of old habit and respect, did the same.

"As you were, ladies and gentlemen." Hakar exchanged some whispered words with the OOD as the rest of the crew went back to work. Rockmore noticed that their backs seemed a little straighter, their work a bit more focused now that the grand admiral was present. He had to admit that even he felt a bit of a thrill standing in the presence of a living legend.

Rockmore studied Hakar surreptitiously. The grand admiral's eyes were open, alert. The Tagean day was far longer than the Terran equivalent, and the Tageans themselves possessed a different biochemistry, with much slower biological clocks. They could go for days without needing more than an hour or two of sleep. Hakar looked surprisingly at ease for someone whose kingdom had just taken the plunge over the precipice of all-out war. The slow pace of their preparations had to be taking its toll on him, too.

Rockmore understood the reason for that inexplicable calm, though. For too long, Grand Admiral Hakar—and most members of the Circle, for that matter—had commanded fleets from a desk on Tagea. A grand admiral's actual presence was rarely required in the field for any reason other than negotiation or public relations, and like much else in the Coalition, they had become largely symbolic, painted figureheads on the bureaucracy's gaudy ship of state. The mercenary commander was sympathetic as he, too, had delegated much of the art of war to his subordinates, a master painter guiding his apprentices. But while many of the Coalition's flag officers had come to accept, even to enjoy, this newfound, enforced lassitude, Hakar had never been among them. No real officer liked to command in absentia, and Hakar was notorious for violating protocol and finding his way to the front on the increasingly rare occasions when there *was* a front. His nickname, "Trenchline Troublemaker," came from loyal sojieri who had never seen a high-ranking officer, much less one of their vaunted grand admirals, standing shoulder to shoulder with them, laughing, joking. On more than one occasion, he had taken up arms with his troops despite the frenzied protests of his command staff. It took years—and an act of parliament during the early months of Kra'al's reign—for Strategic High Command to get him to at least remain on his flagship where, it was argued, he could have the best strategic and tactical information available and therefore make the most informed decisions to protect the troops he cared so much for.

Having been desk-bound for so long, Hakar must enjoy being back on the bridge of a battleship, even in such troubled times. And with a flagship like this one, he must have found it satisfying indeed. He prowled the bridge like an apex predator just released from a zoo, refamiliarizing himself with the geometry of a warship. But he certainly didn't look like he was enjoying himself: he looked distracted and a little sick.

As if sensing Rockmore's gaze, the grand admiral turned and smiled wanly at his friend, the smile of a man under a death sentence. He said something else to the OOD and walked over. "Are your people ready?"

"I was about to ask you the same thing." Rockmore sensed that whatever was distressing Hakar at this moment it wasn't Dobrian. But clearly the grand admiral did not want to discuss it. "Nice ship you have here."

"This old hunk of tin is due for mothball in a few years."

"You're kidding."

"Not by much." Hakar turned serious. "We're both probably due for retirement."

"Don't be crazy."

Hakar didn't seem to hear him. "We've seen more than a few battles, won more than a few wars. But things break down: malfunctions, problems interfacing with newer technology. The universe has changed, my friend. This ship and I have been left behind." Abruptly Hakar switched gears. "What did you mean about Leon not being a Jackal much longer? I hope you're not thinking of letting him go over this. I told you, I'm working on getting him reattached."

"That's not it, Hakar. I admit occasionally Leon has to be reminded that we're a customer service organization and the client is always right. Between you and me, he's not long for the Pack."

Hakar's attention focused in an instant. "If this is about the incident on Tikal, I would hate for that—"

"It's not about your Knights arresting him at gunpoint or the mission to Aethaleia, either. I'd keep him if I could, and I know part of him wants to stay, but.... Did he mention Rachel Case?"

Hakar thought for a moment, tapping his chin. "I'm not as caught up on Leon's life as I wish I were. We didn't have time to get into it, and Traxus doesn't exactly write me a lot of letters. Or call."

Rockmore turned away from the viewport, his head pounding from looking at the conduit for so long. He led Hakar back toward an unoccupied corner of the bridge. "They're in love. They'll probably be married by the end of the year if they don't kill each other first."

"What do you mean?"

"You've been married for a few decades now. Maybe you've forgotten, but not everyone chooses war as a lifestyle. It can be a source of friction."

Hakar looked thoughtful for a moment, unguarded, almost regretful. Was he regretting sending Leon down the path he was on? "So Leon is getting out of the game."

Rockmore didn't comment on it, but he resented Hakar's use of the word "game." Perhaps he *had* been too long behind a desk, watching icons move around a computer screen.

"I still hope he knows that I worked hard to get Her Majesty to relent."

"I don't doubt it, Hakar. Neither does he." Rockmore stroked his beard, tracing his scar. "That Jow Metha makes quite an impression."

The Tagean bristled. "He's not a surrogate for Leon, Jon, if that's what you're implying. I have nothing but respect for both of them, but they couldn't be more different. Considering what Jow has been through...."

"I heard his story. I confess I can't wait to see what he's capable of when you unleash him. Maybe he and Leon are more alike than you think."

Further conversation was forestalled when an alarm began beeping softly but insistently across the bridge. Hakar's ears twitched, and Rockmore glanced over. There was frantic activity in the comm bay, and the alarm stopped. The warrant officer manning the station waved the OOD over. The two conferred briefly, glancing periodically at Hakar, who watched quietly.

A few moments later, the OOD jogged over to Hakar. "Admiral, sir, I apologize for the interruption, but I have to ask you to prepare for emergency reversion."

"What? Why?" Hakar sounded genuinely stunned.

"Sir, I...." The officer hesitated, as though concerned it was a false alarm. "It may be an error with the ansible, but we need to revert to check it properly. We've lost the Signal Fire pulse completely."

Hakar was very still for a moment. "All right, bring us out." He turned to Rockmore, and the old mercenary could tell that the grand admiral was worried. So was he. "Jon, take a seat."

While the OOD contacted Commodore Tarot and the rest of the senior command staff, the two strapped into the observers' seats. Hakar's long arms were poised on the armrests of his seat, muscles taut, as though he were ready to leap out of it. Rockmore felt his heart beating harder and faster. Hakar said nothing. There was nothing to say.

By the time the general quarters alert had sounded and the great ship reverted, many of the senior officers were on the bridge, looking tired and bewildered. Some looked a little embarrassed that they were half-asleep and out of uniform while Hakar still wore his, surprisingly unwrinkled by the day's events.

Rockmore barely noticed as *Condor* dropped out of the conduit in an empty system. A weak, distant star pushed its rays of light at the bridge viewport, a street vendor who knows his wares aren't worth the price he charges. A dusty little planet sat off to the right, revolving sadly in space. The rest of the armada had reverted, as well, ships hanging uncertainly against the black. They were hours yet from Dobrian.

The officers came to full alert quickly enough when Warrant Officer Kisuuj, who was in charge of the comm bay, explained the situation. "Ladies and gentlemen, the Alkyran Signal Fire pulse has failed. We're still trying to determine the reason and origin point for the failure. Our own comm array seems to be functioning normally." Kisuuj glanced around the bridge, but no one interrupted. "We're doing our best to reacquire the signal. Until then, we have to assume that the signal interruption occurred along the Alkyra. Standard operating procedure is to hail PDF and local government leadership. At the moment none has responded."

This time when Kisuuj stopped speaking the silence was deafening. *No one* had responded? It must be an error. Rockmore felt as though a great weight was pushing down on his chest. He just hoped he wasn't having a heart attack.

"We'll continue to hail, and our other ships will do so, as well," the warrant officer assured them all. "In the meantime, you should all be aware that, going back through recent comm logs, we detected an intermittent echo in the Signal Fire pulse. It's too early to say, but initial pattern analysis has led us to believe that an unknown third party was piggybacking the signal. To what end we're not sure. The anomalies were too clean to be background noise or magnetic distortion from nearby stars. Something else was out there."

Rockmore started, feeling himself jolted awake from a particularly bad nightmare. Only he was still on the bridge, still hearing this appalling news. This was his home they were talking about. Without thinking he blurted out, "'Something?' What do you mean by 'something?' Ships?"

Rockmore felt eyes turning to regard him, but the only gaze he cared about was Kisuuj's. "Yes, sir," the comm officer said hesitantly.

"Is there any chance that this is due to the realignment of the trade route systems?" asked one of Hakar's officers hopefully. "Gravitational interference perhaps?"

"It's possible," conceded the comm officer, "but I doubt it."

"Commodore," Hakar said. It was a single word, spoken softly, but with such authority that he might as well have screamed it. Tarot had looked pale and disheveled, but Hakar's voice seemed to jumpstart his heart. He leapt into action.

"All ships signal general quarters. *Canyon Wind* and *Ashes of Pyyran* are still in the D'zen Gulf. They will proceed to Benez and restore contact with the regional government. Scout detachments will head to the other colonized systems of the Alkyra and conduct tactical assessments."

"We're still going to Dobrian?" Rockmore asked in disbelief.

Hakar nodded. "We don't have a choice. Shra and Veraxus will hold the Alkyra until we know more."

The crew had been on full alert already but now sprang into frenzied activity. They would strike at Dobrian and strike hard, revenge for being drawn off so early and leaving the Alkyra open to attack. A volatile, heady atmosphere descended over the bridge.

"We need to hail Eve," Rockmore whispered to Hakar amid the chaos.

The grand admiral gave him an anxious look of comprehension but said nothing. Of course, he knew that Leon was still there, and his own sister might be. He couldn't simply ignore his duty due to personal feelings.

And yet he did. "Warrant Officer Kisuuj, I wonder if you might hail Eve for me."

Kisuuj looked stricken. "Sir, I ... I'm sorry to inform you, but ... we already have."

"Excuse me?"

"The planet's one big busy signal, Admiral. We're being crowded off all the channels."

"Radio chatter? Anything useful?" Hakar's ears had folded back, desperation evident in his voice and his posture.

"Nothing coming out. The planet's blacked out." Kisuuj looked away, unable to meet the admiral's gaze. "We'll keep trying, sir."

Colonel Akida walked onto the bridge, consulting with Hakar's division S-4, the chief quartermaster. He caught sight of Rockmore and made his way over. He snapped a salute, which Rockmore and Hakar returned swiftly. Even in hell, decorum had to be observed.

"Grand Admiral, General, my forces are ready to deploy to Eve immediately."

"I appreciate that, Colonel Akida," Hakar said softly, trying to calm himself. "Hopefully, that won't be necessary."

Akida looked frantically from Hakar to Rockmore, but the general had nothing to offer him. "Stand down, son. As soon as we have a plan of action, we'll be on the move. We still don't know what's going on."

Akida's jaw was set, his hands clenched into fists. He said nothing more, though Rockmore could tell he wanted to. *We're going in the wrong direction,* his eyes pleaded.

It was painful for Rockmore, too, especially knowing there were lives in the balance, lives of people he cared about. He couldn't bring himself to believe in a malfunction or some side-effect of the Alkyra realigning. Hakar was a man of action, he always had been. Rockmore couldn't imagine him keeping them waiting for long.

For once Hakar chose discretion. "Comm High Command and report our status," he ordered. "Meanwhile, I want status reports from all battle groups. Get Shra on the line."

But Shra did not respond.

16: Conquest

I never called Natille back, Leon realized, his mind still foggy with pain. *Will she cancel the wedding if I die here?*

The shooting wouldn't stop. Lying in the back seat, halfway down on the floor of the Hyena, Leon couldn't move or even cry out. One sojier's knee was jammed painfully against his bruised ribs, and it felt like it was grinding its way toward his organs as they rattled over rocks and through the brush. Wind was screaming through the gap where the door had been ripped off. Past his feet Leon could see the blur of the open savannah, dark in the cloudy sunset.

Leon could also see Porter, the saboteur. The terrorist was working to stanch the bleeding stump of his arm, his mouth closed in a thin line, his flesh gray. If he didn't get proper help soon, he would bleed out, and whatever information he had would be lost. The slice was clean, through meat, muscle, and bone in a single swipe. *What could do that? A born weapon.*

"We're going the wrong way!" Leon exclaimed, trying to get their attention. His voice was slurred, even to his own ear. "You need to take us to the Jackal Pack base. I am in charge of planetary defense and I need to get back there."

"Oh, *you're* in charge? You're doing a lousy fucking job, Colonel," snapped the sojieri in the front seat. "There's no way we're going anywhere near there. Those ships are all over your base. It'll be a miracle if your people last another hour."

"Goddammit," Leon snapped back, trying and failing to raise himself up in the back seat, "We have to work together. Get me to my base. My troops will support you."

"Listen, Colonel, we are saving your fucking lives, but you are still prisoners of the Coalition until the commander says otherwise. So sit back, shut up, and enjoy the ride!"

Another blast rocked the Hyena, blowing dirt and rocks into the cabin. Leon and Porter were showered with debris. The sojier fell inward against the back of the seat in front of them. "You okay?" asked Jeric, checking the man for wounds as best he could with his hands tied.

The sojier nodded, his face white. "That was close. I think it cooked off my eyebrows."

Traxus kept up the hurricane of machinegun fire. Stray shell casings fell through the hatch and rattled around on the floor of the Hyena, adding their little jingling contribution to the general cacophony. Bright light filled the cabin of the vehicle as another enemy vehicle exploded alongside. Leon saw the flash reflected in the eyes of Jeric and the sojier who was still lying wounded in the back alongside them.

"Go, Trax!" shouted Jeric, raising his shackled arms triumphantly, blood still streaming from his mangled hand.

"Hold on!" shouted the driver, not a moment too soon: the Hyena jolted hard and went nose-upward, making for the sky. Leon felt himself slide back in the seat as the engine revved, wheels spinning in the air. Looking out through the gap where the driver's-side rear door had been, he saw the ground coming back up at them at a sickening angle. An instant later the vehicle slammed back to earth, and he was thrown hard against the right-hand door. The sojier was thrown against him, knocking the wind out of him. Leon gritted his teeth as pain seized him and twisted him in its grip.

"Holy *shit*!" yelled one of the sojieri.

Jeric's head popped up over the seatback. He looked like he'd been slammed against the door pretty hard, too. His hair was matted with fresh blood on one side, and his nose was bleeding again. The pilot shook his head, trying to clear it, and regarded Leon. He opened his mouth to speak when the Hyena lurched again, slamming him into the ceiling. "Ouch, dammit!" he exclaimed, clutching at his head as he slumped back out of sight.

Leon remained silent, jaw clenched. He wanted nothing more than to squeeze his eyes shut and wait for it to end, but he forced himself to bear witness. He was a prisoner, being taken farther from his base and his duty with every second, farther from Rachel. Being helpless on the floor only made the experience even more harrowing. Had her ship gotten off the ground? Leon had no idea, but he prayed it had.

At least Traxus had taken matters into her own hands, facing death on her own terms, and he was happy his life was in her hands, as well. Flashes of green swirled around them, a jade inferno. Above the steady boom of explosions Leon could hear the shriek of the things chasing them. *Air through intakes, that's all it is*, he assured himself. But it sounded so angry.

Traxus ducked down, looking as though she had been grilled. "Merciful Ancients, it's getting bad out there," she gasped. "I can barely breathe."

The driver looked over his shoulder again, and Leon caught a glimpse of a young man with dark skin and wide eyes. Not looking where he was going seemed to be a bad habit. "Don't worry, we're almost to the perimeter."

"Lead," crackled a voice over the speaker in the dashboard, "we're almost out of commission here!" It was the tank crew. "We still can't raise the base!"

The driver did the talking while skidding around a patch of rocks. "Just hang on, boys! We're almost clear to the line!"

"What if there's no one there?"

"There'll be someone there," the driver assured everyone. *But will it be ally or enemy*? Leon wondered.

Propping himself up to see over the rows of seats and through the windshield, Leon caught a glimpse of a shallow-sloped mountain topped with the ragged rim of a volcanic crater. The Coalition regional base kept a low profile and was closely guarded, but Leon knew that the site had been chosen because the dormant volcano's geothermal vents provided limitless, ecologically sound energy.

Silhouetted against the mackerel sky, the volcano seemed threatening rather than inviting, not least of all because they still didn't know what awaited them within.

The firing continued while the surviving vehicles threaded their way through the brush. There was a loud roar overhead, and one of the sojieri swore. "What was that?"

"Drone fighter!" shouted the driver, pointing. "More ahead!" Sure enough, a cluster of black specks swarmed in the sky, bearing down on them.

"Ours or theirs?" asked the first sojier. "Oh, Jesus, they're going to strafe us."

Leon had just about given up hope when the comm crackled, and a woman's voice said, "Authenticate."

The sojier in the passenger seat grabbed for the mike. "Say again! This is Venom One. Say again!"

The voice returned, full of static but cold and professional. "Venom One, this is Viper Two. I need you to authenticate."

"Viper Two, we are under heavy attack. We've suffered heavy casualties and have noncombatants onboard. We need—"

"Venom One, this is Viper Two Actual." It was a man's voice, calm and even. "Listen, son, we need you to authenticate, or we *will* fire."

The driver grabbed the mike, speaking rapidly but clearly. "Viper Two Actual, this is Venom One Actual. Corporal Omar Bracx speaking. Dancer Violet. I say again, Dancer Violet."

"Acknowledged, Venom One. We're developing a firing solution now. Aerospace support is on station."

The specks had gotten closer, resolving themselves into compact Coalition drone fighters, piloted by rudimentary artificial intelligence. Agile, accurate, and relentless, they flew by at low altitude and tore into the enemy formation, Gatling guns blazing with a sound like a chorus of circular saws. It wasn't enough, though: while they brought down two more of the enemy fighters, they were no match for the invaders.

The driver grabbed the mike again. "Viper, air support is down. We've got half a dozen echoes in close pursuit. Be advised, danger close! Danger *very fucking close*."

The woman's voice responded. "We see them, Venom One. Task Force Venom, shut your eyes on my order. It's about to get very toasty where you are." There was a pause. "Firing in five … four … three … two … *one*. Sending the mail!"

Leon shut his eyes as the blast shot past them. Even so, the light seemed to burn right through his eyelids. The blinding crash was world-ending, and Leon felt the Hyena thrown forward, leaving the ground. The air crackled, standing his hair on end. An alarm sounded, sounding tinny and weak in the aftermath of the explosion.

Gradually the vehicle slowed, and Leon realized they had lost power. The blast had come from a nuclear dispersion cannon, and the resulting electromagnetic pulse had knocked out their electrical systems. Somehow the crew had managed to avoid vaporizing them. The stunned occupants of the Hyena were left unable to speak, and the vehicle coasted in complete silence but for the sound of the brush scraping the undercarriage. What was left of the front bumper came to rest against a rock.

"Everyone out," the driver ordered. "Pavel, you still alive?"

The sojier lying across Leon and Porter spat. "Barely, Omar. That was a fucking close one."

The troops stepped out of the vehicle. Shaking, Traxus helped Leon and Jeric out. The sojieri congratulated her on her relentless defense but made no move to cut their bindings. They left the saboteur lying inside with the corpse of the sergeant. The world they stepped into was nothing like the one they had been in when Leon had shut his eyes. In place of the golden savannah, the earth was blackened, charred. Nearby the skeleton of a tree was burning. A kilometer away Leon spotted the unmistakable glitter of sand fused into glass. The light tank had crashed into a hillock off to the south, and the transport truck had coasted just past the edge of the blast zone. The driver and codriver were helping civilians out. Many were vomiting, but they all appeared relatively unharmed.

"What is that?" Leon finally croaked. He could see a hulking shape in the distance, but his vision was blurry and his head was swimming.

The driver, Bracx, turned to regard him. "You're Colonel Victor, aren't you? I'm sorry I didn't recognize you … with your nose smashed." Bracx remembered that he had been asked a question. "That was one of our long-strikers, sir. And here it comes now." He pointed.

A colossal war machine was moving toward them, a sloped hull bristling with cannon, the largest of which, a capital ship-grade nuclear dispersion cannon, was still smoking. Leon squinted, entranced by the tank even through the haze of pain. It was an LS-133 Long-Striker. Dual fusion reactors charged the NDC and anti-missile lasers while keeping the vehicle aloft on eight two-stage antigrav generators. It was old, an artillery piece from a bygone era, as much a symbol as an actual weapon. What was it doing on Eve?

The thirty-foot barrel of the main cannon was radiating heat, causing the air to shimmer. The jets of steam hissing out of cooling vents along the supertank's armored surface made it look volcanic. The interior of the Hyena had been an oven due to the heat of the enemy's near misses. Being this close to the recently fired cannon, however, left Leon feeling like he was standing on the surface of the sun.

He was barely able to stand or he might have jumped for joy. Bracx and his comrades were working to get the Hyena started again. High up on the turret of the long-striker, a hatch opened. The man who emerged was well into middle-age, disheveled but still somehow dignified. His salt-and-pepper hair was matted beneath his officer's cap. The cap and its shining Rienda emblem were the only things about him that looked clean: his face and battle dress uniform were grimy, smoke-stained, and sweaty. He waved and shouted down, "How 'bout that mushroom cloud!"

"Captain Durand!" shouted Bracx. "Thanks for the save! We've got wounded and prisoners! Why are communications with the base down?"

"Some kind of jamming field has knocked out our comms. All we've got is line of sight. Where's the rest of your unit?"

"Gone, sir." Bracx looked down, focusing on the engine.

"I'm sorry to hear that. But it looks like you boys did some good. Now get that Hyena running and get up the hill. Storm's coming."

"What do you mean, sir?"

"Echoes coming down south of Las Serras. The commander sent the Peregrine to hold them off. All units are pulling back to the crater. It looks like we're on our own." The captain pointed to the west where columns of smoke were visible, scattered across the savannah around the Coalition Regional Base. "Our Triple-A already sent a dozen of them to hell. They stopped bothering us, but they've got plenty of targets to choose from, and we can't defend them all."

The light tank rumbled back to life, and not long afterwards Bracx and his team got the Hyena and the truck running again. The weary refugees piled back into the vehicles and resumed the last leg of the journey, the long-striker plodding along behind. Bracx made his initial report as he drove, relating the harrowing events over the radio with a surprisingly steady voice. The sorry convoy limped up the incline along a rough, rutted road and over matted vegetation, making its way to a gap in the crater rim that had been carved out by Coalition engineers. The gap was guarded by deadly-looking turrets so large they looked capable of knocking a moon out of orbit. A huge blast-gate blocked the path, but it groaned open at their approach. The Hyena led the way into the base, spitting sparks.

§

As the sun's rays chased the night's shadows from the throne room, Empress Kra'al raised her face to them, letting them wash over her, cleansing her. There was warmth in those beams, real warmth. The mosaics stretching across the floor beneath her seemed to come to life, radiant, and she felt herself come to life, as well, rejuvenated by the all-encompassing light.

She had chosen a gown that conjured the sunrise for her audiences this morning, as though to chase away the dark. The light seemed to fuse with it, the fabric rippling in waves of gold, orange, red. Kra'al drew a deep breath and began her prayers, sketching the ancient runes of her clan on the tiled floor, feeling their power shiver up her arm as though conducted by her claws. *I should be in the garden beneath open skies, tracing in the dirt*, she thought irritably. But she forced the thought away and cleared her mind. It was getting more and more difficult to do that each morning.

Her index claw traced the rune for *Guidance* on the tiles, clicking over the edges of each one, that her Clan Father might point her to the right decisions when they came.

She traced the rune for *Knowledge*. She prayed that information would come to her through the agents of the Coalition.

She traced the rune for *Truth*, hoping that she would see with clarity and not falter.

Then, hesitatingly, haltingly, she traced the rune to the Mother Goddess for *Wrath*, that the forces of the CRDF might fall upon their enemies and emerge victorious. She grimaced but knew it had to be.

As the rays of the sun hit the opposite wall and began their swift climb up its tapestry-covered surface, Kra'al gathered her gown around her and stood, reflecting sadly that however warm Tagea's star might be, it was not Prrastra's sun. It was not the sun of her Clan Father, not the sun of the Mother Goddess, not the sun of home and faith, and she received little solace from its light. It was hard enough to keep faith in this cynical galaxy, harder still when there was no sign of her gods on the world she now called home. Standing and moving to the nearest of the tall, arched windows, Kra'al saw a city painted in gold and ivory, fountains and canals a brilliant cerulean, and the sky a mesmerizing violet. *I suppose it's not that bad*, she mused with bittersweet sentiment. Much of the old city still slept, dreaming dreams. All too soon it would wake, rub the sleep from its eyes, and go about its day. The streets would fill with people as would the throne room, and Kra'al's moment of quiet introspection would be left behind. For now she relished the silence, the sight of the mosaics in their entirety, not just contextless patches between the feet of her attendants. When the great carved double doors at the far end of the chamber creaked open and banged against the walls, she started. She had given her orderly strict orders to let no one disturb her.

"Good morning, Your Highness." There was an undercurrent of directionless panic beneath the easy words of Telec's greeting. As the echo of his call ran in diminishing circuits around the great hall, she turned to face her defense advisor. He was running toward her with a bundle of printouts, his shoes snapping smartly on the tiles. His breathing was dry and raspy. Every time she saw the Sanar, the news seemed to get worse and worse. What could he possibly have to tell her now?

"What's wrong, Admiral?"

Telec came to a dead stop before her. She saw the very real fear in his eyes and felt its infectious effects herself. "Raven Blue is on the offensive, Ma'am."

The empress rose, looking down at Telec. "Where?" Had Hakar's fleet drawn them out?

"As expected, they've hit the Alkyra. Twelve worlds along the trade route have fallen or are falling. We've lost contact with the entire sector."

The sun's warmth turned back to cold winter light as Kra'al's heart slowed. Her universe shrank to a spot on the floor of that huge room with its towering columns and windows made up of hundreds of panes of glass. A part of the mosaic showed a young Rukadj girl, blue-skinned and beautiful, the Princess Alkyra, her mouth open in a wordless scream of anguish as she watched her world destroyed, her tears sprinkled across the heavens. *And the tears became the river along which the Prism Ships sailed.* Kra'al knew the tale: Alkyra had been kidnapped, taken to the stronghold of a great villain. Over centuries the legends had become conflated; in some versions she was taken by the Pirate Lord Deschaine, in others by a crusader named Gabriel Tyrell; even the Red Blade himself was occasionally blamed for her abduction. Her avengers had tracked her by the trail of tears she left, to a world presumably at one end or the other of the Alkyra, no one was sure which. None of them had wrought bloodier vengeance than Alkyra herself, who, once freed, had torn her enemy's fortress asunder.

Kra'al knew the tales, yes, and she knew that the Alkyra Trade Route was only a few jumps from the Yangtze Tradeway. From the Yangtze, an enemy could access the Crown Road and raid the interior worlds with impunity, possibly even strike the homeworlds themselves.

"What about ship traffic out?" she asked, hardly daring to hope.

"It's an exodus. Admirals Daris and Najo have already interdicted nearly three hundred vessels, and Winters is watching more flee through the Amanra. Apparently, in addition to severing planetary communications, Raven Blue have managed to jam entire systems."

"What do we have left?"

"Vice-Grand Admiral Veraxus's fleet is holding position without incident, but Shra was in the path of their main advance through Ilieth. His fleet took heavy losses and withdrew to Burlington Station. He … sent an open letter to Coalition High Command."

Telec sifted through his papers to pull out a transcript. He cleared his throat and read, "'Raven Blue ships are continuing to press the attack on all fronts. They are using civilian ships as shields or destroying them outright. While their forces have taken heavy casualties, they show no signs of retreating or even pausing.'" Telec glanced up. "This is where it gets … interesting, Ma'am. 'I am exercising my discretion as the commander in chief of the Iliethi defense to relocate my surviving forces to Burlington Station. We will regroup with elements of the Coalition border patrol and survivors from the Fifth Fleet to prepare a counteroffensive.

'I am requesting that CRDF High Command and the Star Chamber immediately redeploy all available forces to the Alkyra Trade Route. Failure to do so will leave our kingdom vulnerable to deep incursion. We will hold them here as long as we can, but if reinforcements do not come, I cannot waste my forces on a forsaken sector. May the Ancients have mercy on the people of the Alkyra if you don't act. The Krondex will not.'"

Livid, the empress refrained from speaking for long moments. She had not risen to power by losing control of her emotions. "He wrote that? To whom was it addressed?"

"You, Your Highness."

"He went over Hakar's head." It wasn't a question. "What's he thinking, out there?"

"Clearly, Admiral Shra is under substantial pressure. This is his first wartime command...."

"Don't make excuses, Telec. It was insubordinate and inappropriate, and he makes this sound like some religious crusade. Lives are on the line, and I want you—and *Hakar*—to keep close watch on him." Kra'al mulled over the admiral's message, trying to look past the audacity of his words. "And what is 'Krondex?' I've never heard this word."

"Your Majesty, I didn't recognize it, either. I wish I could say that Admiral Shra's message was the first or the last time it's cropped up. Certain ... religious Tageans within Star Command have been using it to refer to Raven Blue. I looked it up. It's part of a Tagean creation myth. The Krondex are the Eaters of Light. I have a translation—"

"That's quite all right." Kra'al sighed. It was a childish moniker, fearful and counterproductive. She moved on. "What of our auxiliaries in the Zoh Hegemony?"

"They fight on, but I don't know that we can count on them if their own territory falls under attack. They will consolidate if threatened and leave our flanks undefended." Telec slid Shra's message back into the stack of papers. "We should discuss Hakar's situation."

"What is there to discuss? He has a job to do, and now a zealot to keep in line."

"Yes, but Eve has come under attack."

"If I hear the name of that planet one more time, I'll scream. Where is he now? If he's taken his fleet back to Eve...." She trailed off, leaving the empty threat unspoken.

"The Second has backtracked to respond to an attack at Dobrian, outside the Yangtze Delta. It appears Raven Blue has sent smaller raiding parties deeper than we had expected, in order to draw off our main battle line."

"We cannot let them tangle us in our own net. The planetary defense forces can secure their own systems. Our fleets must hold the line."

"I will pass that along," Telec said evenly. "Dobrian was a hit-and-fade. Minimal losses. Hakar's fleet is returning to the D'zen presently, but ... he's requesting reinforcements to retake the world, and from there the rest of the Alkyra."

"He's not at Eve already, is he?" Kra'al asked pointedly.

"No, ma'am. He has remained with the fleet. He may have a point, though."

"Losing the Tears would be a huge loss, I agree. But with the trade route moving out of phase, mounting a counterattack would be almost impossible. By the time the conduits reform, linking the arms, it will be too late."

"We may not have a choice."

Kra'al tapped a long claw against her chin. "What have you got there?" she asked, moving the claw from her jaw to point at the bundle of papers. Quickly Telec dumped them to the floor and knelt on the tiles. She crouched beside him, her gown flowing out around her like melting wax. Some of her advisors might have thought her kneeling on the floor like this unseemly, but they could go to hell. Telec scrabbled at a rolled-up sheet, spread it out, and weighted down the corners with what he had in his pockets, as well as one of Kra'al's armbands.

It was a star map, with the jackknifed Coalition territory outlined. Telec had highlighted a number of the crucial trade routes and interstellar highways that allowed for direct, ultrafast travel. The Amanra Crescent at the vertex of blade and handle, the Alkyra, the Yangtze, the Crown Road, the River of Stars ... on and on, crisscrossing, overlapping. The galaxy was full of gravitational quagmires and dense regions, the interplay of stars far greater than anyone had ever imagined. Travel was made possible through the conduits, seams in reality that channeled such enormous energies. Travel was nearly unlimited, yes, but not uninterrupted as the matrix of stars, black holes, and nebulas would draw a fleet out of a conduit, reducing most jumps to single-system traverses. Those were minor conduits. With the major conduits, however, a ship could slip across time and space, across vast distances, from the galactic core to its blurred rim. Throughout history the powers that controlled the access points to those routes controlled every world along them. Looking more closely, Kra'al saw where Telec had scrawled notes, cosmographic equations and lines of projected movements. She frowned. *If Raven Blue gains control of Eve....* "Is that accurate? They didn't say anything about this before."

"They didn't know. The latest data show that the Alkyra is still dephasing. But Eve is being pulled into direct phase with the Yangtze. It's a tenuous line, but the conduit created there would be sufficient to move small fleets directly through, bypassing the D'zen and the Bay of Hope altogether. No telling how long it might hold open."

"If we can figure that out, so can they." It seemed this world Kra'al had never heard of until recently, which revolved near the center of the Tears of Alkyra, might now be the fulcrum about which the universe's balance of power would shift.

"Majesty, should we grant Admiral Hakar's request to return to Eve?" Telec asked after giving her a moment to think.

"No, not yet. If he's in the D'zen Gulf, that's exactly where we need him. Eve hasn't pulled into phase yet, and the D'zen would still be the obvious attack route until it does." There was no time to lose, Kra'al realized. There was no escaping the severity of the situation; it was now close to spiraling dangerously out of control, and there were precious few avenues they could take. The time for downplaying the threat had ended. It was no longer a matter of deflecting public concern. She looked at the map, this static image taken from above the galactic plane. *We might as well set fire to the Valinata's portion of it. And the Coalition, too, if we don't get into gear.* "Telec, listen to me. Tell Hakar to hold in the D'zen at all costs and give Winters the same message. I want all fleets along the Outbound Arc to prepare for attack."

The empress of a kingdom on the verge of invasion drew herself to her feet, feeling her years of experience around her like familiar furniture in the dark. The answers were there; it was simply a matter of carefully reaching out and locating them. "We have to assume the Alkyra is lost, whether or not Eve has fallen. Our priority now has to be reinforcing the sectors leading into the Y.T. Send Motayre and Kan to relieve Hakar. Once the Gulf is secure, then and only then can the Second proceed. Don't wait for Pirsan, divert all available forces to the active sector immediately."

Telec was scribbling his notes on the map, drawing arrows from system to system, noting fleet positions and gravitational bottlenecks. Kra'al let him catch up, taking the time to put her own thoughts in order. He handed back her armband, and she slipped it back on. *I've let them down. Everyone who ever relied on me. I was an agent of renewal, and now I've become an enforcer of stagnation. No, things will have to change. I will have to change.* "Can the forces on Eve hold out?"

Telec laid out another printout and squinted at it, his facial tentacles quivering as he read. "Eve has no PDF, Majesty, and our Falcon outpost there has little in the way of aerospace strength. It seems the Jackal Pack Mercenary Legion accounted for most of the world's naval assets."

"Can we count on them? They could seriously fuck us if they abandon their posts to run to the defense of home."

"If the Kr—Raven Blue—have made groundfall, the remaining Jackal Pack troops would be massacred. And for all Hakar's declarations of their skill, they're still mercenaries. I doubt they're any more loyal to Eve than they are to any other world. It's a base of operations to them, nothing more."

"What options do we have? Bombardment?"

"The Valinata tried that, and the enemy adapted by occupying population centers. I can guarantee that any place they settle will have a healthy number of our own civilians as a living shield to deter attack."

By all the gods of all the faiths, what do we do now? "So, Eve has fallen."

"The planet is not without defenses. According to Hakar's inventory, the Jackal Pack base is equipped with an orbital cannon. The Falcon Guard garrison...." Telec trailed off as he flipped through a packet filled with tables of numbers and coded names for materiel. "Let's just say they're well defended against direct attack. They have a full complement of multipurpose fixed artillery and an airshield to protect against bombardment."

"Not enough to launch a counterattack but maybe enough to act as a foothold." The empress was pacing, but she paused. "Telec, how many people are on Eve?"

"Ten million or so. Maybe more, I'm not sure."

The number was a dagger to Kra'al's heart. Ten million hostages, ten million victims, ten million graves if they didn't act fast. Worse yet, if Eve fell, billions more would be at risk.

Kra'al looked through the windows at the sun trekking across the glorious violet sky. *Perhaps you did some good, after all.* "Last order of business, Telec. I don't want to hear anyone referring to Raven Blue as Krondex. It's defeatist. I won't have our officers ascribing magical powers to these people. Once we find out what they call themselves, we can carve it on their graves."

"Yes, Majesty."

"Get it moving. Now." As her defense advisor retreated, Kra'al put her hands on the sill of one of the tall windows. Lowering her head against the cool glass, she felt the thrum of the wind pulsing against it. *Goddess, help those people on Eve. Alkyra is crying once again.*

17: Asylum

When the vehicles finally shuddered to a stop in the middle of the base, medics were already waiting, bathed in a ring of floodlights. Traxus looked out at the grim wall of downcast faces, sojieri counting the returning vehicles and coming up short. She breathed a sigh of relief to be among allies, tentative though they might be. Leon looked as though he might be going into shock, the whites of his eyes showing all around like those of a frightened animal, and yet he had gotten himself back under control. How could Traxus tell him about the crashed liner? *And what if she was on it?*

The remaining rear door was yanked open, groaning on its hinges. Jeric wearily shook his head and clambered out of the Hyena, coming face-to-barrel with another autorifle. Traxus got out after him, and another rifle muzzle, charcoal-gray metal, swung upwards to stare her down. She slowly raised her hands, the severed trap-cuff wires dangling against her wrists. Her ears were still ringing from the initial explosion and the rambling story of the big machine gun. Even so, her body trembled with the excitement of having engaged and fought off the enemy.

"Identify yourselves," ordered a gruff voice, and another rifle barrel, unseen, jabbed Traxus in the back. *At least, it's not a bayonet.*

Jeric was already getting to his knees, no stranger to being arrested. Blood pumped from the mangled remains of his hand. "I'm a pilot with Jackal Pack. Your neighbors, you know?" Traxus dropped into the dirt beside him.

"Easy, folks, stand down!" came a voice from somewhere in the world beyond the barrels of the guns. "I think we've seen enough violence for one day." The voice was almost saccharine in its marked contrast to how they had been treated thus far.

Reluctantly, the sojieri lowered their weapons, and Traxus got a look at them. These Falcons seemed to have a propensity for shoving guns at people. They stared impassively at her and Jeric but snapped a sharp salute to the approaching officer. Traxus saw now that the perception that the Coalition outpost was a backwater posting crewed by lazy clock-watchers was a myth: these were crack troops with broad shoulders and lantern jaws. Their eyes were cold, as though they hardly cared what was going on just a few kilometers away. But no, that wasn't true: their jaws were clenched too tightly, their knuckles white on the grips of their weapons.

The man who had ordered the troops to stand down jogged over to them. "Hello, hello, I'm Commander Grey Marion. You made it. Great!" he exclaimed. His tone was enthusiastic, welcoming, suggesting that he was hosting a dinner party, nothing more. His rumpled blue BDUs bore a Falcon commander's insignia. Closer inspection of the man revealed sharp, alert eyes and a loose, springy way of carrying himself that suggested he was perpetually ready for anything. He was clean-shaven, sandy brown hair just a little longer than regulation, giving him a surprisingly youthful appearance that belied his rank. Nevertheless, he was haggard-looking, the events of the last few hours having taken a drastic toll. He shook Jeric's remaining hand, which was still cuffed to the other, then Traxus's. His grip was firm. He looked familiar, and Traxus thought she might have met him once.

"We've got wounded down here!" shouted one of the medics, waving for assistance. Somehow, Leon was still standing under his own power, refusing any help.

Commander Marion approached the Hyena and squinted into the smoky interior. He let out a grunt of surprise as the sergeant's body was pulled out. "Shit. My boys," he muttered. "And the rest?"

Corporal Bracx shook his head. He holding a cigarette in shaking fingers and he took a grateful drag. His ebony skin glistened with sweat. Marion put a hand on his shoulder, and the young man nearly jumped out of his skin. "Well done, corporal. You got these people home safe."

"Thank you, sir. I'm sorry we couldn't do more."

"Croyer and the others who stayed behind … did they get away?"

"We didn't stay long enough to see, Commander. I hope they made it. Alpha Flight are all down, too." Bracx pointed at Traxus. "She kept us alive out there."

Marion sniffed and straightened up, turning his icy blue gaze on the mercenaries. "You're Jackals," he said, eying their battered uniforms. "Our neighbors to the east. Your base is putting up quite a fight. Why aren't you there, and who's your friend?" He pointed at Porter as some of the medics loaded the unconscious saboteur onto a stretcher.

Traxus glared at Porter. "It's a long story, and he's no friend. He's collaborating with the invasion force. We captured him."

"Before we captured you?" Marion asked, almost playfully. There was ample suspicion in his voice but no malice. "I expect to hear every detail of your long story if you expect not to be thrown in a cell. For now, I'll settle for IDs." He held out a hand, beckoning.

"Lieutenant Traxus Tachai," Traxus said, fishing out her wallet. She introduced Jeric and Leon, who managed to hand over their own IDs without dropping them.

Marion scrutinized their cards before handing them to another officer who scanned them and nodded. "Welcome to Outpost Hillary, home of the Seventy-Sixth Nebula Corps. Decommissioned, of course. Looks like you all made it out by the skin of your teeth."

Jeric and Traxus turned back to look at the charred Hyena that had carried them to safety. Only now did Traxus realize how close they had come to dying, to being reduced to a blackened patch amid the endless plains. The car looked like it had been barbecued, one tire was missing, and the light armor was dented and scarred.

Shellshocked and battered by an ordeal that had been capped off by front-row seats to an atomic blast, the civilians being helped out of the remaining truck looked even worse. As Traxus watched, the sojieri cut the medics off as they formed a perimeter around the refugees. Murmurs of panic ran through the crowd, and mothers moved their children out of sight. Out here in the Alkyra, trust was in short supply, especially at a time like this.

The commander went over to them, forgetting the Jackals for a moment. "Ladies and gentlemen, please forgive the cold reception. Due to the nature of the attacks, we have to quarantine you all until we can determine just what's going on here. You'll all be given food, water, and medical treatment." He turned his back on them, ignoring their pleas for salvation and explanation.

As the civilians were herded toward a nearby barracks building, Marion returned to the Jackals, looking over his prisoners. "I take it you three have some information to contribute? About the giant fucking mess we're in?"

Leon, an arm wrapped tight around his midsection as though to hold his guts in place, started to speak. As he devolved into a coughing fit, Traxus stepped forward. "We don't know much, commander. Eve was infiltrated by people posing as Valinata refugees with the aim of knocking out planetary communications and hitting critical sites to pave the way for that invasion force. That man, Porter, was one of them."

"Well, they succeeded. All long-comms are down, including our own. It's why we had to put all those refugees in quarantine. There's no way of knowing who's who." Marion sighed. "I'm sure you'll understand that I'll be putting you all under armed guard, too." He nodded toward the unconscious Porter as the medics carried him away. "Especially him."

"What about those people?" Traxus pointed to a hastily built corral where more guards were watching a cluster of nearly a hundred frightened civilians who had already fled the plains.

"Luckily, it's a nice evening. That's a temporary measure, I assure you, but those people infringed upon my hospitality. One of them wiped out our comm array, leaving me no choice but to isolate the rest until we can sort them out."

A sojier ran up, looking harried. "Sir, we've lost contact with the Peregrine."

For a moment, Marion looked despondent. He quickly regained his composure and moved off to confer.

Leaning back against the hot metal of the pummeled Hyena, Traxus took a moment to scan her new surroundings, memorizing everything. The crater housed a fully stocked Coalition base, she noted with surprise. On the rare occasion she thought about the CRB at all, Traxus had assumed it was some remote outpost, a couple of tin shacks and a satellite uplink for the undisciplined to serve their penance. Now that they were sheltering here, she was happy to be proven wrong. A squat tower rose out of the center of the complex, abutted by a raised landing pad. Several choppers were parked on it now, crews looking ready to leap into action at a moment's notice. Low barracks buildings were arranged in a cluster around a small exercise yard. Along the southern edge of the crater, a waterfall spilled out of an underground spring and wound along a narrow stream to end in a pool at the base of the tower. All of it was bathed in the bright white light of spotlights that reminded her of nighttime fútbol matches. It was dreamlike now that night had fallen over the savannah. Being deep in the crater felt somehow cozy, protected, criblike. At the same time, Traxus couldn't help but imagine those menacing black ships everywhere, a dark sky full of them. The CRB may have fought off a wave of attackers, but most of Eve was not lucky enough to have a full battery of aerospace defense cannons.

One of the children held in the corral waved when Traxus caught her eye. Traxus waved back and continued her visual catalog, memorizing the locations of armories, vehicles, defensive emplacements, and escape routes.

Walkways wound up and down the inner lip of the crater, some leading to the turrets that ringed the base. There was a large hangar, too, which merged with the craggy, overgrown crater wall, most likely opening out on the slope of the mountain.

"You like it? I had the underground stream diverted to help the Feng Shui of the place." The commander stood with his arms crossed. His eyes were still and dark. Traxus couldn't tell if he was joking or not.

"It's very nice," she replied guardedly, trying to figure the man out. His fatigues were sky-blue camouflage, hardly in keeping with his troops—or practical against Eve's amber plains, for that matter—but he walked like a flag officer. Military upbringing, maybe? Traxus glanced at his insignia: he wouldn't have worn his commendations with his fatigues, and she wasn't very familiar with Falcon Guard awards anyway, but his ribbon bars were densely packed on his chest and hinted at a highly decorated career across multiple branches. *Interesting.* His face had an openness to it that she liked.

"We did meet once, Lieutenant" he said, as though privy to her earlier thought. "At the Hotel Imperial."

Traxus remembered it now. Rockmore had brought most of his senior command staff, as well as Traxus, to a gala thrown by one of Eve's shabby elite. She couldn't recall if the host had been the architect of an unsuccessful coup or the ruler deposed by a successful one, but it had been quite the evening. She had exchanged only a few words with Marion there, but the somber, elegant Coalition officer of that night bore little resemblance to the faded-looking leader before her.

"Commander, we need a debrief," Leon finally croaked. He sounded like he had broken glass in his throat.

Marion's eyebrows went up. "Colonel, I'm a little too busy right this instant to sit down and talk about your day. Why don't you all head down to medical and get checked out. You look like you need it."

"Sorry, Commander, but I'm not in the habit of sitting on the bench while my team loses the game. Can you at least find out if Benez InterSystem Three-one-three-six made it to Epsilon Merentis?"

Marion hesitated, then glanced at the officer standing behind him. "Gianni, see if CROS pulled any itineraries before the line went dead."

"Yes, sir." The officer dutifully took a note. "But we really need to address the Peregrine's situation. Captain Durand is on-station and awaiting orders."

Marion spun on his heel and began walking toward the headquarters tower. He glanced over his shoulder. "Come on if you're coming."

Leon, Traxus, and Jeric exchanged glances. Heavily armed sojieri fell in beside them, two for each of them. Traxus was almost flattered.

They stopped at a series of blast doors, each shut and guarded, before reaching the base's command center, a massive hexagonal room full of computers and holographics systems that allowed the base staff to monitor everything that was going on in the sector. Every station was full, some occupied by officers in their civvies, possibly roused from sleep. The comm officers looked particularly harried, trying futilely to get a response on any channel.

"Carry on, everyone," Marion said loudly as some of the officers started coming to attention. Catwalks ringed the room, patrolled by several burly men in black t-shirts.

Marion turned to his prisoners. "I'm putting a lot of faith in you right now. Don't move, and don't try anything." He looked at one of their guards. "If they do, kill them all." With that, he crossed his arms to observe. Traxus's jaw dropped, and Leon turned an even whiter shade of pale.

"Echo approaching from the northwest. Altitude twelve thousand meters," announced one of the tracking officers.

"Verified Raven Blue?" asked the chief gunnery officer, walking briskly over.

"Affirmative. ADRs Four through Nine have resolved firing solutions." All eyes turned to Marion.

"Bring it down," the commander said coldly, all trace of good humor gone from his voice.

The crater lit up, and the synchronized report of the Aerospace Defense Railguns reverberated through the glass windows. Traxus started at the sound and light. After a minute, the tracking officer announced that the target had been destroyed. Only then did she realize she had been holding her breath.

"Give me an update on our troops in the field," Marion ordered once the invading ship had been dealt with.

"We've lost all radio contact, but we should have a satellite in range for thermal imaging in another forty-five minutes."

"They may not have that long," the commander said quietly. "Any luck with the comm blackout?"

"Negative, sir. Line-of-sight connections work just fine, everything else is being jammed. There's just too much interference."

Marion turned to the Jackals. "I sent most of our ground complement out to intercept Raven Blue ground forces moving on Las Serras da Estrelas, under the command of Peregrine Noelle," he explained. "She hasn't reported in since engaging the enemy."

Traxus frowned. The Peregrines were the elite among the already elite Falcons; culled from the First Iron Falcons Battalion and clad in the order's sacred armor, they had a fearsome reputation. If the Falcon Guard were often compared derisively to a religious order, one which worshiped war, the Peregrines were their high priests and priestesses. Traxus had not even known there was a Peregrine on Eve. And she had never known a Peregrine to back down from a fight. Would even a Peregrine be enough to hold off the invaders, though? She doubted it.

A nearby speaker crackled. "Commander, this is Shepherd. We've cleared the debris from the ansible resonator, but the news isn't good. The mass itself is cracked, and Doctor Chase tells me that if we try to open a channel, it'll shake the thing to pieces and potentially blow a new crater in our crater."

The stricken look on Commander Marion's face spoke volumes. "What about a pulse? Can we send out a pulse to let someone know we're here?"

"Stand by, Commander." The minutes dragged on while they waited for an answer. Marion's officers were all listening with bated breath. The speakers crackled again, then, "No can do, sir. That bitch blew the hell out of this place. They're still picking pieces of her out of the equipment."

"One of the refugees blew herself up to get at the ansible array," Marion explained.

"A lot of that going around," wheezed Leon. His breathing was growing ragged, and Traxus brought him a chair. He waved her off.

"Commander!" shouted one of the officers in the comm bay. "We're picking up a signal!" The rest of the room went silent.

"From Peregrine Noelle?"

"Hang on, we're cleaning it up."

The tension in the room rose, and eventually the static resolved into a voice. "Castle Bravo, Panther Actual. Do you copy?"

"Go ahead, Panther, this is Castle Bravo Six Actual," Marion said. "Do you have a status update on Task Force Claymore?"

"Comms negative, but we have eyes on. They're in a serious firefight, sir, but they're holding. Hold on, we're seeing…. It looks like a smoke signal. Flores, confirm that."

Traxus glanced at Leon again. His jaw was clenched as he leaned on a railing, listening. What was going through his mind? He appeared barely conscious, seemingly kept upright by grim determination alone. Was he dwelling on the parallels between this and Daltar? Was he thinking about Rachel and whether she had gotten to safety? How much more could he take?

The speakers crackled again. "Castle Bravo, Panther Actual. The Peregrine has deployed an airstrike marker at her position."

"It's got to be a mistake," Marion muttered. "I need confirmation, Panther," he said more loudly.

"We're seeing an airstrike marker, Commander. Clear as day."

Marion turned to his subordinates. "I need visual confirmation. We need overflight. Redirect one of the fighter groups. Now."

As the minutes dragged on, Traxus watched Leon sagging. Jeric had turned white and slumped into a chair. None of them spoke until Leon whispered, "So this is how Aethaleia started."

"What?"

"I never told you. Aethaleia, where we went in the Valinata. Where Asar was nearly killed. These things got there before us, and the whole world—"

"Vic, don't. She doesn't need to hear this." Jeric's voice was quiet, pleading.

"We're *watching* it in realtime, Jeric. What is there to hide?" But Leon said no more.

An officer called out, "We've received confirmation from Vector Flight. Airstrike markers have been deployed along the defensive line."

"Markers?" Commander Marion blurted out. "Plural?"

"Yes, sir. It appears ... Peregrine Noelle is requesting a strike on their position."

"There must be a mistake."

"Castle Bravo, this is Panther Actual. Multiple smoke signals. I repeat, we are seeing multiple ... seven smoke signals."

"Vector Flight is down. Multiple birds downed," the tracking officer announced.

Marion said nothing. His jaw was working back and forth, but no words came out. The officer at his elbow cleared her throat. "Commander, Captain Durand and Captain Paas are ready to move into position."

"No, it must be a mistake. I'm not about to authorize a nuclear strike on our own people."

Leon's voice was whisper-soft. "Commander, you and I both know that if those things get past them, Las Serras will fall, and all the people in those mountains will die."

Marion rounded on Leon, and for the first time, he truly showed the stress of his situation. He looked as though he might crack. "I have four *hundred* of my best men and women out there, fighting to keep those things back."

"They've bought time. Don't waste it."

Marion's eyes narrowed. "This isn't Daltar, Colonel Victor."

Judging by Leon's reaction, those words cut him more deeply than any of the shrapnel. "No, Commander, it's not. It's far, far worse."

The commander studied Leon's face for a moment. "You really believe that, don't you?"

"I've seen what these things can do. They haven't responded to a single hail, have they?"

Marion was silent for a long moment, then, "Move the long-strikers into position." Outside against the gathering dark, two smoking shapes began climbing the rim of the crater. A faint blue flicker lit the sky, probably the Jackal Pack skybeam firing, and illuminated the giant cannons.

"Castle Bravo, this is Panther Actual. The green fire is getting closer. I think they're about to break through Task Force Claymore's lines. Friendlies appear to have deployed white phosphorous at their own position."

Traxus was astonished by the dedication of those Falcons fighting on the plains. They had to know their cause was lost to call down the wrath of their own artillery, and yet they fought on rather than break and run.

The city beneath Las Serras da Estrela was home to hundreds of thousands of people, a series of vast caverns carved from the stone. If the enemy got in there … it would be a slaughter. Leon felt Marion's pain: the man was responsible for the lives of his troops, but he was also tasked with defending Eve's civilian populace. The worst part of it was that sacrificing his men and women would not guarantee that Las Serras would not fall, only that he would have no one left to defend it.

"Commander Marion, Panther Actual. We see some of the enemy ships. They're taking off again. We're running out of time."

"Sir? We need a decision," entreated one of the nearby officers.

Leon stirred, and Traxus put a restraining hand on his shoulder. The advice of the Mourning Star would not be welcome now, she knew.

"Commander?" asked another officer.

Marion was still for a moment longer, then he wiped a tear from his eye. "I can't even tell them how sorry I am." He drew himself up. "Captain Durand, Captain Paas, open fire on Task Force Claymore's position. Full power, maximum spread. All ADMs, empty your racks."

Along the ridge missiles leapt into the night as the Aerospace Defense Missile batteries fired, their deadly payloads shrieking off on tails of fire. The cannons of the long-striker tanks glowed momentarily blue before the energy of the sun tore out of them, flashing toward the horizon. They fired again and again, seeming to rock the very world with their power.

When the firing finally stopped, the command center was eerily silent, the assembled officers collectively holding their breath. A computer beeped, and the tremulous voice of an officer called out, "All targets destroyed, Commander. Long-strikers and ADMs standing down."

Marion drew himself up. "Ladies and Gentlemen, thank you all for carrying out your duty. This was not easy, but it was necessary. The men and women of Task Force Claymore gave their lives to defend us and the rest of this planet. It's up to us to carry on for them." He looked around the room with sorrowful eyes.

Looking at the silent faces all around her, more than a few streaked with tears, Traxus saw cold, rational anger. They were all Falcons, all of them trained for war in a way that no Jackal ever would be. What would life be like, hoping and praying for war? And how did they feel now that those prayers had been answered?

Without a word, Traxus, Leon, and Jeric wearily followed Commander Marion back outside. He led them to the catwalks, stalking up a ramp to the top deck. He paused, looking out at the southern horizon glowing with the light of a thousand fires. To the east, blue lines flicked upwards as the Jackal Pack skybeam stabbed out at its foes. The blasts seemed to be getting fainter, the intervals between them longer.

"They're so close, but we can't even talk to them," Marion muttered, seeing where Traxus was looking.

"Commander, you did the right thing," Leon wheezed.

"Easy for you to say," Marion replied, turning his attention back to the burning savannah. "You didn't just incinerate the men and women who were counting on you."

Leon didn't say anything else for which Traxus was grateful.

The commander wasn't done, though. "I've never felt more helpless. Our planet was just conquered in a matter of hours and right under the nose of the Second Fleet. And if my suspicions are correct, the rest of the Alkyra has just suffered the same fate. Standard Coalition policy will be to quarantine the area, prevent the spread of this infection. If they do come in force, it won't be right away. We're on our own."

"What do we do until then?" Traxus asked, afraid to hear the answer.

Marion turned, and it felt like he was simultaneously staring through her and seeing her for the first time. "We stay alive, Lieutenant Tachai. And we kill any of those things that come near us. Otherwise, we go the way of the Valinata."

It was at that moment that Leon's strength finally left him. Traxus heard him exhale, and as she turned, he collapsed. One of the sojieri guarding them half-caught him before he hit the deck of the catwalk, and Traxus took him in her arms.

"Leon, are you all right?" she asked, touching his cheek. He had been running on pure adrenaline and anger for so long, it had to run out eventually.

His eyes fluttered open. "Help me up. I've got to get back to base." Then his eyes shut again, and his head lolled to the side.

"And on that note, I think it's time all three of you were locked in the infirmary," Commander Marion said behind her, his voice oddly detached. He snapped his fingers, and Traxus felt strong hands grab her shoulders.

§

The D'zen Gulf was so large it could never be considered crowded, but it was certainly hosting an ever-increasing number of ships. Border patrol flotillas had been diverted from the line between the Coalition and the Commonwealth, and regional defense fleets and customs ships had left their posts. A few ships had been detached from the Unified Commonwealth Authority to act as advisors, but the commanders had hinted that more would be on the way if the UCA and the CRDF could agree on terms. At this point, Hakar was willing to wash their ships by hand for some help.

Some privateer outfits had also arrived on the scene, sniffing after contracts, and Hakar was secretly amused by Rockmore's discomfiture. *Competition is good for the market, isn't it?* Some of the units Hakar had heard of; the Sons of Mars, for instance, was a fairly large and well-outfitted group that specialized in naval warfare. Their ships were exotic and painted in a rust-red scheme that reminded the admiral of dried blood. Every ship also bore a dull white skull on the bow that he found a bit ostentatious. But their guns would be welcome if the price was right. He had yet to arrange a meeting with their leader. Other outfits were not so well known; for example, the Exiles of Karuda were a ragtag band of sojieri that seemed more like pirates than mercs. They had come in a flotilla of heavily modified freighters and commercial vessels. Tarot had voiced concern when routine scans identified several of their ships as stolen.

With so much traffic, the tactical coordinators were having trouble managing the area, and they warned Hakar several times about the risk of enemy collaborators attempting to ram CRDF vessels. He had no time to be paranoid. Besides, his worries were focused predominantly on the Eve system, which had fallen silent along with the rest of the Alkyra.

Across the table in the officers' lounge, Rockmore stirred. "Why are we waiting here, with our hands tied behind our backs?" he wondered aloud into his cup of Kaf.

"Because they asked nicely," Hakar said, trying for levity. His voice rang hollow. All he could think about was Traxus. They had not been able to reach her or Jeric, meaning it was almost certain they had been trapped on Eve. It was petty, selfish of him when so many millions of lives were in jeopardy. Yet, who was he fighting for if not his own loved ones? To think he had pushed her toward Jackal Pack as a way to keep her *out* of trouble. Looking at Rockmore, thinking of Leon, Hakar realized how naïve that had been.

"What will you do with those corporate pickets that ran?" Rockmore glanced at the group of ships that had been forcibly docked with by Coalition destroyers trimmed with the purple and yellow checkerboard livery of the border patrol. The privateer crews would be arrested for dereliction of duty, but they were hardly alone: more and more survivors of futile defensive actions were arriving in the D'zen every hour. Most had been genuinely routed, and were eager to regroup as part of a larger fleet, but the desertions could not be ignored.

"What can I do? Part of me wants to execute their captains for abandoning Eve," Hakar admitted. "On the other hand, can I really blame them? They're claiming that a *hundred and fifty* capital ships attacked Eve. That's not exactly a raiding party."

"Exactly why we should hit back now, and hard," Rockmore insisted.

"I have my orders, Jon, and you have yours. Don't make this harder."

"This war is moving at the speed of bureaucracy, Hakar."

Hakar knew that every moment they allowed the enemy would mean more time for Raven Blue to fortify, to dig in, to conquer. As though for the first time, he felt the impatience of the untested sojier, the desire to *act*, to *do*, to *fight* and find out what he was capable of. And yet he understood very well why High Command wanted him to lead the defensive attempt here.

"We should send another scout," Rockmore said forcefully.

"You're not here to advise me, Jon."

"So we're just going to sit here and let the enemy capture as many worlds as they want?"

That's about the size of it. "The hope is that they'll overextend themselves, open their fleets up for an attack when we move back into the area in force."

"And when will that be?" Rockmore knew as well as Hakar how big the CRDF was, how long it might take to get everything in order. "A month? Two?"

Ordinarily, Hakar might have taken umbrage at that. The situation was far from ordinary. "Jon, trust me, we're moving as fast as we can. I think the gears have finally started turning in the heads of the right people."

"A little too late, don't you think?"

"You work with what you have. You know why people are reluctant to start a war, Jon."

"Yes, and I sympathize. I've always seen Jackal Pack as a way to defuse conflicts *before* they become wars." Rockmore was full of conviction, but Hakar couldn't help thinking it was a bit hypocritical. "But it's too fucking late for caution."

"We can't all be the rulers of our own little empires, Jon. The Krondex aren't going to give us any second chances if we don't take this opportunity to secure the Yangtze."

Rockmore frowned, his shadowed eyes darkening further as he looked across the table at Hakar. "*Krondex*, huh? Is that from your boy Shra's letter of protest?"

Hakar felt a pang of shame. "I knew he was a religious man. I just never realized that it went so deeply."

"The man lost half his fleet in a matter of hours. You can't exactly blame him for having a bit of a breakdown." Rockmore took a sip of Kaf. "I have to admit, the name is darkly appropriate for them."

"'And lo, the Krondex came in their ships made of night,'" Hakar recited. "'And the Sun ran before them, but could not outrun.'" He let out a weary sigh. "It's an old legend."

"I hate old legends," Rockmore muttered acidly.

"I haven't thought about that story in a long time. Every day a vendetta, every day a vicious cycle, light against darkness. Forever."

"I don't know, that sounds about right," Rockmore mused.

Hakar only clicked his tongue and sipped at the cup of Kaf that had long gone cold. Two old veterans who had seen too much sat gazing uselessly at each other across the cold metal table, wondering what they were going to do.

§

Later, much later, Rockmore made his way down to the deck where the Jackal Pack troops were berthed. He could taste the anger in the air, mixed with sweat and the tang of carbon dioxide scrubbers.

Troops saluted as he walked past. The general tried to give them some words of encouragement to hold on to, but it couldn't have done much good. It certainly didn't make him feel any better.

How many times could they clean their weapons? How many times could they count their bullets and shells? Would they keep sharpening their knives until nothing was left but the hilts?

He found the man he was looking for at the aft end of the deck, sitting cross-legged before a porthole. Raptor was still, only the tip of his tail flicking back and forth rhythmically. He turned his head a bit as the general walked through the hatch, sniffing.

"Don't get up," Rockmore said kindly.

"It's true," Raptor guessed softly.

"Yes, it's true. We guessed wrong."

"And the Alkyra has fallen."

"Yes."

"Have our troops regrouped?"

Ordinarily, Rockmore didn't invite insubordination, but Raptor wasn't precisely an enlisted Jackal. He came and went as he pleased, and he had earned a little disclosure. "We lost two companies and a frigate at Kurilai. The rest are back or on their way."

"And when do we take Eve?"

"I don't know, Raptor."

The Prross's dorsal spines went erect. "We could go on our own."

"We're under contract."

"That's just a piece of paper. Our home has been taken." It wasn't often that Raptor spoke in such absolute terms. Rockmore didn't know much about his people or their culture, but sometimes Raptor seemed to willfully abandon subtlety and practicality in favor of blunt force trauma.

"If the estimates of enemy strength are correct, we'd be wiped off the map."

"Better to get on with it, then."

Rockmore exhaled tiredly. "I know you don't mean that, Raptor. You want to protect Leon and Heidi and the others, but do you really want to get the rest of the Pack killed for that? We're not enough to save all of Eve. The Second Fleet is."

Raptor's head turned back again, and one of his eyes settled on Rockmore, liquid gold with a pupil of blackest night. "You're right, of course. But promise me one thing, General."

Refusing to rise to the bait, Rockmore said nothing.

"When the time comes, I will have my revenge. Don't get in my way."

"I won't throw your life away, but I know what you can do. I'll support you however I can."

"Thank you. Until you have need of me, I'll be here."

"Get some rest. You're going to need it."

§

Hakar waited determinedly for sleep to come not because he wanted to rest but because he knew he would be more effective if he did. The ordinarily soothing hum of the *Condor*'s stardrives did little to help. Instead, he mulled over the Shra's fleet's losses and the man's peculiar reaction. That letter to High Command should have embarrassed Hakar more than it did; somehow it just made him sad. Still, better to dwell on that than on how completely they had been routed and how likely it was that Traxus was still behind enemy lines.

It was almost a relief when his computer beeped. He rose swiftly from his bunk and crossed to the desk, the light turning on automatically at his approach and bathing the dark wood in a soft glow. He had long since grown accustomed to the long waits associated with retrieving classified documents as the security authenticators handed them off, but this had taken practically forever.

When he logged on, however, he was surprised to find not the files he had asked for but a request that he complete his authentication using *Condor*'s secure comms bay. Annoyed, he dressed and went to the bridge.

The comms bay was cold and silent, an isolated chamber off the bridge. Alone, Hakar keyed in his command override and waited as the signal bounced across relays. He idly smoothed the hem of his jacket until a rotating encryption panel appeared and after that the face of a Human woman. Her face had an ageless quality about it, and she wore the placid gaze of a professional spy.

"Admiral Hakar, I'm Agent Keller," she said simply. "It's an honor."

"Thank you, Agent Keller. I have a request: I attempted to access autopsy results for Simon Munroe and Lydia Gillette."

"The two traitors involved in the deaths of Grand Admiral Mindor and Vice-Grand Admiral Geran," Keller said, unsurprised.

"Access was restricted. I need to see those files."

"Of course, sir," the woman said immediately, and Hakar realized belatedly that the call had been flagged as important enough to warrant a proper realtime ansible tunnel. "We've been asked to cooperate fully with your investigation." She looked a bit embarrassed. "In fact, you should have been alerted as soon as the results were completed. It must have been an oversight when they were sealed."

Hakar didn't believe that for an instant. The Coalition intelligence services rarely made mistakes of that nature. Missing the signs of a full-on invasion on the Coalition's doorstep, on the other hand.... "Can you tell me why they were sealed?"

"I'm afraid I can't, sir, but I have highlighted relevant details for your convenience. I'll have them transmitted by secure packet to your stateroom system. They should arrive in about ten minutes." She paused, affecting embarrassment. "My apologies, but you're not permitted to download them to a personal unit or otherwise disseminate them."

The grand admiral's eyebrows shot up. He wondered what could possibly be in those autopsy files that was so sensitive. What were they trying to hide, and who did the details implicate? "Will that be all, sir?" Keller asked carefully.

"Yes, thank you." They signed off, and Hakar rose to return to his stateroom to study the files. He had walked only a few steps past the hatchway when Tarot intercepted him with an update from the scouts who had been chased out of the Alkyra. As quickly as he could, Hakar disengaged himself and raced to his quarters where he changed back into shorts and a t-shirt, sat at the desk, logged onto the secure terminal, and went through the laborious security clearances needed to get to the actual files. Lydia Gillette's was the less useful of the two as she had blown off most of her own head, including the evidence, to escape capture. *Evidence? What were they looking for in her head?*

When Hakar reached Simon Munroe's file, he found out. It had been established early on that Grand Admiral Mindor's traitorous assassin had succumbed to decompression after his suit was hit by rifle fire. The blood inside his otherwise undamaged helmet bore out that conclusion, and cranial scans had identified nothing other than the expected subdural hematomas and blood clotting. However, Munroe had not died of hypoxia, and his lungs were unruptured, indicating that he had died prior to the complete compromise of the suit. On a hunch, forensic investigators had opened him up, and what they found led to the immediate sealing of the autopsy results. Hakar reread the report several times, unable to keep his eyes from returning to the photographs and scans of the brain biopsy. *What the fuck are we dealing with here? I have to warn them all.*

Hakar was on the verge of returning to the secure comms bay when he remembered the other files he hadn't yet read. He forced himself to sit back down and inspect them. At least, then he would have a clear picture of what was going on.

Or so he thought. He frowned as he began to read what at first glance was an old loss of asset report, wondering what relevance it had. At first it didn't make any sense: it was simply a list of decommissioned ships, many of which were classes that had been retired for decades.

When he flipped to the third page and saw the words "OPERATION PRIMROSE LOSS OF ASSETS," his vision blurred. He pushed his chair back roughly in its track and stood up. "What the fuck?" he asked the empty room. At the top of the list was "INTELLIGENCE ASSET DESIGNATED 'TIGER FLOWER': KILLED IN ACTION."

He paced his quarters several times before rubbing his eyes and looking at the report again. It was no dream and no joke. It must be an error. As though it were dangerous, Hakar gingerly sat back down in front of the computer and resumed reading. He was having trouble focusing, his legs jiggling up and down with nervous energy. "Tiger Flower," he whispered, stricken, when he saw the picture of her face. Was someone fucking with him? If so, this was a profoundly unfunny prank.

Finally, he could take it no more. In defiance of Agent Keller, he transferred the files to a mem and took it to the secure comms bay, his fingertips tingling as though the mem itself was electrified. He had not bothered to change back into his uniform, and he earned startled glances from the bridge crew when he walked through the hatch without saying a word, disheveled in his shirt and shorts.

When the real-time ansible connection to Tagea went through, Telec's face appeared on the screen, alert and curious. Apparently he didn't sleep, either. Hakar wasted no time. "Telec, why the hell is there a report on Tiger Flower with the files I pulled on Sergeant Munroe and Ensign Gillette?"

"I was just wondering why you had requested that," Telec said, unashamed of his snooping.

Hakar should have known Telec would be keeping his own tabs on the investigation, but it still rankled him. He let the matter drop. "Do you realize how bad this is?"

"I assumed it was an error."

"Apparently not. I just can't figure out why the computer picked it based on my request parameters."

"What else was in the report? It couldn't have anything to do with when—"

"Don't you dare say her name," Hakar snapped viciously, and Telec's facial tentacles quivered in surprise at his colleague's reaction.

"Fine, Hakar. I wasn't trying to upset you. Does it have to do with Tiger Flower's last mission?"

"Yes." Clearly Telec wasn't going to be helpful.

Hakar looked down at the mem screen and flipped idly to the end of the document. That was when he realized there were appendices, including comm transcripts and several scans. He began scrolling carefully through them until the computer highlighted a chart. His eyes widened.

Without saying anything, he interfaced the mem and the secure comm system so he could share what he was looking at with Telec.

"May I remind you that this connection is not secured for classified transmissions?"

"Shut the fuck up, Telec, and *read*."

He watched Telec's large, black eyes moving and watched the Sanar grand admiral's expression change, his tendrils contracting. "This must be wrong."

"Telec, when we thought that Raven Blue might be...."

"We had no way of knowing for sure," Telec said hastily.

"There's no mistaking those conserved gene sequences."

Telec held up a hand. "Wait, wait, that doesn't make sense. We checked that composite sample recovered from the battle at Calama, and this never came up. It's not even the same genome morphology. This is a *sphere*."

Hakar had been wondering the same thing, and the answer came to him with a flash of embarrassment. "It wouldn't have come up. The fragment at Calama came from one of those black ships. Tiger Flower sent us Raven Blue's *actual genome*. We just didn't know what to do with it."

"I always assumed it was some last puzzle we were supposed to solve. Instead we just locked it away all this time." Telec's voice was almost reverent. "It looks like they sent along some data on the Aethaleia sequence, too. Another partial match. But I still don't understand, the ships, they're so different from what our people saw before."

"Telec," Hakar said sharply, "people can change their ships, they can't change their genetics. Besides, we only ever saw the one vessel. Who knows what else they had out there?"

"Clearly, a massive fleet of living battleships just waiting to tear the galaxy in half."

§

The hospital ward was full of civilians and frighteningly devoid of survivors of Task Force Claymore's last stand against the enemy. With most of the garrison's field surgeons and medics having perished at the field hospital on the front line, the staff was decimated, leaving only a skeleton crew to treat the wounded. The last refugees had limped in from the plains days ago, fleeing the burning spaceport. Most were dehydrated; all were terrified by what they had seen.

Traxus was lucky to have escaped serious injury. Aside from a pretty severe concussion, some bruised ribs, and a constellation of lacerations, she was remarkably intact. Leon and Jeric, however, more than made up for her lack of injuries. Leon's broken ribs and fractured leg and wrist might not have been too bad if the car crash hadn't compounded everything, leaving him with internal bleeding and several cracked vertebrae.

Of the three, Jeric had suffered the most. His skull was cracked, he had lost several teeth, and a medical robot had amputated what was left of his left hand to make room for a new scaffold. The replacement was a hastily produced vat-grown placeholder. It was functional but clumsy and only nominally a DNA match, but it would keep the nerves and tissue healthy until a permanent clone could be constructed for him. The pilot felt nothing but revulsion when he looked at the foreign appendage.

Of all the injuries visited on them, the deepest were not physical. The feelings of helplessness and uncertainty were hard to stomach. Traxus was unable to sleep, and Leon had barely spoken since waking up after his surgery. He simply lay there, cheeks sunken and hollow, fingers tracing the long scar across his abdomen. His bones had been cemented and his internal bleeding stanched, but he was a shadow of his normally vibrant self. Sometimes he didn't seem to be breathing.

Jeric was in the next bed, staring at the pitted concrete wall beneath the television. The device itself was shut off since there was nothing to watch, all the signals having gone dead when the comm arrays were destroyed. "Have you found anything out?" he finally asked.

"You should really be doing your exercises," Traxus said, motioning at his new hand.

"What's the point? We're going to be dead in a few days, anyway."

"Jeric, that's bullshit. Those things haven't come near this place since...."

"Since they distracted themselves by wiping out our base?"

That hit hard, and Traxus lapsed back into silence. Commander Marion had delivered the news himself two days earlier. The skybeam had stopped firing on the second night. Marion assured them that the Jackals' efforts had saved countless lives and provided air superiority long enough for Las Serras da Estrela to mount a defense. Knowing that her comrades had not let up, even as the enemy cruisers descended upon them, bombarding their home, made her heart swell with pride, edging out some of the grief. They had turned the plains surrounding the Luxor Plateau into a graveyard for dozens of enemy ships, wreaking havoc in the way only cornered Jackals could.

Traxus distracted herself by telling Jeric and Leon—assuming the latter was even listening—what she had discovered while wandering around the base with her armed escort. She moved her chair around to sit on Jeric's left where she could massage his scaffold the way the orderly had shown her. It felt strange and lifeless, she thought, unformed and unfinished. If she lost a hand and had to put up with a temporary substitute like that, she would be disgusted, too.

While exploring the base, Traxus had counted Marion's assets again and again, each time hoping she had missed something. Two squadrons of light fighters remained, but none of them were equipped with gravdrives, which prevented them from traveling far enough to get a message out. What was left of the infantry was supplemented by a few dozen tanks, most of them lightly armed, lightly armored skirmishers. On the other hand, the heavy artillery that surrounded the base was enough to knock a fleet out of orbit or send an army running. It was composed of missile launchers, howitzers, masers, plasma cannons, and railguns. The patrolling long-striker tanks alone were powerful enough to level a small town in a single shot.

None of this lethal arsenal made Traxus feel any safer. They were still isolated, trapped in their cage of weaponry, unable to connect to the outside world. She had never realized how much she took hypercomms for granted or how easily those connections could be severed. The events of the past few days had stirred up a primitive fear in Traxus, the same fear that had kept her ancestors in the trees for millions of years, an almost hardwired and unquestionable instinct. She thought of the things that had attacked them, blue-black and spindly, nightmares made flesh, and she slumped in her chair. *All those spines ... it looked like a beast made of knives.* And yet they had a terrible beauty, as though industrial art sculptures had come to life.

The sound of snoring drew Traxus's attention to Leon. His head was slumped to the side, his arms folded across his chest. Even sleeping, he looked fierce. She took the opportunity to confide in

Jeric. "There's something else," she said, afraid to broach the subject but knowing she had to.

Jeric's interest was piqued by the desperate tone of her voice, and he was suddenly attentive.

"When we were attacked, I mean, when the creatures got to us, I saw a ship crashing."

"The skybeam knocked a lot of them out of the sky, sure."

"No, Jeric. *Listen.* It was one of *ours.* A civilian ship."

Jeric looked away, and realization slowly emerged for Traxus, a bleak dawn over a barren landscape. He must have seen it, too. "You don't know that it was her ship," he said determinedly.

"And you can't tell me it wasn't."

Marion had told them nothing in response to Leon's inquiry about Rachel's flight other than that the base's records hadn't logged any departure information before the comms were lost.

"We can't tell him," Jeric said with finality. "Not until he's back on his feet."

Traxus watched Leon sleeping and wondered what he would do when she told him. She had to tell him, didn't she?

18: Et in Arcadia Ego

It hurt to breathe, Leon realized with dismay. His ribs seemed to rebreak with each intake of air, and his head was throbbing. Every inch of him hurt, turning every movement into a test of will. Far worse than that was the knowledge that Eve had fallen. Heidi, Dawson, Dyran, Sommers, Rosenthal, Vandestan … all the men and women left under his command had likely been killed or captured if they were lucky. Somehow he doubted they would have allowed themselves to be taken alive. He had failed them, failed in his duty to lead them. In the end, he hadn't even been at his post.

He had spent days in a medicated stupor, but the truth was that he had walled himself off, struggling to make sense of the tattered remnants of his life. Every second was an eternity in which he found himself convinced first that Rachel had escaped and then that she had been captured, raped, killed, butchered. On and on it went, hope and despair dancing around one another. It was exhausting, and each day the moments of hope seemed fewer and farther between.

Traxus and Jeric appeared from time to time as he spiraled further into depression, trying to get him to take part in physical therapy, plying him with food and conversation as though he cared.

Leon wasn't sure when the gloom lifted, only that his grief had slowly calcified, frosting over into a hard core of anger. He was furious at everyone: Hakar for abandoning the sector, Jeric for his betrayal, Marion for his inaction, Rockmore, Akida…. He was even angry at the dead: Heidi, for allowing herself to be paralyzed and becoming a victim; Dawson; the civilians who had panicked; the sojieri who had futilely sacrificed themselves. He saved most of his anger for himself when he realized that there was really no one to blame, no one but the saboteurs and the enemy that had so ruthlessly conquered Eve.

And so he had risen and begun his physical therapy, trying to speed the healing process and get himself back into killing shape. He didn't know what had happened to Rachel, but he was going to find out and find her or die trying.

Leon was doing pushups, fighting through the lances of agony that coursed through his arms and chest when a shape appeared in his peripheral vision. "Colonel, good to see you up and moving," said Marion, his voice muffled by the curtain of pain.

"I suppose you could call it that," Leon grunted as he sat up and stretched, rotating his injured arm. He grimaced as the damaged nerves and muscles worked to move the limb, trying to achieve lost harmony. There were angry-sounding pops from the joint, and he lowered his arm. "Thank you for taking us in."

"Don't thank me yet. I've been waiting to interrogate you." Marion's tone was friendly, but there was an unmistakable edge. Whatever else he might be, the man was a Falcon and the commander of a lost garrison on a lost world.

"Feel free to start."

"Your companions have given me plenty to start from, and I trust … Lieutenant Tachai's account of things. Still, you're the one who took off in pursuit of Porter, the terrorist."

"He's confessed to you?"

"Fine, *alleged* terrorist. In fact, he's been in just as bad shape as you. Severe blood loss, and the wound became septic pretty quickly. Doctor Chase had to debride most of the necrotic tissue, and the guy is one arm less than he had. I didn't enjoy wasting medical treatment on him."

"We need whatever information he has," Leon said.

"That's why he's still breathing. He's slowly coming around, and I hoped you might participate in the interrogation. But first things first. Why were you at the cosmodrome, and why did you go after him?" Marion crouched beside Leon in his sky-blue fatigues, a lock of hair plastered to his forehead with sweat.

Leon tried to recall the events after the general's shuttle exploded, but it was a jumble. "I honestly don't remember much of it after the bomb went off. I think I was just running on adrenaline and instinct. As for why I was at the port, I was saying goodbye to my girlfriend."

"Rachel Case."

"Yes," Leon confirmed, fighting past the lump rising in his throat. "After the bombing, I was looking for my friends. We were all wounded, and the whole place was a mess. I don't know how many people were killed in the blast. Most of it actually missed us and took out a nearby freighter, but it blew our shuttle out from under us. I saw this guy at the edge of the crowd. I know what a person in total shock looks like, especially civilians who have just been attacked. He was the only one there who didn't have that look. I don't care how badly things got in the Valinata before he fled, a bomb goes off that close to you, you don't just walk it off. He didn't look surprised, he just looked sick to his stomach. I … trusted my instincts, and when he ran, I knew I was right."

Nodding, the commander seemed satisfied. "That's fair enough. You strike me as a man who's been through enough to know what he's looking at. Before my people found you, did he give up anything of use?"

It took a moment for the memory to coalesce. Leon recalled crawling in the dirt, his body already broken, ears still ringing, the taste of dust and blood, and hazy forms stamping in the dirt, high-pitched laughter. He remembered enormous beasts plummeting from the sky, looking like they had just hauled themselves from the primordial sea, shadowy limbs the length of fútbol pitches reaching, grasping, implacably bitter that they had been left behind by evolution, abandoned to ancestral myths of half-formed grotesqueries. "He admitted that he was working for the things. I don't know if he was responsible for all the bombs at the port or even if he knew who was, but he was clearly part of a larger operation to pave the way for the invasion."

"They did a remarkable fucking job," Marion muttered. "The good news is that Raven Blue is giving us a wide berth. Our batteries give us sufficient air coverage to provide some protection for Las Serras, as well as some of the smaller outlying townships. That being said, if the enemy decides to launch a ground attack on the city under the mountain, we won't be able to do a damn thing about it. Our batteries can't cover the ground in that area, and I don't have the troops left to hold them off."

"It couldn't have been easy—"

"It wasn't," snapped Marion, cutting Leon off. "I'm no stranger to hard decisions, Colonel Victor, but I wasn't on Daltar. I'm not as comfortable with mass destruction as you are."

Leon frowned. He hadn't known Marion more than a few days and had only spent a few hours in his company, but that jab seemed out of character. Was he baiting Leon? Testing him? If so, he wasn't going to rise to it. "You're right. This isn't Daltar, and Raven Blue aren't the Daltari. I've seen what they've done. I've been behind Valinata lines."

The commander crossed his arms. "Yes, I saw a report that you and a team were captured behind Valinata lines. We were asked to monitor you. The report didn't say what you were doing there."

What Leon had seen on Aethaleia was classified, but he didn't suppose that mattered now. "Total destruction. And I mean *total*." Leon shuddered at the memory but he proceeded to give Marion an outline of the mission, the failed rescue, the streets full of the uncounted dead, buildings crumbling as shadowy monsters stalked among them ... and the genetic data that the Coalition had deemed so important.

When Leon finished Marion just shook his head, trying to comprehend it all. On any other day, it might have seemed far-fetched. "They should have told us. Maybe my people would still be alive."

Leon grimaced, empathizing with the man's pain. "Look, I am sorry about your men and women, but they were sojieri. They did what they were trained for."

"So did your Jackals. They acquitted themselves admirably, Colonel. We'll honor their memory by living a little longer. But I take it you've got someone else on your mind."

"My fiancée ... well, she's technically not my fiancée yet. Rachel. She was leaving on the commercial flight I asked you about, and I have no idea what happened to her. That's ... really all I care about."

Marion sighed, disappointed. "Colonel Victor, I don't believe that. Think of the refugees, think of your friends. And don't forget, you were a CRDF officer. The people on this base are your brothers and sisters in arms, after a fashion. As you know, we weren't able to pull anything useful from CROS for you, but I'm sure she got away. You have to work off of that hope."

The commander was right, of course. Leon felt ashamed and selfish. At the same time, he found it difficult to think about anything but Rachel; even his own safety came in a distant second. *I don't even know where she is.*

How long had Marion been waiting, looking expectantly at Leon? "You mentioned an interrogation. Is Porter up to it?"

§

Outside the conference room, the CRB's medical wing was a hornet's nest of activity, but inside all was quiet, and the chairs arrayed around the long wooden table were comfortable. Marion had chosen the location for the meeting to provide a more conducive, neutral atmosphere for the interrogation and also at the request of Doctor Timotej Chase, who wanted his patients kept close to care.

It was something of a shock to meet Chase, who had been left in charge of the wounded since most of the actual base doctors and surgeons had been wiped out with the rest of Task Force Claymore. There was nothing left of the field hospital but ash. Chase wasn't actually a medical doctor but a xenopathologist who had been transferred to the base to conduct a survey of the sector's viral and bacterial diversity. He was short—shorter than Jeric, in fact—and almost spherically rotund. The top of his bald head was tomato-red with sunburn, and a bushy salt-and-pepper moustache obscured his mouth, making him look like a walrus. But he wore a military uniform, the dress whites of a captain in CRDRIG, the Coalition Royal Defense Research Institute for Genetics. He would clearly have been more comfortable in a lab coat than his ill-fitting whites, but he nevertheless carried himself with dignity and authority.

"Doctor, it's an honor to meet you," Leon said, extending his hand. "Thank you for taking care of us."

Chase shook Leon's hand distractedly. "You're welcome, Colonel. I'm sorry I couldn't do a better job on your friend's hand, but I haven't had any experience with scaffolds. All things considered, it went well. I'm lucky the diagnostics robot had such a comprehensive local archive, and the orderlies we have left are competent."

"You won't hear any complaints from us," Leon assured him.

"So you're the little cherub who sliced off the rest of my hand," Jeric said, coming forward. Chase arched an eyebrow but said nothing.

"Don't be an ungrateful little jerk," Leon snapped.

"It's pronounced 'Jeric,'" the pilot said nastily.

Leon resisted the urge to choke the pilot. "Forgive my colleague, Doctor. He has a bizarre sense of humor."

"There's nothing to forgive. You've all been through a lot." *You've all been through a lot.* Chase didn't seem like the type of man to empathize with another person. Was he aware that he, too, was a prisoner on Eve? Did he care?

The door at the far end of the conference room opened, and Commander Marion entered. "The prisoner is on his way. Doctor, will you be staying?"

"I feel I'm obligated to. I'll try not to snore."

Marion smiled disarmingly, seeming a decade younger. He was one of those men who would look perpetually young until old age suddenly broke him. "Doctor Chase has been catching naps between surgeries," he explained.

"Just try to keep this civil," Chase said with a glance at Leon. Had something in the colonel's eyes given him away?

"Doctor, if you don't mind my asking, what's your background?" Leon found himself inquiring. Chase had quite a few medals for someone who spent most of his time indoors.

The look he got from the doctor was one of suspicion, but Chase was clearly a man who enjoyed talking about himself. "A little Blue Lab, a little Red. I didn't exhibit the necessary sociopathy for Clean Room work, so I washed out and joined the CRDRIG. I know about you, though, Colonel. I read your treatise on genetic vulnerabilities in the enterobacteria of Daltari due to their selective breeding practices. It's a good thing no one else did, or they might have acted on it."

Dumbfounded, Leon retreated. They took their seats with Traxus between him and Jeric to provide a buffer. There wasn't much to see in the conference room, but a window in the opposite wall looked out on a busy corridor. Across the hall was a sealed lab with a row of full biosafety suits hanging on the wall inside the airlock. Two orderlies were bringing equipment in and setting it up beside the door. As though he could sense Leon watching them, Marion moved over and drew the blinds for privacy.

Chase sat at the opposite end of the room and stifled a yawn. He leaned back and clasped his hands across his ample stomach. His eyes, though tired, were piercing. He clearly didn't trust the Jackals.

It was good to be back in Pack colors. Leon's Jackal Pack uniform had been laundered and patched up, meaning that he didn't have to slouch around in coveralls or, worse, a hospital gown and robe. Still, the frayed edges and sloppily repaired tears in his jacket made him feel shabby and discarded. Traxus and Jeric both wore civilian attire with visitors' badges prominently displayed. Marion ran a tight ship even now.

Uniform or no, the missing weight of Leon's pistols left him feeling naked, and even his switchblade had been confiscated. That was probably for the best because when the door to the room opened again and two burly Falcon Guard sojieri escorted Porter in, Leon wanted nothing more than to stick a knife in the man.

Porter looked at the white tile walls, the mirror-finished black stone floor, the dark display occupying one wall, everywhere but at the people waiting for him. He wasn't much of an enemy, Leon reflected. His hair was thinning, he had a small potbelly, and his eyes were glazed with pain. And yet the things he worked for … they may have looked primeval, those dark ships, but Leon knew they were somehow connected to that perfect genome that had been partially sequenced on Aethaleia. They were what the Valinata Space Force had codenamed "Abaddon," the enemy that had taken apart their kingdom piece by piece. Abaddon, the Angel of the Abyss. Now these angels of death were at the gates of the Coalition.

Leon pushed those thoughts away, focusing on the here, the now. His horizon was confined to the crater, both literally and figuratively. There was no sense obsessing over anything outside their little world. Not yet. They were in good hands: the Falcons were alert, ready, even if they wore pristine armor and carried pristine weapons. It was comforting that they looked like they knew how to use them.

Traxus touched Leon's arm. "You okay?"

He tried on a smile, decided it didn't fit. "Yeah, thanks."

Porter was led to a chair across from the others. He looked sallow and underfed, with a week's growth of beard on his hollow cheeks. The guards returned to stand by the door, leaving the prisoner manacled. One of them had been in the Hyena when they fled the port. Pavel, Leon remembered vaguely.

"Let's get started." Marion hit a button on the computer in front of him. Cameras and microphones began recording. "Please state your name for the record," he said evenly.

"What are the Jackals doing here?"

"They're here to corroborate your story. Your name, please."

"Dylan Porter."

"How did you come to Eve, and how long have you been here?"

The man said nothing. Leon's eyes snapped to Marion. His blue BDUs were absurd, Leon thought. Who was this clown, playing cops and robbers like it was just business as usual? And how had he gotten command of a Coalition Regional Base near the border with the Valinata? Had everyone gone suddenly mad?

"Answer the questions, please," Marion said, a little more sharply.

"I came here four months ago on the *Mermaid*. I was with a few hundred other Valinata refugees."

"And where did you come from, Dylan Porter?"

"Yesheva. It's in the Valinata."

"What's there? A school for sleeper agents? Special forces training camps?"

"No, nothing like that. I was born there. It's a civilian colony. We export lumber, ore, sulfur. I think there are a couple tritium refineries and mem pad factories in the south."

"And since you got here, what have you been doing?" Marion leaned forward and clasped his hands on the table. "You've been in the camps?"

"Most of the time."

"Did you come here with orders? From Raven Blue?"

Porter looked away. His hand clenched into a fist, and the stump of his other arm twitched, trying to mirror the gesture with muscles and bones that no longer existed. "I didn't have a choice."

"This is ridiculous," Leon muttered. He stood up and moved to the small credenza set against the wall where a carafe of water and another of Kaf stood beside a stack of cups. Hands shaking, he poured himself a glass of water.

"Mister Porter, please describe the circumstances that brought you to Eve and how you entered the employ of Raven Blue."

"The 'employ?' Are you joking? Fuck you, idiots. You have no idea what's going on here."

"Then please enlighten us," Marion was saying, but Leon had already rounded the table, dropping his cup roughly beside Traxus and Jeric, where it spilled.

He grabbed Porter by the collar and hauled him out of his chair, his fingers working into the fabric and the man's throat. He pulled his enemy close, lifting him off the ground. Now the two were eye to eye, and Leon saw fear, real fear, none of the sardonic arrogance he remembered vaguely from after the crash. Hot pain snaked up and down his arm, probing his weaknesses and injuries, but he tightened his grip and felt the man's Adam's apple slide up and down between his fingers. Leon sneered at him. "This is your fault?" It was phrased as a question, but it sounded more like an accusation.

The guards looked at each other from their positions on either side of the door but made no move to intervene. Marion, for his part, looked surprised, his mouth opening. Leon's fingers dug deeper and deeper into the man's neck. "I'm going to kill you, motherfucker," he told Porter quietly through gritted teeth.

"Colonel, let him go," Doctor Chase implored, his chair scraping on the floor as he rose.

Porter's face was turning red and blotchy as blood vessels struggled for oxygen and slowly gave up. He couldn't even get a word out in defense but fixed Leon with an imploring gaze, eyes saucer-wide.

The gentle hand on his face surprised him until he recognized the scent and feel of Traxus's soft fur. She caressed his cheek, and he looked at her, eyes dry. He didn't feel like he would ever cry again. "Leon, let him go. We'll deal with him later." Her hand moved to his arm, his uninjured arm, and gave his biceps a gentle squeeze. "He's not worth it."

"Yes, he is." Leon's lip curled at the traitor, and he heaved the man into the wall, narrowly missing the window. Wheezing, fighting for breath, the one-armed assassin submissively slid to the floor. Leon stood over him, his chest and shoulders heaving. "Later I will kill you." He had felt a familiar coldness settle over him, an icy shroud that seemed to clarify his thinking and dampen his feelings as new-fallen snow muffles footsteps. Squaring his shoulders, calming his nerves, he turned to look at the startled base commander. "I'm sorry, let's continue." All the pain of his injuries returned in a sudden flood, and he sat.

Warily, the others sat back down, as well, and one of the sojieri roughly helped Porter to his seat.

Marion cocked his head and stopped the recorder. "That's not how we usually treat prisoners," he said weakly, whether to Porter or Leon the colonel couldn't tell.

"I don't suppose I blame him," Porter said hoarsely. "Can I have some water?"

Reluctantly, Traxus rose and brought the carafe to the table, along with a glass. She filled it and passed it over to Porter, who drank thirstily.

"To business," Leon said sharply.

"To business," Porter agreed, eying him.

Marion sighed. "Colonel, a moment?" Marion and Leon withdrew to the corridor where the commander's blue eyes went icy. "Listen, Colonel, I understand where you're coming from, but you're in my home now. It's not much, but it's all we've got on Eve. People are trapped here, losing hope. We've got to keep cool, level heads, set the tone, set the mood, got me?"

It was true, and Leon felt ashamed. Without discipline, the base would likely become a mob of frightened sojieri concerned only with fleeing and finding their way back to their families. The base was not impregnable, but it would hold as long as the people within it held. And they were people, after all, with all the inherent strengths and weaknesses that condition implied. "I got you, Commander. You're right."

"Cool."

"Just remember something, Commander. I meant it when I said Rachel was all I care about. And those things are standing between me and her. You're the garrison commander, and since Jackal Pack is under CRDF contract, I consider myself and my team to be under your command. But I will do whatever it takes to get to her. I hope you understand that." Leon hadn't meant to sound melodramatic, but thinking about Rachel made it hard to focus. He was starting to think he couldn't live without her. Every time he looked at Porter's weasely, smug face, it reminded him of what he had lost: purpose, love, future. He would kill whatever got in his way to get those things back.

There was a quiet moment as Marion read Leon's face. He nodded once, sharply, seeming to believe the colonel. "How could I not understand? I've known Peregrine Noelle since she had a different name, before her Ascension."

Marion had exterminated his own troops, but something in the wistful tone of his voice made it sound as though the Peregrine might have been something more. What kind of toll did that take on a man, and how had he not broken? He was either a sociopath or a complete and consummate professional. What were his dark hours like, when he was alone? Leon was beginning to realize that maybe they weren't so different. "Commander, I'm … I'm so sorry."

Marion waved his pity away. "I have to believe that she was already dead when I gave the order. Otherwise…. Listen, I know your history, Colonel. When the time comes to let you off the chain, I'll be happy to. And I hope that when I do, you find Rachel and the two of you live happily ever after. But the stars keep burning, the worlds keep turning, and we have a job to do."

"Yes, sir," Leon said with minimal sarcasm.

"I have a plan, you know, and it was working until you decided to close his windpipe. You still want in, I take it?"

"Absolutely." Leon didn't mean to sound so eager, but the chance to be alone with the saboteur was so attractive an idea it made him sick to his stomach.

"One condition: don't touch him again. I would like a little info out of him first."

"All right. Can we verify his story about Yesheva?"

"Hardly. We don't have much data stored locally, and without the network uplink there's no way to look up the place. Still, he doesn't read like a trained killer."

"No, he doesn't," Leon agreed. "Or he's a hell of an actor."

The commander turned and opened the door again. They reentered the conference room, Leon still rocked back on his heels and more than a little in awe of the seemingly lackadaisical Commander Marion. As it turned out, he was not a man to be trifled with.

Marion slid easily into his seat, while Leon walked around the table again. The commander pulled a wallet out of his own pocket and started flipping through it. He pulled out a business card and a family photo, which he eyed. Porter clearly wanted to look at it, too, and Marion slid it across the table to him. The manacled prisoner grabbed it eagerly, and tears welled in his eyes. "So, Dylan Porter, what have you been doing here since your arrival, other than building bombs?"

"Technical work at the port. I repair engines. I tried to warn people, but no one would listen."

"Listen, Porter. I'm not stupid, okay? I didn't get where I am with a third-grade reading level. I have it on good authority from the colonel here that you have already confessed to espionage on behalf of the enemy. Time is short, so let's not waste it. You're an enemy collaborator."

A pause, then, "Yes."

"All right, I like progress." Marion sat back.

Porter opened his mouth to say more and then suddenly winced, his head twitching to one side. His fingers came up, kneading his temple. "I have a splitting headache. Can I get some aspirin or something?"

"Later. Now talk. You said you came here four months ago. So you got out of the Valinata just before last call. Why come here? Why not flee farther coreward?"

"This is where they sent us."

"'Us'? Who's 'us'? Your fellow traveling engine repairmen?"

"I don't know them. I came here alone. But I only planted the two bombs. There are always others. I meant what I said: I tried to warn people." Porter squeezed his eyes shut. When he opened them, he looked to be on the verge of tears. Leon was less than sympathetic. "It was that way when Yesheva fell."

Leon leaned forward now. "And how did that happen?"

Porter's eyes narrowed. He knew what was going on. "It's not what you think, all right? I didn't know about the Celestials then."

"Celestials, huh?" Marion chuckled darkly. "That's a bit overcooked, don't you think?"

"That's what the others called them. I think it's what *they* like to be called." Porter looked fitfully from the colonel to the commander. "Please, can I have something for this headache?"

Marion rolled his eyes. "Doc, what do you say?"

Chase woke up, startled. Somehow he had fallen asleep after the altercation. "I'm sorry, Commander, what?"

Marion gave the doctor a wry smile. "Why don't you go up and get some real sleep. I promise not to break Mister Porter. But get him some aspirin first." Chase scuttled off, the door shutting softly behind him.

"You were saying?" Leon prodded.

"The Valinata told us nothing, and when I lost contact with my cousin on Terigren Kappa, I assumed it was normal comm trouble. When my planet fell, they approached people like myself—"

"Like yourself?" asked Marion.

"People who would help them to save … ourselves."

"You facilitated the surrender, huh? What, showed them where people were hiding?"

"Something like that, yes."

"What did you do before the fall of Yesheva?" Marion asked pointedly.

"I was a VP at Demuan Aerograde. We had government contracts, so we were a little better informed than most people. I surrendered our facility when it became clear the invaders could not be stopped." Porter swallowed and coughed into his hand, then massaged his throat, buying time. "I saw that if … I helped them, the killing might not be so bad."

An orderly reentered the room and left a bottle of pills on the table. Marion tapped a couple into his palm and handed them to Porter, who swallowed them immediately. "You have to understand,"

Porter continued, "I'm not a warrior. I never wanted to be part of this."

Leon breathed a long sigh. How much of this was bullshit, and how much was true? He sat forward, his eyes filled with a menacing light. "What was the price for turning over Eve?"

"Continued service and the life of my family. They don't have much use for people other than as collaborators."

Leon leaned forward and steepled his fingers. "How many of your little friends were here?"

"I said I don't know."

"In Jackal Pack maybe?" Traxus and Jeric exchanged a worried glance.

"I don't *know*."

"You didn't come here together?"

"No! I haven't seen anyone from my home since I joined the Celestia—them."

Leon pressed the attack. "How many planets? Huh, Porter? How many other planets have you opened the doors to?"

"Three! Three, all right?"

"Coalition?" interjected Marion.

"No, all Valinata until now." Porter fixed his gaze on Leon and pleaded, "Listen, you understand my position. You're a merc. I know Jackal Pack."

"You don't know shit," Leon began.

Marion held up a hand to quiet him. "Easy, Colonel. Porter, I want you to give me a list of names. Any names you know that are involved. On this planet, on any other, it doesn't matter."

"You're right. It doesn't. I know the Coalition laws well enough. Espionage, treason, terrorism, they're all punishable by death."

"That's correct. But I can offer you a certain amount of amnesty if you cooperate fully with me. I'll remove the death sentence. That's a pretty good offer. I could always cart you back to the Valinata."

Porter's smile was anything but happy. "There is no Valinata, Commander. Soon there probably won't be a Coalition, either, or at least not much of one. You talk about law and order like they still matter."

"I *am* law and order as far as you're concerned," Marion said, his voice like steel.

"These things can't be stopped. They've been waiting since the dawn of time for this moment."

"Uh-huh. Forgive me. I love a good story, but this divine retribution angle rings a little false. How do you get in touch with your handlers?"

"They always get in touch with me. By comm or in person."

Leon frowned. "So if you've helped them take three other planets, why did they try to kill you on this one?"

"I don't know. Maybe so that you would bring me here."

Immediately, alarm bells went off in Leon's head, and the others exchanged glances. *What does he mean? What use could he be here?* "And how did you know about General Rockmore's shuttle?"

"I asked around the port. It wasn't that hard. You people are pretty hard to miss. Everyone knows what goes on in Jackal Pack."

"Porter," said Marion evenly, "who within Raven Blue have you had contact with?"

"Other people like me, primarily. Collaborators." He spat that last word out contemptuously. "Sometimes they reach out to me in my—" He was interrupted by a coughing fit.

"Yeah, yeah," muttered Leon, unimpressed. "Keep talking, pal."

When a fine spray of blood hit the table, Leon shut up, his eyes going wide. He planted his hands against the table and pushed his chair back, the legs scraping loudly on the tile. Porter was having trouble breathing, his coughs hard, wet rattles deep within his chest. Marion stood quickly and waved the guards over. "Get him back to infirmary, please," said the commander tiredly. This was becoming an unpleasant routine. "Quarantine!" he called after them.

The guards began helping Porter toward the door. He went meekly, blood all over the front of his shirt and dribbling down his chin. All his resistance and bravado had faded away, and Leon saw a crumpled, frightened man who had done whatever he could to save the ones he loved—if the story he had told them was true. Would Leon have done things any differently?

Leon caught up to him in the corridor. "Porter, wait! You said they took your world, took your family. Do they take hostages?"

"Franca," the man moaned through bubbles of blood coming from his mouth in a pink froth. "Joseph...." He hadn't let go of the picture of his family, had it crumpled in his fist. He let out an anguished cry, and blood began streaming from his nose. "They ... know. That I'm here. In ... *my mind.*" His voice was a whisper, but his words cut through Leon like a knife. "What was I supposed ... to do?"

Before Leon could pursue the point, a door at the end of the corridor opened, and troops rushed in with carts, pushing between Leon and the others. A man and woman with CRDRIG insignia on their uniforms were with them. Two of the carts bore burned Raven Blue sojieri, their long limbs splayed, their armor cracked and pitted. Another cart had a number of rubbery looking canisters on it, each about the size and shape of a rugby ball.

The CRDRIG woman was barking orders. "Put the corpses in Bays Three and Four. Put the ordnance in Bay One." The troops did as she told them before withdrawing.

Porter was still coughing and scrabbling at the side of his head with his hand as though trying to keep it from coming apart. The guards supporting him were professionals, but they couldn't hide their revulsion. It was plain on their faces as the man continued to bleed all over them, coughing and sputtering like he had sprung a leak. Was he sick? Was that why they had wanted him captured? To spread some horrible spaceborne plague? Leon didn't care as he wrenched Porter around.

"Goddammit, whatever happened to your family is going to happen all over the galaxy if you don't tell me! Do they take *hostages? I have to know!*"

Through his coughing fit, bloodshot eyes filling with tears, the traitor spoke, choking out the word. "Sometimes." Porter's wild eyes settled on the cart going into the biosafety lab. "Listen," he croaked, "they're here. They can see through my eyes, and...." He broke off, moaning through gritted teeth. The guards hustled him away.

"I think that went pretty well." Marion sounded bizarrely optimistic. "He'd be a nice guy under different circumstances."

"Yeah. Right." *'Through my eyes,'* he said. *What the fuck did that mean?*

"I don't know, Colonel. It seems to me he didn't have much choice in the matter."

"There's always a choice. You and I know that better than anyone. What now, Commander?"

Marion didn't reply right away. He was staring past Leon, staring at Porter. "What the hell? Do you … hear that?"

Leon paused. Maybe it was the lingering effects of the explosions, but he didn't hear anything out of the ordinary. However, in the conference room where the blinds had been opened, Traxus was wincing and covering her ears.

In the corridor Dylan Porter had fallen to his knees, now clawing at his neck and chest with his remaining hand, the stump where his right arm had been flailing wildly. He clutched at his throat, his coughs growing ragged and violent. His handlers didn't appear to know what to do, looking to their commander, helpless, as several contusions appeared on Porter's face, throat, and around the hollow of his collarbones. Leon recognized them as petechiae immediately, but he was surprised by their size and location as well as the rapidity of onset. Porter spasmed, thrashing out of the guards' hands and falling to the floor. He hit the stump of his arm against the floor, and it began bleeding anew, white bandages turning a startling crimson.

"What the hell is wrong with him?" demanded Marion, a note of panic entering his voice. Was this seizure somehow related to his wounds? Possibly the result of an infection?

"Commander, come see this!" announced a voice from the intercom. "Bay One! We've got movement!"

With their eyes still on Porter, Marion and Leon made their way to the window looking into Bay One. The two orderlies had been moving the canisters into specimen containers, but they had stopped and were regarding them intently.

Two of the canisters were pulsing, and as Leon watched, two more began bulging on the lab table. One of the orderlies was scrambling to get the lab camera running.

"Are those bombs?" Leon asked pointedly.

Marion reached over and hit the intercom button. "Doctor Chase, report to the research wing immediately. You have got to see this." He turned back to see Porter still writhing on the floor. "What is he still doing here? Guys, get him to the infirmary now!"

Things were happening fast, devolving into chaos. One of the guards knelt down to heave Porter upright, but the prisoner's back arched suddenly, making a sickening popping noise. He vomited blood in an arc, frothy and red. It hit the guard square in the face, and the man fell back, spitting. "What the fuck?"

Marion banged on the glass of the lab bay, but the orderlies were enraptured. Leon didn't blame them. He had seen his sister Naomi toward the end of her first pregnancy, when the fetus that would become baby Corrine had been able to push outward against the uterine wall enough that the effects could be seen on her stomach. What Leon was seeing now was that beauty twisted as the head-sized canisters deformed and bulged.

A few moments later, the skin of one of the urns parted like lips pursed for a kiss, and a tiny gray creature poked its head out. It was like a hand-sized, armor-plated caterpillar, its little legs working feebly, unfolding like the petals of a monstrous flower. What they had referred to as ordnance were, in fact, eggs, a clutch of eggs that Raven Blue had brought along to the attack. Leon found himself reminded of Daltar, when he mistook the Daltari exodus for an invasion, bombing not only their sojieri but thousands of civilians, as well.

One of the orderlies picked up the newly hatched creature. It was hideous, Leon thought, although interspecies reactions to newborns were well documented. Traxus had once told him that Human babies looked like the larvae of a certain Tagean cave worm. Having seen some painfully ugly Human babies himself, he didn't disagree.

The orderly was cradling the infant almost tenderly as she examined it. "Limbs are dexterous, ocular response is impressive. The exoskeleton is quite soft, and it appears to be molting already." She turned her head, and her eyes widened in surprise as another hatchling emerged from the egg. Nearby a second egg opened, tiny claws punching through its leathery surface.

"There's a dense pouch attached to the organism's abdomen," the orderly continued serenely. "It may be some sort of … yolk. We need to get these infants into isolation until we can figure out their nutritional requirements and—*ahh*!" The orderly screamed, and the hatchling squirmed out of her grip. Blood was spurting out of her glove, and it looked like one of her fingers might have been torn off. "My … suit's been compromised."

Before she could do anything else, the hatchling reared up on the table and leapt. Somehow its little limbs were able to propel it with enough force to punch through the isolation suit's lining, just beneath the faceplate. The orderly was screaming as the little gray thing writhed against her face. More blood spattered against the inside of the mask, and the orderly fell. Her companion, a look of terror on his face, backed against the far wall of the lab.

Shaking off the momentary shock, Marion hit a wide, red button located beside the intercom control panel. "Lockdown now! We are in lockdown! Biological contaminants in the research wing!"

Leon's hand went to his hip, but there was no pistol there. The commander had unholstered his own sidearm, but Leon still didn't know if he was a real sojier or some academy-pampered paper tiger.

Five, now six, now seven of the things had emerged. Could these really be the infants or larvae of the invaders at the port, those creatures Leon had glimpsed through the smog on Aethaleia? Or were they some sort of organic cluster bomb to be lobbed at the enemy? In the lab, the surviving orderly was flailing, trying to keep them away as the lab locked down. As the little creatures brought him down, the quarantine shutters descended over the window, sealing the room.

"Gas Bay One! Non-lethal!" Marion ordered into the intercom. Through the small, thick-paned windows in the airlock doors, he and Leon could see the shimmering veil of gas descending into the room. The orderly, his positive pressure suit badly compromised, was sinking to the floor as the knockout gas took effect. The diminutive creatures continued to pounce but slowly grew lethargic, stumbling around. One looked through the window at Leon, its yellow eyes glinting, before promptly toppling onto the floor, its little legs splayed.

Eyes wide, Leon and Marion backed away from the window. "That's secure?"

"Biosafety level four with redundant purge fail-safes. It's designed to handle highly pathogenic samples." Marion wiped sweat from his brow. "It should be secure enough."

"That *can't* be standard issue," Leon said breathlessly.

"It's not. It was installed just prior to Doctor Chase's reassignment last year." Marion frowned at Leon. "If you're thinking what I think you're thinking, cut it out. The sector eco survey protocols called for it. It had nothing to do with being so close to the Valinata border and Raven Blue."

Leon was unconvinced. Banging on the shutters drew his attention, and he and Marion watched as a tiny claw slid back and forth between the metal slats, scratching feebly at the glass before withdrawing. "Can they get through that?" asked one of the guards standing over Porter's still form.

"Not a chance," Marion said. "What's his status?" he asked, pointing.

Leon didn't need the guard to check for a pulse to know that Porter was dead. His eyes were red with the blood of burst capillaries, his mouth open in a scream of silent terror. His contorted features made him look less than Human, a gargoyle. What had happened to him? Some raging infection from the attacker that had slashed him at the port? That would have to be some pathogen.

"You think it's safe to pull our man out?" asked Pavel, the guard. He was moving warily toward the door of the lab. Leon admired his willingness to enter.

"We shouldn't open that," Leon cautioned. "You sure it's safe?"

"Reasonably," Marion said, a little too uncertainly for Leon's taste. "You saw them pass out, so at least we know Cendol-121 works on them. If worse comes to worst, the lab can aerosolize a tetrodotoxin. Not a nice way to go."

"Assuming that works on them, too."

The commander said nothing.

The door to the conference room opened, and Traxus stuck her head out. "Is everything okay?" she asked before her gaze settled on Porter's corpse.

"No," Leon said, waving her back. "You and Jeric stay in the conference room where I can see you."

"*What?*" she asked. "What happened to him?" There was something accusatory in her voice as though she thought Leon had beaten Porter to death. Much as he might have wanted to, he strongly doubted his assault on the man could have led to that bizarre and torturous demise.

"Are there any escape routes?" Leon asked Marion.

"What? No, it's a closed system. It's biosafety level four, not a nursery."

"What about ventilation?" Leon pressed. "Where does the air come from?"

"The air supplies for these rooms are isolated. Each one has a dedicated scrubber and filter system. In the event of a lockdown, they seal completely."

"And those seals," Leon said grimly. "How durable are they?" He would have bet they were designed to resist microbes, airborne pathogens, even fire, but probably not claws.

The way the commander's face lost color was all the answer Leon needed. "Okay, boys, pull our people out of there, and then we seal it. They've already killed one person, we can't afford to lose anyone else."

The guards nodded sharply and moved to the door, pistols in hand. Again Leon was impressed by their loyalty to the fallen orderlies. The commander was back at the intercom panel. "Open Bay One," he said with authority. "Override the decon shower procedures."

Leon involuntarily backed away as the door lock clicked off. The guards entered the magnetically sealed airlock, waiting as it cycled. Moments later they had entered the lab, grabbing the fallen orderlies and pulling them back to the airlock. It was only big enough to bring one of them through at a time. At least the man was still alive. "The little things look like they're dead," one sojier said as the hatch opened and they deposited the first orderly on the floor, blood pooling beneath her torn suit. "A couple look like they fucking exploded, Commander." Leon frowned as he looked at the surviving orderly, suspended between two more guards. He was sagging strangely in his suit, looking as though his limbs had broken awkwardly. Marion's eyes settled on the orderly, too, and he frowned as the airlock opened.

"Wait a second," he said just as all hell broke loose.

Leon saw movement, too, and bolted down the hall as the little monsters burst out of the orderly's suit, leaping toward him, toward Marion, toward the guards. "*Trax*, get in the conference room and lock the *fucking door*!" he bellowed.

Was it possible the creatures had gotten bigger? They seemed to be larger than a Human hand, their rubbery gray shells hanging off in strips. The triangular plates covering their backs were now glossy black and looked harder.

Leon counted between ten and fifteen of them, which meant there were still more in the lab. Marion had his wits about him, though: he scrambled to the control panel and ordered the purge. Moments later the lab lit up as the failsafe initiated a controlled burn, incinerating everything, including the dead orderly and whatever little creatures were still inside.

The little swarm spread in all directions, skittering along the floor of the hallway in evasive patterns, leaving pinprick footprints of blood and gore, some trailing strings of tissue or bits of tattered iso suit like gruesome garlands. Their high-pitched squeals filled the corridor like some discordant, hellish choir.

Some part of Leon recognized that these things, comical though they might have looked on their own, were the cruelest kind of commando, infants born to kill, their rubbery eggs some sort of Trojan Horse. Their spread had to be contained at all costs. *This base is only impregnable to an outside force.*

Marion was moving along the sloped wall of the corridor, firing his pistol. He hit one of the creatures dead-on, and it exploded in a black splash against the floor. He yelled into his comm, "This is Commander Marion, we have a priority situation in the research wing, Level One, Section B. Raven Blue out of containment. Blackjack, in here now! C-BURN armor, full kit, *special weapons*!" he roared, firing again.

Standing at the end of the hallway, his back and palms planted against the cold metal of a blast door, Leon watched as one of the things clambered up onto his boot. He kicked and sent it flying. Righting itself, it came running back more quickly than he would have thought possible, with a flashing, terrifying grace. Its gray flesh was flaking off, revealing the new growth of darker chitin beneath. *They're molting. The monsters are molting, and they've only been alive for five minutes. What is this?* Leon threw a chair at it, and it dodged, moving away for the moment.

One of the creatures sank its claws into a guard's leg, climbing up, digging its limbs into his flesh like pitons on a mountain. Screaming, the sojier turned and batted it away with his pistol. As the bug fell, it tore an angry red gash in his thigh and shredded his pant leg in the process. It took a moment for it to right itself, and in that moment the guard shot it.

"Weapons?" Leon cried, hoping there was some sort of locker in the hallway that he had overlooked. Marion shook his head grimly, and a moment later the sojier, limping, was overwhelmed. Pavel was his name, Leon recalled with detachment. The creatures seemed almost drawn to the blood, and three of them flung themselves at him and bounced back. For an instant, it didn't look as though they had done any damage but simply feinted, an attack in pantomime. Then the guard collapsed, thin rivulets of blood pumping from tiny cuts in his flak vest directly over his heart and lungs. They could puncture vest and bone now: they were getting stronger, they were leaping higher. It was all happening so fast.

Seeing his opportunity, Leon ran across the hall, kicking one of the creatures aside as he did so. While they were capable of killing already, they still seemed disoriented. They had clearly feigned being knocked out by the Cendol, but perhaps it had had some effect on them, after all. He fell to his knees in the pool of blood spreading around the fallen guard. The man was still breathing, his eyes dimming but still full of fear and pain. It was a bit of a struggle to get his sidearm away from him, but Leon managed, took the spare clip from the pouch on the man's belt and dropped it in his own pocket. He almost missed seeing the little gray thing running toward him with its swordlike arms held before it like a toy jousting knight come to life. Leon fell on his side to avoid its charge, shooting as it hurdled him. He didn't think he hit it.

Quickly he got his feet back under him, stood, and looked for a target he could hit. One of them leapt at him, and he fired reflexively. The bullet missed, punching a clean hole in the glass of the conference room window. He turned the creature's pounce with his shoulder, feeling its claws rake his arm. He had given them the opening they needed, however: another jumped at the window, which had been sufficiently weakened that it could jump right through. There was a crash and tinkle of glass, and it was in the room with Jeric and Traxus. Leon's heart sank.

Before he could move to help them, Leon saw a pair of the creatures attacking an orderly running to one of the neighboring labs. One of them was on the man's back, hacking its way toward his vital organs. His screams grew feeble as he pounded on a door, begging to be let in, the heels of his hands leaving bloody crescents on the metal. Leon closed in and waited for the moment to take his shot. When he pulled the trigger, the chamber clicked, empty. He swore and fumbled for the spare clip, sliding it in as the spent one dropped to the floor. He fired, and the creature tumbled off its prey. Leon didn't know if the man would survive, but he turned back to help Jeric and Traxus.

They had climbed onto the conference room table for what good that would do them. The creature in there with them charged and pounced. Jeric lashed out with his boot, knocking the thing into a chair. He promptly fell back, screaming, the toe of his boot sliced open, blood dribbling out.

Without thinking, Leon charged, vaulting the windowsill, firing. The chair exploded, stuffing shooting out in every direction, and so did the creature; the bullet that hit it tore it nearly in half. Leon had nearly forgotten how badly he had been injured in the attack on the port, but his landing reminded him. As he hit the floor of the conference room, his knees buckled, his left leg a broken column of fire. He lost his grip on the pistol as his hands spasmed involuntarily, and he sprawled on the cold tile.

A shadow passed over him as Traxus came to his side, pulling him upright. "We have to get out of here," she said desperately.

Leon could only grit his teeth. How many had they killed? Three? Four? He couldn't remember. He knew the one he had shot off the orderly had survived.

It was a relief when a yellow warning light on the ceiling began revolving, casting the whole corridor in an eerie light. The creatures' glossy hides reflected it, appearing to catch fire as they flashed back and forth, back and forth. The wing's main airlock began to open, and Leon glimpsed men in white padded armor sealed at the joints, helmets that locked into a ring at the neck. He and Traxus helped Jeric into the hallway, making their way toward their rescuers. At first he thought they had sent in EMMAs, power-armor-clad marines. The way they moved was wrong, though, too fluid. They were clad in CBRN (Chemical, Biological, Radiological, Nuclear) containment armor, intended for use in hazardous environments. While unpowered, it still provided a self-contained breathing apparatus, and lightweight aluminum plates offered modest protection against shrapnel and small-arms fire.

Their armor may have left something to be desired in terms of sheer bullet-stopping ability, but they certainly did not lack firepower. Each man had a flamethrower mounted under the right arm. These weren't the standard liquid or gas casters Leon was familiar with: the flames were white-hot and focused, almost like fighter afterburners. *Plasma jets*, he realized. The superheated gas was enough to melt metal almost instantaneously and was certainly enough to burn away any pathogen or spill. On the tiny invaders its effect was immediate and perversely marvelous.

The corridor was bathed in the light of day, white streams of fire searching between crates and through vents for the enemy, burning away the crates and vents as they did so. There was no hesitation as one of the men burned out the lab a second time. Leon was revolted by the smell of burning flesh that filled the hallway as the smoke from that sad pyre reached his nose.

Two of the creatures, scrabbling at one of the sealed vents, were immolated, writhing in the flames as they died. Leon estimated they were the size of small dogs by this point, nearly up to his knee. *How?* The answer came to him, unwelcome but unavoidable. *Their perfect genes.*

Porter's beaten corpse caught fire, and Leon quickly stamped out the flames, realizing that he might have some forensic value. The Vali man looked like a mummy, his cheeks completely sunken in, his flesh gray and paperlike. He looked hollow, as though there had never been anything inside of him but fear.

A stream of fire washed over the wall startlingly close to Leon, and he moved farther back, firing. The last thing he wanted after surviving all of this was to get burned alive by his own rescuers. The sojieri were working their way methodically forward in a line, sweeping the corridor with fire. They were well armed, well protected, these men, confident and clear-headed.

They continued their sweep until two of the creatures managed to flit past the wall of fire, leaping onto the leg and arm of one of the men. The faceless helmet turned, and in its expressionless, reflective visor Leon saw only disdain. Casually, a hand punched at the first attacker, unable to dislodge it as it dug through padding and armor weave. Abruptly, the man's movements changed as blood welled up from beneath the pristine white armor. Leon heard a muffled scream and saw blood appear, running down the left leg, as well, as the second creature moved its arms with little, rapid sawing motions. With a sickening ripping noise, the sojier's arm came free beneath the elbow, falling away. He raised his weapon, unthinking now, to cook the beasts rending his flesh. Leon knew that if he did, he could ignite his own fuel tank and they might all burn. He was relieved when one of the other sojieri turned, dropped his hand to his belt, and pulled out a large-caliber pistol. One shot punched right through the front of the helmet and out the back, shattering a wall tile and burying itself within the grout. The dead man in the white suit crumpled to the ground, and the other sojier finished off the attackers, carrying out their duty despite losing one of their own in such grim fashion.

The corridor was a firestorm now, home to clattering demons that shrieked and pounced. The three remaining troopers were the gods' holy cavalry, glowing white and spraying judgmental fire. One wall was alight, two of the labs in flames. The fire itself seemed alive, hot tongues licking greedily at the walls, its deadly caress searching out whatever it could burn, tasting metal but desiring flesh. Leon was having trouble breathing in the smoke; he felt his lungs and his skin seared by the heat. Disgusting popping noises filled the corridor as flaming hatchlings burst. Leon blanched as a gooey mass splattered against his leg.

The commander was cornered at the far end of the corridor, out of ammo. He kicked viciously at one of the creatures, which had somehow grown larger, coming nearly up to his knee. It wrenched his boot off his foot, tearing his pants from the calf down, as well. Another hatchling was working its way along the wall, its claws crunching through the grout around the tiles at Marion's back. How strong they were, how smart, how brutal!

Leon broke into a mad run, tackling the commander and tumbling to the floor with him, out of the path of the leaping hatchling. It slid across the floor with an agitated hiss, its little pincers clicking. Leon raised his pistol and fired from his prone position. The newborn invader jerked and toppled like a tin sojier, its limbs rigid. There weren't many of the creatures left, but they could still kill someone if the troops didn't move fast.

"I owe you one," Marion said breathlessly, helping Leon to his feet.

The sojier who had shot his own man was herding the survivors toward the door at the cleared end of the corridor. One of the creatures made a flying leap, sailing through a jet of fire, and crashed into the sojier's head. Although it was still small, Leon guessed that the thing had to weigh half a kilogram at least, and its momentum threw the sojier forward against the wall. His visor shattered against the tiles, and the man raised his hands to protect himself from his attacker as it worked its way around the helmet toward his exposed face.

"No," Marion breathed, barely audible over the rush of the fire and the keening of the insectlike things.

Though not far, it would be a hell of a shot with such a small, quick target. Leon had made tricky shots before, but it was hard to get a clear sight picture with the flickering fire playing havoc with his eyes and making a mess of the shadows. The heat made it hard to concentrate, the pain even harder. He raised the pistol, noting how unfamiliar he was with it, and steadied his aim.

"Sean, stay still!" Marion screamed, his voice cutting through the chaos with surprising force. The sojier, with iron discipline, braced himself against the wall, hands planted above his head, fingers splayed. The creature continued to work around the left side of his helmet, exposing its back to them. Leon took a deep breath and faltered.

Traxus was beside him, her hand out. Without hesitating, Leon handed her the sidearm. In one fluid motion she raised the weapon, adopted a target shooter's stance, and fired. Five shots rang out.

Leon prayed that the helmet would deflect any shots that went through the target. Sojier and attacker jerked as one, crashing against the wall as two shots tore up the tiles. There were sparks from the man's helmet and a black splash as one bullet found its mark. Finished, the creature rolled off the trooper's shoulder and thumped to the floor, limbs curling like the legs of a spider.

By now the fire was burning out; tiny patches guttered where burned enemies lay smoldering on the floor. The laboratory was still alight, though, burning steadily, the fire destroying research, samples, equipment. It would have been a good day to call in sick, Leon thought. For all of them. The sojieri were clinical in their approach to the slaughter. They had worked their way almost all the way through the corridor, cornering the last of the creatures and cutting off their escape with a carpet of fire.

Leon relaxed a little, surveying the destruction. He barely heard Jeric shout, "*Behind you!*" Leon looked over and saw the pilot pointing, jerking his finger frantically.

The creature was one of the smaller ones, still the size of a small cat, but it felt like it weighed ten pounds when it crashed into Leon's side, dragging him to the floor in a flurry of flashing claws and limbs. Leon managed to grab hold of its thrashing arms and pulled it around. He found himself looking into a face much more expressive than he would have imagined. Perhaps he had expected some soulless grim reaper, but the eyes that blazed in front of his own were full of fear and hate. Its claws cut into his hands where he grabbed it, and it snapped at his throat with its tiny mandibles. Small though they were, one nick to the jugular, and Leon would bleed out. The world sank out of his awareness as he focused all his energy on keeping the hatchling at bay, marveling at its surprising strength. Its sharp, angular exoskeleton dug into his forearm while he wrestled with it, and its legs kicked forcefully against his chest. *But something's wrong, the genes aren't so perfect.* For its limbs were irregular, legs of different lengths, some markedly stunted, one tiny arm shriveled and tucked against its hard torso.

And then Marion was there, grabbing at the hatchling. So was Traxus, trying to protect Leon's face. Together the three of them managed to pinion its limbs, but their hands were cut to ribbons in the process. Traxus had dropped the pistol to help, and Marion scooped it up. He pointed it at the thrashing animal but held his fire for fear of hitting Leon.

"What are you waiting for? Shoot the little fucker!" Leon gasped as one of its scythelike arms, the blade no longer than a steak knife, pushed through his palm and out the back of his left hand. He watched the bloody limb emerge from his skin, mesmerized by the mind-numbing pain.

Screaming, Traxus wrapped her hands around the thing's torso, pulling it off. The blade slid from Leon's hand with the sickening sensation of sutures being tugged, magnified a thousand times. Traxus's grip was strong and resolute as she held the creature away from her body while it flailed, turning her sleeves to ragged tatters and slicing her watch clean through the face.

Suddenly one of the white-clad troopers was there. Leon recognized the broken visor of the man he had saved, a sojier ruthless enough to shoot his own comrade rather than let him burn them all alive. In one armored hand he grabbed the thing away from Traxus. Almost contemptuously, he flung it into a wall and turned his flamethrower on it. The hatchling was cooked in its exoskeleton almost instantly, without even having time to scream.

"Thank you," Leon said, gasping for breath and coughing as he did so. "I thought that was it." He examined his left hand where the creature's organic weapon had punched clean through him. Mirrored rivulets of blood ran down his forearm to his elbow, and for an instant he was terrified that what had happened to Porter would now happen to him, as well. Suddenly his old wounds were not only aching but on fire.

"Sergeant, are things under control?" asked Marion breathlessly.

The sergeant turned to his commander, and Leon got a good look at him. His craggy face was covered in soot and his dark hair, poking out from beneath a rubbery Nomex hood, was shot through with gray. This man had been on the job a while, Leon guessed, but the eyes, blue sapphires, were piercing, with more fight left in them than most people ever had. "We'll be in the clear in a few moments, sir," he said with a rough Irish lilt. *Homegrown Terran*, Leon thought. *And a tough customer*.

"Sergeant O'Reily, this is Colonel—"

"Haven't the time for formalities, sir." The trooper inclined his head and turned around. An instant later he was showering flame across the corridor. He led them to safety, stopping so Leon and Traxus could retrieve Jeric, and they proceeded to the door. Once they were clear, the sergeant turned and rejoined his two comrades. Now, unobstructed by the people they had come to protect, they mercilessly blanketed the hallway with fire. Just to be sure.

The blast door slid open, and Leon stumbled through with Traxus, Jeric, and the commander. They found themselves in an airlock with the few cowering survivors, waiting for the quarantine to lift. A yellow light spun on the ceiling, flickering bright, dark, bright, dark in a dazzling kaleidoscope. Already lightheaded, Leon felt nauseated as the light continued to oscillate.

"I'd say that was close," Jeric said, panting. He was limping heavily, blood pooling beneath his foot.

Leon could only nod, doubled over with his hands planted on his knees. Blood ran down his left pant leg from his injured hand. He looked around. There were only seven of them. He didn't even know how many people had died in that hallway and the surrounding labs.

Narrowly escaping death had cleared Leon's mind but not in the sense that he was thinking more clearly; rather, he wasn't thinking about anything at all. The airlock was a metal oval chamber approximately five feet by five feet square, forcing them to stand nearly shoulder to shoulder. In addition to the expected odors of machine oil and disinfectant, it stank of their sweat and blood, a cloying, metallic smell that settled on their tongues. Still, after the smoke-filled corridor, it was refreshing to be in a room with no corners, where nothing could hide.

The orderly who had been knocked out in the lab, whose suit had played host to those creatures, was leaning on the remaining guard for support. His eyes were wide and wild, and he was jabbering to himself. Waking up covered in those things would be enough to give anyone a nervous breakdown. At least, he would survive.

What had happened in there? Leon's mind was running in circles, trying to comprehend it all: Porter, the creatures, their clearly enhanced development. Worst of all was the clear intelligence behind their behavior. They weren't merely instinctive killers, born precocious like some animals: they had *planned*, feigning unconsciousness when the orderly passed out in order to lull the rest of them into a false sense of security. No, that was impossible. *But I fucking saw it. That little thing made sure I was looking at it when it did its pratfall.*

Too distraught to be analytical, Leon obsessed over that one detail. It had been so long since he had been afraid of monsters that he had forgotten the breathlessness of it, the utter stripping away of any other emotion. It would have been embarrassing to admit his desire to hide under blankets with a flashlight, but somehow Leon knew he was hardly alone in that sentiment.

"Is there a pub on base?" he asked suddenly. There was nervous laughter.

"No, but I think we can find some alcohol if we look," Marion said with the beginnings of a smile. And there it was: their personal defense mechanisms came online.

"We could have distilled something in there if the fuckers had given us ten minutes," said one of the lab technicians, crossing his arms.

There was more hollow laughter that quickly turned hysterical. There was nothing for them to do but laugh. They were still laughing when the yellow light went off and the outer door ground open. Their laughter died as the reality of the situation came crashing back down on them. They weren't walking out into bright sunlight and a warm breeze for cold drinks or into a dark barracks with soft bunks. They were walking into a quarantine room where corpsmen in Level 1 iso-gear waited with hospital gowns and syringes. Nor should they have been surprised by the presence of sojieri in the room with guns, guns which were aimed in their direction.

Doctor Chase met them, looking distraught. "What happened in there? Commander, those samples were invaluable, and you allowed them to be destroyed!"

Marion was too weary to discipline the doctor. "I hope there's something for you to salvage, Doc, but we had other things on our minds."

Looking at the survivors, Chase did a headcount. "My god, how many?..."

"Five, six. I'm not sure who's still in there," Marion admitted.

"You should have waited. Sending Blackjack in there was a mistake."

"Sergeant O'Reily's squad just saved our *lives*," Marion snapped. "Your samples will have to take a back seat to that."

Jeric fell into a chair, and a corpsman began examining his injured foot. "Are we infected with something?" he asked, voice fearful. "After what happened to Porter...."

"Did you see any of that?" Marion interrupted.

Chase nodded. "When I couldn't get past the lockdown, I watched on the security station monitor. I can't believe it. We'll have to download from the lab camera's hard drive to get a better look, though." He turned to Jeric, Leon, and the others who had been wounded by the creatures. "We'll do a full panel on each of you, to make sure there are no foreign bodies in your systems. Hopefully, there's enough left of Porter for me to conduct an autopsy, but it seems likely he picked up some virulent infection from his contact with Raven Blue."

Jeric moaned desperately, and Leon felt bile rising in his throat. Porter's death had been horrible, agonizing. What kind of venom or bacteria could these things carry with them to do such a thing? More importantly, was it contagious?

"I'm certain it's not airborne," Chase said as though to answer Leon's unspoken question. "Still, we'll keep you all under observation until—"

It was hard to tell which they heard first: the explosion, the siren wail, or every comm unit in the room screaming to life. Quarantine procedure forgotten, everyone who could still run made their way to the front doors of the medical building.

As soon as he was outside, Leon regretted it: never before had the old phrase "out of the frying pan and into the fire" seemed more appropriate. Half the batteries along the crater rim were firing, some straight upwards through channels in the airshield, targeting nearly a dozen enemy cruisers that had erupted from the clouds.

His lacerated arms streaming blood, Marion was shouting orders to his command staff over the comm, not missing a beat. Leon, recovering from the shock of their ordeal, watched as a ship directly above them was perforated by shots from three railguns. The guns let out deep oceanic screams as they fired. Missiles struck along the giant black vessel's flank, and it began to tumble and disintegrate as it plummeted toward the base's airshield.

That shield was designed to withstand missiles, orbital laser strikes, and bombs, even a nuclear weapon with a peak output of up to fifty terawatts, *not* crashing ships. The whole sky crackled and seemed to tear apart as the debris rained down against the energy field. Half the hull burned through as the shield shorted, and people ran for their lives as the wreckage crashed into the southern end of the crater, crumpling against the rocky slope.

The force of the impact sent up a gust of wind and dust that nearly knocked Leon down. People were screaming, panicking, and he felt like he was back at the port, watching civilization dissolve into terrified chaos. Spotting Traxus, Leon pushed through the crowd clustered around the entrance to the medical building. It was squat and bunkerlike with thick concrete walls and a sloped roof designed to shrug off attacks. He manhandled Traxus back through the doorway as another explosion above the airshield lit up the crater. This time the shield buckled entirely, shorted by the sustained bombardment, the green haze vanishing, rolling back like bedsheets on a cold morning. They were vulnerable.

The volume of fire intensified, but now green blasts of plasma rained into the base. Buildings were scorched, windows shattered, and doors blew inward. Vehicles were destroyed while sojieri were immolated. Was this the end?

When the answer came, it surprised Leon: it *was* the end, but not for the base. Luckily, Leon was not looking skyward when the first of the antimatter weapons detonated, accompanied by an unholy shriek. A cascade of light sawed across the courtyard, and up above, the sky was awash in a daytime aurora as the antimatter warhead's containment field destabilized. The annihilation reaction simply *consumed* the ship it hit, the surrounding air shrieking as it collapsed into the vacuum left in the explosion's wake. Several more detonations followed as though the horsemen of the Apocalypse had arrived, laying waste to the very sky.

And then, after what had surely been only a minute, the firing stopped, the guns going silent, smoldering. The world braced itself on the brink of collapse, not daring to breathe as the enemy vessels—or what was left of them—dropped out of the sky like burning leaves, decorating the savannah with the embers of their ruin.

A loud hum started, accompanied by a rhythmic thumping that got faster and faster until the geothermal and nuclear backup generators recatalyzed the airshield. Once more, the protective green veil coalesced over them, and the base was again a haven, a prison.

Leon let go of Traxus and allowed himself to exhale. They had survived the end of the world.

19: Paradise, Lost

A dull, cloudy day had never looked so beautiful. When Leon and his companions finally emerged from quarantine three days later, they felt as though they had been embalmed and entombed. Chase and the remnants of his research team were clearly unaccustomed to being thrust into the roles of caretakers: their bedside manner was more suited to dealing with bacteria than living people. They poked, prodded, roughly examined, and drew blood, urine, and stool samples with brusque impersonality. Porter had not died of an infection, that much was clear. What *had* killed him was being kept a closely guarded secret.

Life within the crater base had achieved a weary, resigned monotony. They were a castle under siege, secure for now. Finding themselves in a stalemate with the invaders, they could not let their guard down—the consequences of carelessness were now all too clear. The carcass of the enemy ship leaning against the southern lip of the crater was a testament to how close they had come to being wiped out. The death toll from the attack stood at thirty, including five people killed in the lab outbreak. The enemy bombardment had left the same greasy-smoky smell hanging in the air that Leon remembered from Aethaleia.

It was hard not to obsess over the nature of what had attacked them. Raven Blue was an unfamiliar but clearly highly developed species, with an unprecedented mastery of organic weaponry and ship design, but nothing Leon had seen was beyond comprehension. Nothing except for their offspring, if that's what they were. They certainly seemed to be closely related species, at least. They were vicious and deadly and terrifyingly enough, they seemed to be capable of communicating and strategizing within minutes of birth. They had gone from tiny creatures occupying the space of a Human fist to the size of cats within ten minutes. Clearly, some sort of metabolic manipulation was at work here, something far beyond Leon's understanding.

Creatures built to kill. From the moment they hatch they are lethal, smart, and fast enough to dispatch armed opponents. But disoriented. Small price to pay for the chaos they could have caused. If they had hatched in the open or gotten away ... unless.... Leon's brow furrowed as a painful, horrifying thought occurred to him. *Unless Porter somehow triggered it when he knew Marion and I were in the same place, when he knew a lockdown protocol would trap us with them long enough to kill us.* That was crazy, but it made an upside-down sort of sense, too. If such an attack could be initiated, it would have decapitated the base of the only leadership left on Eve.

Leon flexed his fingers, felt the ache in his palm. It was nothing compared to the rest of his broken body, but the way the little beast had pushed so easily through his hand had been almost perverse. *The fucking thing was five minutes old, and it managed to stab right through my hand.* Traxus walked beside him, a bandage on her arm where she had been slashed. Jeric limped along, short two toes; when he had asked if they would be replaced, Chase had merely shrugged and walked away.

Having sustained minor injuries himself, Commander Marion had nevertheless maintained his good humor (although from time to time the strain had showed through as he kept tabs on everything from his hospital room). Leon liked the man well enough, but he still didn't know if he was up to the task of leading them through this. Either the good humor was put on or the commander had a screw loose. Still, in his own way he mourned the fallen, writing letters to their next of kin even though he had no way of sending them. More than that, the Falcons on the base were clearly devoted to him. If he was good enough for the Falcon Guard, who was Leon to doubt him?

There was an unspoken segregation between the trio of Jackals and the rest of the base. Leon was used to military personnel looking down on them, but that usually stopped once they had seen Jackal Pack in action. There was a certain contempt in the eyes of the Falcons, although Leon suspected they gave the same haughty looks to anyone who didn't wear the screaming falcon badge themselves. No, the distance here was almost a demarcation of territory, professional courtesy between predators. The Jackals had their barracks to themselves, left empty after the destruction of Task Force Claymore, while the civilians remained guarded in two buildings near the outskirts of the base.

Up above, the airshield was a crackling, protective god. Looking at the sky through the green filter offered a view that seemed to be shot through with static. A palpable charge was in the air, as much from tension as the shield. They had seen up close what the enemy was capable of; war and invasion were no longer abstract.

The day might be overcast with a slight bite to the chilly breeze that whipped through the crater, but the grass and trees appeared to have been painted in new, vivid tones. The waterfall was no longer a ragged sprawl of water over rocks but a spill of diamonds, sapphires, emeralds. The sky was not full of clouds but a canopy of silk. The haggard party stopped in awe before the waterfall, listening to its murmur for a few minutes before returning to the center of the base where the smell of exhaust from the Hyenas and light tanks was thick, where the grass had been crushed, the ground torn by booted feet, tires, and treads. After the hellstorm of the corridor and the assault that followed, it was paradise.

And that was too bad. Despite the surreally picturesque setting, they were still on a military base, and the sojieri were drilling. Falcon Guards: the very words dripped with glory and gallantry, conjuring great warriors long centuries moldering in their graves or drifting through the limitless mausoleum of space. Men and women armored in crystal, carrying banners into the fight as the ancients had done, fighting with sword and spear amid laser blasts and rocket fire. They were nobility, nostalgia, and insanity in one.

There were no crystal-clad furies of legend here, not since Peregrine Noelle had perished, but the Falcon Guard infantry could stand toe-to-toe with any army in the galaxy. Like most, Leon and the Jackals had been quick to assume that the Eve CRB was just a placeholder on the galactic map, staffed with misfits and clerks. And they had been wrong, perhaps intentionally misled. Instead, they had been neighbors to a base of crack troops, one which had been preparing for war all this time, quietly, unassumingly, under the cover of apathy.

A squad marched by, adorned in blue and gray. These men and women wore hard, resolute expressions, but there was fear in their eyes, too.

More troops were drilling in EMMA gear, dwarfing their light infantry comrades. Their armor seemed to glow in the diffuse half-light that filtered through clouds and airshield, and they looked powerful, in control. Unconsciously, Leon's hand went to the jack at the base of his skull, feeling its familiar contours. He missed the sense of power, of invulnerability that came with the fusion of a disciplined sojier and a lethal machine. Having seen more than his share of EMMA units in the mud, blood trickling out of holes punched through the armor, he knew that invulnerability was an illusion, though an intoxicating one.

Like dragons the long-striker tanks perched, steaming, on the ridges above, waiting while the base shook itself awake. It was tragic to see the fertile soil of the volcano turned up, the flowers trampled as supplies were trucked out for the eventual mobilization. It seemed to reflect the eternal paradox, that war inevitably led to the destruction of whatever it had been fought to protect.

"I could laugh it's so fucking funny," Leon muttered under his breath.

"What?" Traxus's sensitive ears perked up. "What's funny?"

Leon put his arm around her. "I was supposed to stay away from the fighting. *You* were supposed to stay away from the fighting. A whole war came looking for us."

Traxus couldn't help smiling grimly. "I suppose we should be flattered."

An enormous sojier in jeans and a black t-shirt approached them. Leon cocked his head to look at the insignia on his sleeve. The image was of two playing cards: a Jack of Spades overlaid by an Ace. This guy had to be one of the Blackjack team Marion had called in during the fighting.

"Colonel, Lieutenant...." He looked at Jeric, unsure of how to address him. "Please come with me. Commander Marion has asked for you."

"Only one guard this time?" Jeric jabbed playfully. Leon shot him a warning look. The man could easily subdue all three of them without breaking a sweat, he was sure.

"Lead on, sojier," Leon said evenly. "Anything you can tell us?'

"The commander said the first packet came through while you were still in quarantine." He lapsed into silence as he led them toward the main tower looming out of its decorative moat. The ivy had been singed on two sides of the building, and the metal blast shutters were all down. The idiosyncratic Commander Marion could try his best to make the base look beautiful, but there was no masking its true purpose. Leon couldn't help thinking that Rachel would be highly amused.

"Stop grinding your teeth," Traxus said to him quietly. She softened the words with a warm glance, and Leon forced himself to calm down.

She may still be alive.

Sure, I'll keep telling myself that.

After the attack, security had been tightened even further, and it seemed like half the sojieri left on the base were tasked with watching the doors. Through blast door after blast door and checkpoint after checkpoint, the Jackals submitted themselves to friskings, pat-downs, and scans. No one was taking any chances.

Even now the Falcons were paragons of war; some of them looked a bit rumpled, but their armor and weapons were immaculate. Leon's own outfit was a hodgepodge: while his uniform had survived the bombing and car wreck, it was deemed unsalvageable after the lab attack, and Marion had offered the three of them spare fatigues to wear around the base. He ordered their patches and insignia transferred to the new uniforms, and someone had even gone to the trouble of sewing a red slash of piping down their left sleeves. It wasn't quite the red tiger stripes of Jackal Pack, but it gave them an identity, something they sorely felt they needed. Even so, Jeric looked like a child playing dress-up in BDUs several sizes too large.

In the hallway outside the main command center they encountered Doctor Chase again. The fat little scientist appeared to be everywhere at once, red, sweaty, and breathing hard as he rushed from place to place. He, too, looked like he was about to crack under the pressure. "Colonel, Lieutenant...." He, too, paused when he came to Jeric. "Jeric," he finally said, as though skeptical. "How are you all feeling?"

"Well enough, Doc," Leon answered, flexing his hand to show the mirrored cauterized scars. "Anything you can tell us?"

"You know very well that everything I've been looking into is classified," Chase said scoldingly. "However … the commander and I have been discussing it, and I could use a little extra help in the lab. With the losses to my staff and the destruction of most of my equipment, my sequencing experiments and analysis are going to take far longer than I'm used to. It would be useful to have someone with at least a little experience on hand."

"I'm pretty rusty," Leon admitted, although privately he was flattered and honored by the offer.

"You know A pairs with T, and C with G, right? Then you're qualified. We can clean the rust off on the go."

"Even *I* know that," Jeric muttered.

"Progress has been slow," Chase lamented. "My forensics should have been complete by now. Instead I'm stuck using traditional—no, *archaic*—methods." He glanced at their escort. "*Your* friends didn't leave me much to work with, either."

"Apologies, Doc," the sojier said unconvincingly.

"Is there anything you *can* tell us?" Traxus asked hopefully.

"I've got my theories about our enemy. Just idle speculation, really, until we can get some real data. I've managed to confirm that the organisms you encountered in the lab wing were in fact Raven Blue young."

"Like larvae?" Traxus suggested.

Chase considered this for a moment. "Not precisely. Larvae tend to be relatively immobile and dependent on caretakers, and they usually undergo a complete metamorphosis. As you saw, these were fully capable fighters in their own right, and the resemblance to the adult morphology is strong. They would be more analogous to a … nymphal stage perhaps."

"Careful, Doc," the Blackjack trooper said. "Classified."

Chase waved dismissively. He was clearly excited to share his theories. "Moreover, their actions in the lab suggest a strong bond and communication. It may even be nonverbal. Pheromonal, perhaps, or even telepathic."

"What about their accelerated metabolism?" Leon asked.

"That's what I intend to focus on next. Unfortunately, all their proteins are quite novel. Determining function *in vitro* is going to take time, if it's even possible."

"Well, whatever I can do, I'll do," Leon said.

"Great. I'll have the commander send you over when the time comes." Chase bid them farewell and huffed and puffed off to his next appointment.

The Blackjack trooper led the three of them into the command center. Eyes turned to regard them, particularly from the other Blackjacks on the catwalks. The atmosphere in the room was electric and stank of fear. It was clear even the Falcons knew their chances were slim. To the right was a door guarded by a sojier in powered heavy armor. He stood aside for the expected visitors, dipping his massive Cougar rifle as they passed.

Marion's office was lit by a soothing blue glow, sunlight coming through a large fish tank set in the far wall. The commander was sitting in a plush leather chair, holding something in his hands. Leon blinked in surprise when he realized what it was. The helmet was heavily scarred and dented, the visor shattered. It was something out of another time, a metal death's-head merged with some sort of spiny insect. It was the helmet of a Falcon Guard Peregrine, one of the crystal relics worn by the most elite warriors of the order. Tradition dictated that the helmet and armor of a fallen Peregrine be retrieved at all costs, Leon knew; there were stories of whole battalions of infantry being wiped out simply to bring their dead idols home. Someone had braved the irradiated blast zone where Task Force Claymore had perished in order to bring Noelle's remains home. Leon doubted anyone would go to such trouble for him.

Marion put the helmet down with a last tender caress, his fingers drifting along the ridged, scowling mask. "Thank you for coming," he said, his voice rough. Abruptly, he turned to the aquarium wall. "Do you like it? I always wanted one as a kid. All the fish are local. Here comes one of my favorites." Among the bryozoan colonies, a small blue river crustacean chased an eel-like creature. The white-striped serpent had eyes along its belly which rolled like those of a reeling drunk.

Leon couldn't help looking at the helmet again. The patriot deep within him wished he could have shaken Peregrine Noelle's hand and thanked her for her sacrifice. She almost certainly would have received his overture with contempt: the Iron Falcons and the Peregrines were not known for their patience with fawning admirers. And yet there were reasons for the legends. Although Leon had seen an entire world laid waste by Raven Blue, he was a still shocked that they managed to slay one of the crystalline warriors of the conduits.

"She was very brave," Marion said when he caught Leon's glance. The commander's own personal turmoil was hard to imagine. Not only had he lost a comrade and a superior—was that accurate? Leon didn't actually know where Peregrines fit into the Falcon command structure—he had also lost a friend, possibly a lover.

"My condolences, Commander," Leon said lamely. Jeric and Traxus echoed the sentiment.

"Please, call me Gray. Tea?"

Jeric and Traxus took some, while Leon accepted a glass of water.

"We may have had a breakthrough on comms." Marion pressed his fingertips to the desk. "There was a scout ship a few days ago, one of ours. It got chased out of the system almost immediately. Since then we've been getting blips through the jamming. Nothing concrete, nothing meaningful. But we think they may be parts of a data packet from *Condor*. The Raven Blue jamming field is thick, but they don't appear to be monitoring it—they're just crowding everyone off the air. I'm told that whoever is sending the signal is outside the solar system, and they're modulating frequencies to outrun the jamming. We're trying to find the pattern in their modulation, see if we can synch up with them and maybe get a signal of our own out if we can reach one of the relay satellites. If they're even still up there. We've been trying for a day or two now, no luck, but my guys tell me we're almost there."

"That's incredible," Traxus blurted. Leon, too, felt giddy as though a weight were being lifted from his shoulders. Still, being able to cry for help was a long way from receiving it.

Marion seemed to pick up on his trepidation. "As far as we know, we're still very much alone. We haven't seen any traffic through the system, and cosmographics tells us the Alkyra has fractured. I don't know what that means for any counterattack, but it'll likely slow things down if it doesn't halt them altogether."

That was disquieting, and Leon gulped water while he thought. He didn't know what Raven Blue's fleet strength or ground forces were like. Their whole military could have been on Eve—although Leon strongly doubted it—or this could have been but a token invasion force. The entire Alkyra had likely fallen, and with it the barrier to some of the Coalition's coreward trade routes. If the enemy had sufficient strength, they could press on, clawing out territory one sector at a time. Or they could lure the CRDF into the fragmenting Alkyra and tear into them.

"So what's our game plan, Commander?"

"Well, right now we're a foothold. We may be the only standing loyalists along the Tears. We're certainly the only landing corridor on Eve, and our sensors show us that the enemy has definitive aerospace superiority. There are over two hundred ships in orbit over the planet right now. They could roll right over us, but they know we could do some serious damage before they do."

"The antimatter weapons."

"It was a difficult decision but not nearly as difficult as firing on Claymore." Marion glanced at Peregrine Noelle's helmet again. "It seems I'm on a slippery slope, but I've got far more than my own conscience to protect right now. I will do everything in my power to hold this position."

The comm on the desk beeped. "Commander, this is Aaronson."

"Go ahead, Captain."

"Some of the officers are going into the yard to play rugby."

"That's fine, thank you." Marion sipped at his tea.

"If you don't mind my asking, how's morale? Discipline?" asked Traxus, eying the commander. "Some of the officers seem a little … unkempt."

"We've got discipline in spades, Lieutenant," Marion said. "It depends on what sort of discipline you mean. There are forces where only the rules, only a strict adherence to doctrine, keep them from breaking ranks, becoming insubordinate." He smiled. "The conventional wisdom would seem to suggest that it's a short fall from not shining your boots to shooting your superior officer because you don't like your orders."

Traxus shrugged. Leon, for his part, was curious to hear what Marion had to say.

"I call bullshit on that wisdom. We are Falcons. I trust the men and women of my command to keep themselves in fighting shape. Because ultimately they're fighting for me and for each other. I find that respect and even love are more useful incentives than fear of punishment or some uselessly fat handbook on the proper way to fold your shirt. It's a hell of a lot easier for them to remain loyal and maintain their discipline, their readiness, if the place they're stuck garrisoning isn't a shithole and their commander isn't the asshole shitting into it. Maybe their shirts aren't always tucked in, but I'd wager them against any force in the galaxy."

"Well, now's the time to place your bets," Jeric muttered.

Marion's demeanor turned icy. "I already have. Your base is the one that folded."

His words cut deeply, and he softened. "Make no mistake, your people died as heroes. But they were brawlers, lacking subtlety. They went toe to toe with an enemy fleet. Is it any wonder they were flattened? Lessons are only helpful if you survive to apply them. That being said, they demonstrated more bravery and more loyalty than most armies, never mind mercenaries. They're a credit to you and the Pack."

Marion sat back down and spun in his chair like a child. "When I heard that the Pack was being contracted to sharpen the point of the sword, I thought High Command was grasping at straws. But truly your people have more in common with us than they do with most private rabble."

"Thanks," Leon said hollowly.

"Look, I'm going to level with you three because I like you and because you've demonstrated that you've got the Falcon esprit de corps. Hell, I'd anoint you if I thought you'd say yes. So…"

Leon was about to ask Marion what the hell he was talking about when the comm beeped again. "Commander, we've decrypted another packet."

In a flash the commander was out of his chair and moving toward the door. They followed him out. In the command center a number of officers came to attention, but the vast majority remained at their stations, which Leon could understand, given the urgency of their work. Thirty or forty people were present, stationed at a dizzying array of terminals. He and his companions stood on a platform that ringed the hexagonal command center, staircases leading from it down into the large pit where the consoles stood like some humming metal Stonehenge.

Glowing holographic maps floated over various projectors scattered about the room, and Leon recognized the cosmodrome, the planetary system, and Tesa, all rendered in miniature, revolving slowly as though they were planets in some bizarre, translucent solar system.

Captain Aaronson came to meet them. Leon had encountered her periodically since their arrival, but they had never spoken. At the moment she was wearing PT gear, loose-fitting sweatpants and a tank top. She was fit, incredibly so, her muscles so well defined on her slim frame that she looked like an anatomical study. More importantly, she clearly commanded a great deal of respect among the troops, seemingly just as much as Marion himself.

Leon spotted Sergeant O'Reily leaning casually against one of the handrails along the upper observation platform. His muscles bulged through his black t-shirt, and though one eye was bandaged, the other seemed to have compensated by being twice as piercing. Even out of his armor he was huge, with thick arms, a broad chest, and a boxer's loose, ready body. He nodded to Leon in recognition, and the colonel nodded back. *One tough customer indeed.*

Leon shifted his attention to the large main display that took up an entire wall. The image shifted to a grainy, ultra-long distance feed. It was a black shape, oblong, with gently moving protrusions. Seeing it was like a shock to Leon's system, trauma resurfacing. He was not a superstitious man, not at all. But seeing that image and what had descended on Eve.... *Monsters are real.* How could a ship be composed of organic matter? For these things clearly appeared to be alive, somehow propelling themselves through space. *What the fuck are we even fighting?*

Parts of the ship were being highlighted by the computer, identifying potential weaknesses, navigation- and weapon-related points of interest. Leon would have liked a chance to study it, but just looking at it was making his head spin. It seemed so unnatural, a creature that carried the enemy in its belly like parasites, spilling them out to infect whole worlds.

"Somebody give me some good news," Marion said loudly as he descended the stairs into the pit where the bulk of the activity was going on.

The officer at the main sensor monitoring station turned to them as they approached. "Commander, we just received another encrypted comm burst targeted at the mountain."

"This mountain?" Jeric asked, stupidly, Leon thought. The pilot pointed at the floor as though his question were unclear.

"Yes, sir." The officer pressed a few keys at his terminal, and the big screen changed again, displaying a strategic map of the sector. "As near as I can pinpoint, the signal originated from the edge of the Yangtze Tradeway." He pointed up at the screen, and Leon traced the sinuous line of the Alkyra to the point where it joined the larger Y.T. A large purple star blinked steadily. *That's awfully far away for reinforcements.* "We've decrypted the first packet and authenticated that it's from Grand Admiral Hakar's fleet. It contained instructions for matching a shifting-frequency pattern that *might* give us a narrow window of communication if we can boost a signal to one of the outer comm relays."

"Well, how about that," Marion said, his hands on his hips. "Duplicable?"

"Absolutely, sir."

Marion waved the comms officer over. She stood quickly to attention and made her way through the maze of consoles, at one point stepping through a hologram of one of the eerie squid-ships. "Explain this comm thing to me," he said.

"With the breadth and depth of the jamming field, we've been completely unable to get a signal out using conventional means, not even encrypted bursts. It looks like the team on *Condor* figured out a way to scatter an entire signal through tiny frequency gaps. Too little bandwidth for much real data, but long-wavelength fragments can slide through and be aggregated here."

"Like grains of sand through a closed fist. It'll work?"

"In theory. That first data packet contained rough instructions on which gaps to use so we can exchange coherent messages. We may not get long if the enemy is monitoring the situation."

"How long are we talking?"

"Five minutes, maybe."

Not enough to plan an attack, but maybe enough to let Hakar know there's still someone here listening. If they could touch base, figure out a way to clear a landing corridor for the fleet, the CRDF could bring its infantry and ground forces to bear. With civilian population centers involved, orbital strikes were not an option. A combined-arms assault would be messy, but it was the only way to capture the cosmodrome and the city. *The only way to rescue anyone? Keep dreaming.*

"All right, I'm game. Boot it up," Marion said. "Let's hear the first message."

The comms team went to work in tandem, their fingers flying over keyboards, adjusting gain, amplitude, picking the bits of signal out of the sky. It was a conjuring trick, pure magic. At first the signal was nothing but an eerie moaning sound, like the calls of a shambling, formless terror dwelling far beneath the earth. It was punctuated occasionally by whistles, clicks, and chirps. Then the shadow of a word emerged, incomprehensible but recognizable as speech. " ... ead."

"Ah!" Marion said, flinging his hands out as though to grasp the errant vocalization.

The comms officer grunted. "We can clean it up." *I should hope so*, Leon thought mirthlessly.

The next time the recording played he recognized Hakar's voice, and his heart leapt into his throat. "... miral Hakar to CRB. I h ... to keep this short."

There was a cheer from the assembled officers, and Leon found himself having trouble concentrating. Something was finally going to happen. No one would say it, but the Coalition getting its nose bloodied was an embarrassment. Their worlds had been taken, their fleets routed, their best and brightest military leaders tricked. Now, however, they had a sign that the CRDF might finally go on the offensive, and then they would crush the enemy on Eve. Too long the great empire's mighty armed forces had been marginalized, reduced to a giant, sluggish police force, the lines of communication fractured, the interests of corporations put before the interests of the people they were sworn to defend. The situation was about to change, and for better or worse, Leon Victor would be a part of it.

"Quiet!" Sergeant O'Reily bellowed, his hands on the railing, and the room fell startlingly silent. The big sergeant crossed his arms again and leaned back, evidently satisfied.

"If there is anyone left on the ground, I want you to know how proud I am of you, how proud the Coalition is of you. I know, *we know*, that you will not yield another inch, that you will keep on fighting until help arrives." There was a crackling, pregnant pause, and Leon felt his excitement flag, flickering like a guttering flame. "I wish I had something better to tell you," Hakar continued, "but we've been ordered to hold the D'zen Gulf at the mouth of the Yangtze. I'm not going to insult you by explaining how important it is that we not let the enemy encroach farther, but I know that doesn't make it any easier. I wish I could tell you to look up and see our ships coming down, but they're not. I wish I could tell you when help is coming, but I can't, because I don't know.

"This enemy is one we do not know and cannot name. You must all hold fast, stand strong, shoulder to shoulder as brothers and sisters. But know this: help *will* come. Even now the CRDF is sending fleet after fleet to the Gulf. We will secure it, and then we will move forward in force, and the enemy will know what it is to be afraid. Until then you must not falter, must not fear. Our thoughts and prayers are with you, all of you. More information will follow. Good luck."

The voice faded, replaced by that awful groan with its mocking whistles. Despite Hakar's words, Leon felt confused despair dig its infectious claws into his stomach and seize his reason. *We've been abandoned to the enemy. Sentenced to die. Goddamn them all, they've left us to die.*

"Listen up, all of you!" Commander Marion's words cut through the deafening silence, shattering its hold over those assembled. "You heard the admiral! Help will come. Until then our job is to prepare for it and to make sure that when that glorious, shining fleet arrives, they'll have a clear LZ. I know you're afraid. I know some of you may not be thinking clearly. God knows I'm one of you. But shit, this is what we trained for! We're Falcon Guard and Falcon Guard *do not surrender*." In an instant he had gone from the soft-spoken and occasionally whimsical officer to a fire-and-brimstone commander. It was a marvelous transformation, and Leon found himself wondering which side was the act.

Marion held up his bandaged forearms in a gesture of defiance. "We're outnumbered and outgunned. Surrounded and without relief. But so. Fucking. What. Falcons do not care. I'd wager the companies of this base against the legions of the enemy any day." He pointed at Leon, and the colonel started, stunned that he should be singled out.

"You all know who this man is," Marion said forcefully. "Leon Victor, the *Mourning Star*, has sought refuge here, with us. You can be damn sure he's just as angry about his home being taken as we are. I plan to aim him at Raven Blue and let him go."

Through the room there was a ragged cheer of "Mourning Star!" and Leon felt his veins flush with ice water. Traxus and Jeric looked at him uncertainly but moved closer to stand at his side. He was grateful for that, at least.

Marion was barking orders now, letting his people know he was still in charge. The officers somehow shook off the icy crust of despair and got back to work, running sensor sweeps, preparing to send out a reply to Hakar.

The commander turned back to Leon, mild-mannered once again. "Sorry about the Mourning Star thing. It was for morale."

"I guess you have to do what you have to do." Leon hoped he didn't sound as offended as he felt. At the same time, he understood where the commander was coming from. Wouldn't he have done anything and everything in his power to keep his troops' spirits up? *If I had any left, that is*. The realization that the entire Jackal Pack base was in the grip of the enemy once again hit Leon like a boot to the groin.

Marion had moved off, discussing something with his executive officer, but Traxus and Jeric stayed beside Leon, who felt like his knees might buckle at any second. "Hey, man, sit down," Jeric said, frowning. "You hurting? We can get you back to the medical wing."

"No," Leon said, shaking his head. "I just ... they're all gone, guys."

"The world changed while you were asleep, Leon," Traxus said, beckoning him closer to her and Jeric. The three of them bowed their heads together in the midst of the command center's focused chaos, three friends within the walls of civilization's last bastion. Jeric and Traxus had lost their chance to leave and now they had put their trust in one another, their lives in the hands of strangers. He was a commander in command of nothing, but he had a responsibility to his friends and to the people of Eve. It was never easy living up to such a duty, and Leon found he no longer wanted it. *But what choice do I have?* He didn't know if he could put his trust in this Commander Marion and his sojieri. *Perhaps we would be better off on our own.* He contemplated this idea for a few moments, imagining their lonely trio fleeing across Eve's sun-drenched landscapes in search of ... what? What could they hope to find? *No, Hakar already left us. Those of us who are left have to stick together.* He glanced over at the commander, who was now conversing with Sergeant O'Reily, his hand on the big man's shoulder as they shared a private word. Leon wondered why O'Reily looked so upset, his jaw clenched. *For better or worse, we all have to stick together. And then perhaps we can fight back.*

§

"I appreciate your letting me be a part of this, Doctor Chase." *Anything to get my mind off everything else.*

"Of course, Colonel. I'm sorry if I was a little abrupt earlier. It was hard enough to find good help before the enemy killed half my staff and got most of the others reassigned to medical detail." Was Chase so self-absorbed that he didn't recognize that the lives lost were more than depleted laboratory resources? Then again, what he was doing now was important enough that it was probably an understandable sentiment.

Leon nodded his understanding as he checked the seals on Chase's isolation suit. "You weren't kidding about being reduced to traditional methods," Leon said, looking around the base's remaining undamaged lab. Most of the sequencing equipment and protein simulators had been destroyed. He saw there were still media for plating bacterial colonies, polymerase reactors for amplifying genetic sequences ... but most of the equipment was painfully antiquated, reminding Leon of a survey course he took in historical laboratory methods to pad his grades at university. The course had been harder than expected because everything was so manual. He had a feeling this wouldn't be any easier.

With a sardonic smile, Chase glanced at their tools and shrugged. "It can't be helped, and thankfully we have enough to get started with until better people come along and pick up where we leave off." He flipped a switch and an air scrubber kicked on in the airlock. "If you wouldn't mind grabbing those rebreathers off that shelf there, we can begin." Chase pointed to a shelf that was just out of his reach, and Leon obligingly reached over and pulled two masks down. He pulled one of the rebreather hoods over his head and locked it into the collar of his suit. The scans hadn't turned up any pathogens, but the equipment only looked for contaminants it recognized.

"You think communicable disease may be an issue?" Leon asked.

"Who knows what's inside them? Bacteria, some sort of spore ... I'd just as soon not take any chances."

"No argument there, Doctor."

"Corporal, would you be so kind as to cycle the airlock for us?"

Corporal Tabitha Ilia looked a little resentful at playing second banana to a mercenary, but she did as she was asked. While they were waiting for the air filters to do their job, Chase looked back at the woman who usually served as his lab assistant. "She's a different breed from the others. Takes her work much more seriously, spends most of her time off-duty reading texts I loan her." Leon wasn't surprised. It seemed as though it would be impossible to keep up with Chase without the proper background.

Once the airlock had cycled, the inner door hissed open, and they walked into the remaining undamaged Biosafety Level 4 lab. Through the thick windows Leon could see where fire had left its autograph on the walls. Shattered glass and broken equipment littered the corridor. The salvageable equipment and samples had been crammed into this last lab, creating a narrow, almost unnavigable maze of computers, spectral analyzers, genomics and proteomics amplifiers, polymerase chain reaction sequencing cores, and a number of other machines.

Chase followed his gaze. "Oh, I doubt we'll get that far today, but I wanted to make sure they were available if I needed them. Truth be told, these are a little old, and their archives only contain enough data to recognize conserved regions within some known species. They're really only useful for screening out local contaminants at this point."

"We're focusing on dissection?" Leon asked.

"Yep. The old-fashioned way."

The enemy infiltrators—Leon found it easier not to think of them as infants—had been put in a series of portable freezers. Chase opened one now and pulled out the most complete specimen. "It's a shame," he said as he laid the creature on the operating table. "Only a few of them are intact enough to work with."

Leon suppressed a shudder. Even still and dead, the creature looked capable of wreaking havoc. "Careful with the blade limbs."

"Ah, yes. I will be, but thank you for reminding me." Just looking at them, Leon felt his hand ache. There was a hiss behind them and he almost jumped, but it was only the airlock cycling again, allowing Corporal Ilia to enter. Through her visor her eyes were a startling, beautiful green above the ugly mechanical snout of her rebreather. She shouldered in beside Leon in the cramped space, adjusted a hanging camera over the table, and started it recording.

Chase recited all the basic information, including the identities and ranks of the participants, the date, and the time. "… examining Raven Blue infiltrator, deceased, sample A12. Specimen is approximately thirty-four centimeters in length, weighing one-point-one-four kilograms."

"That heavy?" asked Ilia, surprised.

"That's what the scale is reading, yes," Chase said impatiently. "Specimen is arthroform, exhibiting bilateral symmetry, unknown planet of origin. Eight specialized forelimbs on torso. The uppermost pair is located near the center of the thorax and appears much smaller than the others, possibly vestigial. There appear to have been four dexterous digits, all multidirectionally opposable; however, damage sustained during combat makes it difficult to ascertain. The second set terminates in two long, sharp, stabbing or slashing exoskeletal protrusions approximately ten centimeters long and of extremely dense chitin. The third and fourth sets ... serve an unknown function." Chase paused, lifting one of the lowest limbs, just below the blades, and examined it. It terminated in a curved, paddlelike appendage. "This is entirely speculative, but the third and fourth sets appear to be used for propulsion through a liquid environment. May also be used for social purposes." He dropped the limb. "Shall we begin? Colonel Victor, if you would hand me that scalpel?"

For a moment Leon was confused. A scalpel likely wouldn't cut through the chitinous exoskeleton. Impatiently, Corporal Ilia reached over and delicately plucked a small surgical laser off the tray. "Sorry," Leon whispered.

"Thank you," Chase said, not caring who handed it to him. "If you two would please hold the forelimbs, I'll make an incision in the center of the thoracic plate between the second and third segments. There appears to be a softer tissue around the limb joints which may allow the exoskeleton to hinge open." Carefully, with the precision of a master surgeon, the doctor made a cut, the laser hissing through the tough, hardened material of the creature's shell. Unfortunately, the rebreathers, while filtering out particles as small as viruses, didn't manage to filter out the smell, a delicate aroma of steamed crab meat and hot metal. It wasn't necessarily unpleasant, but it was distracting, and knowing what it came from was sickening. Chase set aside the laser and tugged at the cauterized edges of the exoskeleton, snapping them back. Leon and Ilia leaned forward to look into the chest cavity.

Inside were a cluster of tightly packed organs. Leon hadn't expected anything that looked like a Human thoracic cavity, but the homologies were startling. It was true, Mother Nature had a limited imagination.

Chase was still on the exoskeleton itself, analyzing the glossy epicuticle and the hard, protective procuticle. "The alignment of the chitin fibers and proteins is like nothing I've seen. Overlapping scales appear to have evolved with the aim of distributing impact shock and improving puncture and break resistance while maintaining flexibility. The exocuticle may not be fully developed as the creature appears to have been undergoing rapid growth. The tail is vestigial and does not appear in the adult specimens."

Leon made a sour face in his rebreather. Something about Chase's ultraclinical approach was off-putting. "Any thoughts on the gestation period? Is it possible that the creatures can go dormant for a protracted period of time?"

With a brief, irritated glance, Chase returned to peeling open his specimen. "I would say that cryptobiosis is likely, yes. Once favorable conditions were perceived, metabolism appears to have restarted violently, draining the host vessels of proteins, nutrients, sugars, and fats. Hmm, see here?" Chase had moved aside a whitish flap on the creature's abdomen where the lumpy tail had been attached. "I think … this may not be a tail."

"A mobile yolk?" suggested the corporal, leaning forward to take a look. At a gesture from Chase, she retrieved a syringe with multiple needles and multiple receptacles. Each time she pressed, a new one rotated into place and collected a sample. Once all four syringes had been filled, she deposited them into one of the nearby machines for analysis.

"This is only a guess, but I think we'll find growth hormone analogs as well as something similar to epinephrine and possibly adrenocorticoids to stimulate the accelerated growth we saw. The cells would have to be able to break down fatty acids and protein to provide whatever it metabolizes for energy during their fasting state. A formidable evolutionary trait, to be sure."

Leon's breath caught in his throat. It *was* formidable, terrifyingly so. Tageans weren't considered adults until age thirty, even Humans only reached sexual maturity in their teens. But here was a species that seemed to be born at adult capacity, capable of killing from the moment it took its first breath.

The dissection was continuing, Chase's voice even but clearly charged with excitement at the prospect of helping describe the physiology of a novel species: "…. binary vascular system to facilitate the extraordinary metabolism, three lungs, possibly to supply oxygen to muscles for prolonged periods of exertion … what's this?" He had already encountered a number of organs that would require analysis *in vivo* to determine their functions, but here were two sets of connected glands, attached by a branching duct. Leon craned his neck to see, noting a series of fibrous flaps in which the glands were nested.

"Three glands," Ilia said, probing the creature's left side.

"Three glands," Chase echoed from the right.

"The duct appears to lead directly to the carapace," Leon noted, tracing the slimy canal with one gloved finger. He frowned. "And there's heavy musculature all around the glands, too."

"Yes," Chase agreed, completely absorbed. He hefted one of the glands, gave it a gentle squeeze. "Almost gelatinous. Might be coagulated, whatever it is." He gestured for a conventional scalpel, and Leon handed it to him. "I'm going to make a small incision, in one of the glands." He gingerly made the cut, and a thick, amber liquid began to ooze out. "Corporal Ilia, could you make sure the camera is getting this?"

Ilia reached up to adjust the camera and accidentally bumped the table, just a little, but enough to make Chase nick the next gland over. Almost instantly there was an explosion on the table, a blinding flare like white phosphorous, accompanied by a high-pitched sizzling sound. Leon recoiled, singed, as a green fountain of flame erupted from the creature's chest, shooting a foot into the air. Chase screamed and fell back against the freezer behind him, his arms thrown up before his face. As Ilia had been leaning over the table when it ignited, she caught the brunt of the eruption, fire going up in an emerald burst and engulfing her torso.

Just as suddenly the room filled with fog as haloalkane gas tanks flushed the chamber. Leon began to beat at Ilia's flaming suit, trying to calm her through her screaming. His gloves caught fire and he looked at them, mesmerized, as the insane heat wrapped his hands in its world-muffling blanket. Luckily for him, it was a contact fire, and it quickly died. He began kicking at Ilia, ignoring the flames crawling up his boots. Gradually, the roar from the table subsided, and so did the flames on the corporal's coat, the sickly green glow flickering, guttering, fading. Ilia lay moaning on the floor, moving feebly in the fog. Leon looked around in the haze, blinking away tears as the acrid stink of the gas reached him through the filters.

He moved to Chase, who was trying to stand up. Blood was pouring from the doctor's left ear, and his eyes were wide, terrified. "You all right?" he called, concerned that the doctor had gone deaf.

The man nodded and accepted a hand to help him up. "I ... think that's enough for today."

§

Over the next few days, Leon joined the doctor's small team as they continued to analyze the samples. When Chase finally got a look at the genome, Leon took a certain pride in explaining what he had learned in the wake of his trip to Aethaleia: namely, that Raven Blue possessed a revolutionary and possibly engineered genetic makeup. Rather than the double-helix common to Humans and many other species or even the spironomic or tubulonomic genomes found throughout the galaxy, Raven Blue's chromosomes were densely wrinkled spheres, the bases of which could be read in any direction, allowing for incredible variety and the efficient coding of thousands of genes into the smallest heritable package outside of bacteria.

Chase was beside himself with confusion, then excitement. Even as they began to find answers, the mysteries deepened. Though they could not begin to decode the genome or figure out the functions of the proteins within the Raven Blue infants' "tails," they were, at least, able to directly tie the smaller creatures to the larger warriors which had been retrieved from the battlefield. By the time they got to Dylan Porter's autopsy, Corporal Ilia had been released from the infirmary to rejoin them. They started with the saboteur's chest and lungs, looking for the source of the pulmonary hemorrhaging that had ended with him violently coughing up blood. Leon expected to feel a cold satisfaction in cutting up the man who had caused them so much heartache, but instead he felt only an aloof pity. The man had been a slave, after all, at least, if he was telling the truth. And while Leon privately thought that Porter had deserved his final agony, he was still troubled.

They found that his lungs were fine, but his trachea had been torn to shreds by the force of his heaving and coughing. He had aspirated much of the blood and had possibly drowned in it. Porter's eyes continued to stare at them hopelessly, the burst blood vessels coloring his gaze of accusation. Chase insisted on digging into the cause of the subconjunctival hemorrhaging, too, even though it was entirely plausible it was hastened by the severe coughing fits that tore Porter's tracheal lining.

By his own admission, Chase was a lab researcher, not a doctor or a surgeon. Watching him work on Porter's corpse, Leon was glad he had been out cold for his own surgery. Chase exhibited none of the delicacy he had used on the Raven Blue tissue and protein samples. He sawed, hacked, and broke bone until they were looking into Porter's head.

What they found there shocked them. Ilia went to work with the camera before taking samples. "How did that not come up during the medical scans after his surgery?" Chase asked as Ilia gingerly pulled nearly half a meter of coiled tissue and nerve from Porter's brain. Most surprising was that it was clearly foreign tissue that had been implanted into his skull. It branched at his brain, the roots embedded into the frontal, parietal, occipital, and temporal lobes. A thick probe drove deep, and further dissection revealed that it was fused to Porter's brain stem.

Ilia remained holding the coil of organic material while Chase carefully inspected the connections. "I don't believe this," he said breathlessly while Leon stood back, revolted. Into the microphone the researcher said, "Further analysis is needed, but I think we may have discovered the key to the attack. According to interrogation records, the deceased made mention of Raven Blue seeing through his eyes. If, in fact, Raven Blue communicates by telepathy, as I suspect, they may have developed a method for implanting organic transceivers into psychically mute species. If the connections to the parietal and occipital lobes of the deceased allow the Raven Blue group consciousness to perceive an agent's surroundings through the visual cortex, they might actually be able to send a signal through him."

Leon mulled that over. "Are you suggesting that he saw Commander Marion in the vicinity of those ... eggs ... and Raven Blue sent a signal through him to *wake them up*?"

"It's implausible, I admit," Chase said grudgingly, "but think about it. Commander Marion, Lieutenant Tachai, and several others reported an unpleasant, barely audible tone moments before the deceased collapsed and before the Raven Blue ... organisms hatched."

It was a wild idea, and Leon couldn't bring himself to believe it. Still ... while nothing had prepared him for the things he had already seen, he *knew* that the little monsters had planned their attack, had pretended to fall unconscious just so they could wreak havoc outside the lab. From there was it really such a leap of logic to believe that they could use a man like a comm line? Admitting the possibility made Leon feel like he should be committed to an asylum.

"So they killed him?" Ilia wondered aloud. "They were finished with him, so they killed him?"

"His death may simply have been a result of the implant overloading his brain stem when it sent out the signal." Chase laid his gloved hands on the table, peering at Leon and Ilia over his rebreather. "I think there's a more important possibility we need to consider. If all of this is true, the creatures were triggered by the deceased due to the presence of the commander. They meant to kill Marion and possibly you, too, Colonel. It's no coincidence that those ships attacked us immediately after. I believe they expected the defense to lose cohesion if the commander fell."

"That would certainly support the collective consciousness theory," Leon admitted, feeling a cosmic terror growing inside him. "If they operate as a superorganism or whatever you want to call it, there may be some psychic leadership. Kill the leader, the army loses direction. It makes sense that they would think we behave the same way. But it's still circumstantial, Doc."

"You're right." Chase sighed. "We don't know much about telepathy except that the Talqai can communicate effectively across species boundaries. Now we need to figure out a way to detect these implants and test everyone on the base. Still, I'm ... at a loss."

"It's a start," said Corporal Ilia forcefully, her eyes fierce above her mask. Her hair had been burned off in the previous lab fire, and the stubble made her look vicious and emaciated. "A few days ago we knew nothing about them. Now we know something."

"We just have to find a way to share our knowledge before we get wiped out," Leon said under his breath. His companions regarded him stoically. Being back in the lab was not what Leon wanted. Once he had dreamt of such an opportunity. But sometime in the intervening years, he had grown accustomed to direct action. He found himself craving it now. Even though he knew better, part of him felt that their forays in the lab were simply distractions from their isolation and the constant danger of annihilation. Still, as Marion had said, the stars kept burning, the worlds kept turning, and they had work to do.

§

The dephasing of the Alkyra had gone unobserved. Ordinarily, the severing of a trade route was a time for religious and cultural observances, ancient colonial rites acknowledging every race's infinitesimal role in the universe. Lanterns were lit, special meals were prepared, solemn speeches were made. This time all anyone cared about was that the dephasing made it even less likely that help would come. Their rescuers would be nothing but a burial detail.

The bright sun beat down on Eve, its light tinted a sickly green by the glimmering airshield. Traxus turned her face up to it, welcoming the heat after days of clouds. The dried savannah stretched out for kilometers, broken only by two distant groves of trees that stood out of the muted beige nothingness like lime green eyes. Traxus frowned. Those groves were usually far darker, but she supposed the drought had taken their color as it had taken their water.

Peeking over the horizon as though it were afraid to be seen was the craggy, sunwashed spine of Las Serras da Estrela, the mountains that covered a city. Marion's scouts had restored contact, a trail of brave sojieri huddling in foxholes in order to maintain communication relays over the kilometers. The city was doing its best to fortify, but their shields were there to keep the peace, not repel invasion. They had asked for a garrison, which Marion could not spare, and they had asked to evacuate, but to where? In the end

Marion gave them a few tanks and some mortar crews for the cliffs. The city was guarded by great metal doors that had not been closed in some decades. "Do those big doors of theirs still work, or are they purely decorative?" Marion had asked grimly. When they got the answer, Falcon engineers were dispatched to get them in working order and provide a modicum of protection.

North Bay was, likewise, still free. The small town had been utterly neglected by the enemy after an initial probe. Perhaps they feared that it was within range of the base's artillery although Marion admitted that it was just outside the defensive envelope. Jeric had grown excited, knowing the breweries of North Bay were unconquered, and had suggested garrisoning *them*. Marion had smiled, and some of his sojieri actually went out to retrieve beer in order to boost morale. It was carefully rationed, but somehow Jeric always managed to scrounge some more.

After Hakar's first message, there had been no word, no encrypted orders. Hope was turning to bitter resentment, and soon it might become utter despair. Traxus had been naïve enough to think that the Coalition would never let them fall. It seemed like a lifetime ago. Her trust was waning, and she was beginning to suspect that trust was misplaced wherever one laid it.

Eve had never been what one would call vibrant, had never been a travel or trade hub. Nevertheless, it was heartbreaking not to know if Tesa still existed or not. Marion did not dare send scouts that far into enemy territory though Traxus knew he and his troops were itching to do so. Planets had changed hands hundreds of times in the never-ending cycle of conflicts, border disputes, petty arguments, and legitimate territorial exchanges between the Coalition, the Valinata, the Commonwealth, the Shar'dan, even the far-flung and uninvolved Aradon Dominion. But this was different, and the thought of those lives vanished from history filled Traxus with a melancholy so deep it felt physical, tangible, a sponge soaked in cold water and wrapped around her. It was stifling and chilling at once.

And so she was almost ashamed to be so excited, so thrilled that she was alive when so many others were not. So many friends, so many acquaintances, so many people she didn't know but who had become fixtures in her daily routine—gone. She was embarrassed that she *only* felt relief and not grief, though she knew it would come later. Perhaps most distressing, however, was that her fervent hope, her faith that Hakar would come to their rescue, would not quite die. Her whole life he had been beyond reproach, invincible morally as well as physically, a class of sojier and man unto himself. Though he was nearly one hundred and fifty years her senior, they had been close during her formative years with the clan. Whenever he had returned to visit, a crowd had trailed behind him even as many of the elders snubbed him. A horde had always come to gawk and admire the hero but also to scold him for turning his back on tradition. For him there was only Traxus, and for her there was only Hakar. Many people looked to older siblings as heroes, but it was an unusual feeling indeed to find the rest of the empire held one's brother in similar regard. Of *course*, she had followed in his footsteps as best she knew how. Her path had meandered from his, and now it looked like it might end early. When he returned to Eve in the vanguard, she hoped she was still alive to greet him. *But he's not coming. He's standing a thousand light-years away on the bridge of his ship, fretting but safe. Does he even realize that I never got off the planet?*

"What are you thinking, Trax?" Jeric asked, nudging her. The two of them were sitting in the shallow, east-facing depression of a shapeless boulder, watching the sun drift down to the horizon. The crater was to their backs, deliberately out of sight so they could forget for a few moments the plight of their world. The attempt wasn't working, and as the shadows grew long and ate up the golden grasslands, they found themselves able to think of little else.

The beer in her hand had gone warm long ago. It hadn't been great to begin with, reminding her of a past that was shattered. Eve today was not the Eve she wanted to be on, and it never would be again. "Do you think this is going to end well?" she asked Jeric.

"We can hold out. All we have to do is keep a landing corridor clear for the fleet when they arrive, and Eve is ours again." Traxus knew the look on Jeric's face as he gazed upwards. He was already lost in those far-off clouds, rolling and diving, feeling the shudder of a cannon through his entire body, at one with his ship and the sky and the falling balls of fire.

"I mean ... all of it. The war."

"What war?" Jeric asked innocently. Traxus fixed him with a glare, and he smiled sheepishly. "Yeah, Trax, I mean, come on."

"That's … not really an answer."

"It's the Coalition, Traxus. Fleets so large they could probably reach from one end of the empire to the other if you lined up all the ships. Millions of sojieri, *billions*. Look around you: Marion may be a bit nuts, but his people are good. Fuck 'good,' they're *Falcons*. I walked by the firing range earlier. They've got twenty guys as good as Asar."

"Great, they can hit a target. But can they fight a war, Jeric? You saw those things in the hallway."

"Yeah, a little hard to miss."

"They're bred to kill. Can you imagine a baby Tagean doing that to someone? Or a baby Human?" Traxus found the idea preposterous, something not even her most fevered imaginings could have conjured a week ago. And now she had seen something that was born and attacking people in the span of *seconds*.

Jeric's teeth ground back and forth, his eyes dull with remote anger as his imagination was grounded prematurely. "This *is* a little different than anything that's come before. I don't know what to tell you, Trax. I just do my part and land safely. Or eject, if the situation calls for it."

Traxus decided to let it go. She knew Jeric well enough to understand when he was truly upset, truly at a loss. He was a man with a simple world and an equally simple outlook. When something impinged upon that uncomplicated state of affairs, he shut down, closed out everything else. Traxus knew he would be needing alcohol and lots of it, and she was afraid he would get it. Because, although he might put on an act of nonchalance and try to keep himself apart, she knew that right beneath the surface was a man just as frightened as the rest of them. *And me? I wish I could get lost in those clouds. Hell, I wish I could be anywhere but here. At least, I have Jeric to lean on. I don't think Leon's going to be much good.* Leon was their friend and their leader, and he was a strong man possessed of incredible resiliency, but Traxus wondered if the strain would prove too much for him this time. "We've got to look out for Leon," she blurted. "I'm worried about him."

"Why? After everything we've been through in the last two weeks, he's in better shape than anyone has a right to be. He didn't even get his beard singed when that little dead thing caught fire in the lab." Jeric snorted. "I can't believe they're as dangerous dead as alive."

Traxus rested her chin in her hands and watched the sun depart, abandoning them. At least, they knew it would return. "Rachel—"

"I don't want to hear her name, Trax," Jeric said abruptly, harshly. "I'm sorry for what I did, but I can tell Leon won't let it go."

"He saved you in there. You're his friend, and right now we're all he's got."

Jeric smiled bitterly. "Maybe, but you know him. He has a hard time forgiving, and he never forgets. The way he looks at me when no one else is watching, I get the feeling he wouldn't mind throwing me to those things."

"That's ridiculous."

Jeric took another gulp of beer and grimaced. "Who am I kidding? I have it coming. After everything I've done, this feels about right."

"Stop it, Jeric. Stop it and be thankful. You're lucky you're not dead. We all are."

Jeric drained the bottle and threw it down the mountainside. They heard it crash against the rocks below. "There's always tomorrow."

Finale: Covenant

Her hair hung in front of her face, obscuring her smile as she moved back and forth, back and forth, grinding her pelvis against Leon's, but her eyes were locked on his, two depthless pools of cool, clear water through the curtain of her hair. He reached around, squeezed her buttocks before his hands slid up her back and pulled her to him. They kissed and he made sputtering noises as her unruly hair fell into his mouth and tickled his nose. She laughed and squeezed herself tighter against him until he felt he couldn't breathe. But her hair was the wrong color, the contours of her body weren't right, even the mischievous laugh wasn't hers. He knew he was dreaming ... why was it Heidi and not Rachel?

Leon snapped awake, breathing hard. He hoped that Traxus and Jeric hadn't woken in the darkness, disturbed by a noise he had made in his sleep. Slowly he sat up, wincing at the squeaking springs of the cot and the bright spikes of pain that swarmed up and down his battered body. A clock on the wall glowed faintly, its face reading three in the morning. *Might as well get up now.*

He glanced at Traxus and sighed. The dream of Heidi had been intoxicating, there was no denying it. Waking up only to have it evaporate left an empty pit in his stomach, especially because deep down he knew Heidi was dead. Their base had fallen; how was she going to run when she couldn't even walk? And where was Rachel? If she was still alive, was she free or was she was trapped, a hostage, in terror and pain? Porter had said his family had been kept as bargaining chips. Did the enemy mean to bargain with Leon? Here he was having goddamn wet dreams about another woman while Rachel might be begging for her life. *There's no fucking justice. And it's my fault. She would have been safe on some other world if she hadn't come back for me. If she hadn't met me.* Again he wondered if the enemy meant to use her and whomever else they might have captured in order to get what they wanted. *I would give them the keys to the palace on Tagea if I thought she would be safe.* Leon stretched and felt a rapid popping from his shoulders, back, and neck. He flexed his injured hand, feeling a pain so clear and pure he imagined he could sense the edges of the puncture.

So many dead. The women in his life had dwindled to one: Traxus, subordinate, friend, surrogate sister. How could he protect her? The empty cots in the barracks marched into the distant darkness, standing in mute memorial to the dead of Task Force Claymore. Sojieri had risked life and limb to retrieve Peregrine Noelle's helmet, but no artifacts of the others had come back, only tacked-up postcards and family photos to tell their stories.

I'm used to long odds, Leon told himself, hoping it would be a comfort. Somehow it wasn't. He reached under the cot and grabbed his boots, struggled into them, and limped quietly to the door. As he passed Traxus's cot, her arm shot out and grabbed his wrist.

"Are you all right?" she asked, her eyes glittering in the moonlight that spilled through the window.

"Nope," Leon answered truthfully.

"You want some company?"

Yes. "No, thanks. Get some sleep."

"You, too. I need you—*we* need you—in control. We're depending on you."

He put his hand on top of hers, gave it an affectionate squeeze, and walked out the door. The barren halls of the barracks seemed to ring loudly with each footstep, but Leon wanted to get into the fresh air as quickly as possible. The door to the courtyard stood open, admitting a cold breeze, and he wished he had brought a jacket, anything to supplement the t-shirt he was wearing. Night on Eve could be cold. Did the enemy feel cold? Or maybe sympathy? Leon doubted it. He still couldn't shake what he had seen in the lab, when the dead warrior had nearly killed all three of them with its jet of fiery plasma. Jeric had laughed it off, but Leon was legitimately terrified. What happened when CRDF troops met those things face to face on the field of battle? The silent tomb of the Valinata Enclave was answer enough.

Leon showed his pass to a guard who challenged him, explained that he needed a breather. The man, looking a little tense himself, seemed to understand. Leon asked if he could walk up to the crater rim, and the guard pointed the way. The rocky path was unlit and unmarked, and Leon almost tripped several times. Marion had ordered blackout protocols to make it that much harder on the enemy if they decided to attack again. *Assuming they even use their eyes the way we do.* Aside from the safety of darkness, it felt as though they had been thrown back in time. Before space travel, before interspecies contact, before the discovery of fire.

It was easy to imagine them charging through the dark on spindly legs, childhood nightmares replicated so perfectly by nature— or by something else. There was a rustling sound in the bushes, and Leon's hand snapped to his hip where he normally wore a Sprawler, but, of course, the guns were locked up somewhere. *No one trusts us.* He paused, listened, then heard whatever was making the sound scamper away. He continued his climb.

Commander Marion had offered Jeric a spot in their aerospace defenses, and the way the pilot's eyes had lit up with unhinged joy at the prospect of flying into battle made Leon's head spin. At least, it had gotten him to start physical therapy routines with his new hand. Jeric had always been uneasy on the ground—seemingly even afraid at times—but in the sky he was something else, as close as Leon had ever seen to a Greek god. He made the clouds his home, raining thunder and lightning down on those below, those who would dare fly against him. Leon knew Jeric was made to fly, but for him a fighter felt like little more than a coffin strapped to booster rockets.

Part of Leon wanted to maintain his anger at Jeric, stoking it like a guttering fire, but while the betrayal still stung, he couldn't bring himself to hate the man. Whatever Jeric's actions, whatever his motives, he was still Leon's friend, and they were stuck here together.

And Traxus ... Trax had saved them in the flight from the cosmodrome, reacting the way a great sojier should: bravely, selflessly. It made no difference that Leon had been only half-conscious the entire time; he had seen her shoot. She had fought off nearly a dozen enemy vehicles essentially on her own to protect him and Jeric and the others. He was truly sorry his two friends were trapped on Eve with him.

When he reached the rim of the crater, Leon was out of breath. The rock face was not nearly as shallow as he had thought, and his leg still hurt like hell. He was surprised to see someone else there before him, one foot raised and resting on a rock, elbow leaning on the raised knee. He needed only a moment to recognize the silhouette dimly outlined against the dark clouds as that of the base commander, Marion.

"Who goes there?" asked a voice with only the barest hint of a tremor.

"It's Leon."

"Hey, Leon. Couldn't sleep?"

"Pretty amped up, to tell the truth. You, too?"

"I don't sleep much," the commander confessed. "Especially not lately." Marion turned to Leon in the blackness, and the faint light from one of Eve's Three Sisters cast a pale, ghostly glow on the right side of his face; the left remained in shadow. "I wonder if there's anyone left alive out there."

"If they're smart, they're in hiding."

"How long can they keep that up?"

"Not long," Leon admitted.

"Well, we have to keep up our end, at least. You know the Falcon motto?"

"'Carnage, Ruin, Vengeance, Wrath'?" Leon recalled.

"Those are our virtues," Marion answered patiently. Our motto is, 'Outfight, Outlast, Outlive.'" His eyes glittered worryingly.

"And you know ours?" Leon threw back. "'In Spite of All.' We're with you, Commander. To the bitter end."

A grim smile split Marion's face. "Misery does love company, doesn't it?" The smile died quickly as he ruminated. "You know, it was Noelle who pushed me. We were both Peregrines when we met on Ascension. I saw what she gave up to be a Peregrine. They take a lot from us as it is. I never felt like I fit, but she was everything we're supposed to be, everything the kids' books say we are. They were never going to let us be together, so I resigned my commission, gave them back my armor and my honor. They sent me here as punishment, and they sent her with me to punish her."

"Was it worth it?"

"I'm trapped on this rock and she's dead, but every second I was with her was absolutely worth it. I would have followed that woman to Hell."

Leon didn't want to point out that Marion might very well get his chance, and sooner rather than later. He felt for him. Grief was something he identified with all too well. "I'm sorry, Comma—Gray. Rachel was the one pulling me away from all of this. I was getting ready to leave it all behind, and now I don't even know what's happened to her. I traded my purpose for her, and as far as I know, she's gone." It hurt to admit the possibility out loud, but at the same time, it was freeing.

"Then you have purpose, Leon. There isn't a purpose more pure than revenge."

Leon glanced sidelong at the commander. Marion's tone was light, not a trace of venom beneath his unwaveringly cheerful demeanor. That made his cold words even more terrifying, but Leon could feel himself being guided over the brink by them, nonetheless. It was true, after all. Rachel had taken his heart, and Raven Blue had taken her. He would take everything from them and call it a bargain.

"I wish I knew who they were or what they wanted," Leon said softly. "We need to try harder to communicate with them." He glanced at Marion again. "Don't you think?"

"I do, and I'm insulted that you think I haven't tried. We've been comming them every five minutes, but they haven't responded to a single one of our transmissions. Maybe they don't use radios the same way we do, and maybe they don't understand us, but we've gotten nothing but silence and that weird moaning sound, day in, day out. Who knows, maybe that's them trying to reply. What a shame that would be." He didn't sound convinced. "I'm waiting for them to send another collaborator to try and negotiate our surrender. I'll send them back without a head." They fell quiet for a few minutes, watching the stars wander across the sky.

Suddenly Marion opened the conversation again. "I consider myself a student of history, Colonel. Are you?"

"I suppose I have to be."

"We all should be. Those who don't learn from history are destined to become part of it, isn't that the old saying?"

"Something like that." There was something very odd about this commander, but Leon found himself trusting him, liking him even. While his manner was strange and his methods nothing short of perplexing, he seemed to have a firm grasp of himself and his people.

"The Coalition has had a long history, the Tagean Dynasty before it an even longer one. Conquest was always a part of it until the charter was signed. It's been hundreds of years since the great fleets mobilized."

"You think the Coalition's not ready for a full-scale war," Leon guessed. It seemed to echo the sentiments of almost everyone he had met who understood what it took for an empire the size of the Coalition to shake off the dust.

"Oh no, I think we're *very* ready. Maybe not as a *culture*: as a culture I think we've had a bellyful of the few little fights that have cropped up in the last few decades. But on a technical level, on a logistical level.... We Falcons know better than anyone what preparing for war gets you. Being prepared for it doesn't assure victory, just greater destruction. I won't lie, Leon, I *want* this. All of us in the Guard do. Even those we anoint learn to pray for this. The problem is, sometimes those prayers are answered."

Leon didn't know what to say, so he tried to deflect the conversation. "That's the second time you've mentioned anointing. What do you mean?"

Marion smiled ruefully, and in the darkness his expression took on a macabre aspect. "Veneration: the Falcons' dirty little secret. You're acquainted with Sergeant O'Reily's team, of course. It may surprise you to know that none of them is actually a Falcon or even CRDF, for that matter."

Leon's jaw was hanging open. "I've actually heard of veneration, but I thought it died out." The Falcons had been known to canonize those outside their society who had embodied their warlike virtues, sometimes even from among their enemies. Those venerated were taken into their order and given pride of place as a sort of spiritual weapon.

"Centuries ago. Officially." Marion smiled again. "Star Command doesn't condone it but it gets results so they turn a blind eye. In the days when the Falcons guarded the conduits for ourselves, playing warlord and raider, we often took prisoners, slaves even. They were pressed into service and their descendants taken into our culture, to grow up as Falcons themselves. But we weren't all bad, you know. We rarely hit civilian populations since they didn't put up much of a fight. No, we spoiled for battle, and we would look for it wherever we could." Marion's voice had taken on a startlingly formal tone as though he read from some apocryphal scripture; Falcon history was so elusive and so bizarre Leon wondered if perhaps some codex actually existed. "Maybe we were vicious, once. Maybe we were even violent for the sake of violence. But the enemy of my enemy is my friend, and sometimes something more."

"What did O'Reily do to be worthy of such a dubious honor?"

Far from seeming offended, Marion laughed. "Some lives need saving, some need ending. Like you, O'Reily is a master of both. More than that I can't say: I'm as bound to him as he is to me. He can tell you himself, if he wants." Marion scratched his nose. "You know, I meant what I said before. I would anoint you, if you wanted."

"And I meant what I said. Rachel wanted me to leave this life behind. If she's alive, I'll leave it with her. If she's not, I have to honor her memory. After I chase these things to the gates of Hell." Leon felt the weakness in his own words, though. He *did* want to honor her memory and her wishes. He also wanted to be an agent of justice, to stand between Raven Blue and the other innocent lives they would end. Part of him *belonged* here, facing an enemy he could scarcely hope to defeat.

Marion cocked his head. "Of course, you have to do what you feel is right. I respect that."

Leon sat down on a rock in the darkness, turning away from the commander. "Whatever happens, we have to understand them," he admitted aloud. "We can't have another Daltar."

"I was afraid I had misjudged you," Marion said. "I'm glad to hear you say that. I mean, clearly, we're dealing with something very different. This isn't a clash of nations over trade routes or resources. It's no long-standing feud. Whatever these things call themselves, they're a whole new species no one's ever seen before. Isn't that exciting?"

"The Valinata have seen them before—they just didn't live to tell the tale."

"Valid point," Marion said and snapped his fingers loudly in the dark, startling Leon. "I'm not so naïve as to think this is some simple cultural misunderstanding. Their attack is meticulous, deliberate. But our reaction cannot be one of unreasoning hate. We have to fight with the aim of establishing a peace, and after that, a rapport. Otherwise, it's genocide. You know that."

Leon felt the hairs all over his body stand on end and not just because of the cold. *Here it is again. My chance to travel the galaxy, meet new species, and exterminate them.* "We can't let it come to that."

"Even if it's what they want," Marion agreed. "We could be walking into a war that will never end." He said this last as though it might be true, and Leon was grateful that his voice was leaden, hopeless instead of eager.

Would I secretly love that, a war that never ends? Isn't that what I've been training for, for half my life? Imagine the money, imagine the blood. Leon gritted his teeth. *No*, he told himself.

A bitter laugh cut the night air, and Marion stood up. "Of course, right now we're only two men, talking in the dark. Our words and resolutions will blow away on the wind, and when those things come for us with their blades at our throats, our only thought will be to kill them."

"I hope you're wrong," Leon said, pushing that vicious internal voice away.

"Me, too. This kind of thing picks up momentum, though. Too many people pushing, everyone with an agenda, be it war, peace, stability, chaos, money, whatever. And before they realize it, it's rolling back at them all, with a mind of its own."

"Where do you fall in that spectrum, Commander?"

Marion was silent for a few moments, pondering in the darkness with the faint green haze reflecting far above them. "Right now I just want to keep as many people alive as possible. But in the end, entropy is the only constant in the universe, and I am an agent of change."

It was something Raptor might have said. "Is it that simple?"

"Things never are," Marion agreed. "But to me it almost seems like someone *wants* Raven Blue to break through."

That's just crazy.

"It's crazy, I know," Marion said as though hearing Leon's thoughts. "But since when has any authority truly looked at people as more than pieces on a chess board? Just once it'd be nice to be a king instead of a pawn."

"Ultimately, the kings are only targets." Leon shivered at the thought, or maybe it was just the cold. "One thing's for sure, Commander."

"Mm?"

"Like you said, the stars keep burning, the worlds keep turning. At least, for now."

"And we have a job to do. In spite of all," Marion said through a forced smile. They stood like that, facing the silent night for a few more minutes before the commander roused himself and turned back to the interior of the sleeping base. "I think I'll turn in."

"I'd like to be alone for a little while if that's all right."

"Sure. Want my jacket? Just don't go impersonating me, yeah?"

Leon laughed. "Thanks, but I'm okay." As Marion stumbled down the path in the dark, setting off a small avalanche of pebbles and cursing, the mercenary colonel wrapped his arms around himself, bracing against the cold. A few hundred meters away a missile launcher panned quietly back and forth, vicious-looking warheads gleaming in the moonlight.

Alone on the ridge, looking out at the rolling, charcoal expanse of the savannah, Leon let the faces of his past drift before him. Friends and companions gone forever: Jenn Rada, Tresh, and the others whose bones littered Auriga's golden sands. His Jackals: Buzz, Dawson, Dyran, Vandestan, Mara, Rosenthal, Sommers, Heidi…. He tried hard to keep Rachel apart, keep her to himself, but she joined their silent ranks.

Leon had just come to terms with the hope flowering in his heart, taking root, and now it was gone, stripped from him. But deep within him a cold, dreadful spark ignited. He nursed it, held it close against his soul, relishing its definition and its clarity. It was purpose, singular and ferocious purpose. *I am coming for you, Rachel. Never doubt that I am coming.* And yet when he reached out, trying to touch her heart with his own, he found only the soft confines of memory crowding him. Her laugh, her smile, her silken skin, and he knew he could do little but collect those memories like wilting flower petals and hold them in his mind, trying to approximate the shape of the singular rose to which they had once belonged. *We're safe here, baby. I've got you. I've got you.*

And he knew that redemption, if he was to find it, would come only when he had no more battles to fight, no more enemies to conquer. Had he ever really had a choice in the matter? Had the dream of peace, now seemingly so remote, always been only an illusion? The cold shadows of his past settled over him, a shroud of memory, black armor. *Can you hear me, Abaddon, Celestials, or Raven Blue, or whatever you call yourselves in your barren hearts? Know that I'm coming, and know I won't stop—ever.* He imagined that perhaps this enemy, alone among all others, might very well hear him, and so Leon Victor stood apart, while the universe trembled in its cradle, throwing out his dark promises upon a dark world.

Glossary of Terms

- **Coalition of Worlds**: The largest of the sovereign galactic powers, comprising the home territories of the eleven charter species and governed by a parliament and an elected monarch
- **Conduit**: A gravitational singularity linking celestial bodies, used for faster-than-light travel
- **CRDF**: Coalition Royal Defense Forces, the combined military branches of the Coalition
- **CRAG**: Coalition Royal Army Ground, the ground-based arm of the CRDF
- **CSF**: Coalition Special Forces
- **CRN**: Coalition Royal Navy, the naval branch of the CRDF
- **CRB**: Coalition Regional Base, any of a number of outpost garrisons strategically located within the Coalition territories
- **EMMA**: Enclosed Mechanized Main Armor, used by heavy infantry in main battle line assault roles
- **IORSIRAD**: Information Operations, Reconnaissance, and Strategic Intervention Regulatory Activities Detachment – Leon Victor's former unit within the CSF (disbanded)
- **MMI**: Mind-machine interface, a general term for any direct neural link between a user and machine or computer, commonly used to describe the neural interfaces of powered armor.
- **NDC**: Nuclear Dispersion Cannon, a family of directed energy weapons operating on controlled fusion reactions.
- **PDF**: Planetary Defense Force, general term referring to a planet's domestic garrison and aerospace defense, typically a standing military maintained by the planet's own government
- **SRG**: Shar'dan Republican Guard, the combined military branches of the Shar'dan Confederacy
- **Star Chamber**: The joint chiefs of the Coalition military, composed of eleven grand admirals, each representing one of the charter species

- **Unified Commonwealth**: The second-largest and the wealthiest of the sovereign galactic powers, governed by an elected council of aristocrats
- **UCA**: Unified Commonwealth Authority, the combined military branches of the Unified Commonwealth
- **Valinata Enclave**: One of the principal galactic powers, sharing a contested border with the Coalition and ruled by an oligarchical council known as the Tête
- **VSF**: Valinata Space Force, the combined military branches of the Valinata Enclave

Acknowledgments

The following people were instrumental in getting this story to you, and these words will never be enough to properly express my gratitude. My parents, Mousa and Kristin, supported my passion for writing from a young age, and my mother, Kristin, provided invaluable editing expertise from first draft to last.

Michelle and Mayhem made sure I enjoyed the little things and cheered me on to the finish line.

Kristina Drobny, marketing guru and gourmet, took the photograph for the cover.

Erika Austin, killer ecommerce expert, demystified online marketing and SEO.

Allison Miller, software engineering Voodoo queen and website conjurer, created www.jpishaq.com.

Many friends, relatives, and colleagues supported me from start to finish. Chief among them have always been Chris G. and Naim, Nesreen, and John Q. And back in the day Christina L., Sunder B., and Kim S. told me to "put it in the book," so I did. Cheers to all of them.

Last but certainly not least, I must thank the giants on whose shoulders I've stood to get a better look at the stars: Isaac Asimov, Orson Scott Card, John Scalzi, George R.R. Martin, Frank Herbert, Robert Heinlein, Douglas Adams, and Walter Miller, all legendary writers of science fiction and great literature.

About the Author

JP Ishaq is the author of *In Spite of All* and *Raven Blue* and creator of the Mourning Star series of novels. He grew up visiting far-flung relatives and historical sites, while cultivating a love of adventure and culture as well as a healthy disdain for airports. He learned the art of storytelling from his grandfather's tales of genies and bandits and began writing at a young age, first as a hobby and then as a passion. He attended the University of Vermont, where he studied molecular genetics before entering the tech sector. Vermont is still his base of operations.

www.ingramcontent.com/pod-product-compliance
Lightning Source LLC
Chambersburg PA
CBHW051539250626
47157CB00001B/109